The
Quantum
Conspiracy

A Novel of Possibilities

First published by O Books, 2008
O Books is an imprint of John Hunt Publishing Ltd., The Bothy, Deershot Lodge, Park Lane, Ropley,
Hants, SO24 0BE, UK
office1@o-books.net
www.o-books.net

Distribution in:	South Africa
	Alternative Books
UK and Europe	altbook@peterhyde.co.za
Orca Book Services	Tel: 021 555 4027 Fax: 021 447 1430
orders@orcabookservices.co.uk	
Tel: 01202 665432 Fax: 01202 666219	Text copyright Chuck and Karen Robison 2008
Int. code (44)	
	Design: Stuart Davies
USA and Canada	
NBN	ISBN: 978 1 84694 167 2
custserv@nbnbooks.com	
Tel: 1 800 462 6420 Fax: 1 800 338 4550	All rights reserved. Except for brief quotations
	in critical articles or reviews, no part of this
Australia and New Zealand	book may be reproduced in any manner without
Brumby Books	prior written permission from the publishers.
sales@brumbybooks.com.au	
Tel: 61 3 9761 5535 Fax: 61 3 9761 7095	The rights of Chuck and Karen Robison as
	author have been asserted in accordance with
Far East (offices in Singapore, Thailand,	the Copyright, Designs and Patents Act 1988.
Hong Kong, Taiwan)	
Pansing Distribution Pte Ltd	
kemal@pansing.com	A CIP catalogue record for this book is available
Tel: 65 6319 9939 Fax: 65 6462 5761	from the British Library.

Printed by Chris Fowler International
www.chrisfowler.com

O Books operates a distinctive and ethical publishing philosophy in
all areas of its business, from its global network of authors to
production and worldwide distribution.
This book is produced on FSC certified stock, within ISO14001
standards. The printer plants sufficient trees each year through
the Woodland Trust to absorb the level of emitted carbon in
its production.

The Quantum Conspiracy

A Novel of Possibilities

Chuck and Karen Robison

BOOKS

Winchester, UK
Washington, USA

CONTENTS

For Eleanor Walsh Wasson

In one hundred years, she has learned what others take one thousand years to learn, shared it with more people than most of us will ever know and given of herself, her resources and her home that all of us might see in action the simple truth that we are all one. She guided and continues to guide this book. We give her our deepest love and gratitude. God Bless you, Eleanor.

"It seems to me that rather than spend so much resource and time developing questionable and expensive technology to go places in our solar system, we might do better trying to see what could be done through intergalactic telepathy than by heavy engineering. The idea of the collective memory suggests we are able to tap into a whole lot more than most people are willing to assume. It means expanding our horizon as to what may be possible."

Dr. Rupert Sheldrake speaking during his interview on February 15, 2005 on "What If It Really Works?" on KOTO radio in Telluride, Colorado.

We're Here.

We are the ones you have been waiting for.

The Children of Light

quan·tum field the·o·ry n
a theory developed from quantum mechanics based on the
assumption that elementary particles interact through the
influence of fields around them and the exchange of energy

quan·tum jump n
the sudden transition of an atom or particle from one energy
state to another

quan·tum leap n
a sudden, dramatic, and significant change or advance

*Encarta® World English Dictionary© 1999 Microsoft Corporation.
All rights reserved. Developed for Microsoft by Bloomsbury
Publishing Plc.*

Why I Wrote This Book

In 1950 I was 8 years old and living in Huntington, West Virginia with my parents and my five year old sister. Both sets of grand-parents lived close by. It was the summer. I had ordered my Captain Midnight Decoder Ring and was really excited that it would come any day. That was the period and I was at the age when time crept along so slowly. Each afternoon I would go out to the step of the walkway to the street with my sister and sit there to wait for the postman to come by with the day's mail. While waiting my sister and I would talk about whatever. One subject kept coming up in our conversation and in silence in my mind.

We lived at 2008 Cherry Avenue and my dad had a lamppost placed by the walkway and on it an ornate sign with our address on it. Not a day of waiting for the decoder ring would go by that I would not think about 2008. I would be 66 then, probably famous, and involved in something really important.

Over the next 58 years I would from time to time wonder what would happen in the magic year I had been thinking about for so long. As 2007 dawned, I examined my life and realized I would not be famous nor involved in anything seeming to be important. But it was clear that 2008 was going to be a turning point for us all. As I complete this book I am aware that all around us are signs and wonders that this is a time of profound change. The elections, the environment, the economy, the ethnic struggles, evolution and eternity all signal for our attention…..all around the globe.

2008 looms now in March, as a year of massive and radical change. We are buffeted on all sides with the concept that things could change overnight, but probably won't and if they do it will not be for the better. For decades we have been listening to brilliant scientists, philosophers, leaders and New Age "inner

1

space cadets" talking about a shift in consciousness, whatever that is. We are closer to another World War, led by forces on all sides that seem to have mind control, fear and greed as their main objectives, supported by religious fundamentalists in every religion and region of the world. We seem to be racing toward some sort of event that will communicate we have gone too far and it is time to turn around and find a new path. Either that or perish. And there do not seem to be any leaders who have any truly new ideas to lead us away from what appears to be an immediately pending crisis for the whole species. A recent Albert Einstein quote on Google is chilling in its accuracy:

"Insanity: doing the same thing over and over again and expecting different results."

Many people believe in great ages being introduced by revered spiritual teachers such as Moses, Jesus, Buddha, Mohammed, Krishna and Confucius. The power and effects of these guides are massive. But the vast majority of believers look to the past. Few entertain the idea that a new leader and a new era could be coming. Even the idea that Jesus will return is about the past, the final chapter. But I want this book to open the discussion that a new epoch, a new chapter is at hand, and a new leader is already on the planet to lead us into an evolved future that will release us from the insanity we have created and move us into a higher level of life and evolution. It is a distinct possibility.

If it helps, just think of this as a curious novel written to give you some reading pleasure and just possibly to make you ask some new questions. Of course, it may also be a future history......of the immediate future.

And finally, The Quantum Conspiracy is actually hidden in this book of secrets and possibilities. Pay attention, even to the bibliography. It you are willing to follow the secrets and signs, you will be led into a whole new level of spiritual possibility and discovery.

> "They must find it difficult......
> Those who have taken authority as the truth,
> Rather than the truth as the authority."
>
> *Gerald Massey*

March 21, 2008
Austin, Texas

Chapter 1

The Anna Mitchell-Hedges Crystal Skull was the starting point. The twelve met in one of the alabaster chambers in the great Cathedral of Sirius for a meditation with the Crystal Skull, which had been placed in Belize centuries before as a guide and beacon for the journey they were about to take. The focus of this meditation was to imprint forever the identities of each of the twelve on each other's genetic memories. From this time forward, they would always be able to recognize each other when they met again on Earth regardless of the circumstances. As they gathered in their emerald robes with gold trim and were illumined by the torch sconces on the circular walls, they knew at last the journey was about to begin.

Actually this part of the journey began 80 years ago in Belize when F.A. Mitchell-Hedges anchored his 125 foot yacht off the coast and went inland to build a base camp for his explorations for Mayan ruins and buried treasure. His daughter, Anna, was in her early teens and was required to stay at the compound. One day she was playing at the edge of the compound when she noticed something shining out of a hole in the rocky ground. She called some of the native staff and they helped her dig up the object. As it came out of the ground all the local people began to scream with excitement. They knew exactly what this thing was. They had heard about it from their beginnings. For centuries the mythology of this unique crystal had been told and retold. Reputed to have been used by the Mayans in ceremonies, it had been lost or buried hundreds of years ago awaiting this moment. Finders, keepers. When it came time to leave Belize in 1917, the locals gave the skull to Anna, and she and her father sailed to Boston where it was examined and analyzed at Massachusetts Institute of Technology. The scientists were unable to determine how this had been crafted, as no tools available at the time could have created such a perfect carving in crystal. All they could say for sure was that artists working continuously for 300 years to polish it to perfection must have crafted it.

Anna Mitchell-Hedges kept this skull with her wherever she went from that time forward and it became the focus of her life. She was living in Canada in November 1963 on a large estate. The skull was kept in a locked closet upstairs. One afternoon, after lunch, Anna felt compelled to go upstairs to check on the skull. Normally, the skull remained at a steady temperature of 70 degrees regardless of the environment. She opened the door and went to the skull to check it. She noticed it was wet with "sweat" and very cold to the touch. Very Strange. Other than that, all was well and she locked the door and went back down stairs. The TV news was on and the volume was turned up. Walter Cronkite was just announcing that President Kennedy had been assassinated. This brought back thoughts of the original purpose of the skull.

According to tradition, when a revered elder, such as a shaman, was about to die, a search was conducted to find a young boy who had all the traits of the elder. Once found, the High Priest took the youth and the dying elder to the highest level of the most sacred pyramid for a succession ritual. The old man and the young man were placed on their backs side by side and the skull was placed between them. During the following ritual lasting hours, the old man died and the young man received all of his wisdom. He and the priest then came down from the pyramid and the community celebrated their new shaman.

Anna had many adventures between 1963 and when I met her in 1990 at the Crystal Shop in SOHO in New York. She was there at the request of the owner, Paul, to place the skull on display for visitors to experience whatever power the skull contained. Visitors were allowed 30 minutes with the skull and were encouraged to meditate as they touched the skull to feel its vibrations. Paul later told me the whole store was vibrating at a high level during the thirty minutes I was there with three other people. I was delighted when I was subsequently invited to my friend Ken's home for a private meditation with Paul, Anna, her traveling companion, Charlie and Mark. Anna told us more of the stories of her travels with the skull and revealed that the skull was in fact her life's mission.

After the story telling, Ken led a meditation on the skull. This is where the story begins for me. We sat around a table in the large New York penthouse living room. The table was inlaid with rocks from around the world and made a striking site all by itself. I closed my eyes and the next thing I experienced was sitting with these seven people in a large circular room that was made of alabaster and mysteriously illumined both from within the alabaster itself and also by torches that were burning in sconces around the room. We all wore exquisite robes, like judges robes, but they were made of a wonderful shimmering emerald green cloth, trimmed with gold. Words were not spoken in this place, as everyone communicated telepathically. I don't remember what happened during this time. When it was over and I opened my eyes back in the living room, I was stunned to hear that everyone else in the room had also been transported to where I was in the meditation and they remembered it. They didn't know what it was about either. For years afterward, I would think back to that night and try to imagine what it all meant. All I could figure out was that it was a very important experience in my life and maybe someday I would understand its significance. That someday arrived thirteen years later. This is my story. I am the rememberer and the keeper of the sacred mysteries. I go all the way back to the beginning. I am the whale. This is my music. Sing along with me.

From My Journal.

Chapter 2

How the Messengers Helped Me Discover My Role

Michael

I walked across the street from our old house to the new house we were about to move into. My new wife, Grace Devereaux, was sitting on the front porch with Michael, an old friend and one of the people building the house. They were in a nice conversation and I joined them. "What's going on?" "Michael was just telling me about his tattoo." I had seen it hundreds of times. It was on his right wrist and looked like a dolphin with a rose covering it. "It's a picture of his Merkabah." "His what?" "It's the ship he was captain of on the trip here." "What trip?" They both smiled as if I were the odd man out and they knew the big secret. "The trip that brought us here from Sirius." "I give up, what in the hell are you two talking about?" Grace Devereaux said, "You and I have talked about this before. We came here from Sirius on a special mission." Right then I realized that my new wife and my old friend had just thrown open the big front door of woo-woo-ville. "Space travel and special missions? Please."

Michael told me that several years before; a seer had told him that he was the captain of a group of twelve souls who had traveled across the galaxy to Earth to be here for a special moment. As soon as he heard this, he recognized truth in this and had a space ship tattooed on his wrist to remind him of whom he was. Then he discovered that he did not want to tell people about the meaning of this tattoo. He went back to the tattoo artist and had him turn the space ship into a dolphin, the primary symbol of the Sirians, and then add a rose on top of that to completely obscure what it was all about. And soon I forgot this story from Michael's life. The conversation with him and Grace Devereaux started when she commented that the rose was a symbol of the Ancient Mystical Order of the Rosicrucians, still active today keeping the secrets which they have been promised will someday soon need to be revealed to the entire world.

So Michael was the captain. As I sat there, they went on with their conversation as if the world had not moved when this was revealed to me. "What the hell are you two doing? First you tell me the most amazing thing I have ever heard and then you go on as if you were deciding what salad dressing to have for lunch." "Well, we just know all about it so there was no need to make a big deal of it." Grace Devereaux said. She and I had known since we first met on the Internet that we had a special purpose for being together and she seemed to know all the secrets, which I was trying so hard to understand or at least trying to believe. And then this.

Just a few thoughts got me to thinking about Michael's role in my life. He was younger than me, an Olympic athlete, and a successful stock trader. He befriended me and from the start had a very caring and protective manner in relating to me. I liked him and felt there was a deep bond between us, but on the surface it didn't make sense. We are not alike at all. A year and a half before, when I was still single, I had a car accident resulting in major surgery and Michael served as my nurse when I first got home from the day surgery. He did it all, got the pills, and cooked the food, the whole thing. It was such a kind gesture, but confusing....why me? Why did I deserve such kindness?

Now on the porch it all started to come back to me. He was the captain, both the commander and the keeper for himself and eleven other souls and Grace Devereaux and I were two of them. The three of us were instantly bonded to each other and today that bond is stronger than ever. Now there were three of us who had connected so easily that day on the front porch. And the surprising thing was we knew the adventure had begun in earnest. Just the timing seemed funny. We knew we were real, but we had a sense that we were just visiting Earth. We would go back to Sirius to prepare to return to Earth for the real work to begin in 2008.

It was the spring of 2004. For four years I had been battling my intuition that kept saying, and still does for that matter, that we are headed into a tumultuous and serious time. The 2004 election was several months away and I kept hoping against hope that we would wake up in time to prevent Bush's re-election. If we could wake up fast enough, we might be able to spare America and the world the consequences of four more years of this cancerous affliction affecting our country. I did my best those days to shake people awake, but government sponsored fear is a very powerful sleeping potion and sleep we did, right through the election. And everyone was sleeping so soundly. Many still are. My favourite bumper sticker from that campaign was: "Bush / Cheney 04: Thanks for not paying attention!"

In time the recognition I experienced with Michael lost its shock value and life went on, except I kept thinking about this. The experience in the alabaster chamber came back more frequently until I finally accepted that I was there, was one of whoever "they" might be and I actually had a specific role as one of the twelve under Michael's command. This book is my part of the mission. It comes to me as I write, as if all I have to do is drive the keyboard and the words magically jump onto the screen.

The New Man

The Clan of the Cave Bear is an historical fiction novel by Jean M. Auel. It is a wonderful book and reveals to the reader what it was like when we had different bodies, different DNA, and very different understandings of who we were. At one point a child is born with fair skin and a wobbly neck unlike the stiff necks all the others were born with. Everyone assumed this new and strange child was deformed and as a result was shunned. In reality this new child was a new version of the human species. One day everyone was alike and the next day there were two kinds of man roaming the Earth..........the old cave man and the new man.

The picture painted in this book is there to give us a clue about what is happening right now in America and in the World.........all over the world. A new man has been born. He comes as a child. Many purport he has a new DNA structure, exceptional psychic skills, and a comprehensive and stunning understanding of the world and where we are in time. Just like that wobbly-necked baby, he is often suspect, misunderstood and a problem for members of the old order. But he is here and on purpose. There is an incredible future coming. He is bringing it and it is already happening. Welcome to the Transformation......you don't want to miss this. In fact, you can't miss it.

At times like this, times of great change, tumult and disorder, it is difficult to see and often more difficult to remember there is an order to things. But, even now, there is. When I was a little boy, before I could have remembered all that I know now, I used to doodle the phrase "Now is the time for all good men to come to the aid of their country." I did it so much that I began to believe there would be such a time, long before any of the details of what is happening now were even seeable. But there were hints and guides along the way. They seemed to find me when I least expected it. They would appear, bring me a special message and disappear.

A World Trader's Observation

One afternoon my first wife and I were invited to a garden party at the home of a friend of my parent's who lived in Palo Alto. His back yard was a beautiful Japanese garden and the perfect place for a summer cocktail party. The guests were charming, distinguished and very interesting. The host introduced me to John

Hough, a world trader and a Republican Committeeman from Arizona.....and this was in the time when Barry Goldwater was Mr. Arizona. The host left John and me to talk alone and very quickly he asked me the strangest question: "What do you want out of life?" I had been thinking a lot about that and had a rapid reply answer: "I want to touch the center of the universe and know that I have had the experience." So far so good. Just as quickly, he said the message he was sent there to give me: "I am going to tell you something that will save you years and years of time. Everything you experience in life is total insanity, covered over by the thinnest veneer of rationality to make it palatable." And with that he disappeared into the crowd. I thought about that for a long time. I'm certain that it is not all insanity, but I can see so much that is. That message made it easier, much easier, to take what followed.

My Philosophy Professor

Glenn Maxwell brought me a message. Dr. Maxwell was my philosophy teacher at Austin College. He was a loner, well read beyond reason and even though he appeared cold and aloof, it turned out he had a heart of gold and was observant beyond anyone's awareness at the time. On the day I graduated, he called me into his office and said to me, "Mr. Robison, I have a gift for you on this important day in your life." He handed me a gift-wrapped package that was not much bigger than a stack of 75 index cards. I thanked him and left his office. I never saw him again. I opened the little package when I got home to Dallas and it was an old beat up book and he had underlined and annotated almost every page. What kind of present was this?...I wanted something new and shiny. I put the book on my bookshelf, packed it every time I moved and then one day, fourteen years later, as I walked past the book on a shelf at eye level, I saw it and decided that was the moment to see what was actually in it. It was *As a Man Thinketh*, written in 1880 by James Allen, an obscure professor from New England. It was the transcript of a lecture he had given at that time. Glen Maxwell had given me a profound gift. Not only did he give me a first edition of this classic, but he indeed was a messenger, as the book was the first statement I could understand that contained the truth that our minds and what we think are the real determiners of what we create. In his forward, Allen states:

"The object of this book is to stimulate men and women to the discovery and perception of the truth that "They themselves are makers of themselves" by virtue of the thoughts which they choose and encourage; that mind is the master-weaver, both of the inner garment of character and the outer garment of circumstance, and that, as they have hitherto woven in ignorance and pain, they may now weave in enlightenment and happiness."

Kurt Vonnegurt's Message

Kurt Vonnegurt brought me a message. I read *Cat's Cradle* while I was getting my graduate degree in Theology at Princeton. There I was studying serious Christian Protestant theology and at the same time reading about Bokonon and his claim that all religion was lies. There were a couple of minutes when I was not sure which was which.......but I learned. It took me twenty-five long and difficult years to work through Christianity, but again, I had guides.

A Message from The Grandfathers

The passage of time and the connection of things was a message brought to me by a Lakota Sioux medicine woman, Two Trees. Paul arranged for Two Trees to lead a sweat lodge for myself and four of my best friends from New York. The sweat lodge was to be held on the mesa on the other side of the Rio Grande from Taos, New Mexico on a Sunday afternoon and evening. The afternoon was spent getting ready for the sweat lodge by finding firewood and stones, building the lodge out of saplings to make a structure which was then covered over with canvas to make it light and heat tight. We made strands of tobacco wrapped in cloth as prayers to wear around our necks for the lodge. As we were doing this, at about 3 PM, a major thunderstorm appeared out of the east coming rapidly across the mountains headed right toward us. The Sun was in the west and the high contrast light at 8000 feet made the color of the storm appear almost black as it rushed toward us. I went to Two Trees and asked if we should be leaving. She said, "No, I have already spoken to the thunder gods and they will leave us alone." Right. I could hardly believe what happened next. I was ready to race for the car when this black sheet of rain stopped right in front of us about 30 feet away. It just stopped. On one side was bright sunlight and on the other side a torrential downpour. No wind and no further forward movement. It just stood there. Two Trees explained that the thunder god just wanted to watch us and it did so for what seemed like about a half hour and then it went away.......just drifted back to where it had come from. I had heard about these kinds of things for a long time, but never believed I would see it happen. And this was just the beginning of the sweat lodge magic.

In time the Sun set, the forty-one ceremonial rocks had heated to maximum temperature and we were ready to enter the sweat lodge. We put on bathing suits and crawled in the small opening where several of the hot rocks had already been placed in the center of the circle of the lodge. We sat in the circle with our backs to the lodge wall. The door curtain was closed and all six of us were there together in total darkness. Two Trees explained that the sweat lodge was a purification and prayer ceremony and she led us through that in a series of four prayer rounds. After the first prayer round, one of the guys was too hot and had to get out. The second prayer round ended and another got out. The end of the third prayer round saw another leave. Finally just Two Trees, Mark and I were left. We went through the fourth round of prayers and then Mark left. I was steaming, but unwilling to admit that I was too hot and exhausted to leave. I did not know what to do.

I had kept my hand pushed out under the side of the lodge to try to cool myself off in the outside air and cool ground. Two Trees said, "You have been given a great gift tonight. For the first time in your life you are completely grounded. Now tell me what you see." I looked in the total darkness and suddenly there appeared on the ceiling of the lodge enough stars to look like the Milky Way.....bright stars all over the ceiling. But how could that be? I was in total darkness. I told Two Trees what I was seeing and she said, "What you are seeing are The Grandfathers. They go all the way back to the beginning of time. If you will say three times, 'I will keep you in my heart always, Grandfathers', they will be with you forever." So out loud three times I said, "I will keep you in my heart always, Grandfathers." With that the full ceremony ended and I was able to follow Two Trees out the small door. When I stood up and put on my glasses and looked at the dark sky, there they all were, millions of them. The brightest stars I had ever seen. The Grandfathers. They were right there with me, and are to this day.

When the student is ready!

It took me a long time after I met Gene Kieffer to realize he knew I was one of his special projects and he was the major messenger. Gene was correctly named. He is a genius, and like all geniuses, he felt he had been sentenced to spend his life waiting for everyone else to catch up. He challenged me to catch up and in time I did, but it was like trying to run uphill at 11,000 feet, above the tree line on a scree covered roadway wearing bedroom slippers. Tough going. It's almost impossible to be in the church and not believe that which one is required to preach. I knew several people who did it.......they were cynics, incapable of getting out and unwilling to speak what they thought the real truth was. Vonnegurt's message lay just below the surface for a long time......was it just a pack of lies? Then Gene finally published his book, *The Secret Teachings*, and things began to make sense to me. Even the so-called liberal Christians acted as if the world was started when the Jews showed up. Everything before that was basically unimportant.........in fact, there really wasn't very much before that or so it is taught.

Much of what Gene wrote was based on the writings of Gerald Massey whose book, *A Book of the Beginnings*, is a brilliant attempt to trace backwards to how things got started in the first place. This book, and more importantly, Gene's book stresses that the mythology that Christians take as uniquely theirs, is in fact, as old as time......the same message has been taught from the beginning, and the message is simple on one level and is stated in Gene's sub title: *Unveiling the Luminous Sun Within*. Gene must have worn himself out trying to show me that virtually every detail of the Christian Story of Jesus' life appears first in the Egyptian mythology and that the first Christians, whoever they were, just lifted it out of Egypt and called it their own. But again, that was part of the order of things. That message needed to be kept before us for the next 2000 years. The message of it all is that within each of us, almost seven billion right now, there is God. We are God experiencing himself through us. It's like that old joke about Coach Bobby Knight. St. Peter is showing a new arrival around heaven and they stop by the basketball court and here is this guy running around and screaming and cussing and telling everyone what to do. The new arrival asks St. Peter what is going on and he says, "Oh, that's God, sometimes he likes to play like he is Bobby Knight!"

The Church and the Good News
It took so long for me to work though all of this. Today it is easier

to see that what we know of religion........organized or distraught......is an attempt by some of our brothers and sisters to control the lives of others of our brothers and sisters. Had I known when I left Princeton in 1967 that in five short years the agenda for the Presbyterian Church, for the rest of my life, would be written as "The Definitive Guidance on Homosexuality" which was formally adopted in 1978 as the final word by the Presbyterian Church on the "place" of homosexuals in this church, I probably would have dropped out right then. But I stayed to watch the controllers assign a place for the gays in the church. Basically, the place was at the back of the bus....way back.

Margaret Mead said that the last element that would yield to change in any society was the sexual mores and here we have the seemingly unmovable rock. The Presbyterian Church has been loathe to ordain gays as ministers or even as lay elders and deacons, not to mention allowing gays to be married or even recognized as having holy relationships. In one of the many debates about this in the church, I stood on the floor of the Presbytery of New York City and argued we accept gays thusly: "We have always ordained gays and we always will. The issue before us is simply, are we going to let some of the brothers and sisters tell the truth and prevent others from telling the truth about themselves?" Then I went on to address this 1997 meeting as follows: "Whatever we decide here today, we are still going to have to wrestle with this problem over and over again until we get to the point of seeing God completely in each other. It's like the taxidermist and the veterinarian in west Texas who went into business together to save on expenses. They chose as their motto, 'Either way, you get your dog back'. Now eleven years later, the battle still rages, while the greatest moment in human history is unfolding before us........and the church sleeps on, trying to control the nightmares it is creating for those who still follow the directives of the rulers.

Church is like that. On the one hand it is the designated keeper of the truth. In fact, as an ordained Presbyterian minister, I am allowed to adopt the title, "Keeper of the Sacred Mysteries".....and I am......but keeper does not mean keeping them from everyone else. As Keeper, I am also responsible for insuring that the truth be known as widely as possible. On the other hand, secrecy and control seem to be the order of the day almost anywhere we look. Someone is constantly trying to control someone else for some personal reason. Usually fear is at the center of this process. How fearful would it be if we had to confront the fact that Jesus and the story of his life and birth was a retelling of a myth thousands of years older than we assume. And yet, the story is common.

We are here to discover the Christ within each of us, without the trappings of Church Dogma, doctrine or mind control. In short, the eternal Christ dwells within us all, acknowledged as present or not. Carl Jung had a sign over the door to his office which said: "Bidden or Not Bidden, God is Present". You can call this eternal spirit by whatever name you choose, including Max as one of my friends refers to it. It is the eternal Divine which is the factory setting for who each of us ultimately is.

The Phoenix and the UN

In 1978 Barbara W. Tuchman wrote the classic *A Distant Mirror: The Calamitous 14th Century* about the similarities between our time today and the circumstances that existed just before and just after the year 1500. The parallels are astounding. And they have a ring of truth to them from mythology. The myth of the Phoenix is about a 500 year measure of time. Said to live for 500 years, the phoenix is a bird with beautiful gold and red plumage. At the end of its life-cycle the phoenix builds itself a nest of cinnamon twigs that it then ignites; both nest and bird burn fiercely and are reduced to ashes, from which a new, young phoenix arises. The new phoenix is destined to live, usually, as long as the old one.

Every religion claims that its way is the only way, and each is right on some level. The differences, and they are profound, between the religions of man are powerful separators. But behind these separators is the simple fact that none of these religions is pure within itself. Manly P. Hall in his breathtaking book, *The Secret Teachings of All Ages*, documents how ideas in one religion have interchanged with ideas in others to form a mysterious synergy. Each has exchanged ideas with all the others for thousands of years. This can be easily seen in America today. The lasting souvenir from our tragic trip to Viet Nam and our increasing trade with China is the growing presence and influence of Buddhism. We easily incorporate these thoughts into our way of thinking long before we identify their source. This interchange is possible and profitable precisely because at the core of every revealed and created religion is the truth that there is a God, and his Presence, The Christ, by whatever name, is present in each of us.

I spent the decade preceding the turn of the Millennium as an Adjunct Chaplain at the Church Center of the United Nations in New York City. The view from that pulpit forces one to consider the reality that all the world's religions are valid and useful paths to the evolution of the spirit toward the target set by God for each of us. As a result of my time at the UN, when I use the word "WE" I am referring to all seven billion of us who currently inhabit this part of the universe. Like it or not, we are all in this together. Chaos Theory posits that an action on this side of the world has consequences on the other side of the world, regardless of how small or seemingly insignificant. The Internet and Globalization, like the changes that took place 500 years ago, are bringing us in closer proximity to our neighbors around the world. Sooner or later, hopefully sooner, our religious experiences and statements will reflect this massive change in our way of understanding the world.

The Kundalini Master

The remarkable thing is that we are changing and changing very rapidly. One of the messengers who brought a very special message was Gopi Krishna, who was 83 when I met him in New York when he came to address the United Nations. Gene Kieffer was his agent in this country and Gene arranged an opportunity for me to take Gopi Krishna's portrait, primarily for my own documentation purposes. I had read many of his books by then and was convinced that he was the real thing. His most recent book was *The Present Crisis,* which even today is the very best explanation of where we are right now, twenty-four years later.

He grew up with very little advantage or schooling and at age 35 had what is called a Kundalini experience that expanded not only his consciousness but his intelligence. From that time on, he wrote 13 books, all in English, all exhaustively researched, and each one on such an intellectual level that his work cannot be assailed. He was little known in the world, and may never be, although the New York Times took note of his thoughts on the OpEd page from time to time and remembered him in the obituary when he died a year later at age 84. He was not a guru, did not have worshiping admirers who sat at his feet and brought flowers of devotion, and did not go out of his way to grant time to just anyone. To meet him was an honor and to get time alone with him was a true spiritual gift. I spent an hour with him........alone.

As I photographed, as was my custom, I asked him about his work and thoughts. He was most gracious and treated me with respect and understanding. Finally, when I was sure I had the picture that captured his soul, I asked him the one prepared question I wanted an answer to: "Gopi Krishna, what do I need to do to be enlightened?" I had anticipated he might tell me to repeat a mantra, wear a special color, change my diet, read one of his books, or do some other kind of action or service that might hasten my progress. He looked me right in the eye through those thick glasses of his and said: "Just this; everyday, as often as you can, just think about God, and God will take care of everything else."

Charles D. Robison

Gopi Krishna

Intuitively I knew that real spiritual guidance and insight can be transmitted simply and in simple language and this was about as simple as it gets. I did not need to ask a follow up question, or anything else. I thanked him, packed up my cameras and lights and ran off to my darkroom to develop the prints I knew would be good. In the darkroom, my meditation room, I replayed his advice over and over in my mind. It was so simple, so easy, and so perfect for my limited understanding. So, in October of 1983 I made a commitment right there in my darkroom to follow his advice as faithfully as possible. Twenty-five years later I can tell you it was effortless and the most valuable spiritual practice I have found. I do think about God every day.........and more times each day. I think about where God is, where He is in any given situation, what He sees in situations versus what I see. I think about His plan, and I think about how He is communicating with me and with others. I try to see Him in any way I can. I don't worry about prayers or saying the right word, I don't worry about right belief or purity of dogma. I just think about God. And I am certain that my life is totally different than it would have been had I not received this simple message. Over this period of 25 years I have gone through relationships, careers, illnesses, relocations, ups and downs, loss and challenge, but at the core of each experience I have centered myself on the thought of God. It has made all the difference.

Less than a year after I took Gopi Krishna's portrait and about two months after he finished his last book, *The Way to Self Knowledge*, he died suddenly in India. With less than a years' practice and with immediate results, his words were burned into my brain and nervous system. It is the one spiritual insight I know to be entirely true and correct for me.

I made prints to have him sign before he went back to India the following week and I gave copies of the portrait to several people who asked for them. I decided the portrait was somehow sacred and I was not to push or manipulate the outcome of how it would be used. I just hoped I had a book cover shot. When he died, I was saddened to realize that another dream would not come true. Ten years later a decision was made to publish his autobiography, *Living with Kundalini*, and my portrait was chosen as the only picture of him that would be in the book. I believe in 100 years this book will be as basic to our understanding of who we are, as Darwin's *The Origin of the Species* is today.

The comparison with Darwin is apt. Darwin was asking the question, "Where did we come from?" One of the big five questions. Gopi Krishna was asking the next big question, "Where Are We Going?" Darwin's work got so misinterpreted that we need to put him back on the shelf. It will take a long, long time to misconstrue what Gopi Krishna was teaching. The issue before us is certainly not "where did we come from?", but "where are we going?" *What is the target of evolution?*

We have been so abused with all the science and folklore about randomness that we can scarce think about a goal for evolution or an order to things. Yet it is there, and our ignorance about this issue is at the very core of our *Present Crisis*. Gopi Krishna offered himself as a living laboratory for those wishing to know what Kundalini was about. It ain't your grandmother's yoga. Gopi Krishna was able to prove in his writings and his life that his experiences following his "awakening" at age 35 had actually "rewired" his nervous system and that had resulted in his having become the new man, the evolutionary new step that all of us are capable of becoming.

Where there is no vision, the people perish; but he that keepeth the law, happy is he. (Proverbs 28:8) The Present Crisis goes back to the myth of the Phoenix. All myths are about time and cycles of time. "What Time Is It?" is another one of the big five questions. Looking back with a new perspective, we can see that about five hundred years ago we took a major turn with the Renaissance and the Reformation. We are right now at the 500th anniversary of the most amazing time in this current age......so far. Ships, compasses and explorers' maps created the first globalization. Printing presses created an explosion of knowledge. The Reformation proved individual experience to be more valid than corrupt church authority and the world changed. Science and intellect became the authority and the yardstick by which newly revealed truth was measured. So, again today the Phoenix that symbolized all of this is on fire in its nest of cinnamon and a new Phoenix is about to rise up from the ashes. Or maybe it won't. The message is that we need to correct some of the mistakes we have made in the past five hundred years. Either that or be forced to accept the consequences of those mistakes. It is no accident that our intellectual achievements and scientific world view have simultaneously created the most impressive advances in the way we live our lives and created the two most awesome threats to that life: nuclear war and global environmental degradation, and fueled our disregard for and our inability to recognize the sacred in all of life.

Today, our pursuit of new technologies and increased luxury and wealth more accurately describe what we are about than any search for the sacred in our lives. This includes all of us. Accordingly, when we look at this situation in light of where we are going, toward a new man with new powers and higher spirituality, we can see that a correction is long overdue. Left to continue on our current path, we are likely to blow ourselves up and so pollute the rubble left that we can no longer live on this planet.

That is why, my fellow travelers, we are now here. The correction is upon us. There is an order to things. I have gone over and over in my head searching for the answer to the question: "Why are we incapable of standing up to our corrupt government and recapturing our reputation as really good people in the world?" What happened? It is beyond the issue of the decline of our civilization or America's waning power in the world. It is no accident that we willingly elected and then re-elected the most corrupt and inept leaders in our history. We are dealing with the critical issue of human evolution right now and this is the turning point. We either make the right turn or careen off the road at 90 miles an hour into oblivion. The evidence suggests that nature, God, the universe, or whatever you call the Divine will "spank" us only as hard as we need to be spanked to turn around. But we are very much asleep. Our first order of business is to try to open our eyes and become aware. The scary part is that it is our choice. We are the Decider. It is called free will. It is also called destiny. We are the people we have been waiting for.

Deep In the Heart of Texas

I live in Austin, deep in the heart of Texas. Here in the gentle heart of Texas I find an entire city of people who are dramatically unlike the grandiose image that the rest of Texans actually like to promote about themselves. Yup, boy, howdy! All over this state, at this late moment, there are majorities of people who believe that the current President Bush is the greatest president we have ever had. Even as the nightmare deepens, they would rather go down with the ship than wake up and put on their life vests. I keep wondering how they would feel if he was from, say, North Dakota.

Anyway, Austin is different. Maybe that is why we have as one of our mottos: "Keep Austin Weird!" People here are awake, kind to each other and aware that we are in a spiritual setting. So much so that some speak of Austin as being a vortex, like Sedona or other places that seem to have an inherent spiritual nature. New York City is also a spiritual vortex, but given the choice, and I have been given it, I would rather be here. Amazingly enough, rarely a day goes by that I do not meet someone who has just arrived here and who is aware that there is a special mission for this city and those who live here. We are sure about one thing........we are in the middle of the change that is about to happen to the whole world. We're the early adopters of tomorrow's world.

Evolution: The Message and the Messenger

So how do we answer the question of evolution? God has given us free will and we are heading toward a target for evolution. There are several other rules at work here: The Law of Cause and Effect, The Law of Attraction, The Law of Free Will and The Law of Love. Back in the early 1980's in a *New York Times* Sunday Magazine article Dr. John Wheeler, the astrophysicist, wrote that when the Unified Field Theory is finally written out, Love will be the verb or the subject of the definition. The remarkable thing about these universal spiritual laws, and there are several more as well, is that they are more immutable than any of the physical laws, and the consequences for disobeying them or being ignorant of their existence is total and final.

So the law says, put God at the front of your consciousness or perish. It is your choice, and all the time we thought the issue was the next Lexus we want to park next to the olive tree in some Arabs back yard. America, land of the free thinkers, has the highest percentage of people, worldwide, who do not believe in evolution. The real meaning of that is this: Evolution and the possibility of things being radically different in the future, the possibility of our current answers to important questions being outdated and in need of radical change, is the real threat posed by evolution. As the hymn says, "new truth makes ancient good uncouth." When we use the phrase, "That's history!" we reveal how we value the past and the lessons it teaches.....you know, those who ignore the past are *bound* to repeat it. Given the vast number of people who actually believe that the past is useless, it is hard to believe we oppose evolution on the basis of anything it says about the past.....ours or anyone else's. When it comes to evolution, the past really is prologue.

The problem with evolution is not the past but the future on many levels. The good ole God-fearing Christians hate evolution because it might reveal that total certainty about their belief is wrong. The possibility of wrong answers just does not fit. That is the core of this issue. If we have to change our answers in the immediate future to conform to some evolutionary change or the threat of extinction, then we cannot be so sure of ourselves and of our control of people today through the things we force people to believe or do.

Then when we begin to talk about the possibility that there even is a plan, a target, for evolution and that the new man is going to be really different from who we are today.....I mean really different..........that's pretty scary to anyone who basically thinks human evolution does not even exist.

But listen to what epigeneticist Dr. Bruce Lipton said on July 26, 2007 on the show "What If It Really Works?" (www.whatifitreallyworks.com) about how evolution is now at a point where the whole human organism, the species, is about to change as a result of the need to adapt to a new survival issue that is before us:

"Humanity is at a crossroads. We are having a punctuated jump from one level of human experience to another. Something is going to shake the structure and how we have been doing things right up to that moment. After that, things will simply not work as they have and those who are aware and willing to change will be the ones who continue."

Change or become extinct! Seems far-fetched today, but will

that be the truth six months from now? What if something happens? What if something really big and unexpected happens? Here you are, this big beautiful dinosaur lumbering around in the garden, and then one day, literally out of the blue, this big thing drops down and life is forever changed and if you are unprepared, or unwilling, you are gone....you are history. And then what happens to our cherished American Way of Life?

I am constantly amazed at the really smart people who adamantly deny any possibility that there could be a global climate change and that industrious man could be the cause of it. On the one hand it matters not a whit what they believe, if it is true. Soon enough they will be forced to accept that it is happening as they sit on the upper decks of their beach houses for cocktails at 5:30 as the surf laps at what used to be the front door steps. If it is not true, then those of us who think it is happening, wrongly, will be labeled as "Chicken Littles" and we will be history. Actually, it seems as if any way you shake it, someone and something is about to be history, and soon.

What Time Is It?

"Soon" is the issue. The Johnstown flood is a case in point. The Johnstown Flood disaster occurred on May 31, 1889. It was the result of the failure of the South Fork Dam situated 14 miles upstream of the town of Johnstown, Pennsylvania, made worse by several days of extremely heavy rainfall. The dam's failure unleashed a torrent of 20 million tons of water. The flood killed over 2,200 people and produced $17 million of damage in less than an hour. The sad part was that the flood did not have to happen. For years there were warnings that the dam had been weakened and would break under duress. However, above the dam was a lovely community of vacation homes. Speculators had purchased an abandoned reservoir, modified it, and converted it into a private resort lake for the wealthy of Pittsburgh. The changes included lowering the dam to make its top wide enough to hold a road, putting a fish screen in the spillway (that also trapped debris), and raising the lake level. These alterations are thought to have increased the vulnerability of the dam. They built cottages and a clubhouse to create the South Fork Fishing and Hunting Club, an exclusive and secretive mountain retreat. Members included over 50 wealthy Pittsburgh steel, coal, and railroad industrialists, among them Andrew Carnegie, Andrew Mellon, Henry Clay Frick, Philander Knox, and Robert Pitcairn. Need I tell you who constantly reassured the down stream residents that the dam was perfectly all right and the alarmists were just plain wrong? Just like today, dire warnings were cancelled by the golden rule; he who has the most gold, rules. Of course, that's history. *Credit Wikipedia, http://en.wikipedia.org/wiki/Johnstown_flood*

Suppose the alarmists are wrong and are using their tactics just to get ahead politically. Suppose all they want is to get elected so they can get power and money. Suppose that is the nature of things.........so who do you want getting ahead and making money, people who make weaponry and wars, or people who make cleaner water and solar energy? Now they tell us the war in Iraq is going to have to go on for many more years. Wanna bet? Any feeling person with the slightest degree of intuitive reasoning ability can actually feel what is about to happen. It is in the air. You can breathe it. It's like that prophetic Harry Chapin song, "I believe something's coming and I believe it is something big." Well boys and girls, the wait is almost over.

Suppose there is no global environmental problem, especially if we are cited as being responsible for it. Suppose, as the Mayans believed, we are passing through some kind of equator in the middle of The Milky Way, also known as The Photon Belt and that making this passage is resulting in major Earth changes including unusual climate changes and increased accumulations of pollutants. Even that demands that we somehow have to deal with these changes and adapt to what is going on. There are people out there who refuse to accept any responsibility for what is going on........so just for them: *It ain't us, it's the journey*......now lets figure out how to get through it.

There is a target for the process of evolution. Men and women all over this planet, all seven billion of us, are going to go through a big change. That is why we are here now. All we do now must be done in a sacred manner and in celebration. We are the ones we have been waiting for.

The Cold War is over. All that stuff is gone. Ban the bomb is also gone.....history. So how come we still keep making more and better nuclear bombs and arming our "allies" with them as well? And how come we are totally sound asleep about this? If the public knew the destructive potential of just one current-generation 20-megaton nuclear weapon, we would crawl on our hands and knees (you have seen worshippers doing that in Latin America) to Washington to beg our elected officials to stop this insanity. One of these bombs will so destroy the environment in a 100-mile radius of the drop zone that it will be uninhabitable for a century. Take that New Haven, as you laugh at New York's vulnerability.

An Old Soldier's Warning

It is an amazing thing that just as the Christians have taken such a strong position within our nation's governmental bodies, protecting us from married gay terrorists and biologists with magic cures for most of our physical ills with stem cells, we have also drifted into the fullest expression of the ills of the Military Industrial Complex nightmare. Do you remember what President Eisenhower said in his farewell address on January 17, 1961?

"A vital element in keeping the peace is our military establishment. Our arms must be mighty, ready for instant action, so that no potential aggressor may be tempted to risk his own destruction.

This conjunction of an immense military establishment and a large arms industry is new in the American experience. The total influence — economic, political, even spiritual — is felt in every city, every statehouse, every office of the federal government. We recognize the imperative need for this development. Yet we must not fail to comprehend its grave implications. Our toil, resources and livelihood are all involved; so is the very structure of our society.

In the councils of government, we must guard against the acquisition of unwarranted influence, whether sought or unsought, by the military-industrial complex. The potential for the disastrous rise of misplaced power exists and will persist.

We must never let the weight of this combination endanger our liberties or democratic processes. We should take nothing for granted. Only an alert and knowledgeable citizenry can compel the proper meshing of the huge industrial and military machinery of defense with our peaceful methods and goals so that security and liberty may prosper together."

He warned about the spiritual damage to our country. Can you imagine any country with a true spiritual life turning to war first to settle any issue with another country? Can you imagine what this country and our issues would be like, if our leaders and our followers actually believed in One Powerful God?

Forget the negative stuff, too scary. How about the positive stuff? How about the simple reality that we have come to the end of the road with the use of force? As David Hawkins' book, *Power vs. Force,* so brilliantly shows us, there is most assuredly a better way. Now is the time to find it and use it. Force, military or economic, no longer gets us what we want and need. Now is the time to begin to understand how we can use our divine spiritual POWER to change things. What If *It* Really Works? We chose that name for our mission and radio show because it is what we must attempt to do.....the *It* is using our spiritual center and power to actually change things. Wouldn't it be totally amazing to discover that the collective power of America's 330 million citizens could be used to change things for the better with positive aspects and results all around and at a fraction of the cost? Of course, it might also mean at a fraction of the profit as well. That too can be changed.

The Prophesy

So here is what we see is happening. Sometime in the next 4.5 years, and probably much sooner, events are going to conspire to force us to make an abrupt and irrevocable change. The past, the prologue, will most definitely be over. The only issue is how we are going to handle this change. Fear, as the biologists tell us, makes us create really bad mistakes. Love, as the spiritual people tell us, makes things better for all. (The smart biologists say the same thing.) No one can predict the future. No one can say that this earthquake, or that flood, or that fire or that nuclear bomb will happen to whom or when. Maybe all of these things will happen at once. Or maybe just one asteroid will do the trick. Regardless of the mechanism, nature itself is now about to redirect us toward a new path. In this book we took one possible scenario and set it in 2008, but the story can happen in many ways and in any year in the near future. That is where the Merkabah comes in. Our ancestors will call it evolution. What follows is the fictional part of this book. It is a prophecy of how all this will be resolved. It is purely fictional. So far.

Chapter 3

The Hebrew word Merkabah (הבכרמ "chariot", derived from the consonantal root r-k-b with general meaning "to ride") is used in Ezekiel (1:4-26) to refer to the throne-chariot of God, the four-wheeled vehicle driven by four chayot "living creatures", each of which has four wings and four faces (of a man, lion, ox, and eagle). Jewish biblical commentaries emphasize that the imagery of the Merkabah is not meant to be taken literally; rather the chariot and its accompanying angels are analogies for the various ways that God reveals Himself in this world.

Each knew from childhood that they had been born in this constellation for a real adventure. Now the time had come. They had been completely educated about Earth and the relationship it held with their own Constellation Sirius. Now it was July 23, 2008 on Earth. The exact time that Sirius is aligned each year with Earth and pointed to by the observatory called The Egyptian Pyramids. Their ancestors had somehow built the Pyramids for that purpose and as a guide to get them safely to Earth.

It sure wasn't like the Earth Astronauts suiting up for a launch into local Earth space. In fact, there was no suiting up involved. As Dr. Rupert Sheldrake suggested we on Earth do, the Sirians had learned how to travel in a Body of Light......the Merkabah. The trip across the galaxy would be made by the twelve crewmembers and the other passengers in a Body of Light. It would happen at a speed greater than the speed of light as well. All told there would be 1,728,012 souls on board the Body of Light. How that became the number was as follows. The rules allowed each of the twelve members of the crew, now assembled in the Great Cathedral for a final meditation with the Masters, to be responsible for training and leading 144,000 other souls on the whole mission. By Earth standards, this was clearly impossible. But in Spirit, all things are possible. So it was a big crowd that was going to Earth with The Twelve, and they had a big mission.

Earth writers would probably write a novel about this crowd and have them coming to Earth to repel the asteroid or stop the bomb with three seconds remaining. If only it were going to be that simple. There would be some split second timing to be sure, but the clock was already running and the seismographs on Earth were keeping time, one Earth tremor at a time. They would all get there on time to see the whole sudden drama unfold......but not to stop it. Their mission was to become the "outside experts" as humanity made a forced and abrupt turn back to the direction of the target for human evolution. Funny in a way. There had been more than 80 million copies of a series of books titled *The Left Behind Series* that promoted the idea that the Super Christians would be taken off planet when the action started and the rest of the people would be left on Earth to fight it out. In reality the opposite was true. The only people being left behind were those Sirians not chosen to enter the Body of Light for the mission to Earth.

The Masters' Chapel in the Great Cathedral was large enough for all The Twelve and the Council of the Twenty-Four Ascended Masters plus The King to meet and exerience the Blessing for the mission. That Blessing lasted for 24 hours. The alabaster walls glowed from within, the torches on the sconces added direct light and the copal incense filled the chapel with the aroma of spiritual courage. There was total silence as each Council member communicated with each crewmember one at a time as they all sat in the sacred circle. The communication was a blessing that infused each crewmember with the final knowledge that he or she would need to survive the mission. It was beautiful to see, more beautiful to experience. The glowing light accented the emerald green robes with gold trim worn by all. The chanting of the Gayatri mantra by the 1,728,000 passengers assembled outside the Chapel in the Great Hall of the Cathedral was the only sound. It reverberated off the walls of the Chapel and the Great Hall as if it was going to echo across the entire universe, and it did.

When the blessing was complete, each crewmember was given a gold ring with a piece of the best Lapis Lazuli mounted on it. It symbolized the TRUTH they were about to take to Earth. The Lapis came from the Kieffer Valley in Afghanistan at an altitude of 13,000 feet, which symbolized that all of humanity was now about to rise above all previous experience and wisdom to the new level of evolution ordained by these very Masters.

Then the Masters led the way into the Great Hall and stood before the passengers along with the crew. The High Priest, Metatron, addressed the multitude.

"Today, you begin the most important mission ever undertaken in this galaxy. What you experience and what you create from this moment forward will determine the outcome of all the souls living on Earth. It is the last opportunity that our brothers and sisters will have to regain their spiritual power and create on Earth the Garden it is intended to be. You will not fail. Your victory is ordained and certain. But there are challenges ahead that even we cannot foresee. You will always be accompanied by our presence and power and need only ask and we will be at your side, but the mission is up to you. Go in peace, go with God and celebrate that in the entire Universe, you have been chosen for and entrusted with this sacred task."

As he spoke telepathically, both the passengers and the crew fell to their knees in silence, bowed their heads and felt the cool breeze of pure Spirit move across each one. When he was finished, the vaulted ceiling of the Great Hall opened and slowly the twelve crewmembers rose up, now encased in light and reached down their hands to hold the hands of the 144,000 souls that each would take with them in the Merkabah. As they left the opened Cathedral ceiling headed for Earth, astronomers in Australia saw a huge light leave the constellation Sirius as it rose over the South Pacific to the east just ahead of the Sun on this special morning.

Nine minutes later the Merkabah arrived safely on Earth. It was sunrise, July 23, 2008. From the looks of them, one would never dream that they were from any place other than right down the block. The block turned out to be any one of the seven continents. Each of seven teams had been assigned to one of the seven continents. The remaining five teams were given assignments that supported the first seven; line and staff as we say in Corporate America.

July 23, 2008

Once they were on the ground, Michael called the crewmembers together. They met in the crowded King's Chamber in the Great Pyramid of Giza. Michael chose this spot because it would just hold the crew and was a sacred and ancient space. Nearby was the Queen's Chamber with its shaft that looked up at night directly to Sirius. On a makeshift altar were now arrayed twelve of the crystal skulls that his team had located from the places they were left as beacons for the team many centuries earlier. The fact that the skulls had been located was a positive sign for the future. Metatron appeared via a hologram to congratulate them on their journey and for having so quickly found the crystal skull beacons. He told them that all was in place and the sacred ceremony would begin later that day. He then left.

The full moon had been five days earlier so they knew this evening would have less light than there had been for better than a week. Michael explained the next parts of the plan. The original seven teams had been sent to each continent to immediately be in place as the drama unfolded. Their training had included how to immediately insert themselves into the infrastructures of each region in a way that would give them command over all important services and procedures necessary to secure order. The eighth team was dispatched to every military unit of every country in the world. The ninth team was to be responsible for food on each continent. The tenth team was responsible for health, healing and education throughout the world. The eleventh team was charged with the awesome task of bringing the world's religions together as quickly as possible. The twelfth team was to handle all the executive issues facing the mission.

Michael decided to keep his headquarters in Giza because of the relative safety of the pyramids and the fact that they would be far enough away from the blast zone, should the suspected nuclear attack on Iran take place. Michael's Team Twelve was charged with strategy and organization of the mission, plus complete care of the crew and passengers.

When you think about the size and enormity of the mission, you imagine that the Council would have given the command to somebody like George Patton or Norman Schwarzkopf. Michael was not an imposing military figure. Rather, he was the servant leader, confident about his own safety and direction, but always alert to how he could help those who followed him. He was quiet and always seemed to negotiate well with anyone, but there was one thing everyone knew. When he saw a mistake being made, or an injustice committed, he could move quicker than a hungry submerged crocodile about to grab a gazelle at the edge of the water hole. When Michael was like this, everyone instinctively knew to get out of the way. He prevailed. Always.

Part of his leadership skills had been perfected on earlier trips to Earth. The Olympic thing was a case in point. He had no real desire to compete, but he had to compete in the Olympics to fully understand the human desire for power and the survival thing so common among winners. For him it was easy. In fact, on one of his latter training trips to Earth, he would glide across the back mountain roads in Western Colorado going just as fast as he did in the Olympics. Without the competition huffing behind him, he made it look effortless. Hemingway said that courage is grace under pressure. Michael's picture appears three times in your dictionary....under courage, grace and pressure. He would accomplish his mission.

He liked to build things. As he rode through the mountains he would dream about building a house there someday when the mission had been accomplished. He would design and actually build it with his own hands........right on the side of one of the mountains near Telluride. We met him in Telluride on that trip, as we were also on a training mission to Earth. Part of his training was building the house we were about to buy, but now he had a much bigger thing to build.

The Merkabah members and crew were able to instantly communicate with each other telepathically. As a result, they could gather at any moment for whatever purpose. Tonight was going to be The Invocation, the ceremony that would start the re-direction. There had never been a sacred ceremony like this. This was a first. Michael, the builder, the captain, spent much of the day, between progress reports, creating this ceremony in his head. Each of the twelve crewmembers would invoke the powers of The Council and the Great Spirit to accompany and lead their teams of 144,000 passengers.

Michael went outside when the Sun had set. Darkness covered the Pyramids and the sky was dimly lit by the rising waning moon. The members of his team were there. Several current Earth residents had been brought in to serve as additional staff. They had been on Earth preparing for this moment all their lives.

Grace the Elder was the oldest and was along because she had worked with The Council for most of her life. She was lovingly known by all as *Amazing Grace* because once she was assigned to work with a soul amazing things seemed to happen. She knew this galaxy like the palm of her hand and she could read the heart and soul of anyone who came before her. In two weeks she would celebrate her 86th birthday. Frail now and battling cancers, she was the perfect picture of a crone. She could even shape shift depending of where she found herself. She was bent over and her face showed the record in wrinkles of a fantastic life lived in many dimensions at once. A grandmother and a southerner, in her younger days her wonderful smile and her petite body had opened some of the most impressive doors on the planet. From the Secretary General of the United Nations office to David Rockefeller's 56th floor art-lined suite at 30 Rock on Fifth Avenue to the leadership palaces of the most important men and women in the world, and, of course the international corporate cathedrals, Grace always seemed to have a pass. Wherever she went, she always had her latest pet project with her, and she was always at least 20 years ahead of her time. I met Grace in person for the first time in 2003 and she was anxious to talk about the coming importance of holography as a communications tool for the future. I had heard about this, but she seemed a little off the wall when she talked about all this future stuff, so I took notes and went on. Now I was seeing first hand how the Council actually did communicate with holograms.

It is one thing to see this in the latest installment of Star Wars. It is completely different to see it happen right before your eyes, know you are wide awake and most important, know you are hearing the direct spoken words of the King himself and watch him speak them to you from across the galaxy. This is not long ago in a galaxy far away. This is today, July 23, 2008. Wow!

Grace was famous among those who knew her for being the galactic tour guide. It seems whenever someone had been selected by The Council to make the leap from old human to new human, Grace showed up for a few days to take them on a little tour of the area, The Milky Way and some of the nearby suburbs. Grace loved taking one of the new humans up into one of the gigantic crystal-like space ships that hid behind some of the darker clouds in the afternoon sky. At first it seemed like an imaginary trip until something would happen, like tripping on one of the steps in the ship. Then it felt real enough. Grace wanted me to have the whole tour when she showed up in my life. And that was before Rupert Sheldrake told me about the importance of our traveling through space with our minds and spirit bodies.

We went all the way out to the end of the galaxy and that is when I acquired my addiction to Hubble telescope pictures of our galaxy and others.

NASA

Barred Spiral Galaxy

The pictures are terrific, many better than this one, but in person when you see one of these places the only way to describe how you feel is AWE FULL, which is also the way one feels, I am told, when you are allowed a brief glimpse of God. Seeing the galaxy from that vantage point fully and finally confirms the minuteness of our individual lives.....at least in Earth time and space. It would be like taking one of the 15 year old kids who lives in the tunnels under Grand Central Station and never sees the light of day on a transcontinental trip in the owner's cabin of a private 747-400. It simply is impossible to imagine, but it is out there and we are being invited to make this journey, which is a central part of getting to the target for our evolution. All the new humans on Michael's staff had been given the grand tour by Grace, most since 1977. Grace escorted Ken around the galaxy in 1985. Ken is the only person I personally know who has lived or worked in at least 130 of the world's countries. He once said to me that after all that travel you find that you can easily get home sick for every place at once. Ken traveled so much because he was one of the most curious people I have ever met. He got that way by knowing Margaret Mead. In fact, Ken was her favorite student. So much so that when he completed her graduate course at Columbia and started off as a Life Magazine photographer, she invited him to travel with her on her study adventures in Bali, Samoa, and New Guinea among others. He would photograph the people and behaviors that Professor Mead was studying to illustrate her work in books and lectures. Along the way he learned the encyclopedia of human behavior and relationships. Also along the way, like Grace and me, Ken became one of the new humans.

Ken's purpose here was to use that information for the crew and passengers in understanding cultural differences around the world. I have known Ken since 1982 and have been the willing recipient of his vast knowledge. We used to have lunch outside in New York at busy sidewalk restaurants so he could teach me about what people were expressing with their actions. For example, when two people are walking down the street and one has an arm over the shoulder of the other, that person is exerting control over the situation. Ken is big, and he taught me that big people automatically create fear in smaller people, whether they want to or not. He knew how to reduce that fear. He even told me about a man who was 6'6" tall who learned in college how to "accidentally" fall down when he was meeting people who would be afraid of him, thus giving them reason to see him to be not so fearsome. Extreme, but effective. He showed me how to walk up to anyone on the street with your palms open to them to show you were not carrying anything dangerous. Then he showed me that doing the same thing with animals was a signal that animals automatically recognized and read as a safety signal.

So with the crew, passengers and new humans in Giza, Michael directed each to connect with each other on all the continents of the planet. The Invocation was about to begin. The waning moon was just above the horizon now and its yellow light cast a faint glow on Michael's face as he began chanting the Gayatri mantra.

Om Buhr Bhuvah Svaha (The Earth and the sky and the heavens)
Tat Savitur Vareniyam (The Divine Effulgence we all adore)
Bhargo Devasya Dheemahi (I contemplate on your Divine Glory)

Dhiyo Yo Nah Prachodayaat (Please help me to enlighten my intellect)

This was chanted one hundred and eight times that evening by almost 2 million souls around the world, in perfect harmony and perfect timing. The fact is that all seven billion of us heard the chanting on one of the frequencies we all know and seldom acknowledge. The vibration of this mantra was setting the energy for the mission on Earth and throughout the galaxy.

Michael then led the passengers, crew and new humans in a prayer they all knew and prayed daily:

"I am a Spirit, and as a Spirit, God's Presence and Power is within me.
I am in tune with the Spirit World and open to its' influence.
Please mold me into the best instrument that I can be so that I may serve you with all my heart and all my soul.
I am a child of the universe.
I am Divine Peace.
I am Divine Love.
I am Divine Wisdom.
I am Divine Bliss.
I am the Light.
I am the Light.
I am the Light."

Then there was silence. Some place in the heart of every man, woman and child on Earth at this moment there was profound silence. The time had come. The meditation continued for 30 minutes and then Michael asked each crew member to speak his or her heart about the mission.

The first crewmember to speak was Grace Devereaux. By far she was the most beautiful of them all. Looking at her eyes and facial features you would not have been sure if she was a Native

American, or a native of Sicily or Kashmir. You could even see a little of Bora Bora in her eyes. She was a global spiritual beauty. Her power exceeded her beauty. Her assignment was the most difficult of all; to lead the world's religious adherents to a galactic understanding of who they were and how their individual religions would need to release all those things that divided their members from the members of the other religions. Happy Trails, Grace Devereaux! Her first words dispelled any lingering doubt about the success of her mission or her selection for the responsibility. With a soft smile and her melodic voice she began:

"Our hearts are open to the light in the stars which cover us and the light in our souls which illumines us. The vibrations we have sent out in waves and particles this night to the farthest reaches of the universe will come back to us full of promise and glory. We are here on a true mission from God. This creation, now at the tipping point, is ours to direct toward the goal established by our Father and King. We are here to neither judge nor condemn, but to complete and reconcile, to bring the good news that man, as he knows himself, has come to the end of the road. Untold ages ago, another man came to this moment and he could go no further. The Council sent a mission to Earth to create a new man and a new humanity. The next rung on the ladder toward the target of evolution was taken. Now is the seventh and final time this will happen on Earth."

"I bring you this direct proclamation from the King:

'The day of awakening is here, and the day of reckoning and weeding out is not far away. The cleansing of the world will take place and only those awakened souls will be left to experience life in the divine state. Others will fall by the wayside, left behind, in the world of illusion and darkness. The arrival of the Golden Age will be heralded by a new-coming as well as some upheavals, sufficient to uproot the evil state prevalent today. After the storm, there will be a new beginning and the atmosphere will be completely different. It will be a new age. The age of love, harmony, and cooperation will replace the age of war, fighting, hatred, jealousy, greed, and all these negative aspects of life. Everyone should prepare now for this new change, for I promise that it will come and only those who are ready will survive it. I have given the warning, I have given my message and no one who hears my words can claim ignorance. Do not delay to set right your own lifestyle and change it to the way of God because there is no other way.'

'The Golden Age started in 2002 A.D. In this Era, everyone will be evolved souls. Self-realization will be the main aim of life and not self-adulation, as propagated by some men. Narrow boundaries between nations will vanish. People will see unity in diversity. There is only one religion, the religion of love. There is only one caste, the caste of humanity. There is only one language, the language of the heart. There is only one God and He is omnipresent, omnipotent and omniscient. Education is for life, not for living. Character will be given more importance than skill. There will be sufficient food on Mother Earth for everyone. The power of prayer will avert natural calamities. People will have less desire. During this Era, science and technology will be used for the welfare of mankind. There will be no wars. People will have fear only of sin and will have all love for God. Age-old Sanathana Dharma will prevail on the Earth. People will lead a happy life, with the ultimate goal being self-realization.'

"We will accomplish this with grace and ease and on time because this has been ordained by God and all the Angels in Heaven. I rejoice with you in being included in this most important moment in the history of our galaxy. I recommit to you and to my brothers and sisters my complete life and future that our mission be done on Earth as it is being done in the heavens above us from whence we came."

You could have heard a pin drop in every corner of the world. Although she spoke to the 1,728,000 passengers, twelve crewmembers and the few new humans in the global gathering, all men's hearts were opened as she carefully placed the complete desire for peace in each and every heart on Earth. The silence became a meditation.

Chapter 4

"The cleansing of the world will take place and only those awakened souls will be left to experience life in the divine state. Others will fall by the wayside, left behind, in the world of illusion and darkness."

What's this? These words from the King's proclamation sound way too much like somebody who just put down the last volume of the *Left Behind* series! Surely we have not come to this? Surely we do not expect Jesus to come out of the clouds and take the good people some place and destroy all the others? Or do we?

Yes, it does have the sound of the Super Christians who have been cheering for this war to escalate so we can destroy the infidels who hold up the rebuilding of the Temple, so that Jesus can come back and take all the good Super Christians away while he destroys the world. Surely the "awakened souls" the King refers to are not the ones who want America to prevail in the world through more of the perpetual war for America to be No. 1 in the world!

What is this "new-coming" the King is talking about?

About 1,000,000 years ago, our forefathers lived in small communities close to the equator around the world. That opening scene from *2001: A Space Odyssey* where the apeman uses the first tool still gives me chills. That's us so long ago, but we did progress. At a certain point we set up the rules. Rule One: women rule. At the time it seemed obvious. Women ruled because they had all the power. They gave life; they brought order; and they were the nurturers. Men were good for keeping the borders secure and finding food. But women knew how to run the villages.

All births were virgin births. People would notice that one of the women was growing a large tummy and then one day she would squat down and deliver a baby, just like the animals. There was no thought that birth was a cooperative act between men and women. Then one day, they made one of the most important discoveries in history. It was discovered that about nine months after a man and woman had sex a baby came. Then the relationship became clear. Men, not women, were the cause of babies being born. The change was profound and evolutionary. One day women were the center of the universe. The next day, men all over the world decided that since they were the "first cause", women would from that time forward be second class citizens. Women were demoted and children were given the name of the Father. We all seem to remember the supremacy of women. Some of us are even open to its return.

They put the signs of this change everywhere. They burned it into our memory and just to be sure we didn't forget they created myths about it. It is a 40 week period of gestation between the sexual act and the birth. Everywhere we see the number 40, it has been placed these to help us remember. Noah had 40 days and nights of rain; the Jews fleeing Egypt spent 40 years in the desert; Jesus spent 40 days in the desert. Even today life begins at 40. It was the single most important discovery up to that time. When we see the reminders of the 40 weeks, we remember that birth comes as a result of our fathers. New beginnings are new births.

A million years ago is a long time and a lot can happen, and a lot did. Time itself got some revisions. We discovered the cycles of the moon and the predictability of the seasons as we moved away from the equator. We also discovered that the Sun always went back to the same time and spot after 13 moons had passed. Years became ages. We discovered that after 3750 solar years the location of the Pole Star, Polaris, The North Star, shifted to a new star. Then we discovered that after seven of these 3750 year cycles we were back to the starting point and we call this larger period of 26,250 years the Great Year of Precession of the Equinoxes. Once that cycle was identified, it was divided into twelve equal parts and we called these ages. Myths were made to remind us what time it was in these ages by the position of the stars. All the myths are about time-keeping on a grand scale. The Egyptians kept track of these ages in what Eusebius referred to as the Great Chronicle, which may still exist in papyrus copies of the stone Stele created by the Priests charged with remembering where we were and what time it was.

Each of the twelve ages had a personality and each was marked by where we were in the great year and they became identified as the twelve signs of the zodiac. Today we understand that one age leads to another. The Age of Taurus gave way to the Age of Aries a little over 4000 years ago. About 2000 years ago the Age of Aries gave way to the Age of Pisces. And today we enter the Age of Aquarius. It is said that 2012 is the actual end of this age and the beginning of the next.

The Egyptians believed that the symbols were to change so that everyone would know the age in which they lived. The symbols 6000 years ago were all about the Bull, or Baal. The symbol 4000 years ago became the Lamb led by the Shepherd. "The Lord is my Shepherd." The symbol was changed 2000 years

NASA

Earth

ago to reflect the Age of Pisces and the shepherd became the fisher of men and the symbol was the Fish, adopted by the early Christians. Historically, the Age of Aquarius was symbolized by the water bearer, a young boy with a pitcher on his shoulder that was aimed down and pouring out water. Today we have been given the gift of the real thing. Sir Fred Hoyle, writing in 1948 said, "Once a photograph of the Earth, taken from the outside, is available . . . a new idea as powerful as any in history will let loose." And we all intuitively know what it means. The Earth is the water bearer, the oasis in the black desert. Home.

But new ages mean new beginnings. The Egyptians believed that with each new age, the message had to be recast. The story of Isis and Horus, the child who grew up to become the Father-God contains all of the details of the story of Mary and Jesus. The early Christians, responding to the need for new symbols for the Age of Pisces took the Egyptian story of God's presence and adapted it to the new age 2000 years ago. Yes, there was a man named Jesus and he was a Master and the mold into which the early Christians poured the old mythology. However, 2000 years of dogma and fantasy have skewed that message off its original mark. By the way, "missing the mark" is a literal translation of the meaning of sin. Whoever is coming will not be here to judge and destroy. That will be taken care of by the consequences of our past wrongful actions best described as karma. There will be a time of weeding out and the King says that time is now close at hand. I take that to mean before the end of the age in 2012.

Chapter 5

And a little child shall lead them.

Isaiah 11:1-10

The message behind the message is always the same when the new symbols are applied to the real secret. There is within each of us a Divine spark, a presence that is to grow until it consumes us in its holy embrace. It is called the Christ in the West, the Son or Sun of God. It is the Luminous Sun that has been there from the beginning. Jesus, The Christ, was the first of the new men in this age to fully express this inner Sunship. And now, a new man

Dodecahedron

comes to awaken us to the new age we call Aquarius. This coming, this new man, this new consciousness, this new age will not be a return of anything other than the ages' old knowledge that there is within us all a divinity that demands we see it in each other and treat ourselves and our world accordingly. And the New Man arrives as a child.

He arrives with angels and carries within himself all the messages of the sacred expressed in geometry, innocence and inherent power. The New Man, the new Adam, the seventh and last of the newly evolved humans will come as a little child and as he grows, he will lead them to become the God within themselves. Jesus quoted Psalm 82 when he told his followers: *"I have said, you are gods; and all of you are children of the most High."* So it shall be again as it always has been, with the birth of a child whose mother is a virgin and whose father is God, as in the beginning.

So where is he? Listen to the grandmothers. They all seem to know the secret. Many children being born today are different, very different. They not only know so much more than we did, but they have unusual powers of perception, and completely different skills. I saw a one-year-old child last weekend open up a complex toy designed for a three-year-old. It had batteries and was based on a design of a boom box. This exceptional child quickly understood what this was for and how it worked.

These new children are called Indigo Children and others are called Crystal Children and most are not correctly labeled at all. This is what the pros are saying. The following extract describes the difference between Indigo and Crystal Children. It is from Doreen Virtue's article, *Indigo and Crystal Children*:

"The first thing most people notice about Crystal Children is their eyes, large, penetrating, and wise beyond their years. Their eyes lock on and hypnotize you, while you realize your soul is being laid bare for the child to see. Perhaps you've noticed this special new "breed" of children rapidly populating our planet. They are happy, delightful and forgiving. This generation of new lightworkers, roughly ages 0 through 7, are like no previous generation. Ideal in many ways, they are the pointers for where humanity is headed ... and it's a good direction!

"The older children (approximately age 7 through 25), called "Indigo Children", share some characteristics with the Crystal Children. Both generations are highly sensitive and psychic, and have important life purposes. The main difference is their temperament. Indigos have a warrior spirit, because their collective purpose is to mash down old systems that no longer serve us. They are here to quash government, educational, and legal systems that lack integrity. To accomplish this end, they need tempers and fiery determination.

"Those adults who resist change and who value conformity

may misunderstand the Indigos. They are often mislabeled with psychiatric diagnoses of Attention Deficit with Hyperactivity Disorder (ADHD) or Attention Deficit Disorder (ADD). Sadly, when they are medicated, the Indigos often lose their beautiful sensitivity, spiritual gifts and warrior energy..........In contrast, the Crystal Children are blissful and even-tempered. Sure, they may have tantrums occasionally, but these children are largely forgiving and easy-going. The Crystals are the generation who benefit from the Indigos trailblazing. First, the Indigo Children lead with a machete, cutting down anything that lacks integrity. Then the Crystal Children follow the cleared path, into a safer and more secure world.

"The terms "Indigo" and "Crystal" were given to these two generations because they most accurately describe their aura colours and energy patterns. Indigo children have a lot of indigo blue in their auras. This is the colour of the "third eye chakra", which is the energy center inside the head located between the two eyebrows. This chakra regulates clairvoyance, or the ability to see energy, visions, and spirits. Many of the Indigo children are clairvoyant.

"The Crystal Children have opalescent auras, with beautiful multi-colours in pastel hues. This generation also shows a fascination for crystals and rocks...... Indigo Children can sense dishonesty, like a dog can sense fear. Indigos know when they're being lied to, patronized, or manipulated. And since their collective purpose is to usher us into a new world of integrity, the Indigos inner lie-detectors are integral. As mentioned before, this warrior spirit is threatening to some adults. And the Indigos are unable to conform to dysfunctional situations at home, work, or school. They don't have the ability to dissociate from their feelings and pretend like everything's okay....unless they are medicated or sedated.

"Crystal Children's innate spiritual gifts are also misunder-stood, specifically, their telepathic abilities which lead them to talk later in life. In the new world which the Indigos are ushering in, we will all be much more aware of our intuitive thoughts and feelings. We won't rely so much upon the spoken or written word. Communication will be faster, more direct, and more honest, because it will be mind to mind. Already, increasing numbers of us are getting in touch with our psychic abilities. Our interest in the paranormal is at an all-time high, accompanied by books, television shows, and movies on the topic. So, it's not surprising that the generation following the Indigos are incredibly telepathic. Many of the Crystal Children have delayed speech patterns, and it's not uncommon for them to wait until they're 3 or 4 years old to begin speaking. But parents tell me they have no trouble communicating with their silent children. Far from it! The parents engage in mind-to-mind communication with their Crystal Children. And the Crystals use a combination of telepathy, self-fashioned sign language, and sounds (including song) to get their point across.

"The trouble comes about when the Crystals are judged by medical and educational personnel as having "abnormal" speaking patterns. It's no coincidence that as the number of Crystals are born, that the number of diagnoses for autism is at a record high. It's true that the Crystal Children are different from other generations. But why do we need to pathologize these differences? If the children are successfully communicating at home and the parents aren't reporting any problems... then why try to make a problem? The diagnostic criteria for autism are quite clear. It states that the autistic person lives in his or her own world, and is disconnected from other people. The autistic person doesn't talk because of an indifference to communicating with others. Crystal Children are quite the opposite. They are among the most connected, communicative, caring and cuddly of any generation. They are also quite philosophical and spiritually gifted. And they display an unprecedented level of kindness and sensitivity to this world. Crystal Children spontaneously hug and care for people in need. An autistic person wouldn't do that!

"In my book "The Care and Feeding of Indigo Children", I wrote that ADHD should stand for Attention Dialed into a Higher Dimension. This would more accurately describe that generation. In the same vein, Crystal Children don't warrant a label of autism. They aren't autistic! They're AWE-tistic! These children are worthy of awe, not labels of dysfunction. If anyone is dysfunctional, it's the systems that aren't accommodating the continuing evolution of the human species. If we shame the children with labels, or medicate them into submission, we will have undermined a heaven-sent gift. We will crush a civilization before it's had time to take roots. Fortunately, there are many positive solutions and alternatives. And the same heaven that sent us the Crystal Children can assist those of us who are advocates for the children." From:

http://www.namastecafe.com/evolution/indigo/childadults.htm

So, could it be that there really is something to this leap into a new evolutionary level? Someone once asked Duke Ellington how he knew if a song was good music or not. "If it sounds good, it is good!" was the reply. And the same applies here. God knows we need some new answers and the rich white men working for you in government are not really coming up with anything but the same old answers. The young men are driving around in war zones of our own making with poorly armored HumVees with shoddy body armor. Right now, anybody coming up with the answer to stop perpetual war is a welcome addition to the bankrupt thinking of the warrior class.

So ask yourself, is it possible? The scientists tell us that there is a biological process called punctuated change. This means that an organism is constantly sending sensors out to the borders of its body and these report back to the central processor on what is happening just beyond the borders and what these changing dynamics may require of the organism in order to survive. The punctuation moment occurs when the central processor gathers overwhelming evidence that a major survival or growth opportunity is present and makes a reorganization effort to align itself with the changing environment.

This is clearly one of those moments. We need all the help we can get. On the one hand we can probably survive things going on as they have since the Second World War. However it appears that the dangers of staying this course are life threatening. It also appears that there must be other options, there must be a better way. People have prayed for such a change for long enough. For years I have asked people the question: If you could have peace under any circumstances, would you accept it? I can tell you this is a tough question for many people. The thought process started by this question immediately includes survival issues like, Would I be free?, Would I have enough food and clothing?, Is it better to be "Red or dead?", etc. But the question is: Is peace what you really want? If you could have peace, would you take it under any circumstances? If that is what we want, and most thinkers and spiritual leaders say it is, then that is going to arrive through some sort of jump. Everything else is just part of the problem. As Einstein said, "The solution cannot be found on the same level that created the problem."

In the view from Sirius, the system is no longer able to change or adapt by itself. Outside help is called for. The Indigo and Crystal children are here and they have a very specific purpose: to connect with each other and lead the adults, who are ready, to the next rung on the ladder. They also have a very real responsibility to connect with the crew and passengers on the Merkabah. To do this, these children are being brought together all over the planet for conferences, events and training. A powerful example was the Global Concert for the Environment held in July 2007. The original was Woodstock, the sandbox of the Hippies. When these children are mislabeled and drugged into conformity, they wind up feeling like they have been in a shipwreck and are being asked to survive on a desert island like 21st century Robinson

Crusoes. When brought together to discover they are connected and prepared, a transformation takes places that will ultimately affect the whole planet. They are the people we have been waiting for, and they have been waiting for us. And now they are here with us.

Chapter 6

When Grace Devereaux's presentation was over, Brad got up to speak. He did not have the booming voice of Schwarzkopf, and he was a little bit shorter, but he had the General's heart and a similar steel-trap mind. General Schwarzkopf once told me that he had spent as much time in prayer for his men and his mission as he did in strategy and planning. He was very shy about sharing that information......in fact it was the only thing he was shy about. Brad was the same way. He told me his secret once. "You cannot speak your truth. People do not learn by speaking or listening to someone else's truth. They learn by you living your truth." Brad did that. At 53 he had developed the rugged good looks of someone who had been through a lifetime of adventure. He told me once that when the mission was over, he wanted to stay on an island in the Bahamas and photograph beautiful models and make beautiful spiritual movies. Okay. Sounds like fun to me too, but first there is a war to be won.

Brad had been trained as a commander on Sirius. West Point would have been a cake-walk in comparison. The training was about strategy, values, processes, leadership, and being in alignment with the Divine in all things. Brad could have driven a tank, flown an airplane or commanded a submarine. He could also have been an AK47 sharpshooter. But those skills were not what was needed in the coming global battle. Brad had the right stuff for this too.

For more than eighty years the leaders of the world's major countries had committed their citizens to a global arms race. Those that made the weapons then sold them to nations who could not muster the Promethean effort to make their own. Eighty years of this insured that in every conflict both sides would have similar weapons supplied by the same manufacturers. There were enough nuclear, biological and conventional weapons to kill every man, woman and child in the world, all seven billion of us, several times over in a matter of hours. In fact, that was the vision of many of the world's religious leaders. Muslims, Christians, Jews and fundamentalists of every religion had a vision that there would be a day of reckoning when God would take his chosen off planet for a while and the rest of humanity would be destroyed. People had grown so used to the absurdity of this possibility that they no longer paid it any attention. Evil had not forgotten. Several nations had an advanced missile called the SS-N-22 Sunburn. This sea-to-sea missile had a top speed of just under 3000 miles per hour and flew ten feet over the ocean. Its speed and altitude insured that it was invulnerable to detection or being stopped before it reached its target.

Brad knew that there was a very real possibility that one of these missiles would be used in the Strait of Hormuz to attack an American nuclear aircraft carrier. He also knew that would be the first shot in a lightening nuclear war that would unleash the power of all the arsenals in the world. In 24 hours the few left would truly be back in the Stone Age, ready to start all over again. His job was to stop that missile from ever being fired. The battle was already raging. Eighty years of perpetual war had hardened the hearts and minds of men, and I do mean men, all over the world and the first casualty in that four score of years had been sanity.

He thought about what the King had said in the pronouncement delivered by Grace Devereaux: "The day of awakening is here, and the day of reckoning and weeding out is not far away. The cleansing of the world will take place and only those awakened souls will be left to experience life in the divine state." Of all men on Earth at that moment, Brad knew what was coming and what had to be done. He also knew that the 'day of reckoning and weeding' was not intended to be a day of warfare but of Divine Mercy.

"My Friends," Brad began. "I join you with similar guidance

from the Council. Earth will not be lost. This great blue water bearer in our galaxy will reach the goal set for it by the King and the Council. It will make the transition to the next level of evolution set for it by the Great Law of God. Beginning this day, a new warfare is being introduced to this planet, and for those unprepared, it will look like insanity, maybe even foolishness.

"During the past four score years advance troops have been sent to Earth to prepare for this moment. Very few in number, almost totally ignored by the powerful, and patient beyond comprehension, these masters have perfected the powers given them while they were at our home on Sirius. They are ready to act under my direction. Sometime in the next ten days, pairs of these troops will enter each of the governmental headquarters of every nation in the world. They do not have appointments nor will they be announced. They will not arrive in limousines or caravans of government SUVs. One by one these pairs will appear at the gates and will use the power of their spirits and their mission to instantly and peacefully disarm all guards and set aside all barriers.

"Station by station they will advance to the inner circles of power of every government until they stand before the leader of each nation. When they leave, the leaders will all report that two very tall men, perhaps 7'6" or taller stood before them in bright white business suits and told them to sit down. Each leader will then be asked to ascertain that they are awake and present in their offices. The leaders will look around and pinch themselves and signal that this is not a dream or an illusion. The two men will then speak. "Within the next 24 hours a change of galactic proportion will occur in the hearts of all the leaders of all nations on Earth. You are among them. Beginning now you will cooperate with a new power brought to this planet from Sirius and led by the designate of the Galactic Council. You will follow the specific orders of this power and its leader or you will be instantly replaced. For the next twelve hours you will not leave this office, but sit here and read with incredible speed and understanding *A Book of the Beginnings* which we now hand over to you. Know this: This book and the next 24 hours will change the course of all that has happened since the beginning." They will leave as quickly as they entered and the message will have been delivered.

A dress rehearsal of sorts had happened on December 13, 1968 when these same visitors came to the Iowa Governor's Mansion in Des Moines and paid an identical visit to then Governor Harold Hughes, who had just been elected as Iowa's new Senator. On that visit the two angels said to Governor Hughes, "Within twenty-four hours two books will be found in New York City that will change the history of the world." That same day, Gene Kieffer, on a business trip to New York, found the two volumes of *A Book of the Beginnings* at Weisers Book Store downtown. He did not find out about the visit of the two men in white until he met with the Governor when he got home from New York, and took the books for the Governor to see. Gene uses this event as the opening for his book, *The Secret Teachings*.

Brad continued, "Once these messages have been delivered my team's assignment is to take peaceful command of the armed forces of the world and to use the resources and organization of the world's military to maintain order and to stop violence wherever it starts. Our further orders are to establish supply systems wherever needed, deploy special teams for assistance anywhere in the world, and to insure that no military action takes place outside the control of this team.

"The language on Earth has become as polluted as the environment and the result has been like the Tower of Babel. People the world over neither understand nor believe in what has been told them. This changes now. For hundreds of years, perhaps thousands, invading armies have claimed they came in peace. The most recent example of this had America claiming the citizens of Iraq would welcome them as liberators. That time is now over. We are not claiming to come to bring peace. We are peace. We have superior power, not force, to back up our words. The age of force ends today. We will use the spiritual power, which guides this galaxy, to restore order and sanity to Earth. We anticipate there will be attempts to reassert the use of force and our mission is to immediately halt them.

"During the course of this change, we will employ systems and materials to neutralize and eliminate the world's storehouses of weapons of mass destruction. And we know exactly where these weapons are.

"Finally, like the armies directed by Lincoln, we will be magnanimous in victory. We are here to prove without question that there is a much better way. We follow that way and so too will the citizens of Earth."

Brad was characteristically abrupt and to the point. He was the General. He saluted the gathering and sat down.

Chapter 7

Frank spoke next. In appearance and manner, Frank was the exact opposite of Brad. Where Brad was built like a fullback, Frank was built like a long distance runner. At 6 feet he probably didn't weigh more than 150 pounds and his demeanor did nothing to reveal the immense power he used in his mission. Where Brad chose power words, Frank was the embodiment of gentleness. His power was the power of belief. His training had been all about belief as the ultimate determiner of destiny.

Frank led the team responsible for health and education. This team had the task of seeing to it that every one on Earth would have the equivalent of a grade school education on Sirius. As Frank spoke, visions of the world's current education system raced through his mind: Girls selling fruit in Afghanistan to buy pencils so they could go to secret schools that were officially prohibited by the government; American grade schoolers going through metal detectors to prevent a 7-year old from bringing a hand gun to school; Inuit children going to a community center with the noise of a gas generator in the background which powered the little heat there was and the TV that played Sesame Street and other videos; Brazilian children who left home two hours early for schooling before going out into the rubber plantations for the real work of children; African children trying to understand where skin color ended and wisdom began; Chinese children who could only hear about schools as they made the educational toys that would be sent to America and the rest of the so-called First World; Indian children who would pass the world's oldest holy structures as they went to school with dreams of working for American corporations when they graduated from high school and could make as much as $5 an hour. Frank saw all these mental movies as he spoke.

Frank could see into people the way you or I can see into a

cellophane bag of pretzels. He could see peoples' physical states, their mental issues, their emotional issues and their spiritual alignment. Frank was a healer, and he was passionate. This was why the Council had placed him at the heart of the future of Earth: healing for today and education for the future. When he had been in extensive training for the mission while still on Sirius, he would make holographic field trips through Earth hospitals. The so-called First World countries believed they had the best medical care, and they sure should have. They also had the sickest populations. Eating dead animals is an expensive diet. The costs were in raising animals to kill, growing the crops to feed them and the chemicals for the crops and the polluted water from chemical drain off from the fields, plus the sewage from the animals caged for fattening before slaughter. That is before the brutal killing rooms. Most meat packaging plants in America today are staffed by Mexicans who are here for the money and are willing to put up with the horror of death. Even so, they usually keep these jobs less than six months.

The next step was the selling and cooking of the dead animals. On his holotrips, Frank could not keep from laughing at the folks who could spend $3500 on a stainless steel outside grill from Frontgate to cook their dead animals. This process of animal growing, feeding, killing and cooking too often ended finally in the oncologist wing of the hospitals all over America. We couldn't talk too much about this, because the secret would damage the American and global economy: Eating dead animals causes cancer. Frank had seen it and so had the Council; it was barbaric, ruinous and spiritually damaging.

Frank began. "I too have seen the future of the words Grace Devereaux delivered from the King: 'The cleansing of the world will take place and only those awakened souls will be left to experience life in the divine state. Others will fall by the wayside, left behind, in the world of illusion and darkness.' This is indeed the dividing moment. My heart wants there to be none left by the wayside as we move forward. My mission is to see to it that only those who consciously decide to remain in the darkness will be left behind with their illusions of war, famine, death and destruction. The rest will gladly walk into the light of this new day.

"The cleansing of the world has already started. In every land there is the record in the ground of blood spilt in hatred, fear and the constant struggle for control of one group over another. The floods that have appeared all over the world in the past few years have been to cleanse the land of this ancient spilt blood. The Earthquakes have occurred so that old battlefields and places of true misery will be swallowed up by the Earth itself. What seemed fearful and destructive can now be understood as the process of cleansing the Earth for the coming changes.

"Now it is time to prepare the people living today for tomorrow. This is the moment when actual evolution becomes momentarily visible for those who can see. The great mystic thinker Gopi Krishna put this process in perspective:

'Often we do not give sufficient thought to the colossal task which evolution has to accomplish. It represents a rise from the Earth to the sky. A clod of Earth has to gain the power of thinking, of awakening to the knowledge of itself and then of the universe around it. A handful of insensitive matter has to win a state of awareness where it can mingle with a consciousness which pervades the universe, from a hand full of dust to be one with the All. It is a stupendous transformation, a mighty drama which only an absolute power could design, stage and play. We tend to underestimate the inconceivably vast dimensions of creation and the stupendous proportions of the power of it because our mind and senses, like the brain and the eyes of an ant on a leaf floating upon the surface of an ocean are not able to register our own insignificant position compared to the titanic forces by which we are encompassed.'

Frank continued, "This Great Drama, of which we are a small

part, now requires us to hold hands and jump off the edge of the present together and into a future vastly different from the past. To do this, we must make education the most important mission on Earth. The bumper stickers have been right all along: *The cost of ignorance is much higher than any cost for education.* Health and education go hand in hand.

"There are powerful lessons we cannot learn when eating dead animals. People read the Bible about Daniel and the lions' den and assume it was just a story or better yet an unrepeatable miracle. In fact, it could be repeated any time you want. The lions did not attack Daniel because he had no dead animal matter or energy in his body. There was nothing there for them to eat and they could smell that fact.

"Certain things more important than not being eaten by lions also accrue from not eating dead animals. They are these: The body is built to respond within energy fields. Men fear when they are in the presence of evil, whether it be experienced as a person or as an event. Their fear activates systems that produce predictable effects, like fight or flight. On the other end of that spectrum, positive, open supportive energy produces personal energy described as wholeness, authenticity and spiritual awareness. Because the energies in this spectrum are actual fields, one cannot exist in the same space as the other. Today, the most advanced researchers in the fields of quantum mechanics, biology, and field theory are focusing on energy in the form of light, color and sound vibrations. An early application of this is in the sonograms that are used to peer into the body in the most non-invasive ways. In the future, therapists will be trained to look into the body to find the problem issue and heal it with techniques that will be most like meditations. The current level of mechanical, chemical and electronic methods of healing will continue to be used in trauma cases where emergency situations dictate that something invasive must be done. The future is in energy and the use of readily available sources which might best be described as spiritual.

"Part of my mandate is to bring to Earth the basic curriculum used with the young people of Sirius. We will be greatly helped with this by the young children being born on Earth today who have been characterized as Indigo or Crystal. They already know the dynamics of these types of meditations and they have been given the ability to look deeply into all they meet. Because they are the new man, they will automatically respond and help us teach the other young people how to make the leap into this new element in the plan for man's evolution.

"The teams of passengers we placed on every continent will work together with the children to help educate the adults about the changes that will take place as more and more of the new children are born and then become the majority. Within one hundred years this change will be complete, but the critical moment is now when we must make it clear that the change has happened and that these new children must be treated and educated in ways seemingly foreign to what we have done in the past.

"Beginning tomorrow, our team members on all continents will conduct activities aimed at educating all adults about the change that is taking place, and which must be quickly accommodated so that we can take full advantage of the unique qualities these young children bring to the future of Earth.

Frank did not wait for any response from this audience. He quietly sat down and you could see on his face the look of total absorption in the moment and in the enormity of his task. His face revealed one more clue: he was totally confident that he would achieve his mission with the guidance of the Council which was in constant communication with him and the other members of the crew and passengers.

Chapter 8

Tom was the least like the other crewmembers. He was over seventy, was of slight build and was very direct in his manner. This was not his first major assignment. His training included extensive management of complex systems. In the past, Tom had made many holotrips to Earth to observe, and on one trip he actually got involved with a potential crisis that could have destroyed a whole state. He made the trips to keep himself completely up to date because he knew that he would be a member of the crew when the time came.

The crewmembers and passengers and the men who worked with him on Earth all quickly grew to respect his personal power, his dedication to the work, his unique ability to define problems and then present solutions in ways that easily communicated what needed to be done. He was basically an engineer and he loved how creative thinking could result in machine design that allowed all sorts of processes that others thought impossible. His training had originally been in weaponry when the Council had to use force as the last resort to stop an attack on the galaxy from another galaxy and its malevolent forces. That is history now. So it was not exceptional that Tom was on a holotrip to the Pacific in the early 1950's. He was sent to monitor the progress, if you called it that, being made on the development of the atom bomb. There had been progress. It was no longer an atom bomb......it was now a hydrogen bomb. Tom was able to enter a totally secure facility on the Big Island of Hawaii where final assembly was being conducted on a hydrogen bomb soon to be tested in the South Pacific.

Inside a concrete walled building that was built to at least slow down a nuclear explosion, Tom saw a young officer who led a team chosen to ready this weapon for the test. Bombs then were huge, not like the sleek multiple warheads that are placed on rockets in 2008 that go half way around the world, separate themselves from other bombs on the same rocket, and are guided right down the smoke stacks of civilian targets. These first bombs were so big they had to have a large room for assembly. This room was 100 feet cubed. The young officer was named Bart and Tom was there when the alarm went off. If you go back and watch a James Bond movie from the latter half of the last century, there were frequent scenes where a nuclear bomb was about to go off when a counter reached 000. Many viewers thought of this as a cool movie stunt to add drama. Little did they realize this was not fiction. Tom saw it happen.

Tom was watching Bart and his crew of 7 other military technicians when the red light and Claxton alarm went off. The noise was frightening all by itself. The red light was like a $500 firecracker going off in your face. There was heart stopping panic. Time stopped only for a brief second and then the 180 seconds to detonation started counting down. One of the techs was a tall Nebraskan who everyone thought was a giant of strength. When he saw his shorter teammates break out in panic and tears, he leaned against the wall of the building and just melted to the floor in fear paralysis. As the team came apart, Tom was faced with a decision. He could have left the scene in the holotrip mode and gotten back to Sirius before anything really bad happened. He chose to stay and his first action was to look into Bart's eyes and communicate on the highest spiritual level the following command: "You are not going to die today. Now take charge of these men and stop this tragedy right now." For Bart the message was perfectly clear. He later told a friend he felt that God spoke directly to him and he became calm and in control of the situation.

He immediately focused the team and began the incredibly difficult task of unscrewing 132 large arming bolts on all sides of the bomb. The final bolt was removed as the clock reached one second. The bomb that would have disappeared all of Hawaii was not detonated that day, but there were casualties. Bart was exposed to a lethal dose of radiation.

The doctors were totally upfront. "Bart, there is nothing we can do for you other than try to relieve your pain. We do not think you will live longer than two weeks. That night there was a full moon as Bart walked out to the cliff looking east over the Pacific. As he stood considering the strangeness of the events leading to this moment, he saw Him walking across the water toward him. Bart knew it was Jesus; just the light glowing around him was confirmation enough. Jesus came closer and Bart never felt more secure or more love in his life. This was the peace that would pass all understanding. "Bart, I am with you always, and you are whole and safe. Your response to the command that was given you in this crisis and your success in averting a total disaster will be rewarded. You will be healed from this radiation and you will live to perform many great services. Know that I am always here." With that, the Light of the World walked back across the water and into memory.

The next day the entire medical staff at the facility had to meet in an auditorium because there were too many to meet anywhere else. They all wanted to know what had happened to Bart. He was brought on stage and the three doctors charged with his care announced that as of that moment, there was no evidence of radiation anywhere in Bart's body. He was cured. No one could say why and Bart could not tell of his experience in The Light because he knew these accomplished scientists were not capable of believing such a thing could actually happen.

Tom never forgot that day and he found a way to keep up with Bart. Bart left the Navy and joined Texas Instruments where his distinguished career included computer design and installation for the highest levels of government operations. He was roughly the same age as Tom and was now retired and looking for something to do that would be like the old days. Tom would have reason to call on Bart as the real work began.

The real work for Tom was going to be a truly global project.

The Council had determined that the most direct way to positively effect global pollution and climate issues was to stop the spread of the use of beef and other animals for food. The methane produced by these animals was actually affecting the environment, as strange as that sounded. Additionally the nutrition contained in animal products was offset by the negative physical effects, including cancer. The spiritual effects of animal protein dulling the higher sensitivities had created many of the lost opportunities to ready the global population for the change that was upon it. "Where's the Beef?" was about to become history. The Council had decided that Tom would lead the global team to a healthy non-animal food creation and distribution system across the planet. The nights at Peter Luger's Steak House in Brooklyn were soon to be over.

Tom was ready for the task. The food that was grown all over the world to feed and fatten the animals was enough to feed all the people for the first phase of Food Two as Tom had starting calling his responsibility. The questions that remained were then: how to deal with all the cattle, fowl and other four-legged-animals used for food? And what to do about the economic crisis with the end of this type of food production? And how to distribute the new food supplies that were grown under sustainable systems? Not to mention how to get All American Men to eat their vegetables! After all, it was George H. W. Bush who said: "I am President of the United States and I do not have to eat my broccoli."

Tom addressed the global gathering. "On every continent and for centuries, even millennia, the food customs were constant and organic and dependable. After centuries of the same diet, the effects were known and the resulting deficiencies had been countered with what are now called alternative medicines such as herbs and the use of energy therapies. Then after the Second World War, American business altered the food chain. Beginning in America and spreading across the globe over the past 60 years, these indigenous diets had been replaced with the

MacDonaldization of food. No longer was food grown within 150 miles of where it would be eaten. No longer was food grown in harmony with nature, but today was as much a part of chemistry as it was of nature's processes. And it tasted funny. Ask anybody over 70 if things tasted different than they used to….and that's accounting for taste bud sensitivity being lost to advancing age. Ask any oncologist if there is enough evidence to blame food as much as anything for the increase in cancer. Even if there were not a starvation crisis in many parts of the globe, there is ample reason to address this issue in our work.

"Of all the issues facing Earth today, none is more baffling and damaging than the incredible number of people who go to bed hungry every night and who have no current reason to believe that it will ever change for them. We are here to end this crisis. We are about to create the 21st century version of the Berlin Airlift and it will span all seven continents. The end of hunger is at hand. The beginning of a spiritually supportive food chain is about to begin with our work.

"The elements that will be needed to support this effort will impact each of your missions and all the other systems on Earth, including the political systems. Many will not welcome this change any more than they will welcome the idea that evolution has moved to the new man and the children who are bringing him to the planet.

This is not a voluntary choice; it has been mandated by the goal of evolution itself, and we are but actors on the stage of the future's version of history. We will accomplish this goal before the year 2012 as the Council has mandated.

There was quiet as Tom sat down. The words Tom spoke opened a deep reflection in the hearts of the Sirians who knew the starvation crisis and lack of food was artificial and unnecessary. Their compassion for the starving children on every continent brought tears to their eyes and reminded them again of the high spiritual calling they had answered in coming to Earth.

Since the crew and passengers knew I was there to record and cross-reference the events of the mission, there was little for me to say, but I did say this, through the passion of tears in my eyes: "We know the outcome of this mission and the reason for our being here. What we may not know as we meet here with our feet on Earth is that we are connected to the deepest longings of human history. For millennia and beyond, men have wished for peace, prayed for peace, fought for peace and continued to hope for peace. Many of those same people prayed for outside help in their struggles. We are now here because we are peace. Acting as humans, we may be tempted to forget who we are in the heat of conflict. Observe in this mission, as each one of us continues to remember who we are, millions will also remember who they are. We are here for the lifting of mankind to the next level, the level where we will all know we are peace and will live accordingly. Our mission is to prevent that lesson from having to be learned by the survivors of a global nuclear conflict." The tears were drying as I sat down.

Chapter 9

Next, Michael asked John to speak for the Continental Commanders. "My report is brief. You are soon to hear each of the "ConComs" report in on their readiness for the mission. Although I am assigned to the Antarctic region, I will be on call wherever special missions are needed. I am here to help them and you, and I am ready to stand beside you in solving the toughest parts of the mission." John then called each of the seven commanders of the continental forces to report in. They basically said, "All present and accounted for and ready for action." With this final report to the crew and passengers, Michael concluded the meeting as follows:

"Tomorrow, July 24, will be a new day on Earth. We move immediately as time has run out. Men, women and children everywhere have been prepared for this moment. Others stand guard ready to prevent the completion of our task. There will be conflict, and we will resolve it with our tools and not the Earth tools of death and aggression. We are Divine Peace and we are here to be that peace for all to see. And so it is.

As John sat down, Michael said, "I ask you now to join with me in completing this beginning with the Great Invocation which has been on this planet since the founding of the United Nations." Michael bowed his head and led the project members in a prayer they had learned when they were first selected for the mission by the Council.

The Great Invocation

From the point of Light within the Mind of God. Let light stream forth into the minds of men. Let Light descend on Earth.
From the point of Love within the Heart of God. Let love stream forth into the hearts of men. May Christ return to Earth.

From the centre where the Will of God is known. Let purpose guide the little wills of men – The purpose which the Masters know and serve.

From the centre which we call the race of men. Let the Plan of Love and Light work out. And may it seal the door where evil dwells.

Let Light and Love and Power restore The Plan on Earth.

With the repeating of this prayer by all 1,728,012 souls, The Plan began on Earth.

Chapter 10

Unto us a child is born, a son has been given, and the government shall be upon his shoulders. And he will be called Wonderful, Counselor, the Mighty God, Everlasting Father, The Prince of Peace. Of the increase of his government and peace there shall be no end. Isaiah 9:6

On September 29th, 1982 at 3:40 AM somewhere in central Texas, a child was born. Anne calls him Raul. His mother was Mexican and his father was a real Texan. Anne has never met him, doesn't even know where he is, but now in July 2008, he is almost 26. Anne knew about his birth because she was part of a group of seekers led by Buddhist priests from a Tibetan monastery outside Sedona, Arizona where all the group members lived. On the night of September 28th, on their way to their weekly class, several of Anne's classmates had seen The Star. When they got to the class they invited others who were already inside to come out and see this strange sight. As they watched the sky, it was as if a luminous stairway opened from the ground and climbed straight up to the star, which grew bigger by the moment. All were amazed and speechless as they returned inside to begin their class. Anne's group members were instructed to spend as much time as possible that night meditating and paying attention to what was happening in the environment. Anne went to sleep at 1:30AM after meditating on what might have been happening.

At 3:30AM she woke up with a start. Something drew her to the window and prodded her to look out and up at the Fall sky. Here in the pre-dawn darkness she saw the amazing sight. The Star appeared directly overhead. Although she had no idea what was happening, looking at The Star caused her hair to stand on end, goose bumps to cover her body and tears to stream from her eyes. Although there were no words being spoken, Anne realized that whatever was happening was a profound event, and the only thing she could connect it to was the night that Jesus, the most recent Christ, was born. True, there were no angels and no shepherds, but clearly something was happening and it was totally unusual, cosmic and of profound importance. Anne watched The Star until Sunrise and then it disappeared. It was never mentioned in the media. She never heard anyone other than the members of her group refer to it. The next morning the Buddhist monks asked each member of her group to describe what they had heard or seen the night before. Anne told of her sense that someone special had been born and she told the time it supposedly happened and went so far as to claim that the child was named Raul. The Buddhist monks confirmed her report with beaming smiles. So something had happened.

What Anne spoke to no one was that during her time awake she had the complete sense that a monad was over-shadowing the birth of a monad. In mystic circles, this is a high holy event that almost never happens. Perhaps only once every two thousand years. In Aristotle's "Metaphysics" the monad occurs as the principle of number, itself being devoid of quantity, indivisible and unchangeable. The word monad is used by the neo-Platonists to signify the One. God is described as the Monad of Monads.

Recorded in my journal from a conversation with our friend Anne that happened in Austin on August 28th, 2007

Chapter 11

July 24, 2008

Morning in the urban desert of Cairo. Always unusual as the mica from the sand stirred up by the morning wind changes the light to bright white with an eerie glow. That was common here next to the pyramids.

Giza

There were no other clues of what was about to happen. The remarkable thing about life in the 21st century so far was that everyone seemed to be connected. Internets, cell phones, global TV, private communications networks, the ability to instantly connect with anyone on Earth was matched only by the strange phenomena that the more opportunity there was to communicate, the less people paid attention or communicated anything of deep meaning. It now was obvious that people usually scanned email messages but often missed the critical information they needed to hear. Most people were immersed in multi-tasking and were habitually working on their computers and talking on the phone at the same time. Everyone counted on their Digital Video Recorders to allow them to recall parts of programs that they had been "scanning" while doing other things. The price of attention had become very high indeed.

So it was no surprise that suddenly people began rewinding their DVRs to listen once more to a briefing being given at the White House by The President of the United States. The mystery of The President had only deepened since the book *Dead Certain* by Robert Draper had been published in 2007. The central mystery about The President had been the issue of his intelligence. He just appeared dumb a lot of the time; bad syntax, bad grammar, and to the analytical, bad thinking. However, people who paid little attention to these things liked The President because he seemed like one of them. Draper even devoted twenty pages of the book to a recounting by The President of his physical workouts, blood pressure and calorie expenditures, etc. Never mind that he was a billionaire even before he came to the Presidency. The fact was that his handlers knew that like the perfect secret agent as described by Len Deighton decades before, he had the knack of seeming like a bumbling idiot which he used to cover his uncanny native ability to know what was going on. Sometimes his emotions showed and people thought they could read what he was thinking, but those impressions were so far off the mark of what one would expect from a US President, that people just filed them away; like the time he smiled and gave TV cameras the finger as he walked into the House of Representatives to deliver the State of The Union Speech. Today was no exception.

"………and so I have commanded all United States forces to the top level of war readiness to meet this unprecedented threat of international aggression, should our enemies further threaten our peace efforts in the Middle East." Bling Bling. All of a sudden the price of attention had been paid across the globe, and people were stunned that the one thing they had been most afraid of had now been spoken. By now even street urchins in Calcutta knew that whatever you heard on the news was, at the very best, the top of the iceberg. All the talk about fear over the past seven years since the "attack" on the World Trade Center was nothing compared to the fear that was about to envelop the whole world.

For some strange reason, the leaders and spokespersons of the world's armed countries had been totally silent about the real nature of just one nuclear weapon as they raced to build impressive storehouses of these devices while assuring the populations of their countries that these devices would ensure safety. But you don't buy a Ferrari to run errands at the shopping center. Somewhere, someday, someone was going to drop one of these, and here is the potential for what could be expected from just one of today's 20 megaton nuclear weapons. You have seen the pictures of a vast landscape of rubble created by each of the atomic bombs dropped on Japan in 1945. Today's weapons could turn that landscape into a silicon desert in one instant. Worse yet, the radio active nuclear fallout from such an explosion could render everything within a 100 mile radius of the blast uninhabitable. For example: if your safe deposit box was in White Plains, New York and your home was forty miles north in Somers, New York, an atomic bomb on Wall Street where you worked would destroy your job, but not destroy your bank building in White Plains or your home. You could reach your bank and your gold and valuables in White Plains only by exposing yourself to a fatal dose of radiation that would claim your life within less than two weeks. Bill Reinhart used to say that if Americans had any idea of the power of just one of our nuclear weapons, they would crawl on their hands and knees to Washington to beg our leaders not to use these weapons.

Now our appointment with the big decision had arrived. Fear, the worst and oldest of guides, was now ready to manage the process that would determine the future of mankind, or more likely the end of the wrong turn that evolution had taken some five hundred years ago when we let science belittle the essential spiritual nature of our experience on Earth. There was that funny expression on The President's face. He sounded so serious and sober, but there was that smirk again.........he couldn't hide it. Was he excited about something? Was this another back room trick from the VP's Office?

Chapter 12

Michael was not surprised. He was ready. The Sirians were a truly advanced species and by advanced, it is understood they were highly evolved spiritually. They had nurtured and developed the spiritual skills needed to reach the goals they had all agreed upon. When it came to dealing with Earth, there was extensive research needed for the passengers and crew of the Merkabah. Bishop Fulton J. Sheen once said that Jesus' coming to Earth was like you or I being placed in a pit full of vipers. It was almost as bad for the Sirians of the Merkabah. The ways on Earth seemed almost totally un-evolved to the members of this advanced civilization.

The real reason The President made his speech this morning was that the issue of the human brain and its evolution had come to the moment of punctuation as the biologists call it. Punctuation means that evolution is not a gradual process, but one that builds up over a period of time and then suddenly makes a quantum leap. An organism or a civilization sends out 'scouts' to the perimeters of its existence to see what is on the edge of possibility, including threats. As the scouts report back to the Central Processing Unit of the organism, it assembles the data and when enough information is collected the CPU makes a decision and carries out the necessary changes to adjust to the new circumstances. The various elements of the organism do not know how the change is being researched or planned. Most do not even know a change is in progress until it happens.

Gopi Krishna said, "The process of evolution is active in the body of almost every human being. At its natural pace, the individual has no indication of it throughout his life. His body functions in the normal way, in health and disease, able to sustain stresses and pressures, hardships and privations, overexertion, lack of sleep, and insufficient diet with the strong reserves built into it.

"There are large numbers of men and women in whom the process of this evolution becomes accelerated. The tendency to accelerate evolution is carried by the genes and runs in families, transmitted from the parents to the children.

"Right up to this day mankind, as a whole, has remained entirely in the dark about a momentous secret that is linked to his survival. There has never been an awareness of the fact that the species is still in a state of transition toward a new dimension of consciousness, the result of the slowly occurring organic evolution of the brain. The irony is that in spite of the tremendous strides taken in the science of biology, by a strange trick of fate, this hidden activity to this moment has remained shielded from the eyes of biologists.

"When the secret is unearthed, the shock waves of the discovery are likely to create a revolution in the whole realm of human knowledge that has no precedent in history. The human race is slowly moving in the direction of a titanic consciousness. But the brute force in man is still very much alive. We come across his deprivations in the bloody acts of terrorism, in devastating wars, in oppression and in the exploitation of weak, downtrodden human beings. In the present state of society, these evils appear to be irremediable and have persisted for hundreds of thousands of years. Side by side with the achievements of science, the continued existence of these evils is fraught with the greatest hazard for the race. But in our own present state of knowledge and resourcefulness we are helpless because we do not possess any defense against them.

"On the contrary, the achievements of technology when used for evil can prove to be terribly destructive, obliterating all the benefits they had conferred when employed for good. One all-out nuclear war fought between two super-powers can wipe off every trace of civilization from the Earth.

"One nuclear device in the hands of a desperado or of a

terrorist group can endanger the lives of millions. In the coming ages, with the further irresistible advances in technology, the safety of nations and even of the whole species will always hang by a slender thread, which a single mistake or a single imprudent act can cut asunder in the twinkling of an eye.

"It is not possible to turn back the hands of the clock of time. Our current customs, conventions, laws, values, and standards are not designed for a state of society in possession of the powers that science has placed in our hands.

"Our present ideas of religion, philosophy, justice, and right and wrong are equally inappropriate to the demands of the present or the future.

"The time has come when mankind, as a whole, has to shed the now worn-out scale of current thought and to equip themselves with new ideas and values as a measure of survival in the age to come. The human brain is molding itself imperceptibly in the direction of a superior type of consciousness able to apprehend the subtler levels of creation.

"Compelled by the limited range of our senses to perceive only a fraction of the universe, we are duped into the belief that what we experience throughout our lives is the whole of creation and there is nothing beyond it, hidden from us due to our inability to apprehend beyond the circumscribed periphery. The present-day trend in science to confine itself only to what is perceptible to our senses has been a grave error, of which the vicious harvest is before our eyes in the explosive condition of the world.

"Historians in all ages have assayed to fathom the causes for the virtues that came into play at the time of the rise and the vices that led to the fall. But has anyone tried to enlighten the world about the ferment that occurred in the brain, both at the time of the ascent and the decline in the individuals or the nation as a whole?

"When we critically reflect on this we are completely lost in the major problems of life. What kind of a soul resides in the body of a monstrosity, a criminal, or a genocidal person? How does Karma influence the gene, the structure of the brain, or the circumstances that make one a millionaire and the other a pauper, a king or a beggar, a genius or a blockhead?

"This is the province of science as well as of religion. Why science should ignore some of the most important issues of human existence no one has dared to answer. And why religion should be satisfied with explanations for these riddles, offered thousands of years ago, when space was flat, atoms were solid, and Earth was the center of the universe, is equally unintelligible."

Whatever else you want to say about The President, knowledge of evolution was not in his portfolio. Brute force was the weapon of choice for this western sheriff. Michael had been trained in all of this, especially the issue of the evolution of the brain by the teachers appointed by the Council. All the members of the Merkabah had similar training and knowledge.

Michael had heard The President's entire speech. Starting with the US history since 9/11 which was now almost a tribal mantra, The President reviewed our heroic efforts to change Iraq and Afghanistan, the multiple terrorist attacks his administration had thwarted, the loss of American lives in the quest for Middle East democracy, the need to protect the world's energy resources and, of course, the problem posed by Muslim Jihad theology and the threat posed by weapons of mass destruction. Back in September 07 the retiring Chairman of The Federal Reserve finally came out and said the war in Iraq was mostly about oil. Finally, someone at the top had said the truth. Too bad he did not have the courage to speak about this when he had the power to change things. Back in 2002, I made the statement to a small group that we were now about to see what happens when you give an oilman an army. Oil and the power and future wealth it could confer on its owners was astronomical. In fact, the war on Iraq was the biggest gold rush in the history of man.

Behind this obvious issue was a more powerful one. The need for evolutionary rethinking of most of our assumptions threatened all of the world's religions. Religion kept its hold on its followers by claiming its answers to be final and eternal, not to mention infallible. If evolution posed the threat of making ancient good uncouth, as the hymn says, then evolution must be stopped and discredited. But beyond that, prophesies of three major religions were so deeply held that millions of people were prepared for and anxious to see a final war that would change everything. The Jews would see the Muslims disappear, the Christians would see the Jews relinquish control of Jerusalem and the Muslims disappear, so that Jesus could come back and rebuild the Temple, and the Muslims would see the Jews and the Christians disappear in the final conversions or deaths of the infidels. The payoff for the Jews was that God would help them keep the Promised Land, the Christians would be taken up in the rapture and the Muslims would disappear.

This was pure foolishness. Michael had to stop this madness before the one final act would end the current civilizations on Earth. As he listened to The President who looked all strong in his $6000 custom suit and tie, he wondered how he would look when the nuclear bombs started to fall and his new clothes would be covered with his own urine and feces as a result of the absolute fear that would seize him in the moment the knowledge of the tragedy he had created became apparent.

Michael saw the American wealth machine as a rolling ball of knives. On the one hand we were ready to stop anyone from having weapons of mass destruction. On the other, we were the chief supplier of these weapons to countries around the world. Early in the War on Iraq someone joked that the reason we knew they had weapons of mass destruction was that we had saved the receipts.

And now this.

Chapter 13

For the past few days the daily reports to The President had been increasingly alarming, and oh so welcome. As if following some American presidential dream script, Iran had been playing hide and seek with its weapons and enemies. The Iranian leaders also knew that America had targeted 1200 "military" targets in Iran for a lightening strike with missiles and bombers. Again, America seemed ready to fail in its attempts to use air power to subdue an enemy. It did not work in Viet Nam. It had not worked in Afghanistan or Iraq. But if first you don't succeed, try, try again. Oh boy, the American President was ready to spring his big surprise.

The consensus since the early 80's had been that America would survive a nuclear war. This is one of the more quaint examples:

"VERY late one autumn night in 1981, Thomas K. Jones, the man Ronald Reagan had appointed Deputy Under Secretary of Defense for Research and Engineering, Strategic and Theater Nuclear Forces, told me that the United States could fully recover from an all-out nuclear war with the Soviet Union in just two to four years. T.K., as he prefers to be known, added that nuclear war was not nearly as devastating as we had been led to believe. He said, "If there are enough shovels to go around, everybody's going to make it." The shovels were for digging holes in the ground, which would be covered somehow or other with a couple of doors and with three feet of dirt thrown on top, thereby providing adequate fallout shelters for the millions who had been evacuated from America's cities to the countryside. "It's the dirt that does it," he said."

Its the Dirt That Does It
Robert Scheer

Good thing that the passengers and crew had watched American cartoons as part of their pre-mission education. This quote reminded Michael and many others of a Wiley Coyote cartoon. In fact, when looked at from a certain sick angle, the whole experience looked like a cartoon.

Of course, inside the bubble, things looked real serious and real controllable since this was America after all. The amazing aspect of all of this had been the average guy in America. The American Character so accurately described by Tocqueville years before was still very much intact despite two hundred years of social changes.

"In 1831, twenty-five year old Alexis de Tocqueville and Gustave de Beaumont were sent by the French government to study the American prison system. They arrived in New York City in May of that year and spent nine months traveling the United States, taking notes not only on prisons, but on all aspects of American society including the nation's economy and its political system. The primary focus of *Democracy in America* is an analysis of why republican representative democracy succeeded in the United States while failing in so many other places. He sought to apply the functional aspects of democracy in America to what he saw as the failings of democracy in his native France.

"Tocqueville speculated on the future of democracy in the United States, discussing possible threats *to* democracy and possible dangers *of* democracy. These included his belief that democracy has a tendency to degenerate into "soft despotism" as well as the risk of developing a tyranny of the majority. He observed that the strong role religion played in the United States was due to its separation from the government, a separation all parties found agreeable. He contrasted this to France where there was what he perceived to be an unhealthy antagonism between democrats and the religious, which he related to the connection between church and state.

"Tocqueville's work is often acclaimed for making a number of predictions which were eventually borne out. Tocqueville correctly anticipated the potential of the debate over the abolition of slavery to tear apart the United States. On the other hand, he predicted that any part of the Union would be able to declare independence. He also predicted the rise of the United States and Russia as rival superpowers.

"American democracy was seen to have its potential downside: the despotism of public opinion, the tyranny of the majority, the absence of intellectual freedom which he saw to degrade administration and bring statesmanship, learning, and literature to the level of the lowest. *Democracy in America* predicted the violence of party spirit and the judgment of the wise subordinated to the prejudices of the ignorant." Credit Wikipedia

Americans are still fair minded, independent, resourceful and up front. In the past few years, since 9/11, America had changed. In fact, it had become America 2.0. There was some slight evidence that, despite the benevolent apathy most people used to observe big government at work, people were waking up and at least noticing what was going on in what increasingly appeared to be a state of perpetual war well into the future.

Naomi Wolf, the Feminist writer, was loudly sounding the alarm. "I am traveling across the country at the moment — Colorado to California — speaking to groups of Americans from all walks of life about the assault on liberty and the 10 steps now underway in America to a violently closed society.

"The good news is that Americans are already awake: I thought there would be resistance to or disbelief at this message of gathering darkness — but I am finding crowds of people who don't need me to tell them to worry; they are already scared, already alert to the danger and entirely prepared to hear what the big picture might look like. To my great relief, Americans are smart and brave and they are unflinching in their readiness to hear the worst and take action. And they love their country.

"But I can't stand the stories I am hearing. I can't stand to open my email these days. And wherever I go, it seems, at least once a day, someone very strong starts to cry while they are speaking.

"More times than I can count, courageous and confident men who are telling me about speaking up, but who are risking what they see as the possible loss of job, home or the ability to pay for grown kids' schooling, start to choke up. Yesterday a woman in one gathering started to cry simply while talking about the degradation of her beloved country.

"And always the questions: what do we do?

"It is clear from this inundation of personal stories of abuse and retribution against ordinary Americans that a network of criminal behavior and intention is catching up more and more mainstream citizens in its grasp. It is clear that this is not democracy as usual — or even the corruption of democracy as usual. It is clear that we will need more drastic action than emails to Congress.

"The people I am hearing from are conservatives and independents as well as progressives. The cardinal rule of a closing or closed society is that your alignment with the regime offers no protection; in a true police state no one is safe.

"I read the news in a state of something like walking shock: seven soldiers wrote op-eds critical of the war — in The New York Times; three are dead, one shot in the head. A female soldier who was about to become a whistleblower, possibly about abuses involving taxpayers' money: shot in the head. Pat Tillman, who was contemplating coming forward in a critique of the war: shot in the head. Donald Vance, a contractor himself, who blew the whistle on irregularities involving arms sales in Iraq — taken hostage FROM the U.S. Embassy BY U.S. soldiers and kept without recourse to a lawyer in a U.S. held-prison, abused and terrified for weeks — and scared to talk once he got home. Another whistleblower in Iraq, as reported in Vanity Fair: held in a trailer all night by armed contractors before being ejected from the country.

"The time for weeping has to stop; the time for confronting must begin." *Credit Buzzflash.com* All this in late 2007.

The issue of people waking up was central to the entire drama about to be played out on the world stage. The Buddhists refer to waking up as the process of beginning the spiritual part of life, just as some Christians refer to it as being born again. Being asleep while going through the motions of life is something we have all gone through. Once you wake up you regret what you have missed up to that point. Eternal vigilance is said to be the price of freedom. While we are asleep nightmares with real villains attack our camps and steal our dreams, and we pretend that these are just dreams anyway. Imagine a society supposedly at war with a global enemy, armed with weapons of mass, and I do mean mass, destruction that willingly devotes tons of ink and paper and megawatts of electricity to following the every move of little 20's something girls who prance their mindless egos and tight bodies before us everywhere we turn. If that is not being asleep, what is?

Waking up is another matter. Who among us has found an alarm clock that will make him excited to wake up from the dream every morning? Who remembers being awakened every morning by a gruff parental command? Other than Christmas morning, who looks forward to leaving the dream for reality? The problem was exacerbated by the fact that America had the mother of all thought control machines. The average house in America had a TV on and running 8 hours a day and most adults listened to 4.25 hours of televised information every day. In the formation of America 2.0, the control of who decided what information to present to these television viewers had been given to a very few people, all of whom were very well connected to the government. One of them was not even an American citizen. Rupert Murdock, head of the Fox conglomerate, was a subject of the British Empire and he had also created the information empire that was most closely aligned with the wishes of the American Government, *Fox State TV*. It was hard to even say the words.

So sounding the alarm, getting people to wake up, was going to be Michael's biggest issue on the North American continent. America was content to think of itself as the No. 1 country in the world, despite the fact that it was mostly owned by other nations such as Japan, China, Saudi Arabia and the European power houses. This would prove to be the real strength of America. There was something else that was causing America to be asleep. I am always amazed that people are not as observant as they could or should be. Admittedly, I am hyper-observant, and I am always surprised when other people miss what is obvious to me. Here is a case in point. In the late 90's I noticed there were days when jet contrails would be all over the sky, crisscrossing each other and hanging in the air for long periods of time. Not normally observed for jet contrails and also not normal in that New York was the place all the planes landed, not flew over at 35,000 feet. At the time I did not think anything of it….it was just something else I observed in New York, the living museum of anthropology.

My arrival in Telluride, Colorado changed my awareness in so many ways. I thought I was finally leaving New York after 23 years to move out West. Instead I found I had moved up 10,000 feet. That was a serious jump and to this day I find it hard to explain to anyone the change. It was like living on a completely different part of the planet. The light was much more contrasty, the colors more vivid, the wind more surgical, the humidity always low. There was a sense that you were always surviving against some powerful odds and natural danger was at every turn. One of the glories of getting to the highest peak you could find was the chance to see as much of the sky as possible. I had a favorite spot I visited daily where I could see the sky. The east-west airlines flyway went right over Telluride and when you viewed these massive planes roaring across the sky at 30,000+ feet, they looked so much closer when you were at 10,000 feet yourself. So it was always a surprise when some days the planes would leave these massive and almost permanent contrails. Not all the planes, not all flying in one direction, sometimes flying in very usual directions.

Chemtrails

Big Stock Photo

On these days, as the contrails crossed the sky and stayed there, they began to get "fish tails" on them as they slowly, slowly spread across the sky and within about three hours, they had created a lasting brown haze that actually blocked the sunlight. Several hours later the haze would be gone and by the next morning the skies would be back to that beautiful Colorado high altitude blue. What were these new things? What did it mean?

The doctors at area medical centers reported that within about 24 hours of one of these occurrences, people showed up with respiratory and other related issues. There seemed to be a cause and effect relationship here.

Recently I heard that these sightings had decreased because the planes were laying down these contrails at night when they would be less likely to be seen. In the mean time many theories about what these could be were developed......from governmental attempts to dampen global warming, to metallic seeding of the atmosphere which resulted in outbreaks of Morgalen's Disease, a skin infection that had no cure.

Michael knew what these were. The Sirians had a library of deep space photos and tracks going back to the early 90's. They had also cross-referenced these events with as much information as possible about what was happening on Earth when the newly named chemtrails were in evidence. The best way they had to describe it was it caused a kind of benevolent apathy in those who had been in the area. The more it happened the less people cared about almost everything not related to their immediate life situation.

Despite the apathy, America was still open for the business of being the beacon to the rest of the world to light the way to a better tomorrow. Michael was in constant contact with Jack Socrates, the crew member responsible for the North American continent.

Chapter 14

July 24th Thursday

Socrates was your basic full court press American type guy and came fully equipped for his North American mission. He was smart, more aggressive than almost anyone he had ever met, was a commanding student of the American experience, and had done his homework. There was not a sailor alive who could out cuss, out arm wrestle or beat him in rugby. He was an expert on the effects the American incursion into Viet Nam had on the American psyche. At 60, he was the oldest continental commander among the crew. Forty years earlier he had made a special holotrip alone to Earth to witness the Tet Offensive of 1968. He knew the jungle, the war and the American experience. In fact, the crewmembers would never forget what happened in the training session when they had to watch *Apocalypse Now*, a Viet Nam War movie.

When he had been in Viet Nam, he assumed the identity of a Marine sergeant and had actually seen combat, so he knew what it was like. When the crew was watching the movie, the scene about helicopter gun ships, equipped with external loudspeakers playing the *Ride of the Valkeries*, landing in a school yard seemed really cool and great theatre. When the helicopter landed the soldiers started to get out and just then, on the far right side of the huge wide screen of the multiplayer, a woman came running out toward the craft wearing black. She was on the screen for less than a second when Socrates recognized what was happening, jumped up and screamed as loud as he could: "SHE'S GOT A GRENADE!" For a brief second all the crewmembers went into a real time response as if Socrates had taken them into another dimension and back in time. When they got back to the movie, they realized the power and impact that Socrates carried in his personality. They were impressed.

Michael and the Council had chosen Socrates for the North American Continental Command, because they knew his personality was a perfect match for the times when he would have to confront Americans on all levels and take over command of the processes in which they were involved. It was a wise choice. Most Earth residents, despite their past life experiences, including times in other dimensions, had settled on dealing with things with their five senses and in the here and now. Michael and the Council knew that the North American Continental Command had to relate to people in this fashion as well as practically be a black belt in spiritual judo. Socrates was the quintessential spiritual warrior.

Because the action would center on the east coast, Socrates had taken an office on the corner of Connecticut Avenue and H Street in Washington. From there, he could quickly walk to the White House when the time came. His office spread out over three floors and was staffed by passengers who had been trained in communications and systems. His office faced south and had a view of the White house. Every time he looked at it, he could not help thinking that the sitting President of the United States had chosen to go AWOL for 18 months of his time in the National Guard and had rigged history to hide that issue. When he looked just to the right of the White House at the Executive Office Building he always thought how the Vice President had talked his way out of service in Viet Nam claiming he had more important priorities than going to war. Socrates wanted to jump up and scream as loud as possible. His training and mission demanded he keep a safe distance. There would be plenty of time later to review the character and lives of these fearsome leaders who had not really been chosen by the American people. Even so, every time he looked at the two buildings, he muttered under his breath, "pussies, cowards".

Brad was on the communicator. "OK Socrates, we're running. I suspect we have no more than a week to get everything in place.

Michael and The Council tell me these guys want the war to begin as soon as possible, so people will not automatically think it was a way to stop the American elections and justify the declaration of Martial Law. Our guy in London now says the plan is to have a lightening battle somewhere close to Iran and then have a serious non-nuclear attack in America. He thinks it will be in Dallas. He even laughed when he said it would probably destroy Southern Methodist University and the site chosen for the new Presidential Library…..poetic justice or something. Socrates was up to speed on this one, too. He already had a full team and an office set up on a top floor of the old Meadows building just across Central Expressway from the SMU Campus.

Chapter 15

Michael had chosen Malcolm Newstead as his man for the mission in Europe and had him assume an identity that included growing up in Cape Town, South Africa. Malcolm liked to tell people how he would sit on the deck of his parent's high rise condo every night and watch the Sun set over Bantry Bay and the South Atlantic. And, of course he had the perfect South African accent and that thin and hungry look that British intellectuals all seemed to have.

On the morning of the 24th he just walked into MI-6 Intelligence Headquarters, showed the credentials created for him on Sirius and plugged in. Incredible. That was the way it was supposed to happen, but even so, how could these people not be at least a little more vigilant? Anyway, having access to his European Continental Command right in the heart of the British Secret Service was a very cool thing. The rest of his European Continental Command London staff was in an office space on Catherine Place; close enough to the action to act swiftly should the Queen need to exert any rapid public leadership.

Newstead was balding, blandly dressed, wore glasses and seemed like the nicest guy you would ever meet. Two or three sentences of conversation with him and you would know he was grounded, dependable and not likely to get upset about anything. In the pre-mission training sessions there an extensive segment about the London Bombings of the summer of 2006. Like 9/11, drills were being conducted by the authorities simulating an attack in the subways, just like the armed services in America were in drills in the air on the fateful morning. No one knew if the reports were real world or exercise. And just like Israeli tenants at the World Trade center who unexpectedly moved out just a week prior to 9/11, the former Israeli Prime Minister, who was in London for meetings, was advised not to go out on the streets of the morning of the London attacks. It just seemed like these attacks we coordinated with some elements of the authorities.

Malcolm was not in a position yet to reveal what he knew, but he felt the same way toward the British authorities that Socrates felt toward the "fearless" leaders of America. The European Continental Command seemed to be in the middle of things in every way. The European nations, with the exception of England, had all resisted the US leadership's incursion into Iraq. At the same time, the Muslim incursion into European labor markets had created the gravest possible opportunity for damage from secret cells of terrorists hell bent on destroying any and all expressions of Western Civilization. Worse yet, all of Europe was in closer missile range to the Middle East than any part of North America, although it was seldom mentioned in polite society. Europe had for centuries been the model for global diplomacy and even in the middle of this greatest threat, the majority of people believed that the Europeans' skill in diplomacy would prevent exposure to the issues of real warfare. Malcolm's mission was to use that diplomatic power to communicate with all the other nations. To do this, his operational ally at the United Nations in New York was Steve Nader. Nader and a small group of the passengers had assumed identities of recently returned American ex-patriots who had been stationed in UN posts around the world. Nader's assumed identity included a ten year posting to Georgia, in the USSR, as a researcher. That item on his resume was guaranteed to go unnoticed by the savvy headquarters' power climbers who rated everyone on the basis of their implied access to the top UN power players. Nader used to chuckle when he was ignored by these people who could have no idea of his access to real power.

It was not magic, exactly. It was more like chess. Chess remains, after all these centuries, the ultimate thinking game because it is most like a quantum field of possibilities. Anything can happen and the winner is the person who can visualize the most possibilities through possible successions of other related possible actions. It takes profound concentration to win at chess. Being in the present is the only door to the future on the chess board. The Sirians had the advantage. They knew what was coming on so many levels and dimensions that they could put any future moves in place far in advance of their possible use. Identities were established in the past and as a result, there was rarely a challenge to an identity someone assumed. The pre-mission planning on this level was literally otherworldly.

Nader's job was to be on call to connect any of the UN officials with any of the command sites if a specific government connection was required or was critical to the mission.

Chapter 16

I love you in a place where there's no space or time
I love you for my life 'cause you're a friend of mine
And when my life is over
Remember when we were together, together
When we were alone and I was singing this song for you.

A Song for You (with Herbie Hancock)
Written by Leon Russell

June 6, 2008 Friday

No one is sure how it came to pass that Dubai was suddenly the chic in-spot on the globe. Sometime around 2006, just as Halliburton was moving its headquarters to Dubai from Texas, everybody suddenly got that this was the place to be. Imagine the vision and resources to build a huge building to house a complete ski slope in the middle of the desert. Or how about a series of man-made islands created to look like palm trees and the globe visible from space. The Creek River running through the middle of Dubai is the location for one of the most impressive displays of civic wealth on the planet. Once an American sets foot in Dubai and feels the power and the vision that makes this place hum, a kind of inferiority complex goes into play. This is the future. This is where dreams and luxury meet to bask in the Sun together. It is the triumph of hope over common sense. The desert is turned into a true international oasis and the most dangerous region in the world is the location for the resources of vision and power that guide our path to the future. Or so it was thought.

Margaret Johnson had dreamed of this trip for a whole year. She found the right man at the same time as she was getting packed for the trip. They met one night at the classic SMU hang out, The Egyptian Lounge just east of SMU on Mockingbird

Lane. He was tall, dark and handsome and she was tall, blonde and a knock out. She was energetic, fun and oh so bright, with her new master's degree in Political Science. He was serious, confident and carried himself with an almost regal charm and calm that made him so

NASA

Dubai Palm Island

attractive and at the same time so very distant. It was two days before graduation. Her father had given her everything she wanted from day one, and she wanted only the best. She had focused her considerable intellectual powers on the Middle East as a student and had fallen in love with Dubai long before she ever thought of getting there. She loved to look at Dubai and the Strait of Hormuz on Google Earth. It was like Dallas, in a way: no limits, constant growth, fast paced, glitzy, stylish and wealthy beyond belief.

Billy Johnson had seen to it that his daughter knew best how to mix power and money to create anything she wanted. Her Masters degree was just the beginning. Billy liked airplanes and used only the best in his "little old oil bidness". Margaret loved landing almost anywhere so that she could make a dramatic exit from the G-5 with her dad's initials as the logo. *BJ* was woven into the fabric of all the seating, into the wall coverings, on all the napkins, silverware, crystal and best of all, on each of the gold steps as she would exit or enter the plane. He took me to his plane one day parked at Southwest Airmotive at Love Field and said, "Come here boy. I want you to see this plane." Inside he pointed out to me all the various places where he had cleverly applied his personal *BJ* logo plus all the excesses money could buy. "See this airplane. This is the 56th goddamned airplane I have owned, eighth one just like this. I like to fix them up, if you know what I mean!" We both laughed......he had that Texas way of bragging and laughing at the same time. And yes, I did know what he meant.

When Margaret met him at The Egyptian they were with friends, but later that night when they were alone and talking with each other they shared their heart's desires, their dreams and the goals they had for the immediate future. She told him that her daddy was giving her the plane to take to Dubai for a graduation trip. He told her that he had been offered a position at SMU as an assistant professor at the Perkins School of Theology as an expert in comparative religions and he was going to accept the offer after graduation. He also told her about the times he had spent with Huston Smith, the West's leading scholar on comparative religions. Smith was able to document how all of the world's religions had not kept up with the explosion of man's knowledge, and how in America the Christian Churches had wanted so much to be a part of the society that they had all but abandoned their prophetic voice and positions of moral leadership. She decided right there he was going with her...everywhere.

"Dad, this is Raul Richardson. He's going with me to Dubai next week." Even though Raul was not exactly her father's kind of guy, he sure was her kind of guy. Billy had long ago learned that Margaret had as strong a will as he did and once she made up her mind, that was it.........and anyway, he seemed like a good traveling companion for her trip alone. Bill liked what the investigator turned up on Raul. Clean as a whistle........Dean's list grades, reputable friends, no scrapes with the law, outstanding achievements in and out of school and a good mind for money. There was just that one thing that Bill couldn't figure out. The Richardson name in Dallas and Ft. Worth was like gold, and there was a hint that he was someway connected to the Richardson dynasty, but the investigators also noted that his mother was Mexican and stayed way in the background of her son's life. In fact there were no parents attending Raul's graduation in June of 2008.

It was not just a graduation trip, it was the real thing…..it had been love at first sight, and they both knew it and they both did their best to ignore it. But from his earliest memory, Raul Richardson had known things that he should not have known with his limited experience. He saw connections with people that others never dreamed of. He saw angels, visitors, and space ships, visions of the planet's future and intimations of his own future. He saw Margaret Johnson first when he was 13 and she came to him in the middle of the night and stood at the foot of his bed and watched him until he woke up……….then she winked at him and disappeared. She did that several times over the next 13 years. But when they finally met, he was so stunned that it was her, that he did not know how to react. So he just waited to see when she would reveal herself.

The Burj Alarab Hotel is one of the most dramatic buildings on the planet. It is shaped like a sailing vessel headed toward land and is the most luxurious building inside and out that one can imagine. The least expensive room goes for $2000 per night and Billy Johnson did not send his daughter to cheap rooms. They were on the floor second from the top, and you don't want to know how much it cost.

Dubai Hotel

Then there were the limos, boats and reservations everywhere. All of it first class, of course.

When they were at last in their room after the 18 hour trip from Dallas, she walked to the window to look out to the east on the Persian Gulf, and then she turned and faced him. "I've always known you and I have looked forward to this moment since I was in my early teens. I used to dream you were with me, you would be standing at the foot of my bed and watching me as I slept. Please don't laugh!" He smiled and tears filled his eyes as he said, "You were watching me too, as I slept. There are no accidents.......we are here on purpose and we are here to fall in love." The next seven days were right out of the most romantic of the Arabian nights.

As they left the hotel to meet her dad's plane to go back to Dallas, a black Mercedes 600 limo pulled in front of them and they were instructed to enter the vehicle by a very formal and dapper English chauffer. "Please come with me. Your host wants to meet you before you leave." 'What the hell is this?' Raul wondered to himself.

They went with the driver to a dock in the new World chain of islands where a small yacht was waiting for them. As soon as they boarded they were on their way to the first completed island of this archipelagos. Raul and Margaret were met at the dock by Sheik Mohammed who greeted them and then took them in one of the island carts to the newly finished ultra-modern castle at the center of the island.

After small talk in the large formal presentation room, the Sheik told them he knew they were on their way back to America, but he had something for them to take back with them........actually for Raul to take back. A senior servant came forward with a gold box on a silk pillow. When Raul opened it, it was a very old and worn piece of ivory-like stone and it looked like it was a corner piece of a square with part of a symbol carved on either side it. "You will need this when you meet The Grandfather. He is expecting you and when you present him with this stone, he will reveal the answers to the questions you have been asking yourself since you were a child. I brought this from Switzerland when I had gone there to meet with the Indian mystic Gopi Krishna when he was on his way home to India after speaking at the United Nations in October1983. He told me he had carried it with him to New York, but then had been instructed to give it to me for safe keeping after his death. I have been told to give it to you."

After some additional conversation, Sheik Mohamed said, "You had best be going. I dismissed your father's plane four days ago, so you will be flying in my plane back to the United States. It is the flagship of the Emirates Airlines fleet, and my personal 777. I have some nice amenities on board that will make the trip a little less stressful. I am doing this to give you a hint of things to come, and to wrap up your visit to my country with as much positive energy and power as I can give you. God Speed."

The trip to the boat to the limo to the plane was quiet. Raul was literally shaking because he had suddenly gotten a glimpse of what lay ahead as he looked into the Sheik's eyes when he said goodbye. It was like looking into space and seeing far off galaxies at the speed of light. What could this all mean? And wow, whatever it meant, flying home on the Sheik's private 777-300ER was so cool. It was huge, just two passengers and a crew of ten. Oh yes, Margaret and Raul could get used to this in a hurry. There was everything on board. The best freshly cooked food in the world and the Champagne was not to be believed! The movies and live TV including CNN were in high def on several 60" screens. The master bedroom and beautiful bath were very spacious including a series of small windows over the bed and the massage tables that allowed Raul and Margaret to see into the night sky as they flew across the ocean. Raul could even see Orion and that other bright star just above the belt........was that Sirius?

Once in the air, Raul and Margaret were treated to dual massages and complete body treatments right out of the Grown Ups Book of Joyful Sex. Sensual, romantic music, dim light, hot tub, sauna, colonics, exotic fruits, silk and incense, and hours of spiritual tantric sex all at 40,000 feet. This was indeed the Mile High Club gone wild. When they got up from their post massage love making and sleep, they were still over the Atlantic and headed for Texas as the Sun came up.

Raul went to the library and looked at the art there and caught up on the CNN news and the worsening Middle East Crisis as Margaret was having her hair and nails done. The library and executive office spanned the entire width of the giant plane with just a walkway on the outside of the room's right wall to allow passage to other parts of the plane. In the library were huge comfortable office chairs, a sideboard for coffee, windows along one side, communications gear to call anywhere in the world plus video conferencing gear, valuable art on the walls and another 60" flat screen. It was completely separate from the rest of the plane and, like the bedroom and spa/bath, provided complete and spacious privacy. Raul felt entirely alone and in a very quiet space to think about what lay ahead. He felt his life was moving as fast as this plane was.

Suddenly he was not alone. No door had opened, but when he turned his head a man was standing in front of him. He had on an orange robe, his kinky hair was cut in an afro and he looked like what he was, an Indian mystic or guru. Raul could not understand what was going on or where the man came from, but just looking at him gave Raul the most peaceful feeling he had ever known. "I am Sai Baba. Be at peace. I salute you. In another part of our Galaxy I am known as The King. I have the final say. I am the spiritual leader of this galaxy. I have known you from the beginning. I arranged your auspicious birth. I saw to it that you were identified as a Richardson. I placed the ivory fragment you are carrying to America in Switzerland thousands of years ago for safe keeping until I was ready for your arrival at this moment. I have always been beside you, but you could not perceive me. Now you can. We meet now here high in the air, high above the storm that is gathering on Earth. As in the past, I will be with you every step of the way. I will arrange for everything to be accomplished according to the Divine Plan. You are the most fortunate of men. God created you for the most sacred moment in the history of the species that inhabits Earth. Your mission, indeed your life, is to bring the most powerful evolutionary moment to your fellow humans. There have been six attempts to advance Earth men to the level they now approach again. They failed mainly due to fear and the order of things. The longing for more, that so clearly identifies this age, is about to be met. The only issue now is the willingness of men and women to release their hold on their understanding, and let the new order come forward. You will be the symbol and the leader of this release. You were born for this. You will now see and hear me every moment on this great adventure. Stop now and breathe in the healing power of God and say to yourself: 'I am that.' From now on you will know who you are and I want you to repeat after me the following prayer and definition of who you are:

I am a spirit.
As a spirit, God's Presence and Power is within me.
I am in tune with the spirit world and open to its' influence.
Please mold me into the best instrument I can be, so that I may serve You with all my heart and all my soul.
I am a child of the universe.
I am Divine Peace.
I am Divine Love.
I am Divine Wisdom.
I am Divine Bliss.
I am The Light.

"This is the truth about you and the truth of the New Man you are now to reveal on Earth." The King stood there and kept his peace-giving gaze on Raul's eyes until there was a knock on the library door.

The Captain came in and invited Raul to the cockpit to see how things worked. He could not see The King, but Raul could. It would always be this way. Raul suddenly shifted gears and walked into the cockpit! What a sight........right out of science fiction. The 777's techno science made Billy's G-5 feel like the Wright Brother's first plane by comparison. It was the ultimate computer game, but it was also real and it was hurtling at 580 miles an hour into the future of all mankind.

Once back in Dallas Raul and Margaret found an apartment. Margaret got her new Mac computer to help with the writing she was going to do for her articles in the Dallas Morning News on politics. Raul checked into Perkins School and reported for work preparing for the fall semester. They decided to have a secret wedding at the Chapel at Perkins late one afternoon. Billy was the only family member present. There would be time for a big public wedding later. They both felt they were still on a magic vacation. Now that he was settled, it was time for Raul to find out who this Grandfather character was he was supposed to meet.

Chapter 17

July 6, 2008

This is what Raul found when he started researching The Grandfather: http://www.thedreammasters.org/hopi/martingash-weseoma.php

From Frank Waters' *Book of Hopi*:

"Grandfather Martin Gashweseoma is one of the last remaining traditional elders of the Hopi tribe, located on the third mesa in northern Arizona. He remains steadfast in maintaining the traditional spiritual ways of his people, as assigned by Massau'u at the beginning of this current world. We are now nearing the end of the great cycle, as foretold in the Hopi prophecy. He is highly revered among his people and he predicted 9/11 five years before it happened.

Grandfather

"Another Hopi prophecy warns that nothing should be brought back from the Moon. If this were done, the Hopi warned, the balance of natural and universal laws and forces would be disturbed, resulting in Earthquakes, severe changes in weather patterns, and social unrest. All these things are happening today, though of course not necessarily because of Moon rocks.

"On August 7, 1970, a spectacular UFO sighting was witnessed by dozens of people and photographed by Chuck Roberts of the PreMichael Courier. This occurred after a "UFO calling" by several Hopi Indians and was interpreted by some Hopis as being a partial fulfillment of a certain ancient message inscribed on

Second Mesa, warning of the coming of Purification Day, when the true Hopi will be flown to other planets in "ships without wings."

"The survivors of the Great Deluge thousands of years ago split up into four groups that moved in all four directions. Only one group completed their journey — to the North Pole and back — under the guidance of a brilliant "star" in which the Great Spirit Massau'u traveled. Upon landing, he drew a petroglyph on Second Mesa, showing a maiden riding in a wingless, dome-shaped craft. The petroglyph signified the coming Day of Purification when the true Hopi will fly to other planets in "ships without wings."

"The Hopi also predicted that when the heart of the Hopi land trust is dug up, great disturbances will develop in the balance of nature, for the Hopi holy land is the microcosmic image of the entire planet; any violations of nature in the Four Corners region will be reflected and amplified all over the Earth.

"Martin Gasheseoma said recently that Hopi "elders told us that when the plants blossom in the middle of winter, we would need to go to Santa Fe to warn everyone of suffering and destruction to come unless they change their ways. Last year, in the middle of winter, the plants began to blossom."

"How much suffering and destruction will accompany the time of the purification, and what will be its end result? Martin Gasheseoma foretells judgment in front of a big mirror and death to those who are evil and wicked, with only a handful of people surviving in every nation overseas who will then come to this continent, "which we call heaven."

"All the suffering going on in this country with the tornadoes, floods, and Earthquakes is carried on the breath of Mother Earth because she is in pain," says Roberta Blackgoat, an elder of the Independent Dineh (Navajo) Nation at Big Mountain. She explains that the Four Corners area is particularly sacred because it literally holds Mother Earth's internal organs — coal and uranium which the Bureau of Indian Affairs has allowed the Peabody Coal Company to mine. "They are trying to take her precious guts out for money," says Blackgoat. "My Grandfather told me that coal is like the liver, and uranium is both the heart and lungs of Mother Earth." Hopi and Navajo traditionalists are fighting the mining.

"These life and death matters will be determined when Pahana returns and theories abound as to Pahana's identity. Since Pahana has also been called the White Brother, and since he is to return from the east, Hopi of past centuries wondered whether he could have been a Spaniard or an Anglo and devised tests for determining the true Pahana, including knowledge of the greeting of brotherhood, similarities of religious beliefs, and possession of the missing piece of the stone tablet. Many were tested, including Catholics, Baptists, and Mormons, but none passed to the satisfaction of traditional Hopi.

Hopi Stone Tablets

There was the cycle of the mineral, the rock. There was the cycle of the plant. And now we are in the cycle of the animals coming to the end of that and beginning the cycle of the human being.

When we get into the cycle of the human being the highest and greatest powers that we have will be released to us.

They will be released from that light or soul that we carry to the mind. But right now we're coming to the end of the animal cycle and we have investigated ourselves and learned what it is to be like an animal on this Earth.

"At the beginning of this cycle of time, long ago, the Great Spirit came down and He made an appearance and He gathered the peoples of this Earth together they say on an island which is now beneath the water and He said to the human beings, "I'm going to send you to four directions and over time I'm going to change you to four colors, but I'm going to give you some teachings and you will call these the Original Teachings and when you come back together with each other you will share these so that you can live and have peace on Earth, and a great civilization will come about."

"And he said, "During the cycle of time I'm going to give each of you Two Stone Tablets. When I give you those stone tablets, don't cast those upon the ground. If any of the brothers and sisters of the four directions and the four colors cast their tablets on the ground, not only, will human beings have a hard time, but almost the Earth itself will die."

"And so he gave each of us a responsibility and we call that the Guardianship.

"To the Indian people, the red people, he gave the Guardianship of the Earth. We were to learn during this cycle of time the teachings of the Earth, the plants that grow from the Earth, the foods that you can eat, and the herbs that are healing so that when we came back together with the other brothers and sisters we could share this knowledge with them. Something good was to happen on the Earth.

"To the South, he gave the yellow race of people the Guardianship of the wind. They were to learn about the sky and breathing and how to take that within ourselves for spiritual advancement. They were to share that with us at this time.

"To the West He gave the black race of people the Guardianship of the water. They were to learn the teachings of the water which is the chief of the elements, being the most humble and the most powerful.

"To the North He gave the white race of people the Guardianship of the fire. If you look at the center of many of the things they do you will find the fire. They say a light bulb is the white man's fire. If you look at the center of a car you will find a spark. If you look at the center of the airplane and the train you will find the fire. The fire consumes, and also moves. This is why it was the white brothers and sisters who began to move upon the face of the Earth and reunite us as a human family.

"And so a long time passed, and the Great Spirit gave each of the four races two stone tablets. Ours are kept at the Hopi Reservation in Arizona at Four Corners Area on Third Mesa. "I talked to people from the black race and their stone tablets are at the foot of Mount Kenya. They are kept by the Kukuyu Tribe.

"I once had the honor of presenting a sacred pipe at the Kukuyu Tribe carved from the red pipe stone of Mount Kenya. I was at an Indian spiritual gathering about 15 years ago. A medicine man from South Dakota put a beaded medicine wheel in the middle of the gathering. It had the four colors from the four directions; He asked the people, "Where is this from?" They said, "Probably Montana, or South Dakota, maybe Seskatchewan." He said, "This is from Kenya." It was beaded just like ours, with the same color.

"The stone tablets of the yellow race of people are kept by the Tibetans, in Tibet. If you went straight through the Hopi Reservation to the other side of the world, you would come out in Tibet. The Tibetan word for "Sun" is the Hopi word for "moon" and the Hopi word for "Sun" is the Tibetan word for "moon".

"The guardians of the traditions of the people of Europe are the Swiss. In Switzerland, they still have a day when each family brings out its mask. They still know the colors of the families; they still know the symbols, some of them. I went to school with some people from Switzerland at the University of Washington and they shared this with me.

"Each of these four peoples happens to be people that live in the mountains.

"In 1976 America had its bicentennial celebrating 200 years of freedom. Some of the Native people thought this was significant and they carried a sacred pipe bundle from the West Coast to the East Coast of this land.

"They said that the roads of this land should either go North-South or East-West. If they went North-South we would come together as brothers and sisters, but if they went East-West there would be destruction and almost the Earth itself would have a hard time. So you all know the roads went East-West.

"They said then things would be lost from the East to the West and from the South to the North and that they would come back again from the West to the East and from the North to the South.

"So nine years ago in 1976 from the West to East Coast of this land, from San Francisco to Washington, D.C. people carried a sacred pipe bundle by hand, on foot. My aunt had dreamt 15 years ago that people that didn't like them would throw rocks and bottles at that pipe bundle as they carried it across the land. And sure enough that came about. But, as was in my aunt's dream, the rocks only came so close and then they dropped, and nothing touched it.

"They said a spiritual fire would be lit in the North and would come down the Northwest Coast of this land. When it gets to the Puget Sound, it would go inland. I think this, nine years later, is the gathering in the North, myself. That's why I came here. This is it. We have the capacity to start the spiritual fire now, here. The old people long ago saw it and foretold it and I'm going to come to that.

"So we went through this cycle of time and each of the four races went to their directions and they learned their teachings.

"We were given a sacred handshake to show when we came back together as brothers and sisters that we still remembered the teachings. It was indicated on the stone tablets that the Hopis had that the first brothers and sisters that would come back to them would come as turtles across the land. They would be human beings, but they would come as turtles.

"So when the time came close the Hopis were at a special village to welcome the turtles that would come across the land and they got up in the morning and looked out at the Sunrise. They looked out across the desert and they saw the Spanish Conquistadores coming, covered in armour, like turtles across the land. So this was them. So they went out to the Spanish man and they extended their hand hoping for the handshake but into the hand the Spanish man dropped a trinket.

"People came on the east coast and they went across this land to the east and they were told in the prophecies that we should try to remind all the people that would come here of the sacredness of all things. If we could do that, then there would be peace on Earth. But if we did not do that, when the roads went clear from east to west, and when the other races and colors of the Earth had walked clear across this land, if by that time we had not come together as a human family, the Great Spirit would grab the Earth with his hand and shake it.

"And so if you read the treaty negotiations from Red Jacket of the Six Nations on the east coast of this land clear to Chief Joseph and Chief Seattle on the west coast of this land, they all said the same thing. Chief Joseph said, "I accord you the right, and I hope you accord me the right, to live in this land." Always we were trying to live together. But instead of living together, you all know there was separation, there was segregation. They separated the races: they separated the Indians, and they separated the blacks.

"So when they got to the west coast of this land the elders that were made aware of these prophecies said they would then begin to build a black ribbon. And on this black ribbon there would move a bug. And when you begin to see this bug moving on the land, that was the sign for the First Shaking of the Earth.

"The First Shaking of the Earth would be so violent that this bug would be shaken off the Earth into the air and it would begin to move and fly in the air. And by the end of this shaking this bug will be in the air around the world. Behind it would be a trail of dirt and eventually the whole sky of the entire Earth would become dirty from these trails of dirt, and this would cause many diseases that would get more and more complicated. So the bug moving on the land, of course it's easy to see now.

"In 1908 the Model-T Ford was mass produced for the first

time. So the elders knew the First Shaking of the Earth was about to come about - that's the First World War. In the First World War the airplane came into wide usage for the first time. That was that bug moving into the sky. And so they knew something very important would happen.

"There would be an attempt to make peace on Earth on the west coast of this land and so the elders began to watch for this. They began to hear that there was going to be a League of Nations in San Francisco so the elders gathered in Arizona around 1920 or so and they wrote a letter to Woodrow Wilson. They asked if the Indian people could be included in the League of Nations.

"At that time the United States Supreme Court had held that a reservation is a separate and semi-sovereign nation, not a part of the United States but protected by it. This became a concern because people didn't want the reservations to become more and more separate. They didn't want them to be considered nations. So they did not write back and the Native people were left out of the League of Nations, so that circle was incomplete.

"In the League of Nations circle there was a southern door, the yellow people; there was a western door, the black people; there was a northern door, the white people; but the eastern door was not attended. The elders knew that peace would not come on the Earth until the circle of humanity is complete, until all the four colors sat in the circle and shared their teachings, and then peace would come on Earth.

"So they knew things would happen. Things would speed up a little bit. There would be a cobweb built around the Earth, and people would talk across this cobweb. When this talking cobweb, the telephone, was built around the Earth, a sign of life would appear in the east, but it would tilt and bring death. It would come with the Sun.

"But the Sun itself would rise one day not in the east but in the west. So the elders said when you see the Sun rising in the east and you see the sign of life reversed and tilted in the east, you know that the Great Death is to come upon the Earth, and now the Great Spirit will grab the Earth again in His hand and shake it and this shaking will be worse than the first.

"So the sign of life reversed and tilted, we call that the Swastika, and the rising Sun in the east was the rising Sun of Japan. These two symbols are carved in stone in Arizona. When the elders saw these two flags, these were the signs that the Earth was to be shaken again.

'The worse misuse of the Guardianship of the fire is called the "gourd of ashes". They said the gourd of ashes will fall from the air. It will make the people like blades of grass in the prairie fire and things will not grow for many seasons. I saw on television not too long ago that they were talking about the atomic bomb, the gourd of ashes. They said it was the best-kept secret in the history of the United States. The elders wanted to speak about it in 1920.

"They would have spoken of it and foretold it's coming if they could have entered into the League of Nations.

"The elders tried to contact President Roosevelt and ask him not to use the gourd of ashes because it would have a great effect on the Earth and eventually cause even greater destruction and a the Third Shaking of the Earth, the Third World War. I'll get to that in a few minutes.

"So they knew after the Second Shaking of the Earth when they saw the gourd of ashes fall from the sky then there would be an attempt to make peace on the other side of this land. And because the peace attempt on the west coast had failed, they would build a special house on the east coast of this Turtle Island, and all the nations and peoples of the Earth would come to this house and it would be called the House of Mica and it would shine like the mica on the desert shines.

"So the elders began to see they were building the United Nations made out of glass that reflects like the mica on the desert so they knew this was the House of Mica and all the peoples of the Earth should go to it. So they met and talked about this. They said that in the 1920's they had written and they had not been responded to, so they said this time we better go to the front door of the House of Mica because things might get a lot worse.

"So elders representing a number of tribes I believe drove to New York City. When the United Nations opened they went to the front door of the House of Mica and they said these words:

"We represent the indigenous people of North America and we wish to address the nations of the Earth. We're going to give you four days to consider whether or not we will be allowed to speak."

"They retreated to one of the Six Nations Reserves in New York State. The Six Nations Reserves are keepers of the Great Law of Peace of the prophet that appeared here in North America, Dagonnorida. And this Law of Peace is still recited; it takes four days between Sunrise and noon. Each year an Indian, by memory, must recite it about this time of year.

"Four days later they came back and I believe the nations of the Earth heard that the Indians had come to the door. And they voted to let the Indians in. They wanted to hear what they had to say. But the United States is one of five nations of the United Nations with a veto power and still they were concerned because this time the Native sovereignty was even stronger. And I believe they vetoed the entrance of the Native people.

"So then they knew other things would happen on the Earth, and the United Nations would not bring peace on Earth but there would be continuing and deepening confusion. And that the little wars would get worse. So they retreated to the Six Nations Reserve and they talked about this and they said the time is really getting close now, 1949.

"They said, "We're going to divide the United States into four sections and each year we're going to have a gathering. We're going to call these the 'White of Peace Gatherings'." They began to have these around 1950. And they authorized certain men to speak in English for the first time about these prophecies.

"One that I used to listen to many times, over and over, was Thomas Benyaka. He is a Hopi man. I believe he is still living. He was authorized to speak in English about what was on the stone tablets and he has dedicated his lifetime to doing this. And they began to tell us at these gatherings, they said "In your lifetime you're going to see things happen."

'It was strange when they said it in the 1950's and 1960's but now it seems very clear. But then it was unusual. They said, "You're going to see a time in your life when men are going to become women. The Great Spirit is going to make a man on the Earth. He made him a man but this man is going to say, "I know more than the Great Spirit. I'm going to change myself to be a woman:" And they will even nurse children. The Great Spirit is going to make the woman on the Earth. She's going to say, "I know more than the Great Spirit. I want to be a man. And she will be physically a man."

"They said "You're going to see a time in your lifetime when the human beings are going to find the blueprint that makes us." They call that now, DNA, deoxyribonucleic acid. They said, "They re going to cut this blueprint." They call that now, genetic splicing.

"And they said, "They're going to make new animals upon the Earth, and they're going to think these are going to help us. And it's going to seem like they do help us. But maybe the grandchildren and great-grandchildren are going to suffer."

"They are making new animals. The elders talked about this. They said, "You will see new animals, and even the old animals will come back, animals that people thought had disappeared. They will find them here and there. They'll begin to reappear."

"They said (and I know many of you are from tribes that also have this prophecy), "You're going to see a time when the eagle will fly its highest in the night and it will land upon the moon." Some tribes say the eagle will circle the moon. Some tribes say the eagle will fly it's highest in the night. "And at that time," they say,

"Many of the Native people will be sleeping," which symbolically means they have lost their teachings. There are some tribes that say it will be as if they are frozen: they've been through the long winter.

"But they say, "When the eagle flies it's highest in the night that will be the first light of a new day. That will be the first thawing of spring." Of course, at the first light of a new day, if you've stayed up all night, you notice it's really dark. And the first light, you want to see it, but you can't. It sneaks up on you. You want to see it change but it's dark and then pretty soon it's getting light before you know it.

"We're at that time now. The Eagle has landed on the moon, 1969. When that spaceship landed they sent back the message, "The Eagle has landed." Traditionally, Native people from clear up in the Inuit region, they have shared with us this prophecy, clear down to the Quechuas in South America. They shared with us that they have this prophecy. When they heard those first words, "The Eagle has landed," they knew that was the start of a new time and a new power for Native people. There was absolutely nothing strong before us now. We may do anything we wish.

"In 1776 when the United States Government printed the dollar, in one claw [of the eagle], if you've ever noticed, there is an olive branch in this claw. They said that represented peace. The Indian elders shared with me in South Dakota that to them that represents the enslavement of black people.

"In the prophecies of the Six Nations people say there will be two great uprisings by black people to free themselves. We've seen one about 1964. There will be a second, more violent one to come. I'll get back to what that means in a minute. In the other claw are 13 arrows. The founding fathers of the United States said that represents the 13 States. But the elders say that represents the enslavement of the Native people.

"When the Eagle landed on the moon, they decided to print a

118

special silver dollar to commemorate that. I don't know how many of you noticed it. The original design showed the spaceship landing on the moon but at the last minute it was changed to an actual eagle. And in the eagle's claws is the olive branch, but the arrows are gone. The elders said, "That's our prophecy, we have been released."

"There was one more uprising coming for the black race of people and then they will be released and this is also going to have an effect on Native people, a good effect. There's a whole new set of prophecies from the Iroquois people about that and I won't have time to go into that this morning.

"But we're in that time now. We're between the first light of a new day and the Sunrise. The Sunrise is about to come and when it comes up everyone is going to see it. But you know how it is in the village there's a few people that get up early, and there are some that sleep until noon. I'm probably one of those that sleep until noon. They said when that Eagle lands on the moon, the powers will begin to come back to us.

"Within seven days of the time the Eagle landed on the moon, the Freedom of Indian Religion Act was introduced into the United States Congress. The legislation was introduced in 1969, less than seven days after the Eagle landed on the moon. Eventually it was passed in November of 1978, signed by President Carter. These are the physical manifestations of the spiritual prophecies that we have.

"So he said at this time you're going to see that things will speed up, that people on the Earth will move faster and faster. Grandchildren will not have time for grandparents. Parents will not have time for children. It will seem like time is going faster and faster. The elders advised us that as things speed up, you yourself should slow down. The faster things go, the slower you go and there's going to come a time when the Earth is going to be shaken a third time.

"The Great Spirit has been shaking the Earth two times: the

First and Second World Wars to remind us that we are a human family, to remind us that we should have greeted each other as brothers and sisters. We had a chance after each shaking to come together in a circle that would have brought peace on Earth, but we missed that.

"Tonight they were talking on the news about the sign for the Third Shaking of the Earth. I heard it while sitting in the airport after I missed my plane. They said they're going to build what the elders called the "house in the sky".

"In the 1950's they talked about this: they will build a house and throw it in the sky. When you see people living in the sky on a permanent basis, you will know the Great Spirit is about to grab the Earth, this time not with one hand, but with both hands.

"Many of you of Native background may have heard "the spirits will warn you twice, but the third time you stand alone." We've had two warnings, the first two World Wars, but now we stand alone in the third one. As it says in the Baha'i Writings, there will be no-one protected. When this house is in the sky, the Great Spirit is going to shake the Earth a third time and whoever dropped that gourd of ashes, upon them it is going to drop.

"They say at that time there will be villages in this land so great that when you stand in the villages you will not be able to see out, and in the prophecies these are called "villages of stone", or "prairies of stone". And they said the stone will grow up from the ground and you will not be able to see beyond the village. At the center of each and every one of these villages will be Native people, and they will walk as "hollow" shells upon a "prairie of stone". They said "hollow shells" which means they will have lost any of their traditional understandings; they will be empty within.

"They said after the Eagle lands on the moon some of these people will begin to leave these "prairies of stone" and come home and take up some of the old ways and begin to make themselves reborn, because it's a new day. But many will not. And they said there's going to come a time when in the morning the Sun is going to rise and this village of stone will be there, and in the evening there would just be steam coming from the ground. They will be as steam. And in the center of many of those villages of stone when they turn to steam, the Native people will turn to steam also because they never woke up and left the village.

"An interesting exploration of the Hopi prophecies is provided by Thomas O. Mills. Mills grew up on the Hopi Reservation in Second Mesa, Arizona. As a boy, he helped his Mom run the newly built Hopi Cultural Preservation Office, which today is the main stopping point for outsiders.

"The Hopi tablets that were given to the ancient ones by Musawa. The story is told as follows:

"The Hopis also have in their possession the stone tablets that Muasaw gave to them. These are not ordinary stones that could have been made in America, but ivory stones with hieroglyphs cut into them with strange figures... like those carved in Egypt on the temples.

"Figures of headless men, swastikas, and snakes. One corner

This is a replica of the stone that is to be returned from the East.

of the Fire Clan Tablet has a corner missing. It was broken off when Masawa gave the stone to the Hopi, and this piece was given to the White Brother as proof that he could return and join in the Ceremonies, finally completing the Cycle making this a paradise on Earth, complete with joyful songs to the Creator from the rooftops. Old Oribia will be rejuvenated and rain will come for all the crops for all four brothers on Mother Earth.

"One of the tablets Masaw gave to the Fire Clan was very small, about four inches square, made of dark colored stone, and with a piece broken off from one corner. On one side were marked several symbols, and on the other the figure of a man without a head. Masaw was the deity of the Fire Clan; and he gave them this tablet just before he turned his face from them, becoming invisible, so that they would have a record of his words.

"This is what he said, as marked on the tablet: After the Fire Clan had migrated to their permanent home, the time would come when they would be overcome by a strange people. They would be forced to develop their land and lives according to the dictates of a new ruler, or else they would be treated as criminals and punished. But they were not to resist. They were to wait for the person who would deliver them. This person was their lost white brother, Pahana, who would return to them with the missing corner piece of the tablet, deliver them from their prosecutors, and work out with them a new and universal brotherhood of man. But, warned Masawa, if their leader accepted any other religion, he must assent to having his head cut off. This would dispel the evil and save his people.

Return of the Star Nations During Our Time of Purification: Report on the Star Knowledge Conference – Sedona by Richard Boylan, Ph.D. (c)1998

"In 1989 an 80-year-old grandmother gave Minneconjou Sioux elder, Woableza a gift of a stone. This charismatic medicine man spoke next, telling of Spirit saying to him that the stone was from

Chief Sitting Bull, and designated Woableza as a messenger. Four years ago, he was directed by Spirit to go to the Elder level of teaching. He added that the stone has acted as a spirit to arrange ways for him to accomplish his mission. He declared: "There is hope beyond the coming chaos. We cannot escape it, but we can pray to get beyond the chaos. Spirit says that there is a New World coming, a beautiful World, but we have to prepare that world, with love in our hearts. The Star People are messengers from Creator to say that we have the power to heal the Earth ourselves. We need to share this message with family, friends, relatives, neighbors. We need to fast, do Sweat Lodge, purify ourselves for what is coming. Turtle Island will be the continent of teachers for the next thousand years, according to the Star People."

"Hopi Grandfather Martin spoke through an interpreter as Prophecy-Keeper for the Hopi people, sharing information given by his elders. He has been advised to speak now, "because it is time for this information to come out." In 1990 he went to Santa Fe, because anomalous things were happening: plants growing out of season; wild animals being where they are not supposed to be, such as cities; and pets attacking their masters. These were signs that it is time to bring the Prophecies out in the open about where we stand in relation to the Time of Purification. There are some Sacred Teachings which it is not yet time to release. He consulted with the Dalai Lama about these still-withheld Teachings.

"We are heading into a future more intense than the devastation you see today. What is coming is larger than you think. You need to prepare for what is coming. Pretty shortly there will be World War III, somewhere around 2000. Before this World, there were earlier Worlds (Atlantis, Lemuria and earlier macro-historical epochs). At that time people went through the same things we are going through now. We are seeing it happen again. We were told not to make the same mistakes again. The Crop

Circles are teachings, telling us about our times and what we are headed towards, and that it is very close. We need to get back on track. We need to pray for a better world.

"Two years ago the Time of Alignment took place, but the Alignment (of Earth with Solstice Sun) didn't reach the path it was supposed to reach. So the Elders got together and put the Alignment back. Because Tewa (the Sun) is a sophisticated spirit and only likes things of value, the Elders gathered together their best jewelry with turquoise, an offering to persuade the Sun to realign its path. The Sun agreed and took the offerings. But now the Sun is off its path again. A lot of places are going to have different weather patterns: it'll be hot in cold places, cold in hot places; reversals of weather will affect many things. Temperatures will rise higher, so that nothing will grow. The misalignment of the Sun is a correlate of the Pole Shift: when the Purification comes, the Earth will turn over four times.

"The Kachinas (Spirits) are connected to the Prophecies, including the Blue Star Kachina, who represents something. The Koshares (Clowns) in the sacred dances represent mankind in the gradual degradation of our lifestyle and need for purification. The people are more and more distracted from the proper way, and when people are totally distracted, then the Purification will come. Hopi lineage extends to the Aztecs and Mayans, whose teachings are very similar." Grandfather Martin is not sure if the Dalai Lama is keeper of a set of spiritual prophecy tablets which correspond to the Hopi prophecy tablets, "but the Lama does have a lot of sacred knowledge." He described an aborted private meeting with the Dalai Lama, spoiled by uninvited persons barging in, but declared that there will be another opportunity for the Dalai Lama and him to meet.

"What goes on in Hopiland affects the rest of the world. Hopiland has spiritual lines that connect to the rest of the world. Hopi prayer is for the entire world. Hopi tradition tells about a group of people from the Pleiades that would come and help the people here when something big and unfortunate happens. Hopi Elders had the knowledge of how to visit other planets, and knew that there was life on other planets.

"We are all brothers and sisters here, as we were in the beginning, then went our separate ways. It was prophesied that we will come together again. With this Conference we hope to mend the circle (Sacred Hoop) again, make a better world, and alleviate some of the harsher disasters coming our way. The Purifier is the Bahana (Brother) returning from the East. His return will be the Purifying Times. He will know what to do, how to help us. His job is to make us understand and behave ourselves. If we don't, the Ones from the West will come to purify us, like World War III. The Brother is powerful enough to stop the Ones from the West. When Bahana comes, it will be too late to correct your path. The Creator looks at your heart over time. It is already too late to start changing.

"To prepare for the Changes coming, you need to have belief and live the sacred ways. There are not many, even among the Indians, who are keeping to the traditional beliefs. It is foretold that when the Changes start, people will come back to the old ways. Those who do not follow the old ways have a lot of questions. There will be even stronger winds, fires, Earthquakes, weather changes, natural disasters and other things than you are seeing now. The Changes will especially affect those in the big cities, because of much corruption in the cities. People need to prepare themselves, prepare food for storage to use. Money will become obsolete. People will need to be able to live off the land, get their food that way. We will go through a Depression, where food will be scarce. You need to stockpile dry goods. There will be 2-3 months without food or water (available). There will be starvation. There will be a holocaust, a lot of lives lost. The intensity will be less if you settle down and pray. The evil people will be eliminated. Only the good-hearted people will make it.

"Grandfather Martin said there is no precise date set for the Time of Purification that we are to watch the signs and prepare ourselves.

"After the Purification is over, there will be one language, one law. Togetherness will come about, as was once before. The altars and shrines of the Hopi Societies will be eliminated, because they will no longer have power. There will be one government, but not the New World Order some talk about, because freedom will be of the essence."

After Raul had read this information, it felt like a veil had been lifted that had been in front of him all his life. He felt a connection between this news, the Hopi and his mother and Arizona. Way too early to tell what it might all mean, but the need to meet The Grandfather was now the most urgent thing on his agenda. Plans were put into motion immediately.

Chapter 18

From My Journal:

October 18, 1983

I went to the UN tonight to the main lobby for a ceremony hosted by the Hopi leaders who had invited Gopi Krishna to address the UN at this event. The Hopi's led the crowd into the building. We waited outside for the leaders to come into the building and then we followed them. It was a clear night and it was about 45 degrees. The Hopi leaders walked in with Gopi Krishna. They explained to the crowd of about 400 that they had hoped to address the General Assembly but had been turned down with their request at the insistence of the US Delegation. They were therefore giving their speech inside the building and at night and that this would be the last time they would attempt to bring their message to the UN. This is a sign that the changes are upon us.

After the Hopi leaders spoke, Gopi Krishna walked up to the podium and presented an address detailing the leap that the species would have to make as a result of the dictates of evolution that is constantly at work in the minds of all men.

Tomorrow I am to meet and photograph Gopi Krishna at Gene's apartment at the "Fertile Crescent" apartment on 36th street just outside the Mid Town Tunnel.

Chapter 19

July 24, Thursday

Our man in Dallas had been given the identity of a native. He went to Dallas schools, made the obligatory stab at getting a "higher" education at "The University" in Austin, joined a band and dropped out into a life of one strange adventure after another. Or so the dossier said. Nice cover. Actually, he was one of the brightest minds among the passengers, was adept at seeing patterns emerge in relationships long before others did, and he loved confrontation.

From his office on the southwest corner of the old Meadows Building on Central Expressway he could see all of SMU's campus, a sliver of the skyline of downtown Dallas and perfect views of those wonderful Dallas sunsets. The main décor in his office was his collection of rubber chickens, his scuba gear and a very large computer. The coat rack held his collection of unique hats. Clearly he had a sense of humor. He knew how to talk with anyone on any level of this unique part of American society.

At lunch time on the 24th our man Davis Russell drove across campus to Snider Plaza to eat at Food From Galilee, a greasy spoon that the Middle Eastern students liked. He liked the food too, but there was another reason he ate there. He could meet members of the small Muslim community and hear all kinds of gossip. Anyone looking at Davis would know he was a little weird. No one would suspect he knew several of the most important Middle Eastern languages and dialects.

After The President's announcement this morning, Socrates and Newstead had both confirmed to Brad and Michael that something was up in Dallas. The reports indicated that the Iranians planned a special surprise for The President in what would be his new hometown and the location of his looming Presidential Library at SMU. Russell's job was to find out exactly what was happening with this plan. Although he ate alone most days, he listened in to the conversations around him, knowing that someday he would hear the cue he was waiting for.

Dedman College is centered in a beautiful building with a rotunda at the center and facing the main quad of the campus. It is the humanities center of the campus and as such it has the major share of foreign students. Because it is a Methodist institution it has unique connections to mission fields of the Methodist Church and numerous scholarships exist to insure that students from mission fields are given a first class education. The Reverend Scotty Callahan was a missionary to Palestine and was responsible for sending many students to scholarship programs at Dedman. He was also responsible for a little devious underground work with Palestinian and Iranian contacts while in the Middle East. Two students in particular were of interest.

Davis listened to their conversation during lunch. The Gaza International Airport opened in 1998, but it closed in 2001 after being severely damaged by Israeli military forces. Abdullah Mububaarik was twenty at the time and his father, an airplane mechanic, was killed in the attack. This tragedy brought Abdullah to SMU on a scholarship arranged for by Scotty Callahan. Absman Ayaad got to SMU the same way, except there was no tragedy to start his journey. He was identified as a potential computer genius and he wanted to get a real American education. Scotty saw to that as well. Davis listened to them and the three exchanged curious glances several times. Finally, Absman said to Davis, "Haven't I seen you on campus?" "Yes, I'm at the computer center from time to time." A nice introductory lie, but it worked. The three talked and Abdullah and Absman were cautiously interested in what this real Texan did and why he seemed so comfortable talking with them. He told them he also had an office in the Meadows Building and that he was involved with international trade. They did not suspect that he had been listening into their conversation in their own language, or that he had telepathically done a complete check on their backgrounds.

They had been talking about 'the project' and Samad, apparently a third friend. Their talk was excited by the repetition of August 2, as some kind of signal. Seemed like a big signal and Davis knew he was at the right place. Somehow the subject of The Presidential Library came up and Abdullah and Absman both laughed. They also looked a little skittish and seemed to be checking to see if anyone could hear what they were saying. Davis knew this was part of what he was looking for.

The two foreign students were definitely not what they seemed. In addition to studies and grades, they had also gotten themselves into what appeared to be a business relationship with Wilkins Electronics, a security firm in Dallas. They also had friends in other businesses like oil field explosives and military supplies. How they got into these deals as students remained to be understood, but somehow, right here on the 24th, Russell got lucky. "Hope to see you guys here again." Then Russell left.

He came back every day and saw them again on the 29th. They were not alone. Abdullah and Absman re-introduced themselves to Davis and then introduced Samad Hussein as a friend who was helping them with some work. Davis already knew about Samad. His famous and common last name was a strange calling card to use in conservative Dallas, but it worked. Samad had the money that allowed the other two to do business in Dallas and complete their plans for the Big Surprise planned for August 2. But what the hell was it?

National boundaries meant nothing to the Sirians. National allegiances meant less. They saw connections and these always transcended the others. It was no leap at all for the Sirians to understand what happened on 9/11, though most Americans could not make the connections. Eighteen Arabs flying stolen planes was good enough. The idea of pre-wired buildings, mini nukes and advance notices that allowed all kinds of people to be absent from the World Trade Center on 9/11 and our armed forces to be on training exercises somewhere else was just too far fetched. We liked our tragedies to be simple, like out of the old west and *High Noon*.

But it was about to happen again. The Reverend Scotty Callahan, The Missionary, was not what he seemed either. He had his foot in all the camps. Somehow he had used his old school connections to help Wilkins Electronics quote and successfully bid on a new security system for the campus that was to be completed and tested by August 2. Scotty placed his three students into the security game just in time to be part of the last three months work before the test date. The system was campus wide and monitored at two sites, one on campus and one in the Campbell Building on Northwest Highway at Central. SMU maintained a comprehensive Emergency Response Plan that met state standards, and was in compliance with the National Response Plan. At the heart of the plan were two fundamental ideas: the protection of human life, and secondarily, the protection of property. The contract was let in 2007 when The Presidential Library was announced for SMU. The campus, on its own, was getting ready for this wonderful addition, which would add to its' fame around the world. So were the Muslims and Scotty Callahan.

On the weekend before 9/11 in 2001, both the North and South Towers of the World Trade Center were closed above the 78th floors for "construction". No one other than work crews were allowed on the upper floors. Beginning on the 28th of July, each of the major buildings on the SMU campus was closed for a day as the final adjustments were made to the new security system. These adjustments were just as complex as the construction on the WTC the weekend before 9/11. Both building closures were about the placement of explosives in strategic places. SMU was about to go down. Somebody needed a really good excuse to deliver payback to Iran, and Davis' new friends at SMU had been chosen by somebody to light the fuse.

Chapter 20

CNN Breaking News Flash, July 29th, 4:04 PM EST: "..........As you know, five days ago I commanded all United States forces to the top level of war readiness to meet this unprecedented threat of international aggression. We have known for a long time that Iran has been willing to do anything to topple America and our leadership of the free world. We have known and you have seen all this year Iran's attempts to destroy American ships in the Persian Gulf beginning on January 7, 2008 when five Iranian speedboats harassed three US Navy ships in the Strait of Hormuz, approaching them and radioing a threat to blow them up. Since then there have been six other incidents of increasing danger. Early this morning another attempt was made on the USS Nimitz, one of our carriers currently in the Gulf.

A major confrontation was narrowly averted, but intelligence indicates that Iran has stepped up its plans to attack America. Of course, we would never attack another country without clear provocation, as was the case with the weapons of mass destruction harbored by Iraq. This, also, looks like a situation that may demand we take steps to rule Iran out of the international community. As a result, we are continuing the military high alert I commanded five days ago around the globe. Our military forces are superior throughout the world and there is no need for American citizens to be concerned for our safety. We are confident our systems can avert and control any threat from Iran. This alert is in response to aggression from the evil of Iran and we will fulfill our destiny and confront this evil wherever it raises its ugly head. I will personally speak to the American people and the international community as this situation develops. There will be no further comment or questions at this time"

"Huh?.........that's all? Goddamn it. 'Of course, we would never attack another country without clear provocation.........who does this guy think he is kidding?" Socrates was shocked at the trickery these jerks continued to pull on the American public.....and get away with it. Everybody had seen the videos from both sides of the tiny little boats from Iran supposedly threatening the American cruiser and other ships. The idea of taking on an aircraft carrier with one of these little boats was completely ridiculous. If Iran was going to attack our ships, real missiles would have to be used from ground positions or large ships; more smoke and mirrors to keep everyone's attention from wandering to the real issues.

Some people see what is reported to be happening and take that as the basic reality. I see things that make me see other things. On Saturday, February 1, 2003 the Columbia Shuttle exploded over Dallas as it was returning to Florida after a long mission in space. Everyone was shocked and saddened, and yet not so concerned, as we were more interested in the coming revenge war on Iraq. But I noticed something. Here was a high noon clear message from the heavens for those with eyes to see. Here was America's technical and military might rocketing across the sky in another space trip victory and then all of a sudden it exploded, killing all aboard and raining pieces across northeast Texas. Pretty straight forward. But what if there was another reality? What if this event coming down from heaven was a sign? What if the future was sending us a warning that our technology and military might were not as powerful or as invulnerable as we hoped? What if the future was sending us a message that all the shock and awe in the world would not win a war, based on lies, in a country we little understood, nor cared much about more than for just getting the oil that was under the ground? Of course when I proposed that thought to friends, they assumed, again, that I was just a little too *woo-woo* for polite society to take seriously, and why didn't I just go along with everyone else.

And what happened? All the predictions that the war would be over in three weeks, the carrier landing to proclaim Mission

Accomplished, the anticipated crowds rushing to the streets to shower us with flowers and proclaim us as liberators........all of that a stupid joke, a very bad bet, a snare and a delusion. Here we were years later, no end of the war in sight, the payoff of the war from captured oil no where to be found and the cost approaching three trillion dollars and 4000 lives lost, and two countries torn asunder by this ego trip of a man who continued his alcoholic sickness even though he had stopped drinking. Or so it was assumed. John Bradshaw, the theologian and psychologist, famous for his revealing studies on the Inner Child had explained this so clearly when on September 21, 2006 he appeared on the radio show What If It Really Works? (www.whatifitreally-works.com)

And then on the 27th of January of this year, the US Government announced that a bus sized military spy satellite had lost power and would fall to Earth by the end of March and that its dangerous material might contaminate wherever it fell. There would be nuclear radiation or deadly chemicals. The satellite crashed in Belize after an unsuccessful attempt to shoot it down over Hawaii on February 20th during a full eclipse of the moon. People all through Central America saw it crash into the land, but the government was able to cover it up, sweep up and hide the nuclear materials and declare the area off limits for a long, long time. Strangely though, the contaminated part of the satellite landed 100 feet away from where Anna Mitchell Hedges found the crystal skull. And it was a sign all right. Our safety from nuclear events was nowhere to be had.

Chapter 21

July 29, Tuesday

"Hey, Socrates, we gotta move right now!" It was 4:30 when Russell phoned Socrates at the Continental Headquarters on Connecticut Avenue. The President had just finished his briefing on the 'attack' on the Nimitz. "Get Brad at Headquarters to alert Nader at the UN and Newstead at European Headquarters to circle the wagons. These two guys I met last week have a third partner and they are running a scam to provide security systems to SMU and have it all in place by Saturday for a system wide test. We also need our guys in the Middle East to bring in The Reverend Scotty Callahan for a 'little discussion' about who he is actually working for. And I need a crew of 200 weapons experts here tomorrow morning. We have to comb every inch of SMU, because I am pretty sure they have wired the entire place for a lot more than security.

Socrates was in action immediately. He had to support Russell in this threat that he too knew was coming, and he had to act completely outside the US government apparatus, as no one was considered trustworthy.

Brad, as the head of the military aspect of the mission, made the final decisions on issues like this. He and Michael stayed in constant communication and they knew that the supposed attacks on the Nimitz were a ruse, orchestrated by what Michael was calling the International Terrorist Organization (ITO). He thought of it as a super Mafia-like organization that went across all national boundaries and was for hire by any interest that needed some really bad stuff to go down. Michael had become a student of the Harvard and MIT Professor Noam Chomsky whose articles so brilliantly explained how this was all connected and how it worked. Earlier this year Chomsky published his understanding of how America owns the world.

http://www.chomsky.info/articles/20080101.htm

Basically Michael knew America's leadership of the ITO was not unlike that of Milo Minderbender in Catch-22, although not nearly as funny as Milo. Milo had the "corporation", a foretaste of the multi-nationals of today. They worked with all sides in the Second World War and did whatever helped the "corporation" grow. They would bomb anybody, including their own bases, for a price. The situation developing with Iran was a case in point. The history of this coming event was about interlocking relationships. America had supported the Shah of Iran, then supported Iraq in fighting Iran, then supported Osama Bin Laden in fighting the Russians in Afghanistan. Funny how the *Charlie Wilson's War* movie did not even mention Bin Laden working for America! First America supported the Taliban, then they were against them, then America supported Pakistan, then invaded them, and on and on and on, while the Russians were supporting Iran. So these guys who worked for "the corporation" were now about to take out SMU, so that another division of the same corporation could take out Iran, and then the American division of 'the corporation' could claim all the oil that seemingly never showed any profit in the greatest gold rush in the history of man. This is why no one could trust the American government. Who the hell's side were they on?

Socrates had 200 specialists on a plane to Dallas at 6:30 that night, fully geared and briefed for the mission that would start as soon as the charter plane landed at Love Field.

"This is Michael. We have an update here. It seems the anticipated Iranian attack turned out to be the 'raid' on the USS Nimitz...another dud. You will love the videos CNN and the others received from the White House to prove how we averted this attack. Fox State TV even has a great classical orchestral sound track for the video. The Nimitz under full speed being chased by these little sport fishing boats looks like a freight train about to run over a colony of ants trying to cross the tracks. They really do think they can convince the Americans of anything. We are now receiving reports that another false flag terrorist attack is being planned for America. We need the following: pick up Scotty Callahan, last reported in Palestine and working as a Methodist missionary at a children's hospital. We need him right now. Next, Newstead needs to alert M1-6 to block any response the British might give in the event of another attack on the US. Nader, you need to alert your group at the UN that any UN response to any US attack is first to be cleared directly with me. Our special team in Dallas has uncovered the path for the attack, which will be to take out SMU and the site already under construction for the new Presidential Library. We have enough resources to stop this one and we do not have any reports of alternate sites that would be used if this one fails. The thinking seems to be that by attacking the SMU site, the 'terrorists' would automatically galvanize American public opinion for the planned war on Iran. Everybody seems to be running out of time here and this one is about to go live by Saturday. Heads up."

Michael had been on the communicators with all the continental commands almost hourly. With the exception of North America and Europe and the Middle East, things were going well and according to plan. So far the Asians were staying out of the way and South America was willing to deal with the rain forests and the educational issues. Africa was on its way with the schools and food problems and Tom had already gotten a provisional food transportation and distribution operation in place. Imagine, within just a few days the man-made, greed-driven hunger crisis would no longer exist. No more starving children pushing through crowds to get small chunks of bread or packets of rice to stave off what was already terminal hunger. It wasn't simple, but from Michael's vantage point, it really was obvious. Tom and Brad had spent a lot of their mission time on the food thing.

Frank had given the most impetus to the issue of food.

Without proper nourishment, kids and adults could not learn or function properly, let alone make the spiritual leap needed to continue forward in what was about to happen all over the world.

America, since the First World War, had been the leader in so many good things. Not the least was the massive and total war effort to stop the Japanese and German ambitions in the Second World War. But conquered ambitions lead to new ones. America in just less than 70 years had changed the diet directions of the whole world. The common denominator was beef. Prior to that time, diets in countries around the world had been the same for generations and were locally grown and managed. But beef had become the symbol of having arrived in the new imperial global American culture. It connected so many things especially the need for oil to create chemicals for farming, transportation, and even disposable packaging.

Late last year Frank had made a holotrip to America to get ready for the food war about to happen. Frank knew about all the issues with beef. The dead animals were filled with chemicals and hormones and infected with disease. In the trip Frank posed as a meat plant worker and used a hidden camera to record the awful abuses against living creatures that were resulting in the growing ill health of America and other First World Countries. The findings appeared in The Washington Post, to little or no effect. No surprise there.

"Video footage being released today shows workers at a California slaughterhouse delivering repeated electric shocks to cows too sick or weak to stand on their own; drivers using forklifts to roll the "downer" cows on the ground in efforts to get them to stand up for inspection; and even a veterinary version of waterboarding in which high-intensity water sprays are shot up animals' noses — all violations of state and federal laws designed to prevent animal cruelty and to keep unhealthy animals, such as those with mad cow disease, out of the food supply.

"Moreover, the companies where these practices allegedly

occurred are major suppliers of meat for the nation's school lunch programs according to a company official and federal documents.

"The footage was taken by an undercover investigator for an animal welfare group, who wore a customized video camera under his clothes while working at the facility last year. It is evidence that anti-cruelty and food safety rules are inadequate, and that Agriculture Department inspection and enforcement need to be enhanced, said officials with the Humane Society of the United States, which coordinated the project."

Washington Post Wednesday, January 30, 2008

It was all connected. Sick cattle being fed to sick kids who were being dumbed down in what was a sick educational system. But now the change was just a few days away.

Frank found it curious that the coming attack on SMU would hit an educational institution that had fostered the Texas beef connection. Yet, just a few years before, the various Texas beef associations had taken on Oprah because she was trying to get this word out to the whole country. As a result of this case, even less could be legally said about the dangers of beef.

Chapter 22

July 30, Wednesday

John Buck had made many holotrips to Earth posing as an adventurer and author. On one trip he shipped out on a freighter when he was posing as a sixteen year old kid. Another trip had him taking part in an ascent on Mt. Everest's North Wall at twenty. He hitchhiked around the world at twenty-two then used another holotrip to pose as a Foreign Service Officer for several years. He holotripped into the middle of the revolution in Libya and the war in Vietnam. One time he was a member of NATO's top-secret Nuclear Planning Group. Another trip placed him as a foreign policy advisor to Senator Harold Hughes of Iowa, and another got him assigned as an assistant to the US Ambassador to the United Nations. His trips got him deeply involved in U.S. initiatives in southern Africa, South Asia and Cuba. By most holotripping measures, he was very successful. However, something was missing. He could not see where all of these connections and experiences were heading, for him or for the world itself. It had been one hell of a series of adventures.

He had known for eight years that he would be one of the Sirius crewmembers. It turned out that the Council made him Co-Commander of the Antarctic continent, which was a big surprise, because he figured he was less prepared to deal with penguins than people. Such is life. He was not told that he was given that assignment because there would be very little to do with the South Pole other that dealing with its role in the environmental crisis which was part of the agenda for the whole crew. The Council knew that John would be the most capable crewmember for single person undercover assignments critical to the whole mission.

"John, they just called your play". Michael thought of himself as a quarterback for the team and he liked to use that kind of language in speaking with the crew……and they liked the added drama that only they were in on. "I have a guy we need to talk to right now, and he has to be brought in undercover. I don't think he will be all that easy to find or bring in. Scotty Callahan is a small time Methodist minister who left America after three disappointing attempts at being a local church pastor. He wanted to be a missionary and for some reason was assigned to Palestine and a children's hospital. He is a true believer, buying all that Christian fundamentalist nonsense starting with the seven days stuff. We're not sure what his job is at the hospital, but he somehow gets kids to America and sets them up with great educations. The only problem is that these same kids, in one particular instance, are actually ITO operatives, and they are about to take out SMU. He must be stopped, and you're it." "OK. I'll start now. I assume this means you want me in Gaza?" "Go for it and stay connected. This guy may need some of our kind of roughing up."

All the crewmembers and some of the passengers had made repeated holotrips to Earth prior to the mission. They could fully participate in Earth events and environments, but there was that magic techno distance between them as holotrippers and the real Earth people they were working with. It was like surgeons doing remote surgery on a patient 1000 miles away through the use of computers, satellite communications and remote tools. The only feeling at that distance was a feeling of techno wonder as all the gear worked perfectly. It was like being the pilot of a B-1 bomber and flying from Maine to Miami and knowing that you had sixteen nuclear bombs aboard that would allow you to take out every major city on the way down the coast and all you would experience would be the bright light as each of sixteen bombs exploded in your rear view mirrors. No burning children. No hospitals exploding in a fire ball. No beautiful 20's something couples making Tantric love as the world exploded. No grandparents helping each other up the steps. No football stadiums full of fans listening to a great rock concert as the sky exploded above them in a vaporizing fire.

For the crew and passengers, being here as real Earth people, fully human and fully Sirian, made for a completely different experience. All of a sudden the five senses and the millions of feelings flooded the time here with what it really felt like to be a Human, and the fear was amazing. Here they were, with a complete array of super-human abilities, and yet they felt the fear, the depression, the greed, the passion and the rush of time and events that was the human experience in the new millennium. Most of them slogged on with the mission, but even the very best of them had to stop from time to time to compensate for the light-headedness and nausea that came over them when they had to experience something that would never happen on Sirius.

John wasn't prepared for Palestine and the Gaza Strip. Faced on one side with the Mediterranean and the other side Israel, it should have been an urban garden. But the Google Earth landmarks in Gaza were listed in numbers marking where bombs had been dropped in the 60 year struggle to secure a non-war zone life for its inhabitants. There was always something that made life constantly intolerable. The 60 years of deaths, murders, terrorist and military attacks and destruction on both sides of the Israeli-Arab conflict had resulted in a perpetual stalemate that refused to yield to the best intentions and ideas of all concerned. And no side was right. It was just endless conflict with no end in sight. When Israel was founded after World War II with the blessing of almost the whole world community, appeals were made to the other Arab countries to take in the Palestinian refugees. The Arab neighbors, for their own purposes, decided not to help the Palestinians and left them there to further create the agony that is felt both by the Israelis and Arabs, indeed the whole world. Now, 60 years later, the Israelis wanted to keep Palestine contained behind enforced borders and the results were blockades that kept out everything needed to just exist. Israel was able to stop anything getting in the country. And today, John was going to have the Palestinian side of the war pushed right in his face. He had to cover his nose and mouth as he walked through the latest catastrophe created with a border sealing. From the news:

Feces Change the Face of Gaza by Mohammed Omer, Inter Press Service

"Gaza City - A stream of dark and putrid sludge snakes through Gaza's streets. It is a noxious mix of human and animal waste. The stench is overwhelming. The occasional passer-by vomits.

"Over recent days this has been a more common sight than the sale of food on the streets of Gaza, choked by a relentless Israeli siege.

"Hundreds of thousands of Gazans, almost all of its able male adults among a population of 1.5 million, crossed over into Egypt last week to buy essential provisions - and a new lease on life. That has staved off starvation. But streets continue as sewers.

"The rain has not helped. The sludge has spread, and the stench with it. Starved of timely income and essential supplies, municipal services have all but ceased.

"The smell," says Ayoub al-Saifi, 56, grimacing as he holds a handkerchief over his nose and mouth. "The stench of the sewage ... my wife has asthma, and she can't breathe."

"Saifi lives next to what has become a newly formed pool of waste. This used to be the street leading to home. "It's getting worse day by day," says neighbour Said Ammar, an engineer, and father of four.

"The sewage treatment plant in al-Zaytoun neighbourhood in Gaza City requires 20,000 litres of fuel a day. Last week Israel ceased delivery of all fuel and supplies to Gaza. The consequences have been catastrophic.

"Without fuel to pump it away, the waste backs up, flooding the streets and clogging the plumbing. The local ministry of health has declared this an environmental catastrophe.

"Doctors have warned that a medical catastrophe could follow by way of spread of cholera and other diseases. That is at a time when not even life-saving medical services are on offer any more.

"We have to choose between cutting the electricity on babies in the maternity ward, cutting it to heart patients, or shutting down our operating rooms," says Dr. Mawia Hasaneen, director of emergency at al-Shifa Hospital, the largest in Gaza.

"The World Health Organisation released a statement warning of serious health difficulties arising in Gaza Strip, isolated by the Israeli siege, the Egyptian border and the Mediterranean Sea.

"Frequent electricity cuts and the limited power available to run hospital generators are of particular concern, as they disrupt the functioning of intensive care units, operating theatres, and emergency rooms," the WHO said. "In the central pharmacy, power shortages have interrupted refrigeration of perishable medical supplies, including vaccine."

"Christine McNab, acting director in the communications department in Geneva adds that "our current concerns are about the supply of electricity to health facilities, the ability to move medical supplies into the region, and the ability of people to seek care outside of Gaza."

"McNab notes that even if the full blockade is lifted, additional measures would need to be taken by the international community against any further disruptions."

The stench was overpowering and the horror on every face was deadening and suddenly John could not get beamed up to end a holotrip. He was stuck in hell, and it was worse than what he had seen in Viet Nam or Iraq, and it had been going on endlessly for sixty years.

As he struggled through the sewage past the place where the Israelis bombed a corner building in 2002, another American made F-16 flew overhead and released two missiles that landed right down the block in the direction he was headed. The combined sounds of the plane and the explosions were deafening and the screams coming from every building in the path ahead would never have been heard on Sirius. He had noticed that being in a human body had amplified his hearing sensitivity to such a level that human screams actually produced extreme pain in his whole body and he began shaking as he tried to walk on in the debris and small fires lit by the missile. People were rushing out of the buildings into the street.

The hospital was four blocks ahead. He could only get there by going through the blast zone. As he approached where the missiles landed, he saw a sight that instantly took him back to Viet Nam: a little girl, maybe eight years old, came screaming out of a building with no clothes on and she was covered with burned skin, on her arms and stomach and she was running wildly through the street.

John's vomit added to the filth and chaos of the scene as he struggled to reach his goal. Other people came to the street, all mangled, all screaming, all in panic. He had to find The Reverend who had the power to do much worse than this to people a half a world away with hidden nuclear bombs. This scene was burned into John's memory so powerfully that in the hidden weeks ahead he would wake night after night with the fierce anger that made him want to find any way possible to get back at the American support of the Israelis and their total war on their ill equipped neighbors as they signed peace agreements and then turned around and unleashed their American arms on these neighborhoods of children. No wonder people chose to use their bodies as weapons…..it was all they had. These scenes that kept rushing through his mind were the factories where suicide bombers were being made every day. And for John, they became the amnesia drug that made him forget everything, especially who he was.

Sirens raced to the scene of the blast and the injured were taken out by friends and placed in ambulances for delivery to near-by hospitals. The stench and the mess seemed to have multiplied by the blast and covered anyone in the area, including John. He got through the worst of it and kept going to the Children's

Hospital. "I'm looking for The Reverend Scotty Callahan who works here." "And you are?" "John Buck and I am from the American Headquarters of the Methodist Church and have come here with good news for him." "We're a little busy right now. Fifteen kids have just been brought in from the missile attack down the street. I know you can't help with that, but I can't help you under these circumstances. He's on the second floor, the end office on the right of the south wing." The nurse quickly left to assist in the ER.

"OK, I can sure follow those directions." he said, mostly to himself. He walked to the steps and took them two at a time. The hall to the south was about 125 feet long and there was little sound as he made the trip. It was a wood door and he stopped long enough to catch his breath before he pushed the door open. It sounded like someone was moving something or doing some kind of heavy work inside. HOLY SHIT. Callahan was there all right, and he was making noise and his back was to the opening door and he didn't hear John come in. He was completely involved in the contents of his computer screen which showed picture after picture of young children, nude, being sexually abused by men whose faces could not be seen by the viewer. "So this is how the holy man recruits his agents to America." John was stunned. When John caught Callahan's eye as he turned toward the door, it was like being hit with a death ray....pure evil and demonic anger. "Get out of here......who are you?.........you're not authorized.......get out." John stood in the open doorway and watched as Callahan adjusted his pants to cover a wet spot before getting up. "We need to talk, Callahan."

"Michael, I have made contact with Callahan. We are leaving now." Then John spoke to Callahan. "We're going to our headquarters." That's all John said to Scotty as he led him down the stairs. In a totally matter of fact and non judgmental way, John led the way out of the building taking the long way back to the destroyed airport close to the Egyptian border in a blood stained cab that had stopped at the hospital to let off one of the victims of the missile attack. The command chopper was waiting on the bombed out main parking area in front of the dilapidated main terminal. Once aboard, again with no talking to Callahan, the chopper lifted off for Cairo and landed at the western edge of El-Giza which included a great view of the local pyramids. The Headquarters was a short van ride ahead.

Headquarters was still close to the Great Pyramid but the relocation closer to El-Giza had meant they could build temporary buildings with complete services and still have total access to the pyramids and their ancient energy. The Egyptian Minister of Antiquities, Zahee Hakas, had always suspected that the real mystery of his charge was to be revealed outside Earth and the history of these pyramids. He was not overly surprised when Michael met with him and revealed the bare essentials of the plan and requested his help. Hakas was a uniquely powerful and self-made man. He could call any shot he wanted in Egypt and was happy to help Michael. Headquarters was a series of nice offices, a dormitory, commissary, and the other services that were needed for the global command. Michael liked to laugh that he could run the most powerful operation on Earth from what was a very modest location, when just a thousand miles away the new US Embassy in Iraq had now exceeded two billion dollars and was still not functioning and probably never would be. Anyway, the main room of the headquarters was circular with a glass dome as its roof and about 100 feet in diameter. The circumference was given to a padded seating arrangement around the wall that allowed large numbers of people to be in the room for meditations. There was also room for people to bring in comfortable cushions to sit on the floor for these times.

Earth people thought it made sense to torture people to make them reveal secrets. Of course, much of this was aided by high tech tools like cattle prods, but the ancient water tortures were also used. Small bare rooms and crude furniture seemed to complete the current torture panache.

The Sirians knew better. Callahan was taken into the building, fed a light vegetarian meal, given shower privileges, dressed in a yellow and orange gown with Sirian markings on it and led into the meditation room and placed in a straight chair in the very center that rotated at a very slow pace on a lazy Susan device, thus allowing him to see everyone in the room. Two hundred twenty three of the passengers filed in and sat around the circumference and on the floor. No one spoke. Callahan's face became a grotesque mask of fear. The death ray in his eyes shone like a beacon in all directions as the chair turned him round and round. The passengers all closed their eyes and began the meditation that was among the oldest traditions on Sirius.

Throughout the universe when a person is born they bring a certain vibration, almost like a song, with them. This can be learned. Repeating the song will instantly get the person's complete attention and will dial in the highest level of consciousness of that person. It is irresistible. One of the indigenous tribes of Earth, which happens to worship the Dog Star, or Sirius, does this when a child is conceived. The tribe meditates with the mother during the pregnancy to learn what the song is. As the child is being born, all the tribe members sing the song they have learned and the child is born knowing and hearing that song. At every major point in that person's life, including moments of failure, the song is sung. They do not use judgment, fear or punishment. They just call out the highest level of that person with the song, and behavior is changed. The song is also sung by tribe members as the person dies.

The passengers focused their meditation on Callahan's song. Their awareness was so tuned in that within fifteen minutes they knew the song and they began singing it. Callahan almost melted before their eyes. His death ray became tears which became loud sobs and then a stream of consciousness confession revealed his work as a broker for the ITO who arranged and recruited the right people for specific ITO assignments. He named the three candidates he had recruited for the SMU assignment and revealed all the details of the plan, including where the bombs were to be placed. The whole process took less than 45 minutes and when it was over, Callahan was taken to a surgery suite and a device was inserted under his skin. The device would play his song for him for the rest of his life, regardless where he went and he would finally become the spiritual person he had pretended to be all his life.

Michael and Brad had been in the meditation and when it was over, they went to the communications room and dialed up all the needed players. "Socrates, we got the skinny on this guy. There are four mini-nukes planted on the SMU campus. We know one is in Dedman, one at the Cox School, one at the Meadows School Museum and one at another location and that may be somewhere in the Perkins buildings. Russell will have to use the crew you sent him last night to find the exact locations. They must be defused by 10AM Saturday the 2nd. Nader will notify the UN Secretary General's Office of the possibility of this thing going down. Everybody else stand by.

It was 10AM on the 30th in Dallas when Russell put his crew on campus and they just started looking around. Michael's research report on Callahan finally came through at 4:30. They had 60 hours to find the bombs and disarm the bombs, stay invisible while doing so, and protect the campus without any outside help. They were good, really good. Russell figured the Perkins complex was the last place he needed to look because the real power was not in religious studies. Wrong.

By 3pm on the 31st they had the first bomb in the Dedman building. They had the Cox bomb partially done by noon on the 1st and Russell decided he better have lunch at Food From Galilee to see if he would meet Abdullah, Absman and Samad. Damn, they were there! But the energy at their table was chaotic and dangerous. All of a sudden Davis wished he had brought one of his rubber chickens with him to lighten things up and detract any attention from his mission here at lunch. "You boys doin all right?" "Yeah." "What's happening?" "We're just working on a rush computer project. We thought we had until tomorrow morning to finish it up but they want it done by tonight at 8 and this is going be to the only chance we have for about ten hours to have some really good food." *Oh God, how am I going to beat their schedule?*

Russell's phone rang just at the right time and he said, "OK, I'll be back across Central Expressway as fast as I can. Bye" "Hey, I have another so called emergency over at the office, hope to see you next week." He was out of there and back on the phone. "Socrates, this just got serious. I thought these guys were going to run their test at 10am tomorrow, but something happened and they are going to do something right after 8pm tonight. Light up the communications tree, we're on double time." "Copy that, Russell."

Russell was quick with his orders to the specialists on the project. "Get a crew into the Meadows School Museum right now and give me a crew for the Perkins School." Russell went first to the Meadows School Museum and gave maximum attention to the problem including the decision to x-ray all of the large art. This had to be done with exquisite care and in a way to not set off alarms, mechanical or in people's minds.

Next on the agenda was the Perkins School. Not much of value here to be worried about in terms of ancient art or great buildings. He got the crew there started at 2PM. Finally his tour took him to the Chapel. It was beautiful, simple and expensive. The recent complete renovation of Perkins Chapel had included the renovation of the Aeolian-Skinner organ Opus 1167. The upgrade project in 2002 had added 1,250 pipes to the existing 2,500 and included a Musical Instrument Digital Interface (MIDI) system. *Oh My God! 3750 pipes! We're gonna do this before 8PM?*

"We have an issue here." Socrates could hardly believe

Russell's report. Finding a bomb in a pipe organ that must not be destroyed in the secret process was a tall order. "OK, go for it and I will have Headquarters do the backup." Next Socrates had Brad and Michael on the line. We have about 6 hours to find the last bomb and tearing the place up to find it risks a booby trap and the loss of the whole campus. We have to take apart more than 3750 pipes on this big deal organ. Michael, this sounds like an alert for the whole Merkabah." "We'll find it." Michael was more than a little concerned. They had been so successful to this point. Two hundred passenger/specialists climbing all over a pipe organ and each other posed all sorts of issues.

Chapter 23

Lost in the Stars

Before Lord God made the sea and the land,
He held all the stars in the palm of his hand.
And they ran through his fingers like grains of sand,
And one little star fell alone.
Then the Lord God hunted through the wide night air
For the little dark star on the wind down there.
And he stated and promised he'd take special care
So it wouldn't get lost again.
Now a man don't mind if the stars grow dim
And the clouds blow over and darken him,
So long as the Lord God's watching over them,
Keeping track of how it all goes on.
But I've been walking all the night and the day,
Till my eyes get weary and my head turns gray.
And sometimes it seems maybe God's gone away,
And we're lost out here in the stars.
Little stars, big stars, blowing through the night,
And we're lost out here in the stars.

By Maxwell Anderson & Kurt Weill

July 30

John was exhausted and did not understand why. He had as much experience on Earth as anybody else on the crew and much of it in really difficult situations. But today had been the first time his experiences had been as a full human. He was drained. More than that, he was disillusioned. He hurt. Seeing those kids in the middle of the bombs, sewage and blood was too much all at once. He had done a good job of hiding his feelings from everybody and especially himself, but now that Callahan was being fixed in surgery, John felt the full force of what he had experienced so far this day. He wanted out. Now. He took a cab across the Nile to the Cairo Grand Hyatt and went to the lounge at the top floor. The Sun was setting and he could see the pyramids to the west as he did something completely outside the book. He ordered the dirtiest martini possible with Sapphire Bombay Gin and five olives. He didn't like the taste but it was gone quicker than the sunset and he ordered another.

These people were not just un-evolved; they were damned. They were monsters. He understood the mission and knew they could complete it. But the pain. Today he had seen the bombings, the injuries, the depravity of a child molester, the potential panic with the nuke strike about to hit Dallas, and the nagging feeling that Earth people had just gone immune to understanding or feeling the massive tragedy they were constantly creating for themselves. And this was only the beginning. The Sirians had waited until the last minute. Time was up. All the forces of conflict and negative change had been rushing toward each other since the Second World War. It had created a psychic super highway to the looming Third and really final World War. What was this thing in these people that allowed and encouraged them to act as if killing someone or millions of someones could solve anything? Imagine! Thirty thousand nuclear weapons scattered about the Earth and in the air on bombers and now in satellites parked in space waiting for the big day. Might makes right. They had been wrestling with this same concept for thousands of years and the answer was right there in the formulation of the idea. Right makes right. All the great masters had said the same thing. Do unto others as you want them to do unto you. That is not just a great idea. It's the law. People will do unto you, just as you do unto them, and you are the initiator of the doing. We create our own reality. And, Oh God, this place was hell.

John did not realize the power of the juniper berry from the nearby desert. It was almost like a drug. Actually, it was a drug hiding out in a gin bottle and like most drugs it created a different reality.......and not a good one. Normally, depression does not overtake one all at once; the body chemistry needs time to adjust to the new state, but the Sirian's had a slightly more rapid chemical ability, even in human bodies. When the Sun had set, John was so far into depression that he did not even recognize the signs. His soul was heading down faster than the elevator was carrying his body to the ground floor so he could make his escape. The depression and the chemical changes it created in his body dampened the built-in communications systems the crew used. They would not be able to find or contact him in the normal or any other way. Now he and his depression were in control and he would decide where to hide out and when, if ever, to reconnect with the crew and the mission. John walked out the main door, hailed a cab and disappeared into the dark night of his soul.

Chapter 24

August 1, Friday

"Get those three pricks in here and get them here right now." Russell smiled as he realized he had been working too long with Socrates. Socrates was the galaxy's greatest cusser and he was also a carrier of graphic language. It helped to relieve the emotional weight of the moment. That thought fled as he sent out the command to bring in Abdullah, Absman and Samad for a little nuclear recreation.

An hour later one of the passengers brought in Absman. Fifteen minutes later Abdullah arrived and Samad followed 10 minutes later. Russell brought them down to the front row of the Chapel for their first visit to a real American Christian church. "Well, if it isn't my little Falafel lunch bunch. Welcome gentlemen. You're going to sit here and you are going to tell me where this bomb is. I already know you are not suicide bombers and I also know you know I have found the other three bombs with no mistakes. I have a crew working in your back yard back home right now. They're in Cairo and they're working on you. In a few moments you are going to experience nausea, disorientation and finally, excruciating pain as your mind goes into combat with your soul. You soul is going to win, but you are the only person who can determine how hard a battle it turns out to be. My advice is to give in now and quickly, to avoid pain. We will not hurt you, but your resistance to our power will cause you great distress.

The three looked at each other as if to say, "Is this dude crazy or what?" Absman was the first to vomit.......all over himself. Then Samad, then Abdullah. When Absman looked up it was like being on LSD.........and a bad trip at that. His eyes were spinning in their sockets. And then the pain hit. Then Samad, then Abdullah. Then screams. "STOP IT, STOP IT!" "Sure. I'll get it stopped as soon as you stop wasting my time and tell me where you put this last bomb." Fear filled the souls of these would-be terrorists. They had nothing in their past to prepare them for this. Finally Samad broke. "It is in the third largest pipe....at the rear." His pain immediately stopped. Russell looked at the other two. "You want the pain to stop too?" "YES, YES, YES." "Tell me he is right." "This is the truth. Just tell them to stop." "OK." They started to regain normal consciousness and their vision and they were each given a bucket of water and a towel and were told to clean themselves up. This successful "torture" took less than 5 minutes, and no one was touched. It was all done with prayer and meditation by passengers and crew a half a world away. When this was all over, the message to Earth people would be unmistakable.

"OK guys.....the third largest pipe at the rear..........and somebody dial up E. Power Biggs and J.S Bach on that boom box over there........we need some mood music for this take down." Russell could be under the most severe pressure and still make it seem like he was having fun. He laughed at the contrast between the music coming out of the boom box and the real music the 3750 pipes against the walls would still be making when this was all over.

"Socrates, I'm pretty sure we're going to be clear on this in about 90 minutes. This frees up Brad and Michael to start working on the announcement with the guys on the East River in New York and our outpost on Catherine Place in London. I'd sure like to see The President's expression when he discovers we saved the plot of land for his library, and destroyed the plot for his attack on Iran!" "Russell, you're the best. I owe you one."

Chapter 25

August 1, Friday

The summer in Dallas had been hotter than usual, but that was the norm, since 1996 each summer had been hotter than the last. Most people just complained about it, but few were willing to discuss the real issue. After all, everyone agreed it was not happening as a result of man-made things. Raul and Margaret had been playing house all summer and getting Raul ready to teach and Margaret ready to write for the Dallas Morning News. They were excited to get out of town for the mysterious trip to Arizona that had been planned for four weeks. It would be a nice long weekend. They would leave Friday morning and come back Monday afternoon.

Billy was curious about the trip, but did not ask to join them. He just gave them the plane and said it would be easier getting into Second Mesa in Hopi Land with their own plane. Raul had grown truly fond of Billy over the summer, and Billy was always surprised at how respectful he was toward Raul even though Billy was the main player in that circle, and he generally thought the God Squad types were a little too off the wall. Before they left Love Field that morning, Raul rechecked his shoulder bike messenger's bag to see if he still had the case with the stone fragment. This would be the entry into Hopi Land that would be like no other.

Raul had done his homework. He had read all of Frank Waters books on the Hopis, seen all the videos and other documentation about the Hopi, had spoken to Bill Chambers, the Hopi art collector in Sante Fe, and Ann Roberly, the patron of Hopi projects in New York. Ann agreed to introduce Raul when he explained the gift the Sheik had given him in Dubai. So The Grandfather knew about Raul on several levels before he arrived. The Grandfather also knew exactly what time it was.

Now that he had flown in one of the really big boy's planes, Raul thought of Billy's G-5 as "the little plane" as it touched down at the airstrip at Second Mesa. Margaret sat in the chair on the other side of the small table facing forward and toward the back, visible only to Raul, was The King. As usual, Billy had provided a wonderful brunch of spectacular "airplane food" as he liked to call it from his favourite Highland Park caterer, delivered right to the door of the plane minutes before wheels up at 9:09. When the pilot landed and opened the door to the hot dry Arizona air, everybody was ready for the day ahead.

The plan was to have someone from The Grandfather's group pick them up for the ride to his place. No one was there to meet them until an hour later when a rusty brown pickup truck ambled up to the plane and a young man about Raul's age got out. "I am Horse and I am supposed to take you to see the Grandfather. Is this all your luggage?" "Yes, we travel light." They squeezed into the truck and slowly left the strip as the pilot fired up the two engines for the trip back to Dallas. As the take off sound went away, Raul asked Horse about his work here. "I normally live in LA and manage education projects for young people who come from here to UCLA for special training for my people. We are making real progress toward bringing our ways and the white ways together and these young people are leading us.......and The Grandfather is leading them. When Bill told me that you had a meeting with The Grandfather, I decided to come home to meet you and help The Grandfather. Bill says you have a special mission?"

"Well, I'm not real sure, frankly. This seems like an adventure all right, and the last episode ended when I left Dubai with a present for The Grandfather, but as far as what it all means, I really can't say. How long have you known The Grandfather?" "Since I was a little boy." They talked like that during the ride to Third Mesa and the small house where The Grandfather lived. When they got there both men felt like they knew each other pretty well. Margaret felt like she had been eavesdropping on the typical male bonding thing and she made a mental note to remember the feeling she perceived between the men as a footnote for her later writing about the event. She had a sense that a record of this trip would make great reading some day.

Raul didn't know exactly how to greet The Grandfather, so he decided to use all three greetings he knew about. At the door, before he walked in he put his hands together and spoke the Namaste, then he put his right hand in the air as a salute and then he offered his right hand in a handshake. The Grandfather smiled and let him in along with Margaret and The King slipped in behind her. Horse stayed outside and eventually drove off. Once inside, The King telepathed Raul to look The Grandfather directly in his left eye and open both hands palm up, and say simply, "I am from the east and I have a gift for you." This was the secret greeting The Grandfather had been waiting for. "Come sit with me." The mysterious introduction had been made and Raul, Margaret and The Grandfather sat in the small chairs in the room. The King stood to the side where he could hear and not be seen, but he also knew The Grandfather could easily see him.

"Show me the gift, please." Raul took out the small box and handed it to The Grandfather who slowly opened it and examined the small fragment of what must have been a larger square tablet. The Grandfather closed his eyes and held the piece in both hands for several minutes. When he opened his eyes, he looked at Raul intensely for a long time and then said, "Great Pahana, I have waited since I was a little boy hoping to see this moment. I salute you. I am at your service." Raul did not understand. This was the Great Man. How could he be at Raul's service?

"I knew in 1982 that you had been born. Many people in this area and south of here saw your birth star. I knew you would be here soon. That star confirmed that the prophesy was about to be made real, and this is that long awaited day. You complete a long journey my people have made from all four directions. Your arrival signals to all my people that the day of purification has arrived. We have waited for this day to reclaim our place in this land, and now it is here. I will help you with our power granted us for this moment."

This became the ritual beginning of Raul's mission. Had you been there you would have felt like you were at Jesus' Baptism by John. The King brought a unique vibrational energy that elevated the whole cottage and the people in it, almost as if they were being levitated.

The Grandfather's home was on the most powerful energy vortex on Third Mesa and it was the perfect setting for this to happen. It seemed like a conversation between The Grandfather, Margaret and Raul with The King watching.......slow and casual and circling around and around the same subjects at higher and higher levels of revelation. It seemed so normal that Raul was startled when he glanced out the window and saw the last light of the setting Sun. It felt like they had only been there for 30 minutes, but now it was obvious it was more like seven hours......and it was clear this was going to be a long process. Already Dallas and Perkins and being a professor seemed grandly unimportant and in the distant past. Raul heard the barking of dogs down the road and they seemed to announce the arrival of Earth animals and totems into the process.

When the Sun had set, a group of young Hopi men came to the front yard and waited for a signal from inside the house. The Grandfather went around the room and lit candles in all four corners and one candle in the center of the circle where they were sitting. That was the signal for the music to begin. Outside the young men started chanting and beating two powerful drums. Another of the men played a flute that sounded like Kokopelli, himself, about to preside over the birth of a new creature. The music seemed to create an additional vibration field around the house as The Grandfather opened a clay pot and handed Raul, Margaret and himself each a small peyote button and instructed them to take it in their mouths, chew and swallow. In another tradition this would have been called communion.

The long night had begun. Thirty minutes of no speaking and quiet meditation to the music outside ended when Raul threw up and Margaret was ready to do so herself, as The Grandfather told them this was all right, safe and part of the process. When they had cleaned up and had some water, the music took on a completely different sound. It was like hearing the song of Earth.......it was a vibration and sound they seemed to know somewhere, but did not remember having ever heard. Raul looked to the corner at his left and sitting beside the candle, at attention, was the most beautiful white wolf he could have imagined. The Grandfather smiled when he noticed Raul saw the white protector. In another corner Raul saw an eagle perched on a coat rack. In the third corner, standing next to The King, was an old Hopi Chief in full ceremonial dress. In the fourth corner was the biggest rattlesnake Raul had ever seen, and that included all the rattlers he had seen as a kid in Texas at the Big Spring Rattler Roundups. His whole body shook and he saw Margaret recognize the same beings present as well. He snapped to attention when the chanting outside stopped and The Grandfather started his own chant. This chant had its own rhythm and tone and suddenly Raul and Margaret, The Grandfather, The King and the totems left Earth and found themselves in a large circular room of alabaster walls that glowed from within and was also lit by torch light from the sconces on the walls.

The King and The Grandfather and the totems all knew where they were. But for Raul and Margaret, the Masters' Chapel in the Great Cathedral was the most powerful place they had ever been. They were dressed differently than they had been at Third Mesa. They all had green robes trimmed with gold that seemed to shine. The King also was wearing a gold crown. It was a beautiful 24 carat deep yellow gold with two snakes intertwined around a large Lapis stone shaped like a tear, and called the Tear of Isis, to symbolize the mercy of the feminine energy throughout this galaxy.

The King spoke. "This is the beginning now that we have all waited for. There have been six times in the past that I have sent my people to Earth to bring men the power I want them to have as their inheritance. Each time, Earthmen's' fear combined with their brilliant technological advances have resulted in unimaginable tragedy as they have destroyed their worlds. You may have heard some of these so called myths, poorly remembered and never understood. The disappearance of Atlantis is the one event most people seem to entertain as being possible. It was the sixth and most recent destruction of a global civilization. Very little remains; a submerged road bed off the coast of Florida, the dreams of Edgar Cayce, and a persistent myth that this society found enormous powers it was not capable of using wisely, which created a global tragedy that ended this super advanced civilization. This is about all Earth people know about this event. There were five other similar cataclysmic events and civilizations before that.

"This evening, back on Earth, there are forces at work whose success, if it occurs, will mean another global cataclysm and the end forever of Earth as an evolutionary incubator for the galaxy. Raul, I have chosen you to bring the long prophesied Day of Purification in such a way, that this time, man will accept the power he was created with and will lay down the force that can destroy him. Power versus Force. The history of your world has been about force and might making right. Earlier in your last century I sent many prophets to Earth to set the agenda for this moment. One of them was Dr. David Hawkins, who was given the task of clearly delineating the difference between real power and the destructive use of force, which he did in his book *Power vs. Force*. He has been wonderfully successful, so much so that throughout the world my children all recognize the wisdom of his work and many are already using it.

"You, Raul, are unique among men. Your birth, little noticed, was a remarkable supernatural event signifying that I created you to be fully human and fully Sirian. No one else is like you and yet I have given you the power to awaken in all men the dormant side of themselves, which is also Sirian in nature and ability. Right now on Earth, waiting for you, are almost two million Sirians who will accomplish this mission with you. I have also placed millions of advanced Earth children, who carry a new strain of DNA, at your disposal. Most are under twenty-five years old. They have been trained in what we call 'night school' or 'mystery school' which occurs at night during sleep. They are ready now and your appearance will activate them to their mission. Up until now, they have not understood that their uniqueness was preparing them to step forward to be recognized as the new humans, the next step in man's successful evolution. Their uniqueness has fooled others into thinking these children are wastoids or badly adjusted, and they have been shunned, drugged, ignored, made fun of, mistreated, and otherwise misunderstood and rarely appreciated. Lucky are those who have had aware parents and teachers who encouraged the development of their powers. All of that is about to change.

"You will be surprised when you wake up again in The Grandfather's house and discover how much time has elapsed since you left, but you will not be surprised at what you know." The King made a signal with his head and two servants came forward with a platter that had a beautiful brilliant crystal skull on it, and they placed it on an altar that was in the center of the Chapel and quietly left the room. "I placed twelve of these on Earth in special places before Atlantis disappeared. They were made in Atlantis and they are unique memory devices. This thirteenth skull is the most powerful of them all and it was made here. I have given the twelve Earth skulls to the twelve Sirians who are now preparing for the Purification you are about to introduce.

"I have brought you here to the Chapel to conduct this ritual in what you will now know to be your true home. This is the place you used to dream about when you were young, but could not understand. When you were thirteen, before one of these 'dreams' I sent Margaret to you as a sign that you were safe and headed toward this moment. She is to take care of you, although this is the first complete sign she has seen that tells her who she is.

The King motioned to Raul to come before him and to lie on his back on the altar with his head toward The King's feet. As Raul was getting up on the altar, the twenty-four Masters filed into the Chapel and sat around the edge to witness this sacred event and to add their power to the coming transformation of Raul. The King then motioned for The Grandfather to lie down beside Raul. He then placed the crystal skull between Raul's and The Grandfather's heads. With a brief prayer, Raul and The Grandfather went to sleep in a ritual that went back many thousands of years. While asleep, The King used the skull to transfer all of The Grandfather's wisdom to Raul. Once accomplished, The King transferred additional information from his own memory bank to Raul. Thus making Raul the most informed man on Earth.

The King continued the incantations over The Grandfather and Raul for a very long time. Then the Masters came around to the edge of the altar and placed their hands on both men and offered silent prayers. As The King was finishing, the sounds of what could only be understood as angelic music increased in volume and Raul, Margaret, The Grandfather and the others sensed they were leaving The Chapel and Sirius to return to Earth. As they neared Third Mesa, the music changed from angels to chanting, drums and Kokopelli's flute. As they came back to normal consciousness, it was late afternoon light and the totems were gone and The Grandfather, Raul and Margaret were more hungry than they remembered ever being. When the music stopped, almost as if on cue, three women arrived at the door carrying plates of food and spring water. The three ate quietly as the Sun set. Raul looked at his watch for the first time and discovered it was Wednesday, August 6th. So much for the long weekend get away. And on top of that, Raul sensed he had seen the last of Dallas for a long, long time to come.

As he finished eating, Raul remembered the last words The King had said to him before they left Sirius. "I will be with you when you arrive back at Third Mesa, but I will be in the background as I have been in the past. Trust me in this process. We will succeed. There is a divine order to things." In the background was The King. Next, The Grandfather spoke and said that a final ritual of purification was in order and all three went out the back door, which faced to the east, and looked down the sharp slope of the Mesa. It was a moonless night as the new moon was two nights away on August 8th. In the back yard was a domed small structure, about five feet high and ten feet in diameter and the men who did the chanting and drumming and flute playing were now there with their music. Horse was there too, tending a roaring fire that surrounded a cage contraption that held forty-one glowing hot stones. The Grandfather motioned for Raul and Margaret to go through the small door into the sweat lodge. The King went in next and finally The Grandfather who closed the curtain door.

They sat quietly and could hear the muffled sounds of the chanting outside. Then the curtain was opened and Horse used a shovel to put eight of the hot stones in the center of the lodge and closed the door again. The heat was instantaneous and power-fully hot. The Grandfather started offering opening prayers to The Great Spirit and they invited Raul and Margaret to do the same. Again Horse brought in eight more stones for the first prayers of thanksgiving in the steaming hot lodge. Then again eight more stones and another round of prayers this time for forgiveness, and then the fourth group of stones was piled on for the prayers of guidance for the mission. The final group of nine stones was for the prayers of intercession for the whole world and for peace. When they were finished The Grandfather led the group outside where the women had made four very comfortable beds on the ground. The four laid down and were covered by warm blankets as they watched the stars above them and listened to the chanting of the men. Each could clearly see Sirius. Raul and Margaret were in awe at the thought they had been right there less than twelve hours ago. They went to sleep in the stars with the sound of the desert coyotes echoing all around them.

Sun up on Thursday found them full of excited energy. Raul intuitively knew the little plane would be back shortly and they would be off for the next part of the adventure. Horse came around the house to the back yard with the three women bringing wonderful breakfast foods and most welcome coffee. Out of nowhere, the scream of a fast low flying small jet blasted their outdoor kitchen and Margaret started to laugh. She knew who was on board. Only Billy would pull a stunt like that, and she could almost hear him laughing as the plane streaked forward to the landing strip. "Well, here we go." she thought to herself.

Horse was pretty dressed up for a truck driving Indian, and he had a great smile on his face. Raul and Margaret's luggage was in the back of the truck along with a bag for Horse. The Grandfather walked them to the truck and took Raul aside. "Horse is like a son to me. I have asked him to be with you as a guard and guide. He will know what you need before you do and he will provide anything you need. He carries my power for you." "Thank you Grandfather" then The Grandfather placed a perfect sacred eagle feather in Raul's hand and their time together was complete.

The drive to the plane was quiet, and no one spoke even as they approached the plane. When the truck stopped, Billy rushed out of the plane to hug both Margaret and Raul. "Hope you all don't mind me butting in like this but a guy who rents an office on one of my floors at the Meadows Building stopped by yesterday afternoon to give me a heads up about what you all are up to. He thought I might like to be part of this, sort of a Texas Ambassador to the mission, what with me knowing The President and all. He suggested I be the tour guide, so if you all are ready, let's jump into my little ole plane and we'll be gone. I brought some airplane food for lunch during the trip." He winked at Margaret who knew when Billy traveled airplane food was almost as good as the Sheik's.

At Second Mesa it was wheels up at 10:08 and it was 1:08 in Washington. Before take off, Billy, who was in the front seat of the passengers' cabin, turned to Raul, Margaret and Horse and told them to be in forward facing seats and strapped in real good. Margaret started to laugh, and Raul had a question mark on his face, but Billy was the consummate jet owner, and the pilot followed his orders, which were are follows: They would take off to the west and fly 200 feet above the ground until they reached a speed of 500 MPH and then the pilot would pull back on the yoke and they would go straight up like being on the big roller coaster in the sky. As they started the climb, the sound of Billy's "Whoopee!" was louder than that of the jets. They gradually leveled off at 45,000 feet and headed for National Airport in Washington.

Thursday, August 7th was a hell of a time to be headed into Washington. Raul and Margaret had no way of knowing that they were headed into a Capital about to be battered by the perfect geopolitical storm.

Chapter 26

"All that is essential for the triumph of evil is that good men do nothing."
Edmund Burke

August 1, Friday

Michael had accomplished the seemingly impossible while Russell and the crew rampaged through the organ loft at Perkins. The meditation room at the Giza headquarters had almost been scorched by the energy and power of the meditation work that was done there to help the Dallas crew find the last bomb. It had to be found by 7:59 when the so-called test was going to happen. They defused the bomb by 6:30.

That should have been enough for one day, but there was more. The news services were all a flutter with the latest rumors about what was going on in the Gulf. Analysts questioned what the Administration stood to gain by putting out the news of a possible confrontation. Many thought it was another attempt to cover the damage done to the Administration's credibility after its claims about Iran's nuclear ambitions were seriously undercut by the latest National Intelligence Estimate on Iran, released in March, which again found that the country had terminated its nuclear weapons program four years earlier.

As had been the case throughout this current Administration, the alerts seemed to go up when the Administration wanted to pull off a fast one and needed everyone to be looking the other way. The rumor mill seemed to be working just fine for this purpose. At every water cooler in America, people were talking about the "attack on the Nimitz" as if it made more sense to believe what the Administration was telling them, rather than their own eyes and ears..........and the government was supplying the footage!

The cute little blond selected to speak for The President at press briefings had that seductive and hard look that telegraphed that something was up, but of course, she could not say what it was. It could only be hinted at. So late Friday afternoon she announced there were indications another effort by Iran was afoot which might possibly involve an effort to disrupt the American Home Land. That was all that was said. She noted that it would be crucial to stay alert for any concrete warnings that might be issued by the government, should anything actually be discovered that would affect the situation.

Michael had anticipated all of this and had Nader arrange a video conference with The Secretary General of the United Nations. The whole crew, including Grace Devereaux and myself, were included. The subject was the first formal step in neutralizing the United States. Ban Ki-moon was almost a new face on the world scene. U Thant, who left office in 1971, was the only other Far Eastern leader of the world organization, and a lot had happened in the intervening thirty-seven years. Despite the numerous rumors of conflict and danger, Ban Ki-moon's name and accomplishments were not household words in America. Additionally, anyone from Korea was suspect in this country. So here was a looming test for all the players: would Americans openly rebel if the UN, under new Asian leadership, exerted its first real influence into what America thought to be its own business and sovereignty?

"Mr. Secretary General, this is the most dangerous of situations, as you know. The US President has waited and deliberated for more than ten months now about this attack on Iran. Back in February the Administration, led by the Vice President, thought that an attack on Iran could be easily pulled off. They also thought they could win the upcoming elections and stay securely in power. They didn't count on the possibility that providence itself would send a man like the current front-runner to change all the projections. The US interests were such that any threat to the long-term secret strategy must be stopped. The hidden government of the US was not about to let all the work of the past seven years be stopped by any charismatic leader, and they knew they dare not kill him with the economic situation being so grim. So a false flag terrorist attack had been arranged by the ITO. In typical "make them look the other way for sure" style, the attack was to have damaged the Highland Park section of Dallas and Southern Methodist University, just to be sure no one would ever suspect The President would destroy his own back yard to justify putting Iran to sleep.

"Two hours ago, our global team, who are participating in this video conference, solved the mystery of this attack and the secret US plan to justify the beginning of the Iran war. There will be no attack on the US. But the failed plan itself must be revealed to the world in a way that prevents the US from doing anything about what has just happened, including substituting another plan for the same purpose. That is why we come to you. We need you, with the backing of the whole Security Council, minus the US, to make the announcement that UN Security Forces, acting against an international threat, have stopped a plan to destroy the SMU campus and the site for The Presidential Library. This threat included the planned detonation of four mini-nuclear weapons which would have rendered a portion of Dallas uninhabitable for the next hundred years, and would have destroyed the lives of thousands of Americans. We believe this approach, with you as the leader, will stop the American regime from the planned retaliatory attack on Iran and will force both the American people and the Administration to turn to the UN for leadership.

"Unfortunately, we know that the Administration will not actually follow the UN, but your involvement will at least focus the world and the US population on the need for International cooperation on this 'threat'. That will allow us enough time to deal with the other issues that the ITO has contracted with the Administration to carry out."

Ban Ki-moon, despite his newness as The Secretary General, knew very well what was afoot and the importance of the UN's involvement in stopping it. Still, the open incursion into American politics, by surprise and without invitation, was a big risk for the international diplomatic visitors working in the mica palace beside the fast waters of Turtle Bay on the East River. Ki-moon was very quiet as he looked at the camera and the Sirian force assembled around the world. He knew this proposition was being delivered to the UN by a superior power. So how to go along to get along. "Ok, Commander, when and how do you expect the Administration to react to the interruption of the plans for the attack on Dallas?"

"Well first, they will go into conflict mode as soon as the 8PM CDT deadline passes without Dallas going lights out. We have silenced everyone connected in Dallas with the attack, so the failure will be a surprise. No Big Bang in Dallas means a Big Bang in The White House at 9:01. They will not be able to come up with an alternative plan much before Sunday morning. As a cover, they have The President attending a function tonight at the Hilton where he will give a brief speech at 9:15. I can almost see him sitting there when someone walks up at 9:05 and whispers in his ear that there is a problem in Dallas. He will probably just sit there like he did in Florida on the morning of 9/11. He will find out about the failure soon enough.

The Big Wheel starts a rollin! Ban Ki-moon went to work to convince the Security Council and Nader assisted by mobilizing the passengers' diplomacy teams. By midnight there was agreement on the Secretary General's plan. Newstead was ready in London where it was early Saturday morning. It had been agreed by the members of the crew that a joint news conference between Ban Ki-moon and The Queen would be broadcast at 7 AM EDT Saturday morning.

Newstead liked the walk from the Continental Command center on Catherine Place to the Buckingham Palace Road side entrance to the palace. Walking reduced the possibility that he might call attention to himself. He looked just like another cog in the wheel of royal government. Again he was amazed at the ease with which he got into the palace and through the maze of hallways and offices that ended in the large high tech conference room, where the British Prime Minister was waiting with a small staff. After introductions and questioning looks by the staff about who this guy Newstead was, another door to the room opened and one of the Queen's staff asked all to rise as the Queen entered. She noted those present and took her seat at the head of the table.

This was not the kindly old monarch who greeted guests in her ornate residential offices. This was all business with the ruling member of one of the wealthiest family businesses on the planet. She was not interested in royal niceties. "Now then, please tell me why we are here." She used the power of her royal gaze to bring The PM into action as he explained that a suspicious plot had been uncovered in America and its discovery must be revealed as an international UN based investigation whose results were to be jointly announced by The Queen and by the Secretary General of the UN. The PM then introduced Newstead as a special envoy of the International Investigative Unit (IIU) who went on to explain that this unusual request to The Queen was necessitated by the fact that aspects of the investigation revealed that other normally cooperative government bodies might be working against the best interests of the US, Great Britain and many of the Middle East governments. The current plan being presented to The Queen was designed to short-circuit any cover stories these rogue elements of the opposition might put forth as a means to hide what was going on so their plan could continue. Newstead didn't feel the absolute need to state just then that both The President and The Vice President were the leaders of this wretched plan.

"Please tell me, Mr. Newstead, what other elements are you monitoring?" "Your Highness, we believe there is an American plan in place to attack Iran in the immediate future, and what we uncovered yesterday in Dallas is a ruse to justify that plan. By our having short-circuited the Dallas part, the US will try to hide that failure and come up with another reason to attack. By involving the UN and Your Majesty's government, we bring this plot into the world arena before further damage can be done."

"I see. So you want me to expose the American plan to invade Iran?" "Yes. We know this might seem to you like a conflict with the commitments your government has made to the US, but Iran has done its homework. Since January, they have built diplomatic and military bridges to all the Middle East Muslim governments and are now in a position, even in Iraq, to call the shots. If Iran is attacked, the short fuse on a regional and perhaps global nuclear war will have been lit, and no one and I mean NO ONE can predict the outcome." "If I do this for you, are you telling me this war will be averted?" "No, Your Majesty. I am telling you that your positive decision will buy us some more time to work with the rapidly changing dynamics of this situation. The end is not in sight, if we keep working. If we stop working, we must immediately confront a larger conflict." "What say you, Mister Prime Minister?" The Queen's look when she spoke to The PM was later described to the crew by Newstead as her royal death ray.

"Your Majesty, we have reached a point where someone is going to have to reveal the hidden governments at work around the world. The Secretary General and Your Highness are on the short list of world leaders who can call upon a strong residue of moral credit to lead toward the right decision in handling this situation. I believe we can steer our government through this passage and continue to receive the commendation of the world Public Relations court. This is Your Majesty's decision alone. You are very much in a situation also faced by King Arthur. You now have the final say for the future."

The old lady Queen thought briefly about what her son would do were he in her place. She also considered her grandson's action, were he King at that moment. She looked down at her folded hands, closed her eyes and accepted the place time and the river had led her to. She did nothing. Then she looked up, first at The Prime Minister and then at Newstead using her death ray again at both. "Proceed." As she got up to leave, all the others rose to watch her determinedly walk out of the room.

Chapter 27

"Goodbye," said the fox. "And now here is my secret, a very simple secret: It is only with the heart that one can see rightly; what is essential is invisible to the eye."
The Little Prince
Antoine de Saint-Exuprey

Part of Grace Devereaux's training prior to the mission had been to learn about the role of women on Earth. It was a lot different than that of women on Sirius. The Sirians knew that women had been created with vastly different powers and missions than men. If Grace Devereaux might have been impressed by the majesty surrounding The Queen and her holdings, she was even more impressed by the majesty of the organizations and holdings of all the world's major religions. Every one of the religions was anchored in the past. In fact, it was well known and understood that religions usually take as long as three hundred years to make a significant change in their thinking or ways of doing things. It was a slow business. But people who were slow were drawn to these religions and their organizations for that very reason. Slow seemed secure.

Well, yes until about 1960. Then things began to change. It's hard to say what all the elements of the change were, but Paul Tillich, the great theologian, looked out toward the future in the late 1950's and saw that things would change and that the major religions would experience a massive downsizing in the decades ahead. This is easily seen in America today where all the major religions that have been identified with America have experienced losses of members and money. It has happened all over the world. The age of information has simply overcome the religions of the world. The power has moved out of the cathedrals and into the fast lane of the information super highway.

Nowhere is this more apparent than in the networks of women all over the world. In the past twenty years leading up to this moment, several women have come forward as the spokespersons for women all over the world. Oprah is a name everybody recognizes. But there are many others. As Oprah is to Chicago, Sulou Rogers is to Atlanta. She is a white woman from the south who has been creating an empire that allows her to speak to and influence the thinking of additional millions of women worldwide! Her radio, television and publishing entities were recognized in America, but unlike Oprah, she had an equally large audience world wide and many of her show segments were produced and broadcast from remote locations including Russia, China, Italy and even Dubai. Because of her international appeal, her influence was greater in the world than that of Oprah.

First there was Woodstock where we discovered we could all get along, then the big global concerts like the Earth Concert during the summer of 2007 to the most recent and exciting of them all, The Sulou Rogers International Spiritual Web Seminars, which always attracted huge audiences. It was not uncommon for as many as 2,000,000 people to tune in for each installment of these webinars. And because she was international, teachers from all traditions were featured. The Dalai Lama broke the record for attendees when he gave a one night three hour seminar on Happiness which attracted 5,000,000 visitors. Two to five million people in a world of seven billion is a small number, but in terms of influence, it is unequaled. Not regulated by any government, not condemned or condoned by any religion, translated into many languages, this event served to demonstrate the new power of the information superhighway. It also served to focus the attention of these souls on a vastly different kind of spiritual experience: the journey inward to the divinity within each person on Earth, with none of the trappings of the old time religions. Here in the twinkling of an eye, a change took place that would have taken several three hundred year cycles prior to 1960.

Why did that happen so quickly? Grace Devereaux had several holotrip meetings with Sulou Rogers during the twenty years leading up to 2008. Sulou could never reveal these sessions that happened in the secret spaces in Sulou's homes, but they started high in the mountains in Telluride, Colorado in 1988 just as George H. W. Bush had won the presidency. The Buddhists say, 'The Bigger the Front, The Bigger the Back', meaning that when one force exerts itself, an equal and opposite force comes forward to create a balance. Sulou had been drawn to the small community by the mountains and her sense that it was a spiritual place despite its reputation for being a drug fueled party town without parallel. Her home was at 11,000 feet and most of the rooms faced west toward Wilson Peak, best known as the Coors Beer Mountain. As the Sun was setting over the mountain on the evening of Wednesday, November 8th, Sulou took time to watch the breathtaking beauty of this sunset and think about what the election of the Connecticut Yankee in Texas cowboy boots was going to mean for America. She laughed as she remembered Gloria Steinam saying that the new president reminded most women of their first husbands.

Across the room, Grace Devereaux walked quietly toward where Sulou was sitting and joined her on the couch to share the sunset. "What is this? How come I'm not calling for the guard? Who is this woman?" and the questions kept silently walking through Sulou's mind until Grace Devereaux spoke. "Thank you for allowing me here, Sulou. I have come a long way to meet you and to tell you about the future." Sulou was having another spell. That's what she called that almost panic feeling when the altitude would hit her and she could not get enough high altitude air. It hurt and it scared her....it didn't seem like a vacation, it seemed like a medical emergency.....so much so that she was glad to have someone, anyone, sitting beside her in case it got worse. It never did, but it was always a distinct possibility. Grace Devereaux continued, "I have a message you have been waiting for all your life. You have been chosen to be a major agent for a global, even galactic, moment in the immediate future. We are about to process the human species through a long awaited evolutionary advance. It has been building for a long, long time, but this will be what the biologists call a moment of punctuation. Overnight, or perhaps in one morning, humankind will reorder everything about how life is lived and understood. You have been chosen to be the focal point for the re-entry of the feminine energy into an openly superior position in the world."

The waning half moon finally came up over the mountain at the back of the house and lit up the new snow on Mt. Wilson as their talk ended. Grace Devereaux got up sad to leave the nighttime Remington landscape out the window, but enough had been said. "We will talk many times in the years ahead. I will help you discover all that has been planned for you. We have a bonded communication and you can call on me whenever you want help and I will appear. In the meantime, I suggest you let this house go to someone who likes the high altitude panic feeling that seems to make you so uneasy here. There are other places. This place has served its purpose for you. Good night." And she was gone. Sulou would not sleep that night. She would be awake to see the moon set over Mt. Wilson. In fact, spiritually, she would be wide awake from then on.

As promised, there were many trips to Sulou's houses, many conversations, and many nudges in the direction she was being led in order to fulfill her part in the divine drama unfolding around the world. The Masters' Council had decided at the beginning that they would simply bypass the established religions. They were not going to change and they had a valid place in keeping many people opiated and out of the way while the world hurtled toward the moment just ahead. Trouble was they didn't hold still. The closer the moment came, the more powerful the Fundamentalists in every sect and religion of the world became. Yes, even the Buddhists. They were angry, backward, fearful, doctrinaire, controlling and oh so very good at using guilt to have their way with peoples' minds. The worst of them wanted to see a showdown across the board. They wanted to win and like the famous lieutenant in Viet Nam, they were willing to destroy the global village in order to save it. And, of course, they were sure that God was on their side. Sulou's role was to show the world that in oneness, there are no sides, just us, all seven billion of us.

The religions didn't pay her any attention. Some ditsy white chick on the afternoon women's talk show circuit, really......who cared? Every once in a while they would hear that she had met with this person or that Pope, or started a club, or a school, or endorsed a writer like Gary Zukav and his book *The Seat of the Soul*. The subtitle read: *The Library Journal called it a remarkable treatment of Thought, Evolution and Reincarnation,* but the religious leaders paid no attention. In a holotrip I took to Earth in 1991 I did a favour for Grace Devereaux and took that book to Princeton and the President of the Theological Seminary and suggested he allow me to teach this book and James Allen's book, *As a Man Thinketh* to any interested students in a non-credit seminar. He took one look at the cover and the Library Journal quote and literally threw the book over his shoulder behind his chair and announced that no one at Princeton would be reading anything about reincarnation. Fine. Nothing like being blind-sided just as you are also being forcefully marginalized. So the churches, the religions, were so sure of their place in the scheme of things that they didn't even remember what had happened five hundred years earlier when science had started the church's long march to the back of the bus. Now they were about to be thrown under the bus.

It happened on March 21st this year. It was a triple threat day. It was the Vernal Equinox, the full moon and Good Friday. There was enough high energy in the air to create almost anything and two things were being created. For weeks Sulou had planned to spend the weekend in Maui, in her beautiful private retreat alone. She left in her G-5 on Friday morning for the six hour flight. The crew, as was her custom, was asked to stay on the flight deck and she did not travel with an attendant. She was alone in the cabin with her version of "airplane food" which was quite different than what Billy and The Sheik would have been comfortable with. As the plane passed over the Rocky Mountains she was aware that Grace Devereaux had come aboard with someone else. She turned her chair sideways to see the couch along the other side of the plane.

Grace Devereaux was seated along with a strange looking man who almost looked African with his Afro and long orange robe. He spoke English with a distinct British accent that identified him as being from India, assuming he was "from Earth" in the first place, which was an incorrect assumption. He spoke first. "I am the King. In this Galaxy I have the final say. We meet here in the air over this magnificent mountain range as a symbol to you on this momentous day. You are traveling to be alone this weekend, but I say you will be alone from now on with the news I bring you. Earlier this morning a decision was made by the US President and his closest advisors. You will remember that last week, one of the best and the brightest of your military men, an Admiral, was forced to quit his post over a disagreement with The President about the strategy your country has been following in regard to the Muslim countries. He was my hand picked military man and when he spoke, he spoke my words. I told him to say: 'I expect that there will be no war, and that is what we ought to be working for. We ought to try to do our utmost to create different conditions.' He was to be the one man that could stop an invasion of Iran. The Vice President convinced The President to abandon this Admiral who had become the road-block to the long pass the Administration was ready to make at the very end of their game.

"The plan put into motion this morning will be to attack Iran, of course with good cause, in August, before the conventions and the election, so that regardless of who is elected, we will be committed to and fully engaged in an all out war with Iran. It further assumes when the election is held the American public will not want to change horses in mid-stream, so the Republican will stand the best chance of being elected. However, another more dangerous plan is also in place. Should the American public push back and agitate to stop any such attack, the Administration has all plans in place to lock the country down under martial law. The most serious resisters will be permanently placed in secret detention centers set up around the country. In 2005 a Congressional bill authorized $385,000,000 to build these secret centers and the contract was given to the Halliburton companies. These centers are ready to receive the prisoners whenever the Administration gives the order. I will not permit this to happen for the simple reason that an attack at this time, with these leaders in all the involved countries, would result in a lightening nuclear war which would set humanity back thousands of years, and for the last time.

"Grace Devereaux has been visiting you these past twenty years in anticipation of the role you are about to play. In the beginning women were the rulers, the nurturers, the networkers, the planners, the child bearers and the spiritual leaders of the race. In time men usurped many of those roles and we come now to the result. You have been chosen now to use your voice as the new voice of religion in the world. I am not talking about buildings and funny men running around in colorful dresses and hats. I am talking about activating the spiritual center in each person on the planet. It is done by the use of energy and by example. Grace Devereaux and I are supplying the energy and you have been chosen to supply the example. When you next appear on your show, people will notice the change in you, and your every move will be directed toward a rapid expansion of the creative energy needed to move us through this time. Grace Devereaux will be with you and she is set to answer any question you may have along the way. In essence, you are about to introduce a global spiritual experience to the human race, and you have been chosen because you have consistently asked to be used by our power and to be of service. You are the example. That is who you have become and that is who you shall be."

The King stayed in the plane until it cleared the west coast. Once over water, he left Grace Devereaux and Sulou to explore together what lay ahead. Sulou had not stopped crying since she learned of the plan The President had authorized that morning. How could it be that one man, pretending to know the Mind of God, could throw all the progress of the current leap man was about to make, into total chaos? She would have preferred not to know this, but she had asked to be used in the highest service and this was indeed the highest service. The tears and the dreams lasted that weekend and Grace Devereaux was chosen to be Sulou's guest on the first show after Easter.

No one who tuned in to the afternoon show that Monday could have guessed that when Grace Devereaux walked on the stage with the most minimal of introductions, their hearts would have been opened. But hearts were opened, tears flowed and people around the globe went to their Tivos to see what had actually happened. Of course, the news did not pick up on this, but the phones did and so did the casual coffee chat and the meetings of moms, and word got around that something had happened. About the best way to compare this was what happened after the death of John Paul II. When he was gone, people around the world, people who would never have paid any attention to the Roman Catholic Church, reported over and over again that they had seen the Pope on one of his journeys, or in Rome or on television and the mere sight of him trudging along through the holy aisles of life had produced uncontrollable tears, mysterious tears, moving tears that rolled down the face and opened the heart, if only for an instant......an unforgettable instant. So Easter 2008 had brought a secret resurrection of women's spirituality around the globe.

Chapter 28

August 1, Friday Night

"OK, I'll be there as quickly as possible. Somebody wheel POTUS over here from the party at the Hilton and I hope he didn't sit there like a dumb ass bump on a log like he did in Florida when he got the 9/11 news." The Vice President correctly guessed. That was exactly what POTUS had done, but he recovered in time to give his brief speech and then be rushed off to the White House basement. All the old gang was there and VPOTUS was really pissed off. How could anybody screw up this vital plan? "How the hell could anybody find four frigging nuclear bombs so perfectly hidden? There were only seven of us who knew, and that includes those towel head kids we had doing the hiding?" Now they were all exposed if the plot was made public. They didn't have a back up and time was running out. They could not keep the fear level from the Nimitz attack up forever, and the news networks were starting to get a little critical about the details of the supposed attack. This was going to be a night to remember. This was the White House version of the Mafia tactic of going to the mattresses. Just another gang of thugs getting ready to wage war when almost any other strategy would have been preferable. "Patch me into Gen. Cowden, and I mean now." Cowden, as the CIA director, had become accustomed to these emergency visits with the Vice President, so he knew it would be a night out with the boys, but he was shocked when he heard the VP say, "Listen you sonofabitch, you have made your last screw-up......I've got the most important moment in my Presidency, I mean Vice Presidency, going on here and somehow it got loose and now we have to fix it."

At 3:30 AM, POTUS nodded off and it was decided to break and take a nap for everyone. Nothing was going to happen in the middle of the night anyway and so far nobody had a workable plan to create another false flag attack to use as the excuse for the Iran war, which was scheduled for next Friday. At 6:30 the phones rang upstairs and Nader called from the UN to The President's Chief of Staff, who was already up on this Saturday morning. David Aldrich Pollen was looking forward to his fifty-fourth birthday on the 16th of the month. He sure as hell was going to take that Saturday off. This business of all nighters and plots within plots was getting a little old. He thought about his name. David won the battle with Goliath, and now thousands of years later, same neighborhood, different war, same problem. He also thought about the Aldrich heritage and what it had always meant to be, one of the first families of the country. Pollen…there was the problem. Although they were not related, people somehow always got him mixed up with John Polton, the nut case POTUS had appointed to the UN Ambassadorship apparently to piss off the entire global diplomatic corp. And he was a superb success. They all hated America and the arrogance with which Polton treated them. The UN wasn't the cocktail party on the East River anymore. It had become a global experiment in anger management.

"Mr. Pollen, I am Steve Nader and I am working with the Secretary General of the United Nations. I am calling to report to you and your staff that a major development has occurred overnight. No one in the US Government has been informed about this, and I am not to inform you now. In thirty minutes, at 7 AM, an international press conference will take place with the UN Secretary General and the The Queen of England. Afterward they would like to speak with The President and his team at 7:30 in a video conference. Please prepare your staff to receive this news." "What the hell is this?" Pollen was caught truly off guard and he raced for the elevator and the gang hiding out in the basement.

They were all up and now the new plan was being devised as quickly as possible. They could not risk a hit on Dallas because that might risk another screw up, and they were not likely to figure out how the SMU attack got sabotaged in time to make any changes. But just to be sure, the CIA, the DIA and the FBI were about to cover SMU like white on rice. Russell was still asleep as the Feds got on the move and he smiled as he turned over in his sleep at how he had "fought the law and the law lost."

"OK, we still have to find a way to mobilize public opinion to absolutely insure they will be with us on this. I suppose a hit on Houston would be a perfect cover for us all." The Vice President's voice was as manipulative as always. "I wonder what we would do with Mom and Dad if we hit Houston?" POTUS thought. Just then Pollen came in the door and announced the coming press conference. You might have thought the underground bunker had been hit with an Earthquake. "WHAT? The Queen....of England? What the hell is she doing messing with the UN on Saturday Morning?" VPOTUS got everybody's attention with that, because his face turned red and Pollen was ready to jump for the defibrillator if necessary. It was now 6:43.

At the UN, the Secretary General had checked with his staff, had his make-up applied and was on the phone with Nader to double check how Pollen and the White House had handled the news. "Well, I think it could be said that it is giving them a feeling of not being in control." Nader had become the master of the understatement. "Just to be sure, I'll call headquarters and see if everything is in order."

Chapter 29

August 2, Saturday, CNN Atlanta

"We have just received word to stand by for a special press briefing from the United Nations to be broadcast at 7AM, roughly sixteen minutes from now. We have no idea what this means, but at this time of day it is a most unusual moment. We go live to the UN Plaza in Manhattan and Jake Morris." "Thanks Ted, we are a little at odds here to guess what this all means, but multiple media buses started showing up here at 6:15 and they have all been in a rush to get set up for what is happening. The last time we saw anything like this was the invasion of Iraq, so one is left with the feeling that something big must be up. Other than that, we know nothing." Several black Mercedes Benzs entered the circular driveway and discharged important looking people with serious looks on their faces. "It looks like the German Ambassador and the French Ambassador have just arrived and the Chinese Ambassador is pulling in right now. So far, no one from the American Embassy has crossed 45th Street looking official, and we're not sure why they are not here. Back to you Ted." "Well, we'll just have to wait now to see what this is all about. Our networks and reporters across the globe have neither seen nor heard of anything unusual happening. There was a report of a hazmat emergency in Dallas last night, but that seems to have been a false alarm. This is August and Saturday and we normally expect things to be quiet.

Chapter 30

August 4, Monday

In the middle of the action in Dallas, London, Cairo and the UN, Michael and Brad had been finalizing the military plans. Brad often remembered a conversation he had heard at the Academy, long before the current mission to Earth. "What we ought to do is take all the members of the warrior class on Earth and give them a big island someplace with all the weapons and just let them fight it out until they are all dead." Great idea, little possibility of success. The work had to be done in place. Brad had exceptional resources at his disposal.

Like the problem faced by Grace Devereaux and the world's religions, trying to change the military was like swimming against the tide. They were not going to change through any kind of enlightened self-interest. In the military's case, they would have to change and immediately. So it was decided to get to the military organizations through the governmental leaders.

Michael and Brad assembled the special team under Brad's command that would deal with this problem. There are almost 200 internationally recognized governments in the world, most with military units under their command. Brad assembled his elite corps of five thousand "warriors" for a briefing on Monday morning August 4th at Headquarters in Giza.

Michael began the briefing. "The most entrenched element of the world's ruling bodies has always been the military. They are the ultimate expression of the belief that might makes right. In many cases, these armies have stood for the highest aspirations of man against the lowest expressions of his unawareness. That has changed in the past fifty years. Now the race for technological supremacy and the resulting profits have outstripped every other issue around military might. It will not correct itself. Our mission is to make that correction by being who we are. We are going to show each one of the leaders of the world's governments that it is both the time and imperative to convert military might into a global power for right. Specifically, weapons for killing will be replaced with tools for rebuilding all the societies of the Earth. Brad is going to give you the plan."

"This Thursday the 7th has been set as the beginning for the conversion." Brad began his briefing. "At exactly 3PM at the International Date Line and moving west, pairs of our special forces will appear at the gates of every executive headquarters of every government in the world. They will use the power of their spirits and their mission to instantly and peacefully disarm all guards and set aside all barriers. Station by station they will advance to the inner circles of power of every government until they stand before the leader of each nation.

When they leave, the leaders will all report that two tall men, perhaps 7'6" or taller stood before them in bright white business suits and told the leaders to sit down. Each leader will then be asked to ascertain that he or she is awake and present in their offices. The leaders will look around and pinch themselves and signal that this is not a dream or an illusion.

The two men will then speak. "Within the next 24 hours a change of galactic proportion will occur in the hearts of all the leaders of all nations on Earth. You are among them. Beginning now you will cooperate with a new power brought to this planet from Sirius and led by the designate of the Galactic Council. You will follow the specific orders of this power and its leader or you will be instantly replaced. Until 10AM tomorrow, Eastern Daylight Time in America you will not leave this office, but sit and read with incredible speed and understanding *A Book of the Beginnings*, a copy of which we now hand over to you. Know this: This book and the plan we are delivering with it will change the course of all that has happened since the beginning. During the course of this change, we will employ systems and material to neutralize and eliminate the world's storehouse of weapons of mass destruction. And we know exactly where these weapons are."

"Finally, like the armies directed by Lincoln, we will be magnanimous in our treatment of you and your country. We are here to prove without question that there is a much better way. We follow that way and so, too, will the citizens of Earth. You no longer have the option, on any level, to destroy your fellow beings."

Brad, steel jawed and unflappable as always could not hide his excitement about what his crew was about to create. Things were beginning to feel a lot like progress.

Chapter 31

August 5, Tuesday

On Tuesday morning, Michael took the crewmembers who were present at the headquarters in a van to the Great Pyramid. Zahee Hakas had arranged to have the pyramid off limits to everyone but the crew and was waiting when the van pulled as close to the entrance as possible. "Dr. Hakas, thank you for accommodating our special request." "Think nothing of it. As a man who lives in antiquity all the time, it is a true honor to live these few moments in the future." The crew for this entry into the pyramid included all the continental commanders and the headquarters staff. Only John was missing.

Once inside, Michael revealed that his bowling bag actually contained the headquarters crystal skull. He placed it on the altar and lit twelve candles in a circle around it. "The last we know of John is that he left the Grand Hyatt across the river in a cab about an hour after sundown. He shows up nowhere in the various data bases, has been contacted by no one and all our efforts to scan for him have failed. We know he is alive due to the DNA plan, but he is gone. I do not suspect foul play, sabotage, or being captured by hostile forces. I believe something went wrong in his emotional reaction to the Gaza mission. I want him back and I want us to work on that in this meeting. With that, both Metatron and The King holotripped into the King's Chamber of the pyramid. Metatron spoke. "Your crewmember will be safe, but his absence makes it necessary to create a new part of the plan." Then The King spoke. "I will aid you in this plan and it may turn out to be the most important part of our work, but it is too soon to know that. We are now going to connect with the entire council to discuss what steps we will take next."

The room became quiet as the crewmembers felt the seriousness of the moment and the presence of the Masters inside the pyramid. Something very powerful was about to happen.

Chapter 32

August 2, Saturday

"This is Jake Morris at the UN with news that a very unusual press conference is about to begin. We still do not know the nature of what we are about to hear, but it promises to be unique in that nothing like this has happened in the UN history. Here is the feed from the UN Media Department."

They really did it up right. The opening showed the parade of flags outside the main building as they fluttered along First Avenue in the light of sunrise and early morning wind blowing off the river. The UN logo was superimposed on that scene which then dissolved to a split screen with The Secretary General and The Queen. Ban Ki-moon opened the press conference. "Good Morning. The Queen of England and I have called this press briefing to report to the world a major incident that happened yesterday in Dallas, Texas. An international terrorist attack was averted that would have resulted in massive loss of life, nuclear contamination for much of Dallas and the destruction of the Southern Methodist University Campus. This attack was interrupted through the heroic efforts of the British Secret Service and a UN Anti-Terrorist team working together to prevent this calamity from reaching its full potential. In the process, neither loss of life nor physical damage occurred in Dallas." The Queen went to her script for the rest of the narrative. "My government's leadership discovered this plot last Wednesday and we immediately took steps to halt this potentially catastrophic plot from being completed. In so doing we spanned international boundaries to enlist cooperation of the UN and its worldwide resources. Later today we will distribute the necessary details of this operation to the press. My Government wishes to thank Secretary General Ban Ki-moon for the cooperation he arranged through the UN to stop this international plot."

Ban Ki-moon spoke next. "We are grateful to Her Majesty's Government for so selflessly acting in the best interests of the entire international community. My office will follow up this announcement with any further pertinent details as they become available. At this point, however, a major chapter in international terrorism comes to a close and for that, we are all grateful." Fade to the flags and lights off.

"Well, Ted, there you have it. That has to be the most unusual press briefing ever to come out of the glass palace here in New York. If you have just joined us, the UN Secretary General and The Queen of England have just announced the exposure and elimination of a threatened nuclear attack on Dallas. If I heard correctly, the Americans were not involved in this action. Ted, looks like you are going to have an interesting weekend." "Right, Jake. We're going to take a break here and we'll be right back with more on this astounding story."

Chapter 33

August 2, Saturday

"WHAT?" VPOTUS was stunned and so was everyone else in the war room. How could this happen? "The Queen of England rummaging around in my country and no one tells us? Her forces stop our efforts to get this attack started? Our Ally?" POTUS was thinking about the really nice meal he had at the Palace when he finally visited England two years before, and how The Queen had not made him wear formal gear. "Get me the Chairman of the Joint Chiefs......now!" VPOTUS was all over this problem and everyone was so stunned by this turn that they did not notice his physical change. "Mr. Vice President, Adm. Miller is on the line." "Bobby, we've got a real problem here. Get here as fast as you can and bring your top Navy Guy." Ever since he had fired the Admiral in March, VPOTUS could not remember the new guy's name. Miller got Admiral Gary Roughneck, Chief of Naval Operations, and they were both in their limos within five minutes and walked into the War Room just as the Queen's Call was put through. "Good Morning, Mr. President." "Hello, Your Majesty." "Mr. President, I am sorry I had to withhold information from your government until now, but we have been dealing with this threat with the knowledge that the possible security breaches could have gone anywhere, and would have been disastrous. The security force of The UN and My Government's security force made the decision to act independently of the US until we got this issue solved. We believe we have stopped this plot and there will be no more exposure."

VPOTUS was totally infuriated, and he had a permanently red face of anger as he thought about what he had just heard. 'Who did this bitch think she was? I'm running this and she pokes her head into my most important plan, and then acts like her limo just changed lanes right in front of mine and called to say I'm sorry.'

POTUS finished the conversation with The Queen and handed the call off to Pollen who would take care of making all the connections to see that everyone in the non-military side of this mess was alerted and put into action.

As if on some kind of cue, POTUS decided to lead. "Bobby, this deal with the UN and The Queen is as serious as a heart attack. This settles the issue of Iran planning an attack to provoke us. We have to move now to neutralize them. We cannot wait any longer." Miller shifted in his chair and had the same feelings he had when he was forced to let Admiral Falloff go in March. They were going to do it and there would be no stopping them now. The UN had pulled the plug on the Administration's best plan to get the attack started, but had at the same time given them every reason to put together another plan. "Let's just go ahead with the plan to attack Iran this Friday. Put everyone in place. Set up some kind of attack on one of our military installations somewhere in the Gulf and leave Kuwait, Qatar, and Dubai out of it. Make it as serious as is needed to instantly get the public totally insane to get back at the Iranians." Admiral Roughneck was stunned. He knew he was getting the order to sacrifice some of his assets this week. This went against everything he believed and knew. He was surprised that Miller gave no sign of feeling like he was in The President's vise and being squeezed as hard as possible. He was a good soldier.

Chapter 34

Tom had been doing his design work while all the international intrigue was unfolding. He had been fascinated with the issue of instantly stopping the world's hunger problem. Unlike Earth men, he *knew* that it was a manufactured crisis. The system design of the Earth itself assured there would be enough food, usually locally grown, to feed all the souls who came here for this part of their educations. However, over the past five hundred years and especially the past sixty years, the system had been corrupted and Earth now had a system that saw huge numbers of people living on the edge of starvation every day of their lives.

Tom had just caught a Science Channel program that described the Volkswagen parts system, and he was stunned to see the solution to the problem in this show. He called Brad at Headquarters. "Brad, when you convert the military, do you think you can turn it around in a reasonable time frame? These guys are all focused on killing and victory and I am concerned that reorienting them to the real mission may take a lot of time." "Tom that has been the issue with me as well until last Friday. By this Friday, I expect to have the plan fully operational, and I do not think I am being overly optimistic. All of the Continental Commanders have placed teams of passengers at every military installation on every continent. These passengers are now safely in place at every level of command in every military organization in the world. They know their mission and are prepared, with our help and that of the Council, to see to it that we turn this thing around on a dime. What do you want to do?"

Imagine this. Volkswagen has dealerships all around the world. They all need parts and service items all the time. The cost and inefficiency of having parts depots all over the world has been avoided by this incredible system. They own one of the world's largest warehouses in Germany and it is right beside a major manufacturing facility. The warehouse is fully computerized and mechanized. They have a constant supply of parts for every product they have manufactured for the past fifteen years. That is not entirely unusual. What is unusual is the airport right down the road. Many companies today take as long as a month to get parts for anything to the end user. At Volkswagen, order a part today and it will be in your hands tomorrow anywhere in the world. Through a computer network that directly accesses the warehouse in Germany, parts are pulled, packed and trucked to the airport and flown to their destination and then delivered the next day... and it actually works." So Tom figured, why just parts?

"Brad, I want the military air forces on my project. I want to make daily deliveries of food and supplies, including medicines, anywhere in the world when they need them. If we can fix sick cars overnight, we ought to be able to fix sick people just as quickly. Your military system has all the gear and personnel we will ever need to do this right now." Brad had a big smile he was glad Tom could not see. Tom was as bright as ever and he had a totally workable plan. Brad knew there were things the military could do: building schools, roads and hospitals being among them. And they could build warehouses, airports and bridges, but this plan would include all of that plus a "just in time" inventory system for food and medicine all around the world. The world's militaries had a plane for every purpose. Even the most remote village in the Congo or Mongolia or the Arctic was easily accessible by planes designed for heavy duty work there, and they were already on station. It had always amazed Tom that after the Berlin blockade more such missions were not taken around the world. It was a matter of priorities. The military mind was willing to take humanitarian measures, but only so far. Killing was so much more "romantic" as The President had indicated in a public statement the week before Easter. (Credit CNN)

Brad kept thinking. 'If I could make this work and Tom can get it organized, in a month the poorest person in the most remote village in the world can have FEDEX-like service for the things he really needs, including the money to pay for it. WOW!' In prior conversations Brad and Tom had imagined what could happen if they had control of the now THREE TRILLION dollars spent in the past five years to subdue the twenty-two million people of Iraq. Three trillion dollars would have housed, clothed, fed, educated and healed every man, woman and child of the seven billion people on Earth. Hell, there would have been money enough to send anyone who wanted to go to Disney World. The War on Iraq really had been the biggest gold rush in the history of man. No wonder VPOTUS was so angry all the time. Those people should have welcomed his forces with roses and open arms, just like the guys back at the old company in Houston had done when it became clear that Halliburton was going to be the major recipient of much of this spending. So now, instead of giving an oil man an army, Brad, Tom and Michael were about to give an army to the people of the world to rebuild all the things those same armies had destroyed or derailed.

"Tom, Michael tells me that the 8th is the current focus point for the US action. Things might get busy that day, but by the 9th we will be up and running with your plan." Tom wished Brad could see the smile on his face now. "We may never be known for doing this, what with our covers and all, but I know in my heart that we have just solved one of the most tragic problems in the world......and you know what?........Einstein was right. Even the most difficult problems can be solved if you have the right vantage point."

Chapter 35

Grace Devereaux's work was also progressing. After the global course with The Dalai Lama, Sulou had geared her daily shows to a more spiritual path. She continued to feature discussions on food, but the focus was on the use of food to promote spiritual growth, which was a really new direction in people's thinking. The reaction was predictable. Companies that made processed, canned and synthetic foods all started screaming in the news and the courts that she was misrepresenting the truth and causing all sorts of problems. It made Oprah's scrape with the Texas Beef Lobby look like a school outing.

She changed the focus of the interior decorating portions of her shows and productions to promote using space for spiritual healing and harmony. Vashtu architecture and Feng Shui became interlocked as the way to design spaces and place objects in them for maximum spiritual alignment. She also held a week's series of programs at Giza and in the middle of the Pyramids and she exposed her global audience to the ancient mysteries and even the alignment of the pyramids with Sirius. One of her guests was Gene Kieffer talking about The Secret Teachings and how opening people to the ancient truths would radically change how people relate to each other around the world.

The shows and the focus of Sulou's life got so far out that people on the outside thought she was just about to spin out of control, but under Grace Devereaux's guidance and her work behind the scenes with women's groups around the world, Sulou's audience and influence kept growing. In June, Sulou had a remarkable guest on her show. Eleanor Wasson had turned 100 in February and her autobiography, *28,000 Martinis and Counting* had been featured as an alternate selection in the Sulou Book Club. Grace got Sulou to read the book prior to selection and she was amazed at the remarkable life this vigorous woman was still leading. After speaking to her on the phone, Sulou sent a crew to Santa Cruz to film Eleanor in her hilltop Japanese-style house with the waterfall down the side, the koi pond off the deck and the art and artifacts that defined this woman of the world and her massive achievements. They decided to have members of one of Eleanor's projects, Women Rise, be in the taping session as a way to emphasize the powerful work she was still doing at 100. Sulou played the video of the interview in Eleanor's home and then Eleanor came out on stage to meet the studio audience to a standing ovation. Sulou described Eleanor as a true hero and then asked her to speak.

"Well Dear, in my 100 years I know this to be the most profound moment of them all, not for me, but for all of us. This is the moment women around the world have been waiting centuries to see. I do not know what is going to happen, but I refuse to think on anything that is not positive, so I believe that we are right now at the point where the direction of our race is about to tip in a most positive way." Eleanor's gentle spirit and the witness of her life's accomplishments communicated to women all over the world a message that no one else had been able to deliver. No one watching could doubt they were hearing something from another realm, a special spiritual message from this dignified and beautiful woman who must have had one foot planted soundly on Earth and the other planted soundly in Heaven. When she finished her eloquent and all too brief statement, Sulou's tears were reflected in the tears of every audience member in the studio and around the world. Clearly something way out of the ordinary was happening and Sulou could see Grace standing behind the last row of seats smiling at her.

Grace Devereaux was making the impossible plan work more easily than virtually anyone, including the members of The Council and The King, could have anticipated. Clearly, what no one knew was that the women's centuries of prayers and dreams were now being answered, and their prayers for their children and families were creating this shift in the world's conventional thought. The women would not be content to keep silent any longer. Their power and their numbers, all over the world, were about to create a change in the world's religions that would feel like a tsunami to the crafty old men who guarded the old religions from change and confronting new realities.

Chapter 36

Frank approached the global issues of health and education from his Sirian perspective. He was constantly aware of the part of The King's proclamation that involved his work:

"Education is for life, not for living. Character will be given more importance than skill. There will be sufficient food on Mother Earth for everyone. The power of prayer will avert natural calamities. People will have less desire. During this Era, science and technology will be used for the welfare of mankind."

'Education for life, what a concept.' Frank thought about all the children all over the world who understood education to be about getting ahead....getting ahead of others and ultimately ahead of themselves, only to discover that all the getting ahead had put them behind in the line to understand what life is about. When he thought about what was coming, the changes at hand, he was in pain thinking what the children would have to learn so quickly. He knew, of course, that for the adults, the changes would seem almost insurmountable. So the question was how to make the changes work as easily as possible.

Frank knew that at the beginning was the answer to the question: What Is Important? The Sirians could never have gotten to Earth this time, or the many times they had been here from the beginning, if they had been focused on competition, acquiring things, beating their neighbors or destroying their enemies. Instead they had created a Garden of Eden on their planet. Having a King helped. Kings are primarily responsible for the spiritual and physical welfare of their subjects. Emperors, on the other hand, were seeking conquest and control. It seemed like Earth rulers were working with the Emperor model. America's leader was a glaring example. So how do we get people to seek Kingly leadership? The King was right there beside Frank as these thoughts went through his mind.

The Queen of England was a role model of sorts. She stood apart from the government administration issues, but those who knew what was going on were clear that she was still head of an empire and as such was very much in the play of empire building. The Pope was another role model, but the death of John Paul II had ended the example of a real spiritual leader. Throughout his life he did battle with the forces of empire in the Roman Catholic Church, for he was the King/Pope. His successor was an Emperor/Pope, lacking a real spiritual connection to his subjects. So who could it be?

The short list had one person: The Dalai Lama. His stature and presence had been enhanced in the spring of this year when the uprising in Tibet brought the world's attention once again to the destruction of an entire culture by the Chinese. They destroyed the landmarks and sacred temples, ran the leadership into exile and in return built a fast railway line from Beijing to Lahaska. Sooner or later things would have to change. The Dalai Lama led like a king, keeping sight of the spiritual welfare of his followers. From that vantage point, he was the most powerful leader on Earth, and his influence was global. "Frank, get the Dalai Lama", The King whispered to Frank.

Grace Devereaux was in contact. "Grace, help us arrange a meeting with the Dalai Lama.", Frank requested. "OK, he is the last stop on my list, let's see what we can do!" Frank felt closer to Grace than to the other crewmembers, perhaps because they were working on the soft sciences of education and religion. There was an easy connection between the two that made accomplishing all that had to be done that much easier. Frank did not know that Grace had arranged for Sulou to go to Dharmasala with a crew to produce her show for the week of August 4th. She was way ahead of the curve.

Frank knew that working with the Indigo and Crystal children was at the heart of his mission, and he also knew that educating the parents to support these children was a revolution in the making. Public and private schools the world over seemed to be working with form and function from the past. These new children and the DNA they brought to Earth would never fit into the structured "reading, writing and 'rithmitic taught to the tune of a hickory stick" that had worked more or less until the time of their arrival. They really weren't liked, because they caused problems in everything they did......the old rules simply did not work. The frustration was summed up by a grade school teacher who had too many of these kids in her class, when she said, "These children are our future, unless we can stop them now!"

The secret would be in redefining education as being for life. The King felt life itself was learning, and when approached that way, each moment was a learning experience. There was no goal or degree for the process, just the opportunity to keep learning. The solution was another, but much more sophisticated, global networked educational community. With a play on words, Frank named it the CCN, The Crystal Children's Network. It was a voluntary association, but one had to be recommended to gain admittance. Frank estimated there were now almost 1,400,000,000 children between the ages of 0-20 who were destined to be a part of this network.

One of the difficult things was defining how the values emphasis would work: so many cultures and so many traditions. The King made one rule. Get it right early or get out. Children would be taught from the beginning that the issue in life was being loving and acting responsibly. In every community there would be educators there to help new parents learn the steps to teaching children how to know the difference between right and wrong, based simply on the golden rule, which cuts across all boundaries. Here was the hard part: by the time a child was seven an assessment would be made of his progress. If he showed that he understood the values, he would be allowed to continue as far as he liked. If these same values were not demonstrated, his education in the issues of commerce, technology and communication would stop so that he would be able to hurt only people close to him geographically. Too many people had already risen with education enough to create all manner of evil in every culture. This would put an end to that.

The CCN would provide the higher levels of education, thus finally outdating schools and providing a global forum for children and for parents. This high tech effort, available everywhere, would level the playing field for children around the world, and allow affinity groups around every subject and curiosity to benefit from global input from the children's and parent's knowledge base.

"Frank, get over to Dharmasala as fast as you can. We are here with the Dalai Lama and he will be making some announcements and requests on the Thursday and Friday Sulou shows. This is going to be a big deal and I suspect there will be some synergy between this event and what Michael and Brad are working on." "OK, I'll be there. Could you do some background work for me with the people there about the global health issues as well?" "Frank, I think we may have that one covered already. Tom has the food distribution system up and running with Brad. They have taken your thoughts about pure food and phasing out eating dead animals, and they are going to ask you and Tom to put together a global healthy growing plan that will, among other things, create oxygenation systems and reduce methane gas production."

"Frank, here is the amazing thing. We knew about the Dalai Lama and his considerable powers, and how so many people feel he is basically a diplomat, but it turns out, here in his own capital he is recognized as a true spiritual genius. He has known we were coming and that we would be here now, for the past twenty years.

He knows, understands and fully supports our plans. He's up to speed. Be here for Thursday."

"Roger that, Grace."

Chapter 37

Tuesday, August 5

Back in the pyramid the crew at the Tuesday morning meeting was about to hear the answer the Council had devised to complete the plan.

The King spoke. "John is safe and in my care, but his absence from you and your effort is actually the key to the ultimate success of the plan. He will reappear at the most amazing moment, completely unexpected. However other elements of the new plan must be put in place.

"Begin today to contact and organize the plan with Sir Richard Branson and "The Elders". They have been in existence now for a year and they are ready for this assignment. Founded in Johannesburg with Nelson Mandela on his 89th birthday, The Elders had melded serious statesmanship and a large slug of audacity in a crew of world-famous figures to launch diplomatic assaults on the globe's most intractable problems. So far their efforts have been little noticed or cited for major results. The members include the retired Anglican Archbishop Desmond Tutu; Jimmy Carter, the former U.S. President; the retired United Nations Secretary General Kofi Annan, and Mary Robinson, the human-rights activist and former President of Ireland. The group has resisted being guided by ideology or geopolitical pressures and have been early and harsh critics of American foreign policy, particularly toward Iraq and the Israeli-Palestinian conflict. Mandela and Branson believe the fact that none of The Elders holds public office allows them to work for the common good, not for outside interests. (Credit: The International Herald Tribune, Richard Branson forms a band of 'Elders' with Mandela, Carter, Tutu and others. By Michael Wines Published: July 17, 2007)

A little known but important member of The Elders is Claes Nobel of the Nobel family of Sweden. His efforts to found the first

Earth Day Celebration in 1972 and his tireless efforts for peace have resulted in a global understanding of the crisis facing the Earth.

"This group needs to be brought to Washington for a totally secret meeting this Thursday. You are to find a secure location and we are asking Socrates to secure this place within walking distance of the White House even if it is necessary to build the facility on our floors at the H Street Continental Headquarters. The meeting will last until Sunday the 10th.

"We are confident that this plan will work, although the test is still ahead. We are working now inside the White House to set their part of the plan in motion. Michael will keep you informed about the details of the plan. We are hours away from the most massive change in all of human history, and that covers a million years."

Socrates was all over the meeting plans. He decided to have The Elders stay in seven instantly rented and refurbished townhouses in Georgetown, each with full hospitality and communications facilities. A fleet of unmarked cars would move them around town and they would be in a media blackout. They would be requested to speak only with crewmembers and passengers and each other.

"Mr. Nobel, I'm Jack Socrates and I am in command of a national team charged with creating an emergency meeting here in Washington this Thursday. I cannot discuss the nature of this meeting until you and I are face to face, but I need your help in setting it up, since you are an American and not as well known as some of the other meeting attendees. I will have a special plane at the airport close to your home in Oregon within an hour and I want you to join me here in Washington later today. *'What's this? This sounds important. I have dreamed so long for something special to happen and this could be it'* Nobel thought to himself. "All right, Mr. Socrates. But I have one question. Is Sir Richard Branson in anyway involved with this?" "I cannot answer that question until we meet, other than to say I know Sir Richard and he is a very important man." "OK, I'm always packed and ready to go. I assume your driver knows how to reach our farm?" "He will be there in 25 minutes by chopper, and thank you, Mr. Nobel. I'll reveal all when I see you in about 2 hours."

It would not have been fair to tell the Elder Nobel he was about to go cross country in the fastest reconnaissance plane ever built. They would meet in two hours time with minutes to spare. Giza Headquarters asked Brad to start rounding up the other Elders and getting them to Washington for the Thursday meeting.

The Sirians had the security advantage at every turn. No one knew they were there, they had hidden the identities of all 1,728,012 of them and they could commandeer anything they needed with the false identities they had created for themselves, no questions asked.

"Hey, you old fart, I just thought you'd like to know that your little nuclear rumble at SMU sure started something. I think you might want to mosey on up to Washington for dinner and a drink Thursday night. I understand your friend and landlord Billy Johnson will be in town and, well, you just never know when a little rubber chicken humor will be needed. See you here at the cocktail hour." And Socrates hung up. "I fought the law and I won!" Russell smiled as he said it again to himself on his way to lunch at Food From Galilee. He knew he would be eating alone, unless, of course, that beautiful blond with the long hair and the picture perfect breasts sat down at a table beside him like he had been dreaming she would every time he had seen her there.

"Newstead, this is Michael. I have another assignment for you. I need it done right now. Find Sir Richard Branson and meet with him wherever he is. You have all the planes and everything else you need to get his Council of Elders together in Washington for a meeting that runs from Thursday to Sunday, no absentees allowed, no excuses, and no delays. You cannot tell them the nature of this meeting, but you have to make this happen and now. Stay in touch with Socrates in Washington and Brad will back you up with anything you need, including a fully portable hospital if anyone wants to claim sickness as an excuse not to attend." "Thanks, Michael. I'll have this done. I'm assuming I will travel with Sir Richard to Washington?" "All depends on what airline he uses! He may be able to get you a free first class seat if he has enough frequent flyer miles. Ha!"

Chapter 38

10:00 AM New York time, Thursday, August 7

"This is Jake Morris at the UN and we have little to report. Things are expectedly quiet at the UN during this August break. Little traffic and the weekend's British surprise has been eclipsed again by the push back of the Iraqi forces the US is now calling *The Radical Terrorist Sympathizers*. UN sources report that the fighting has moved to the southern portion of Iraq after the rocket attacks on Tuesday again damaged much of the new US Green Zone Embassy in Baghdad. Rumors are that skirmishes on the border with Iran are increasing. There is no confirmation yet of that resulting in any significant change in the stalemate situation."

"This is Monty Fortz and we interrupt this report to bring you a Breaking News statement from Secretary of Defense Robert N. Hinge emerging from a meeting at the White House with The President and his top advisors."

Hinge always looked unflappable and confident, but close observers saw something in his demeanor that suggested he was at least 'out of sorts'. Actually, he looked worried when he spoke. "The attacks on the Green Zone on Tuesday are a clear indication that Iran has moved into a much more powerful involvement with anti-American forces in Iraq. We believe this to be a serious incursion that is bringing in supplies and munitions, some of which are being stored in the southern area around Al Qushlah. American forces are in that area to stop any further interdiction of munitions or enemy troops. The USS Nimitz has been stationed off this coastal border of Iraq and is flying missions in the area to stop the delivery of supplies to the enemy. The President and I are confident there is no major threat posed by this development, but steps are being taken to insure that it does not escalate further. Thank You."

"We go back to Jake Morris at the UN. Jake, what does this

mean?" "Monty, it's hard to say. I think the US was hurt on Tuesday, but they have chosen to completely hide that fact in light of the end run The Queen and the UN conducted last Friday. The American press machine seems a little touchy about what The Queen accomplished with her own "invasion" of the US." "OK, Jake, we will be back to you, but first a message from our sponsor Abistart." The diuretic commercial ran as unmarked cars were pulling in front of the H Street Office in Washington.

Chapter 39

August 7, Thursday

The top three floors of the H Street Building were now off limits to everyone but Socrates's staff, The Elders, and the expected crewmembers. Socrates had a meeting room on the south side of the building that gave the participants a full view of the White House. Everything would take place in that room. The opening luncheon was the first time the Elders had been together since Earth Day when they had been interviewed by Sulou at a meeting at Sir Richard's island home.

Michael opened the meeting and introduced Socrates. He further explained the unusual nature of the meeting and the need for secrecy. He then asked Claes Nobel to briefly describe the growing influence of The Elders and to suggest that the time had come for them to exert real power. With that he welcomed The Elders to his adopted country and Sir Richard began to explain what was actually happening. Sir Richard went on in some detail and then he finished with, "…..so that is why we are here today and why we have, now, less than 20 hours to make our plan and take action." As he spoke, passenger teams were at the side of the room and in an anteroom adjusting the security systems to insure no one would be able to eavesdrop on the proceedings.

At 5:25 Billy's G5 landed at National Airport and at 5:45 Russell's commercial flight disembarked its passengers. Billy fired up his satellite phone and reached Russell. "Hey, meet us out front, I got one of them drivers that will take us to the hotel." "Cool."

The drive to the Willard Hotel was uneventful. Russell felt like the odd man out. Nobody seemed to need any rubber chicken humor. Horse held back and fiddled with his phone that Billy had bought him for the trip. Billy was being the magnanimous host and concerned for everyone. Raul was the only one watching The

King who seemed to be enjoying the ride. Margaret kept looking at her dad wondering what his real role was and how involved he was in all of this.

At 5:30 Michael turned on the cable TV and suggested The Elders watch The Sulou Show. They liked her, and they were ready to have a break from the incredible news that had filled the afternoon meeting.

"We are here in Dharmasala, India for a once in a life time meeting with The Dalai Lama. This quaint town with its hillside villas and temples is one of the last places I ever expected to do a show, but we're here at the invitation of The Dalai Lama himself.

The interview took place in a special temple-like room in The Dalai Lama's residence overlooking a beautiful mountain. Frank and Grace Devereaux had prepared Sulou for a discussion on global spirituality and the need for advanced education and health systems. They had been instructed not to mention the meeting of The Elders or the agenda going on right that afternoon.

Chapter 40

In everyone's life, at some time, our inner fire goes out. It is then burst into flame by an encounter with another human being. We should all be thankful for those people who rekindle the inner spirit.

Albert Schweitzer

August 8, Friday

He had that damned smirk on his face from the minute he woke up. This was going to be the big day. He was going to give his big Mont Blanc pen a mighty work out. Hell, it would be easy to write the date beside his signatures: 08-08-08. He might even wind up being President for longer than he thought. There was a lot about being President that was fun. He loved that big plane and flying around in it and making such a commotion when he landed. Too bad it had taken three years to figure out he could take it outside the United States. He hated having to deal with those damned uptight foreigners, though. The great food! he got anything he wanted......they even flew in barbeque that he loved from that greasy spoon in Midland anytime he wanted it.

"But, what the hell was this deal last night? I'm sure I wasn't dreaming, and even though I've seen some pretty strange things with all the coke I've taken and weed I've smoked, I think it must have been some kind of real people. Bigger than shit, for sure, and those white suits were too weird. The book they handed me! It was big and the title, *A Book of the Beginnings*....what was that, some kind of bedtime story for idiots? These two giants actually thought I would read that book before today? Oh, I read it all right. Gobbledygook, bullshit... all this stuff about Egypt, and in the past. Who the hell cares about ancient history? Hell, I wouldn't go to Egypt even today. I knew these guys were not to be trusted. I looked in the index and table of contents and there was nothing about Jesus there, or the church, or salvation. That did it for me.

They were of the devil. Hell, I was asleep by 10 even with all that research. Some weird stuff happens in this place. After this deal last night, I'm almost ready to believe that people really were healed just by pleading to Nixon. I've often heard that rumor, but I've never believed it."

Such was The President's self talk at 7AM this day. The President's valet noticed the smirk, but he also noticed that The President was a little nervous. As he was adjusting his tie, a call came in which The President answered. "Yes, make the announcement." That's all he said.

Last night had been unusual for lots of people. Brad and his crew had sent out the teams of two giants in white to every government and military leader in the world, each with the same set of instructions. At 7:00AM Washington time, Brad got the final reports that the mission had gone without a hitch. The world's leadership was now in a period of transition.

After the Sulou Show, The Elders had a wonderful dinner, still at the H Street offices, and Claes Nobel and Jack Socrates had managed the evening which began with another briefing from Michael who gave two directions for the group: One, each would have a private briefing once they were in their quarters tonight about the activities planned for tomorrow. Two, breakfast would be held promptly at 8 AM here in the building and the rest of the schedule for tomorrow would be discussed at that meeting. There was no hint, just yet, as to what tomorrow would mean, but if today's briefing was an indication, tomorrow was not going to be like any other day.

Michael left the H Street Offices and took a car the short distance to the Willard. He called Russell's room and Russell agreed to get the others to meet him right away at the hotel dining room. Elegant. Washington. Powerful. Someone recognized Billy when he walked in the room, but nothing was said. Raul, Margaret, Billy, Horse, Russell and Michael were all seated. The King was standing behind Raul, but only he and Michael could see him. The conversation was as good as the food, especially since they were essentially strangers. Toward the end of the evening, Michael simply told them that all was set for tomorrow and they need not be concerned about being further briefed. "Later tonight, when you are settled in your rooms, you will be visited by members of my team who will give you a secure and complete briefing for tomorrow." That was it. Raul had started thinking of himself as a crew member and understood Michael's message. The others were a little on edge.

When he got back to H Street, Michael got all the crewmembers together along with the full corps of passengers. "All is ready. Our instructions are to begin the meditation at midnight Washington time. I have spoken with The King and he assures me that all is well, but I cannot stress enough the importance of this meditation. With that, he asked Grace Devereaux to lead all 1,728,012 Sirians in the prayer that had guided them since before the journey had begun. Before beginning her prayer, Grace announced that she and Frank had been working with Sulou and the Dalai Lama to produce what would be the most remarkable of all of Sulou's shows tomorrow. Then she quietly intoned for all to hear:

"*I am* a Spirit, and as a spirit, God's Presence and Power is within me.
I am in tune with the Spirit World and open to its' influence.
Please mold me into the best instrument that I can be so that I may serve you with all my heart and all my soul.
I am a child of the universe.
I am Divine Peace.
I am Divine Love.
I am Divine Wisdom.
I am Divine Bliss.
I am the Light.
I am the Light.
I am the Light."

VPOTUS and Hinge had also met Thursday night. It was finalized. The troops in Al Qushlah and the surrounding neighborhood would retreat toward Basra and a special forces squad would leave that area for just inside the Iranian border. They would set up a site to use the Sunburn Missile when the command came from the White House. The missile was contained in a travel locker and none of the squad knew what it was, just something that had to be set off in Iran to promote the next part of the battle. These things happened all the time, especially on the trips in and out of Iran that were constantly happening for all kinds of purposes.

As had been the case all over the planet in the past hours, each member of the Elders was visited in his or her room by a team of the men in white and each was given a copy of *A Book of the Beginnings*. These Elders were then told of the complete plan and sworn to secrecy. They were also promised that they were about to write the first page of a new book of beginnings for the whole species.

Of course, Billy was Billy, full of stories and optimistic and always joking. The two men that came to his room that night were very relaxed as well. They gave him the consciousness test and then they told him what was actually going to happen and asked him if he was sure he wanted to continue. "Hell, boys I wouldn't miss this even if it was my own hanging!" No one had ever seen the two men smile before, but they did for Billy and he had an unusually hard time going to sleep when they disappeared out the door. Even so, reading the big book was just a little over his head. Seemed a lot like history to him.

They also visited Horse and they brought The Grandfather with them. "Horse, I always knew I would not get to make the trip you are making now, but I have prepared you all of your life for this moment. Your presence will be my presence, I will be beside you all of the way. Your supreme focus is to be on Raul and Margaret, now and forever. You have been chosen for this and you will not fail." With that, one of the men in white gave the book to The Grandfather, who in turn gave it to Horse. "This is the book that is before our own record, so now you will have all of the beginnings. The third book is at its' beginning now, and you will help write it. You have my blessing."

Finally, Raul and Margaret were alone, too excited to even make love, and full of wonder. "So this is what I saw in the Sheik's eyes when we said goodbye. I feel totally incapable of understanding this, not to mention taking any reasonable action tomorrow." He entered quietly and for the first time, Margaret actually saw The King here on Earth. She broke out in tears. Up until this moment there had been doubt and a tiny amount of suspicion. His presence here wiped that away faster than she was able to wipe away her tears.

"Dear Children, you are prepared; you are supported; you will both see me from now on. You are the gift that I am giving this planet. You will not fail. As you sleep tonight I will give you all the information you need for tomorrow and every tomorrow. Good night." They went right to sleep and neither woke up all night as The King kept his vigil at their bedside.

7:15 POTUS enters the Oval Office

7:30 VPOTUS enters the Oval Office with the Secretaries of State and Defense accompanied by Pollen and National Security Advisor Sam Bradley.

Pollen announced that the networks had been alerted and that the speech would run at 10AM from the Oval Office. What was left was a final review of the plan, document signing and then the speech. VPOTUS led the final discussion. All were agreed that the Sunburn attack on the USS Kitty Hawk had to happen to close all future discussion about the threat posed by Iran. It was an old ship that had been brought in from Japan again in May and it was as close as you could get to calling an aircraft carrier a throw away. Hinge couldn't look anybody in the eye at this point. He was about to send thousands of our best sailors and pilots to their death. Of course, it was also like the strikes on Japan sixty-three years ago right now. We had to destroy a lot of people to protect many more. The difference between then and now was that then we were destroying the Jap enemy and now we

Kitty Hawk

Big Stock Photo

were about to sacrifice our own people.

Various check-ins were made, coffee was served, a photographer came in to take the historical record and at 9:15 POTUS sat down at his desk as VPOTUS handed him order after order to sign. "Hell, I'm gonna run out of ink at the rate he has me signing these damned things." As quick as they were signed, they were taken to the war room down stairs where they were communicated to the appropriate military units. Go time was set for 9:50. "What's this one, VP?" "OK, we're calling that one your encore order. That will establish martial law and allow you to postpone the elections until this issue is under control." "Cool. I think we may all deserve a longer term in office after today."

9:15 at H Street and Connecticut Avenues

Michael had The Elders ready to walk to the main entrance of The White House. The security was invisible, but traffic stopped by itself as drivers started to recognize the famous people walking together toward the north side of Pennsylvania Avenue. When they got there, Billy and his charges were waiting for them and they all walked across the street. Well, game time. Michael and Raul led the team to the security gate. The King told him exactly what to say and as he did so, the whole group was given unchallenged access to the White House. From this point forward they merely needed to open a door and they were not challenged, but simply observed and ushered to the next stop along the way. The surprised staffers along the way were shocked to see these people walking in their White House. One of the younger staffers told her girlfriend, "Branson is even sexier than he looks on TV!"

9:35 They entered the Oval Office and the surprise was just like ice. The TV crews were waiting outside ready to do a quick set up for the 10AM presentation. The camera man left after the history photo session. No one would forget the looks on the faces in the Oval Office when the door opened and Raul and Michael walked in with the others. POTUS stood up from his signing labors and Raul moved to meet him, but they did not shake hands. "And you are?" "Mr. President, I am Raul Richardson." POTUS looked at the group a little more closely and spotted Billy who smiled at him. 'OK, this must be some sort of surprise, but my birthday was last month' he mused to himself. "Go on." "I am here to relieve you of your responsibilities as President of the United States. This will be effective immediately. I represent a large and very powerful group of people in this room and around the world. We are not going to let you continue on the course you have just authorized." "Bullshit........somebody get these people out of here now....and by the way, the orders, which you seem to think you know all about, have already been given....you're too damn late. Five more minutes and every American in the world will want Iran off the map, and I've already set that in motion."

"Mr. President and your staff. We represent a power you have never even considered as possible. You were given an opportunity last night to consider this and you rejected it out of hand. You do not have a choice. A document is being drawn up right now, right outside that door, which will be the last thing you will ever sign as President. It is your resignation letter. Here it is now. Please sign this, Sir.'

The funny thing was the way Raul's voice seemed to have changed from last night. Billy was in shock. Hell, this was no geeky theology professor. His words and his voice were commands. The President got that too. It took him less than a minute to sit down and open the big Mont Blanc for action. "OK, Secretaries and staff, I order you to stand down."

VPOTUS was standing up when The President gave the command and the intensity of the moment was so strong that no one reacted as the red faced Vice President slammed to the floor. He didn't move and Pollen pushed the emergency medical button and in seconds The White House Medical Staff entered the Oval Office to aid VPOTUS. They had the defibrillator, all the drugs and every other item that had been waiting for just this moment. The work was fast and furious and the ambulance was called up and VPOTUS was put on a stretcher, with medics carrying all the gear that was already hooked up to the dead man's body. When the call came that the VP had died at the hospital minutes later, the Constitutional plan of succession was put in order, and the Speaker of The House of Representatives was enroute to the White House to be sworn in as President. She was in shock.

9:55 "This is Ed Henry at The White House. We were notified earlier that The President would be making a major announcement at 10 AM and we have just received word that the announcement has been delayed. We will break into our regular programming when the announcement is set to roll. Back to you Elaine."

Michael came forward. "Mr. President, I am Michael Anderson. I represent a superior power that has been sent here to prevent a global catastrophe. My troops paid you a visit last night, but you failed to hear their warning. You have no choice sir. There is no one in the world that can walk in this room now and stop what I am commanding you to do. Please sit down and sign the document."

Once again he had his pen ready. His mind was reeling. He felt faint. *'What's Dad going to do when he hears this?'*....and then he remembered how Nixon had cried for his mother when he resigned. *'Shit'* "OK, signed! Now what?"

"You are going to read that letter to the press instead of the announcement you were going to make this morning and then you will be escorted out of the White House with your family. You will be in Dallas this afternoon to begin your work as ex President. You will make no further comments to the press until ordered to do so. And that will be a long time from now." Raul was listening to The King for instructions as Michael finished his orders to the ex President of the United States.

The Administration members were in shock, but they had the presence to act when the new President walked into the room. She looked terrible. She was not ready to be the first woman President, she was not ready to be President at all. The King motioned to Margaret to go to the new President and comfort her. This surprised Billy too. All of a sudden his cute little girl had taken on her authority and she acted more powerful than the new President was able to act at that moment. 'Hell, I really wouldn't have missed this for anything. They'll never believe me about this one back home.' It was kind of fun being in the middle of this, even though his job was to be the cheerleader and rustle everybody up when it came time to move.

Michael and Raul were in the corner with The King when the TV crews entered. Suddenly there was a crowd. Make-up was called in for the old President whose grey shade was going to need a lot of help. The new President needed some work too. Raul was radiant, as were the other non-administration members of the crowd. Branson was all smiles. He was giddy. He hadn't had this much fun since he shot the glass of water at Colbert on TV! "Crickers, mates, this is history!"

Mr. President, the cameras are ready and it's time to stand.

10:15 "This is Ed Henry at The White House. We have just received word that The President is ready to make his announcement.

People just could not believe it. He had aged over night. He slumped in his custom made suit. His skin was ashen. All across the country people were screaming at someone in the next room, "Get in here and look at this!"

He held the paper. He looked at the cameras. He looked down. He looked up. He looked like he was looking for his father to come into the Oval Office and fix this for him, like he had fixed almost everything until 2001. Then he just stared as the nation saw again what it had seen on 9/11. The President of the United States was totally lost, confused and unsure of how to proceed. Finally, Pollen came beside him and said quietly, "Just read, Mr. President." "It is in the best interests of our country that I now resign my position as President of the United States effective at 10:05 this morning." Pollen took him by the arm and led him out of the room. Pollen was a superb administrator. Somehow or another he had even thought to call The Chief Justice of the Supreme Court, James G. Rollins, Jr. who would administer the oath of office to the first woman President.

The cameras rolled as Michael received the confirmation he had been most concerned about. Brad reported in that the global meditation had resulted in the Sunburn missile malfunctioning in mid-flight on its way to the Kitty Hawk. Something happened to its guidance system and it went under water without exploding.....yet. Brad had a team at the site and they were already working on bringing it up to defuse it.

Michael spoke to Raul with the news from Iran. Raul smiled knowing that the hard part was over. Michael then guided Raul to the microphones.

"I am Raul Richardson, an American citizen from Texas. I appear before you as a messenger for certain powers that have come to our aid in this time of crisis. Earlier this morning an order was signed in this office that would have created a nuclear attack on Iran. It would have involved the destruction of one of our aircraft carriers and the engagement of the entire Persian Gulf fleet in an attack on Iran. This has been stopped and is no longer a threat to the peace of the world community.

"It was not possible to stop this event without the help of almost two million people whose presence on Earth at this time is an expression of the love the Universe has for us. We are not now, nor are we ever going to enter another moment when the possibility of destroying ourselves is an option." The TV cameras focused on Michael and his name was identified on the crawler as 'a representative of other governments'.

"Since last night leaders of every nation and every military have gone through an opportunity to redirect their efforts and those of their countries toward peaceful issues and actions. A small number of leaders in both fields have chosen not to make the necessary changes, and as is happening right now in America, these leaders are resigning their positions to be replaced with new leadership who will understand the critical urgency before us to solve the problems that have brought us to this point. As of today, we will no longer tolerate war, nor killing, nor any other attempt to settle differences through use of force.

"Hunger, shortages, and ignorance will be eradicated from the planet as we move forward. Please note, I am not a politician and these are not empty promises. You will see this happen in the weeks ahead.

"Here is what is behind all of this. We are having the experience you have all wondered about. Beings from another part of our galaxy have come to Earth to help us do what we could not do ourselves. They have brought a superior technology and an ability to solve problems on a level above that on which the problems were created. They came at this time because we have reached the critical moment that biologists call a 'punctuation point'. The species has already changed. In addition to the almost two million beings from the other side of the galaxy, there have been born around the world in the past twenty years young people whose DNA is not the same as that which most of us share. They are the new people and they number almost twenty percent of the global population. More than anyone else, they have dreamed of a day like this. I can assure you that some member of this group is among your acquaintances.

"These young people have been misunderstood and labeled with all sorts of negative implications. They have received an inferior education that would never challenge their hidden skills and talents. Today, that changes.

"I am now announcing to the world community that it is time for these young people and those of the same order who have been on Earth, preparing the way for them for almost seventy years, to come forward. These people are the real future. They will transform life throughout the planet in the next forty years. All the dire and grossly negative predictions about the future are going into retirement along with the negative people who professed them as truth. This is the golden age we have been promised, and because we have been able to act now, the day of purification will be a peaceful one as we simply leave behind the tools and trophies of the old order and assume the blessings of the new.

"The news from now on is likely to be filled with massive education programs to help all of us catch up. I have two additional items. First, one of the most important members of the crew that came here to help us is missing. We believe he is unhurt, but needs a signal. Here it is. You may not even remember why you came here, or with whom, or how long you have been here. But it is time to wake back up and join us. Your heart knows who you are. You have had thoughts from the beginning that a day like this would come. Throw off the dream and come join us NOW. Second, the young people who are here as the true future need to connect with each other. To that end, we are setting up networks and educational processes immediately for them, their families and their teachers. The long wait is over.

"According to the plan, I am here to serve America and the rest of the world as the human symbol for the leap we have taken. I, along with my wife, Margaret, am honored to carry the confidence of the future for all to experience as we live our lives." Margaret joined Raul at the microphones and people could actually see how their auras overlapped and became one at the center. No one at the networks or in the entire technology industry could explain how this could have happened, but it was seen by billions of people around the world.

"Next, I would like to introduce you to Captain Michael Anderson. Michael is the leader of the mission to Earth from Sirius. He and his crew have been on Earth many times in preparation for this mission prior to their formal arrival on July 23rd." Michael came forward and said only, "As Raul said, this is indeed a new day on Earth. We celebrate this moment with you. The God of all ages blesses this moment and all seven billion of you."

"Finally," Raul continued, "I wish you to meet The Elders. These powerful and well known men and women have come together to create a guidance system for the race as we move through this transformation. They now stand ready to speak for all nations and their leaders." The cameras panned around the room to show the Elders beaming.

"Although this message is being broadcast from Washington, DC, in every capital and statehouse and in every military headquarters in the world, people have already made their decisions to welcome a new future. We have no need to control or manage any country in this process. The talent and direction are already in place. The Vice President of the United States suffered a fatal heart attack earlier this morning. Our sympathy goes out to his family and our thanks, too, for the work he did for our country. According to the Constitution, the replacement for The President in this circumstance will be The Speaker of the House of Representatives. The Chief Justice of the Supreme Court will now administer the oath of office to the new President."

The cameras followed the swearing in and the very brief remarks the new President used to open her time in office. When the lights were turned out the visitors to the office noticed no members of the old administration were around. It was over!

Epilogue

Of course the phone lines and every other avenue of communication were jammed around the world all day and for many days thereafter. The feared panic that many instantly predicted never materialized, primarily because every leader in every country was out in front with the same message: this is peace at last. At eight the next morning, local time, an aircraft arrived in Darfur. Massive amounts of food, clothing and medicines arrived all day as huge aircraft from all over the world came to Darfur. Tom was the first off the first plane, and he could not control the tears that welled up in his eyes as he saw what his work was already accomplishing.

Brad already had plans in place to use the combined armies of the world to build much needed water purification plants, schools, hospitals and homes in every country in the world. Yes, even in America. Word raced through cities like Sao Paulo, Mexico City, Hong Kong and Calcutta as the news spread that the change would positively affect every person in the world, no exceptions.

Grace Devereaux and Frank stayed with Sulou and the Dalai Lama through the weekend and throughout the following week to feature His Holiness teaching for the new order of consciousness. Sulou finally realized why she had worked so hard to get to this point. She immediately put together a global network and systems to help locate these new DNA children and help promote understanding for the work they were here to do. She closed her Friday program on the 8th with a plea for the lost crew member to come back and join his comrades in this bright new day. The Dalai Lama closed his portion of the program that day by repeating Jesus words: "Bring me the little children for such is the Kingdom of Heaven." (Matt. 19:14) People on every continent started to wake up and remember they, too, had been on a long trip across the galaxy. They did not know if they were the lost crewmember, but they did know that they had a mission now, and the power to fulfill it.

The Continental Commanders stayed at their posts to coordinate all the various elements that characterized their continents.

Ban Ki-moon guided the UN toward its original mission of peace. Steve Nader retired from the UN and bought a big 'fixer upper' home in Vermont.

The Queen decided it was time to let go and arranged for her grandson William to take the throne in 2010. Her son, Prince Charles, joined Sir Richard Branson on one adventure after another to help people decide for themselves the kind of a world that was possible, and the Prince loved every minute of his life without having to deal with being King himself. His mother lived until 2025. Newstead was recruited by the Royal Family to become chief of operations.

Russell went back to Dallas and decided he and Billy were cut out of the same cloth. They went into business together. Billy had all the money and Russell had all the fun ideas. They ran a series of scuba companies and high-end resorts around the world. The bar in every resort was named The Rubber Chicken. Billy was such a happy parent that he gave Raul and Margaret the treat of a flight to India and a chance to be with Sulou and the Dalai Lama all week. He called in a favour and got the Sheik to give them his plane again for the trip.

Jack Socrates wanted to get back to what he loved. He convinced the new President to appoint him Secretary of Defense and he quickly ended the war in Iraq.

Frank stayed with the Dalai Lama and ran his health and education mission from high in the mountains. Grace Devereaux and Sulou decided to continue the work of the world's spirituality on a global mission.

The Grandfather was found Saturday morning in his bed. He died of natural causes in his sleep. His work was truly done and he left to join the other The Grandfathers in the sky.

Sir Richard Branson and The Elders grew in importance over the next ten years. Their commitment and experience formed the basis for almost all of the new systems that moved the evolutionary leap ahead. They were most proud that their appearance at the White House marked the end of war-making and the beginning of children being trained from an early age to be exceptional leaders.

Within 20 years of the White House meeting, the work of Gene Kieffer and Gopi Krishna and their two best books, *The Secret Teachings* and *Living with Kundalini* had become standard text books in schools around the world. Gerald Massey's *A Book of the Beginnings* was required freshman reading at every major university in the world.

Michael went back to the mountains and his bike and the dream of his hand crafted house. I called him and told him I had kept a good record of the mission and I planned to publish it in a book. "Of course, please do and recount all of it. It will be the start of *A New Book of the Beginnings.*" There was a smile in his voice as he told me he had already found the perfect piece of land for his house. It would be at 11,000 feet and face southwest toward Mount Wilson. He had decided to stay on earth just in case something else happened. He also said he had taken up snow boarding and loved hanging out with the kids. If you look for him in Telluride, he's the one with a tattoo on his right wrist that looks like a rocket ship disguised as a dolphin and covered by a rose.

The ex-President is now in Dallas, again running the Rangers and much happier. Dallas finally has a living former US President, a major improvement over the Kennedy assassination memory, and SMU is safe and secure with a massive presidential library. In 2058 the papers he signed on the morning of August 8, 2008 will be opened. It will be a very minor moment in the long forgotten life of the man who wanted to bring on Armageddon.

Arthur C. Clark died in March of 2008, too early to see the

events described in this narrative. Vijita Galkisse Fonseka, a Buddhist monk and advisor to Clark, was by his bedside when he died. They had been friends for a very long time and I met 'VJ' when he traveled with Clark to New York to make a speech at the United Nations in October of 1983. In his last words to 'VJ', Clark said, "Now you can tell them that the movie *2001: A Space Odyssey* was not fiction. We really did leap to a new level and a completely new species. Remember my saying this later this year when it will all be revealed." Clark knew all along it was not science fiction.

Raul and Margaret are going to live happily ever after, but that will be the subject of another book sometime in the future.

And finally, I take a break. I am so grateful I have had this trip and lived to see this day. *Never Cry Wolf* is my favourite Disney movie and the last words of that movie come back to me now as a way to end my own past and begin the future:

"I think over again my small adventures, my fears.....those small ones that seemed so big.
For all the vital things I had to get and to reach.
And yet there is only one great thing. The Only Thing.
To live to see the Great Day that dawns and the light that fills the world."

Old Inuit Hymn from the movie Never Cry Wolf

Biographical Note on the Authors as it appeared in the book, How To Believe, written by Jon Spayde and Published by Random House in 2008

Focus on the Good
Chuck Robison, Interviewee

The interview for this chapter took place live, on the air and in cyberspace at the same time, as a fifty-five-minute segment of an Internet radio show called "What If It Really Works?", which highlights New Age and "new paradigm" thinkers and writers. The founders and hosts of "What If It Really Works?" are Chuck Robison and his wife, Karen.

I'd met Chuck Robison when he was pastor of Christ Presbyterian Church in Telluride, Colorado, and was impressed by the energy of his presence and personality - he's a large sixtyish man who seems to fill any room he's in - and the breadth of his experience. Aside from preaching and pastoring, he had been a professional photographer and a high-octane businessman, among other things. He's an unconventional Christian - a thinker who worships God and The Christ in the light of a spirituality that encompasses other faiths, advanced science, and what many see as a spiritual revolution under way planetwide.

I was intrigued by what he told a Telluride journalist at Christmastime in 2004: "The discovery of infinitesimal particles, such as photons for example, the particles composing light and forms of electromagnetic radiation, confirms for me that our world is all about light. My God does not have a long white beard, nor does He sit up there in heaven on a throne as William Blake pictured Him. I believe God exists in these particles without charge or mass. He is also in those charged particles that collide with photons. He occupies the spaces in between the smallest particles of nature. He is omnipotent, omnipresent, and omniscient. Therefore, all allusions to the 'universal light of God' are apt. So the celebration of the birth of Christ is all about light coming to the Earth, God's gift to mankind. This holiday is about accepting that gift and coming to understand that light is also love. Where there is light, darkness disappears. Where there is love, fear cannot exist."

Robison, who now lives in Texas, told me he'd be happy to be interviewed, and he wondered if I'd like to do it on his show, as a sort of turning the tables. Normally, Chuck and Karen interview spiritual teachers and authors; this time, I'd be both the guest and the interviewer, by phone, and Chuck would answer the most probing questions I had about his spiritual life.

Now, I have a very modest background in broadcasting: three years (1967-1969) part-time on a 250-watt AM station in rural Iowa while I was a high school kid. I spun easy-listening vinyl, read the news off an AP teletype machine, and recorded ads for local businesses such as Leck's Dairy Crème and Flamingo Bowling Lanes. This was only about two rungs above ham radio, but I flatter myself that I can sound pretty smooth on the air - or on Wi-Fi, for that matter.

So I agreed to do the interview on July 27, 2006, at 5 p.m., Pacific Standard Time, under the deterritorialized conditions of the digital age. The engineer was at the Contact studio in Bellevue, Washington; the Robisons were broadcasting from the Unity Church of the Hills in Austin, Texas; as I was at home in St. Paul, with our cat sleeping on my laptop keyboard. I was better prepared than usual but still plenty self-conscious as I tried for pear-shaped vocal tones.

I led off with a question about Robison's childhood openings to the spirit, and in his rich West Virginia-Texas-bred baritone, he told me about the altar call in a Dallas Presbyterian church to which he responded at fifteen.

"I don't know what happened," he said. "I came down to the altar when the minister asked people to let Jesus be their leader, or whatever the magic words were at the time. I didn't know I was doing it; it just happened before I understood what was going on. From that point forward, I simply *knew*. Of course, I didn't know all the twists and turns my life would take - nobody does - but I certainly knew that I was supposed to be part of something big. And it seemed natural for me to become a minister; there were plenty of good role models for that in Dallas.

"But my first priority was to get out of high school! As my friends could have told you, that wasn't necessarily an easy thing to do. I was way better known as a hell-raiser than as a scholar."

By leaving hell where it was for a while, Robison managed to obtain a diploma and then go on to undergrad work at Austin College, the leading Presbyterian liberal arts school in Texas. He was serious enough about his studies and his faith to decide to apply to Union Seminary in Richmond, Virginia, then the number-one Presbyterian seminary in the South. But as it turned out, he was headed to an even more prestigious academic perch. On a visit to Austin College, the late Dr. James I. McCord, president of Princeton Theological Seminary, met the young clergyman-to-be and was impressed. "He said, 'I want you to come to Princeton, and I'll make it possible," Robison told me.

At Princeton, he threw himself into the civil-rights and anti-war ferment of the sixties, taking part in demonstrations and protests and developing a social conscience that is still an important facet of his personality and calling. Robison's first post-seminary church posting, back in his native West Virginia, coincided with the birth of another passion: photography. With his very first pastoral paycheck, he bought his first camera, and right away he found himself relating photography and faith. "Once I had taken a few pictures, I knew I was *supposed* to be doing this," he said. "I believe that, when I take a picture of somebody, I can connect with their soul. When I can hand them a piece of paper that reveals that soul in a positive way, I'm doing healing and ministry."

Robison was then posted to a church in Philadelphia, and he eventually found himself on another track as well: doing marketing for the Presbyterian Ministers' Fund (now Covenant Life Insurance), the oldest insurance company in the country. Whether he knew it or not, he was taking his first steps out of organ-and-altar ministry and into something else.

"I never, ever doubted that God exists and is present with us," he said. "But what started eating me up was that I didn't seem to fit anyplace in the church as it was structured then. I spent a lot of time going to afternoon coffees with charming elderly ladies. I could be very nice to them, but it just wasn't *me*. I was looking for something that was simply beyond the church of that time."

Eventually, he left Philly for Manhattan and a job with Metropolitan Life. He also divorced his first wife. It was a difficult time but full of promise too. Perhaps the most dramatic pivot point in this unsettled period came in a hospital room in Dallas at the moment his father died. "He died in 1975, at the age of seventy-one," said Robison. "I had fed him his last meal the night before. I asked him to be a guardian angel and protect my son. I watched him and my mother exchange their last words - and then he died."

"As he died, this strong wind rattled the venetian blinds and swept through the room, I felt it and had no idea what it was. But it was so powerful as it rushed through me that I knew right there my life was going to change forever."

Experiences like this made him alert to the free-floating, many-faceted, and more or less countercultural spirituality that was flourishing in the seventies, and he wondered why its energy and questing spirit hadn't penetrated the stained-glass windows of the church. "In the seminary," he said, "we talked all the time about what went on in the Bible, but never once did we talk about things such as the experiences that living people were having with angels. I had learned all this ministerial stuff, and I knew how to do it, but there was something else going on out there, and I wanted to know what it was. So I started asking questions, questions the church wasn't asking, and things started to open up for me."

His insurance career was taking off too. At MetLife, he was an agent-recruitment whiz. Then, at New York Life, he designed the company's mass marketing plan and became the youngest officer in its history. At the age of forty, he went solo as a consultant on training, outplacement, and other human resource issues.

"Forgive me if this is an impertinent question," I said at this point in the interview, "but the insurance industry wouldn't be the first place I would go to widen my spiritual horizons. What did it mean to you?"

Robison was ready for that one. The corporate office suite may not have been a meditation room at Esalen, but it allowed him to regain a sense of vocation - a sense that he was ministering to people under the battle conditions of our business culture. This increased when he began HR work in the outplacement field.

"Say there's a guy who makes two hundred and fifty grand a year at the age of thirty-one, and he has a deal sheet that's three pages long," he said. "He comes to me ten minutes after he's been fired, and he's hit the wall. All he can think about is, 'Hey, I can't do deals anymore. What am I going to do with my life?' I could help somebody through that. I could give him a chance to take a breath and ask, 'Is this really about deal making, or is it about something else?' As a minister, I had something very concrete to do, something measurable. And I didn't have to be in a church with an organ playing behind me to do it."

Robison was so good at this real-world ministry that he was asked to give seminars to senior officers in the New York Police Department. "I stood up in front of three hundred of these tough guys and said, 'Life is about having a vision of where you are going, and I can help you find one,'" he told me. "After panicking for about five minutes, they realized that they were getting a day off and they might as well sit back in their chairs and enjoy it. I talked, and they learned some things. And I learned that they were good guys, good officers. The cream really does rise to the top in an organization like that."

Meanwhile, he was commanding good money as a formal portrait photographer and studying *A Course in Miracles*, a text very influential in the New Age movement that has been described by one scholar as a Christianized version of India's Vedanta. And he was having powerful psychic experiences - seeing visions of departed family members and hearing phrases and sentences from passersby in the street that felt like spiritual truths. One epiphany in particular has remained with him.

"I saw a woman approaching me on crutches," he said. "She had a beautiful face, but you could tell that she had never had the feeling that she possessed real beauty. As I looked at her I thought, 'This is a whole life right in front of me. I am going to make a conscious decision to see her as beautiful as she is. I am going to see her as healthy and whole.'

"I began to realize that I'm not really a Jesusian; I'm a Christian. Jesus was the man and the teacher, the sainted one. But the Christ is the Son of God. The Christ will not come back because the Christ never left and is here always, in all of us, whether we recognize it or not. The trick, of course, is that lots of us don't recognize it or see it only fleetingly. So I see it as my responsibility – and I'm not very good at this – to look for it in each person I meet, on the off-chance that they have forgotten it and my seeing it will help them remember.

"I once sat down and counted the places in the New Testament where Jesus used the words *sin, sinning, sinner,*" he went on. "And I found fewer than twenty instances. I don't believe it was a big concept for him. And I don't believe it's about Jesus dying for our sins. I think it's all about us realizing that Christ *lives* in us!"

Robison's spirituality was re-energized to the point that he began preaching again, as a volunteer, in various churches around the New York area, and his message was profoundly positive. "These were not Fifth Avenue churches," he said. "They were in the Bronx and Brooklyn and Queens. I preached about

'Ask and ye shall receive,' 'seek and ye shall find,' 'knock and it shall be opened.' I preached about God's presence. About the fact that we are all one, and I mean all seven billion of us; that's not an easy concept to get, but it's real." He was experiencing global reality regularly too, as an adjunct chaplain at the United Nations Church Center.

In 2000, after living in Manhattan for a period for twenty-three years (which he called "the adult dose"), Robison followed the suggestion of a friend, the *echt*-sixties folksinger Peter Yarrow, to move to Telluride, Colorado, the picture-perfect mining-town-turned-ski-Mecca. There he returned to something like old-time ministering, running the historic Christ Church along traditional Presbyterian lines while extending the church into the community by hosting AA and the local choral society, and operating a food bank.

In 2002 he met Karen, another lifelong spiritual seeker, via the Internet, and they were married two months later. Three years after that, the Robisons decamped for the White Bluff Resort in Whitney, Texas, about eighty-five miles southwest of Dallas. From this comfortable base, they lead seminars on spiritual growth and carry on their broadcast work. They subsequently moved to Austin, Texas in 2006.

I didn't want the interview to end without asking Robison about sin and evil, which, to me, seem ubiquitous in our world and which his optimistic and generous Christianity, with its New Age feel, seems to discount. Again, he didn't hesitate to respond and to remind me of his moral convictions. "Questions like the war in Iraq are seen solely as political issues, but they are really moral issues," he said. "Is it moral for a country to believe that because it might be threatened, it is okay to go and destroy another country? The church seems willing to talk about sin as long as it doesn't make one go against the grain."

"I do know this: as an individual, I have a choice. On a minute-by-minute basis, I can choose to look at the bad stuff or the good stuff. If I choose to look at the bad stuff, I am not going to simply bemoan it or become depressed by it. My only realistic option is to try and make it better. It is not easy, and I don't claim to be good at it, but I am getting better at it."

It was something for me to chew on. When I look at evil, I like to think I am realistic about it, but often this "realism" is little more than a sort of frisson of negativity, a boost to my feeling of superiority over the Pollyanna's and my political opponents, followed by paralysis, during which I do nothing against the evil. Chuck and Karen Robison believe, as he told me, that "if enough of us decide to look to the good stuff, there isn't going to be room for the bad stuff." That sounds a little childlike to me, but then Robison has been doing the good stuff his whole life. Do I believe in the good stuff strongly enough to try to do it, by my own lights? Can I remember that the Christian faith is a path to walk and work to do, not just a set of ideas to ponder?

And what if it really works?

Karen J. Partain-Robison

Karen has been a Youth and Family Ministry Director for the past 12 years and was the founding director of the Angels Rainbow Camps for at-risk children providing camping and educational experiences for children living in the projects in Dallas, Texas.

Karen is a Religious Science Practitioner who provides Prayer and Guidance to anyone in need of assistance. She has studied with many of the leading spiritual teachers in America over the past eighteen years. She began her spiritual adventures in 1990 when she had a spontaneous awakening that revealed her many spiritual gifts including the ability to connect with and understand angels present in all situations.

She is a recognized spiritual teacher. Together with Chuck, she leads seminars which help attendees rapidly connect with their guides and assist in the next step of their spiritual understanding. This book is her first exploration using fiction to communicate powerful spiritual information.

If you would like to know more about her experience in contacting angels and spiritual guides, visit her website www.angelreadingsbykaren.com.

Additional information about the progress of this book can be found at www.thequantumconspiracy.com

References

(In Order of Appearance)

The Clan of the Cave Bear by JEAN M. AUEL (Paperback - Jun 25, 2002)

As A Man Thinketh by James Allen (Paperback - Nov 7, 2007)

Cat's Cradle by Kurt Vonnegut (Paperback - Sep 8, 1998)

The Secret Teachings : Unveiling the Luminous Sun Within by Gene Kieffer (Hardcover - Dec 13, 2000)

A Book of the Beginnings, Vol.1 by Gerald Massey (Paperback - Sep 1, 2007) See also http://www.zeitgeistmovie.com/main.htm for a summary of Massey's insights.

A Book of the Beginnings, Vol.2 by Gerald Massey (Paperback - Sep 1, 2007) See also http://www.zeitgeistmovie.com/main.htm for a summary of Massey's insights.

A Distant Mirror: The Calamitous 14th Century by Barbara W. Tuchman (Paperback - Jul 12, 1987)

The Secret Teachings of all Ages by Manly P. Hall (Paperback - Oct 31, 2007)

The Present Crisis: A Critical Analysis of the Human Mind by Gopi Krishna (Paperback - Dec 1981)

The Way to Self-Knowledge by Gopi Krishna (Paperback - Jan 1, 1987)

Living with Kundalini (Shambhala Dragon Editions) by Gopi Krishna (Paperback - Nov 9, 1993)

On the Origin of Species: By Means of Natural Selection (Thrift Edition) by Charles Darwin (Paperback - Jun 23, 2006)

Power vs. Force: The Hidden Determinants of Human Behavior by David R. Hawkins (Paperback - April 2002)

Left Behind softcover books 1-6 boxed set (Left Behind) by Jerry B. Jenkins, Tim LaHaye, and Jerry Jenkins (Paperback - Aug 1, 2000)

The Seat of the Soul by Gary Zukav (Hardcover - Mar 17, 1999)

28,000 Martinis and Counting by Eleanor Wasson (Hardcover - Sep 2004)

How To Believe by Jon Spayde, Random House 2008

Portions of the following articles also appeared in the text:

Page 22-23, *The Johnstown Flood,* http://en.wikipedia.org/wiki/Johnstown_flood

Page 39-41 Doreen Virtue's article, "Indigo and Crystal": http://www.angeltherapy.com/ and also http://www.nam astecafe.com/evolution/indigo/childadults.htm

Page 47 and 59-61 Gopi Krishna, "A New Dimension of Consciousness" The Kundalini Research Foundation, Ltd. © 2007

Page 63-64 Alexis de Tocqueville article from: http://en.wikipedia.org/wiki/Alexis_de_Tocqueville

Page 64-65 Naomi Wolf interview about her book, *The End of America: A Letter of Warning to a Young Patriot* at the BuzzFlash web site: http://www.buzzflash.com/articles/interviews/077

Pages 74-91 one article from *The Book of Hopi* by Frank Waters and one by Richard Boylan, Ph.D. (c) 1998 both of which appeared on:

http://www.thedreammasters.org/hopi/martingashweseoma.php

Page 100 Washington Post Wednesday, January 30, 2008

Page 102-104 "Feces Change the Face of Gaza" by Mohammed Omer; Inter Press Service, Monday 28 January 2008

The Dolphin on the cover was taken by Chuck Robison from the bow of the sailboat "The Violaine". Robison was sailing inside the reef in Bora Bora when the dolphin appeared and "posed" for this portrait. The photograph is not manipulated in any way from the original 35mm negative.

BOOKS

SOME RECENT O BOOKS

The Barefoot Indian
The Making of a Messiahress
Julia Heywood

The book is warm, funny, but altogether life changing. It teaches lessons that are infinitely valuable, on life itself and the nature of the cosmos and the ailments of the human race. They are so many answers, and my old self is itching to show off and tell you some, but I am not able to. The book is one you must journey through and reflect upon by yourself. A touching and life changing read, "The Barefoot Indian" is definitely one to pick up the next time you visit your local bookstore. It is an easy and essential read for all ages. **She Unlimited Magazine**
1846940400 112pp **£7.99 $16.95**

The God of the New Millennium
A search for balance in an age of spin
Gregory Dark

It works, if you try. A little quiet will have you reading words that will inspire you to ask yourself the questions that matter most. Thoughts that will open your mind, set apart successful goals from the poor choices that lead to failure. Words that will clarify doubt and end negativity.
Lallouz International Magazine
9781846940637 144pp **£9.99 $22.95**

Thinking through Thomas Merton

Thinking through Thomas Merton
Contemplation for Contemporary Times

ROBERT INCHAUSTI

SUNY PRESS

Cover art: Drawing by Thomas Merton. Used with permission of the Merton Legacy Trust and the Thomas Merton Center at Bellarmine University.

Published by State University of New York Press, Albany

© 2014 State University of New York

All rights reserved

Printed in the United States of America

For information, contact State University of New York Press, Albany, NY
www.sunypress.edu

Production by Diane Ganeles
Marketing by Michael Campochiaro

Library of Congress Cataloging-in-Publication Data

Inchausti, Robert.
    Thinking through Thomas Merton : contemplation for contemporary times / Robert Inchausti.
        pages cm
    Includes bibliographical references and index.
    ISBN 978-1-4384-4945-6 (hardcover : alk. paper)
    ISBN 978-1-4384-4946-3 (pbk. : alk. paper)
    1. Merton, Thomas, 1915–1968.   2. Contemplation.   I. Title.

BX4705.M5421527 2014
271'.12502—dc23   2013004184

10 9 8 7 6 5 4 3 2 1

"The rediscovery of Christianity is made possible by the dissolution of metaphysics, that is, by the end of objectivistic-dogmatic philosophies as well as of European culture's claim to have discovered and realized the 'true' nature of humanity."[1]

—Gianni Vattimo

"There is, however, another world—it is this world properly received."[2]

—Mark Johnston

Contents

Introduction

Everything Old Is New Again

Upon first reading the works of Thomas Merton, many Christians (especially Catholics) felt that religious thinking had finally come to life again. The cultural treasures of the Christian past were at last being made to speak more powerfully than the trite, pious bromides they were commonly thought to express. Here at last was someone who could reanimate the sacred tradition, interpret its value, and bring it into dialogue with the problems of our time.[1]

Merton's best-selling memoir, *The Seven Storey Mountain* (1948), was a compelling, first-person description of the clash between the imperatives of the inner life and the demands of modern social existence. But Merton added a surprising and unexpected final chapter to his account in which the soul triumphed over its circumstances through a return to contemplative living.

At the heart of this return was Merton's reaffirmation of the fourfold biblical hermeneutic articulated in the Patristic Age. This approach to reading scripture was refined during the high Medieval Synthesis and corrected to meet modern epistemological concerns by powerful twentieth-century Catholic theologians such as Henri de Lubac,[2] Jean Danielou, Hans Von Balthasar,[3] and Etienne Gilson. These thinkers—arguing against both biblical fundamentalism and the so-called "higher criticism"—argue that the Bible *makes sense only when read devotionally*. That is to say, when Jesus is

1

quoted as saying "I and the Father are one," he is not making a logical metaphysical assertion or a historical claim open to archeological correction, but rather a prophetic pronouncement more in line with the epistemology of modernist poetics and its non-dualistic perspective on existence. The same can be said for the multivalent, overdetermined content of the Prophets, the Psalms, and the Old and New Testaments.

By reading Holy Scripture in this way, a contemplative Christian is inoculated against the heresies of literalism, "cheap grace,"[4] and "cheap supernaturalism," which substitute magical thinking for a sincere transcendental reflection.[5] Merton understood, as did his patristic and monastic precursors, that the interpretive problems raised by ambiguous stories and changing circumstances, problems involving persons and purposes, cannot be *solved* (if by "solved" you mean explained away) by any simple procedure. They can only be understood through multiple shifts in perspective, where the antinomies that generated them in the first place are brought in dialogue with our own evolving categories of self-understanding— categories that are themselves constantly changing as we deepen and grow as persons. Thus, reading scripture, if done with integrity, raises as many questions as it solves, and by so doing generates many more meanings, paradoxes, and ironies than any single ideology can decipher or decode.

In this sense, biblical interpretation is not a normal science but a spiritual practice requiring self-knowledge, piety, discernment, and humility—not indoctrination. It does not yield its secrets to ideologues or fanatics. And so by adopting this ancient, devotional approach, Merton was able to reanimate the Great Chain of Being—once so central to Western philosophy and theology—by incorporating its assumptions within his own interpretive practice. But he didn't do this by reasserting its value as an antique metaphysical absolute—but rather as an interpretive heuristic necessary for the comprehension of biblical images and tropes. This merging of the sociohistorical horizon of the present with the unique existential assumptions built into the biblical text was an achievement largely lost on post-Enlightenment thinkers—atheists and believers alike—who were so deeply entrenched in their Cartesian notions of the self that they could only read the Bible as pseudo-history or as the proof text for various religious doctrines.

Merton's application of the fourfold hermeneutic made it possible for him to employ a conscience driven version of what Roland Barthes once described as "the structuralist activity"[6] to his reading of the Bible and tradition. This imaginative act of finding new meanings in old forms ends up transforming the reader in the process of reading.[7] Another way of putting this is that the contemplative meaning of scripture, its existential challenges and inspirations, like the challenges and inspirations we experience in our everyday lives, takes on its true value only *after* we see through the niggling, ideologically ridden content of our binary codes and historical moment so that we may fathom our place within a larger, yet to be discerned ontological mystery. It is only then that new, more important questions arise for us, and the larger literary and final messianic challenge can emerge.

By writing out of and through this eschatological point of view, Merton revealed a depth to religious thought previously lost on his more literal-minded contemporaries—both secular and religious. He showed that what they thought they knew about religion, Christianity in general and Catholicism in particular, had been fatally compromised by materialism and reductionist metaphysics. And yet *The Seven Storey Mountain* was no simple call for a return to the old-time religion. Merton brought the monastic contemplative tradition forward into the twentieth century, freeing it from its ethnocentric prejudices and antique cosmological assumptions to reveal its constructionist and communitarian roots in the practices of the early Church. He took the notion of Christian self-forgetting (kenosis) and rendered it concrete by bringing it into dialogue with the social and existential realities of modernity (not the least of which was the struggle for human rights and the search for personal meaning in an increasingly politicized, militarized, and commercialized world).[8]

Unfortunately, the deep theological underpinnings of Merton's thought were often overshadowed by his controversial stands on issues of the moment—such as his criticisms of the Vietnam War and his defense of the civil rights movement. As a result, he was more popularly seen as a social critic, as opposed to an Orthodox contemplative diagnosing the spiritual crises of the age. And though it is true that he was an admirer and friend of Dorothy Day and Dan and Phil Berrigan, he was not an active participant in their protests and remained both inside and outside the Catholic Peace Fellowship during the Vietnam War—joining it briefly, then quitting over the self-immolation of former Cistercian novice Roger Laporte, only to rejoin it again several months later.[9]

Merton's relationship to Catholic social thought actually follows more closely the work of Charles Peguy, who argued for a new, more socially engaged Catholicism,[10] and the work of Jacques Maritain,[11] who intellectualized that vision in his philosophical teachings. Henri de Lubac along with Urs Von Balthasar then welded those progressive social views to patristic scholarship, providing the Orthodox theological foundation for the reforms of Vatican II. Merton then translated this emerging perspective into psychologically compelling, first-person poetry and prose—authenticating its contemporary existential significance, extending its influence, and bringing it into dialogue with contemporary culture.

This more general project of a return to spirituality is something very different from Christian apologetics per se or even theology per se, for it can be seen in the works of secular as well as religious figures. Modern writers as diverse as Honoré de Balzac, Leo Tolstoy, Fyodor Dostoyevsky, Rainer Maria Rilke, Martin Heidegger, Aldous Huxley, T. S. Eliot, G. K. Chesterton, Soren Kierkegaard, and even Jack Kerouac[12] all start from the same basic premise that the integrity and freedom of the human person need to be defended against the dehumanizing forces inherent to contemporary civilization. For Kierkegaard, this led to his critique of Christendom as a superficial reduction of the interior life; for Balzac, to a multileveled narrative exposé of the capitalist unmaking of Christian civilization; for Tolstoy, to a radical questioning of all forms of social authority; for Heidegger, to a temporal resituating of Kantian metaphysics; and for Huxley, to a rearticulation of

The Perennial Philosophy amid forebodings of a coming *Brave New World*, where the interior life (and along with it art, science, and religion) might very well disappear amid a plethora of distractions, entertainments, and automation.

Merton, for his part, tried to rescue Christianity from its contemporary misrepresentation—both within and without the Church—by exposing the false distinction between the active and contemplative life that had plagued Western thought at least since the Reformation, and probably as early as the Renaissance—a distinction that defined the active life in terms of worldly ambition and gave it priority over contemplative existence. Merton, by contrast, believed that the contemplative life, based upon God's self-emptying in and through Christ, served as the corrective to the worldly excesses of the active life and to the theological scholasticism both ancient and modern that was crippling the spiritual vitality and intellectual reach of the Church.[13]

"Christianity," Merton wrote, "can not only throw light on the most typical and most urgent problems of the modern world but that there is a certain light which Christianity alone can provide. But this light does not shine all by itself. It is not always clearly apparent to the Church, but it must be made evident *by the creative activity of Christians themselves as they participate in the solution of contemporary problems on which the very future of man depends.*"[14] (author's italics.)

After *The Seven Storey Mountain* became an international best-seller, Merton became the most famous monk in American history. Since then, his reputation has only continued to grow— not only as a modern spokesman for monasticism (although that would have been enough to establish his importance), but also for his unique capacity to throw new light on contemporary issues as a spiritual master, political dissident, popular essayist, and avant-garde poet. His works have spawned hundreds, if not thousands, of critical commentaries, study groups, retreat centers, scholarly associations, and political action committees.

Yet, despite his renown, or perhaps because of it, certain fundamental questions remain as to the significance of Merton's legacy. Exactly what is the relationship of Christian monasticism to contemporary thought in general and to theology in particular? How seriously can moderns (or postmoderns) take his existential version of the medieval synthesis? And what exactly is the significance of his embrace of monasticism in the middle of the twentieth century or the meaning of his ambivalent relationship to the New Left and 1960s counterculture? Do his views speak to the recent theological turn in European philosophy or to the contemporary breakthroughs in neuroscience? Or are they more of a throwback to the spirituality of Pope John XXIII than the harbinger of anything really new? And what is the relationship of contemplation to dialectics, philosophical analysis, phenomenology, or deconstruction, anyway? Is it a method among methods, a subject matter among subject matters, an anti-philosophy, an ascetic practice, or something altogether different—a new form of thinking after reason itself has been seen through as a kind of metaphysical shadow play?

These are tricky questions because Thomas Merton was not, strictly speaking, a theologian. He was a creative writer who was also a monk. He was an essayist, a stylist, a Christian disciple, and poet who lived and wrote in a monastery—that unique liminal space between ancient and modern existence. In this sense, he was a kind of performance artist to his secular literary peers—testing the integrity of his vision through a life of daily devotion and asceticism. Moreover, Merton transformed the genre of spiritual autobiography from an exercise in doctrinal piety into an in-depth analysis of the interior life. He then brought that analysis—along with his monastic commitments—into conversation with a variety of different intellectual and spiritual traditions.

To this day, the Catholic Church does not know exactly what to make of Thomas Merton—acknowledging his faith and his genius but flinching at his interest in progressive politics and avant-garde literature. A short biography of Merton was to be included in the official U.S. Catholic Catechism for Adults, published in 2006. But the profile of Merton was replaced shortly before publication with one about Elizabeth Seton, the first native-born American saint. Seton was, after all, a far less controversial figure.[15] Merton's conservative critics still remembered that Merton gave a talk on Marxism at the height of the Cold War and spoke admiringly of the works of Herbert Marcuse, Eric Fromm, and D. T. Suzuki. He also counseled conscientious objectors during the Vietnam War, wrote experimental poetry in praise of pre-Columbian civilizations, and, at the height of the civil rights movement, publicly questioned the sincerity of white liberals' commitment to African American equality.

So the questions remain: was Merton a traditionalist or a heretic; a beatnik, a Buddhist, or a saint? The Church, of course, will have to make its own official assessment for itself; my task here is to place Merton's contribution within the context of contemporary thought. For, in the larger scheme of things, the mere fact that Merton joined the Church at all, let alone became a monk, was itself a radical response to the secular crisis of modernity and marked a significant transition from literary modernity to postmodern religious belief. But, unlike other popular twentieth-century religious figures, Merton did not see his status as a believer as a license to ignore contemporary intellectual developments; rather, he saw it as giving him a responsibility to name and expose the spiritually deadening positivisms of his day—including those of cheap grace and religious superstition.

What follows is a thinking through of the significance of what Merton accomplished and a look at contemporary thought through the lens of those accomplishments. As such, the book describes Merton's perspective from a contemporary point of view and interprets contemporary thought from Merton's perspective. In other words, it considers not just who Merton was, but who he is still in the process of becoming. It seeks to reintroduce the reader to Merton's originality by going beyond "the already explicated Merton" in order to rediscover "the ever-radical Merton" whose work has yet to be—and perhaps never will be—fully understood because it is not so much a set of ideas as a domain of interior experience.

The first chapter looks at Merton's life as a Kierkegaardian leap into the dangerous imperatives of the True Self. Chapter 2 considers his view of contemplation as a radical alternative to modern philosophical methods—including phenomenology and dialectics. Chapter 3 examines Merton's embrace of avant-garde poetics as the idiom best capable of giving popular expression to contemplative experience. Chapter 4 looks at the role of the monk "at the end of history." Chapter 5 considers pacifism as Merton's most dangerous idea—calling into question the monopolies of power and violence that pass themselves off as agents of law and order. The conclusion offers an overview of Catholicism in the light of Merton's witness.

1

An Experimental Life

"To be a saint means to be myself. Therefore the problem of sanctity and salvation is in fact the problem of finding out who I am and discovering my true self."

—Thomas Merton[1]

Thomas Merton's mother died in 1921 when he was only six years old, and his father died in 1931 when he was only seventeen. This left him and his younger brother, John Paul, virtually alone in the world. As a consequence, Merton lived a rather wild youth—flunking out of Cambridge in his freshman year after fathering a child out of wedlock and participating in a drunken fraternity stunt in which he played the victim in a mock crucifixion.

After being kicked out of Cambridge, he moved to Long Island in 1934 to live with his mother's family. In New York, he attended Columbia University, briefly joined the Communist Party, and eventually discovered his calling as a writer through contact with a series of influential teachers and friends that included Robert Giroux, Joseph Wood Krutch, Mark Van Doren, Robert Lax, and the avant-garde painter Ad Reinhart.

It was at Columbia that Merton first grasped the need to move beyond modernism and his literary hero, James Joyce. He discovered William Blake and the Christian critical romanticism that would influence him for the rest of his life.[2]

By Christian critical romanticism, I am referring to that set of writers who first translated the spiritual traditions of the West into secular terms—figures like Blake, Coleridge, Emerson, Whitman, Tolstoy, and Dostoyevsky—writers who celebrated the interior life yet also emphasized the need for a prophetic public witness over and against the powers that be. Blake's claim that it was possible to attain a second innocence on the far side of worldly experience appealed to Merton so much that he wrote his thesis on Blake's vision of art and nature.

Merton's interest in Blake prefigured his ultimate transition from an aspiring novelist to full-fledged Christian contemplative. And it also helps to explain the perpetual tension throughout his life between his calling as a writer and his calling as a monk. Merton was, like Blake, forever of two minds, always thinking in terms of antipathies, contrasts, dialectical tensions, and reconfigurations.

Moreover, Blake gave Merton another way to understand his terrible first year at Cambridge. Education is always a move into experience—and, as such, a fall from innocence. It is, by its very nature, tainted with corruption—that is, unless one acquires a second innocence on the far side of worldly experience. In Merton's case, this worldliness was a heady stew of Marxism, Bohemianism, and literary ambition. But his mature works, written after his conversion, express his second innocence (or rebirth in Christ), with Blakean reflections on overcoming life's antitheses through the transcendent experience of a higher Self.

At the time of his conversion to Christianity, Merton's college friend Robert Lax confronted him with a question: "What do you want to be?"

Merton answered that he wanted to be "a good Catholic."

Lax replied that if he wanted to be a good Catholic, then he should say that he wanted to become a saint, for hadn't Augustine himself said that we must be emptied of all with which we are full so that we may be filled with that of which we are empty? Merton demurred, telling Lax he couldn't be a saint, but immediately realized that in denying that aspiration, he was indulging in "the false humility which makes people say they cannot do the things they must."[3] This was the turning point in Merton's life, for in that moment he recognized that even Christian converts could deny their our own true selves—their souls' true destiny—in the name of their own personal, lesser conception of the faith. But to truly be a "good Catholic" meant more than that. It meant living in accord with the Christ within, the saint within, your own true Self that knows you better than you know yourself.

Saints know that their concepts of God get in the way of their own souls' truth, and so conversion of manners, that is to say, of behavior and belief, has no simple pattern. Each of us has to take on the difficult, individualized task of seeing through ourself and even beyond the petty pride that fuels our first nascent ambitions to become a "good" Christian. A greater love calls.

And so from that very moment forward, Catholicism became for Merton a pathway to sainthood—not merely the acceptance of a particular religious dogma. To be a "good Catholic," one could just follow the rules of canon law, but to aspire to sainthood meant dedicating oneself to living out the highest values, meaning, and witness of Christ. It meant embarking on a voyage.

Saints are men and women of faith who embark on that voyage and by so doing become transparent vehicles of the Holy Spirit. Their creative acts of love and gratitude challenge the values of empire and push the envelope of conventional spirituality. Saints redefine the norms of moral behavior within the Church and sometimes even redefine the Church's own understanding of itself. As such, they help us all overcome the false separations between theory and practice, theology and personal life, will and conscience. They accomplish this by personalizing God's providence through moment-by-moment spiritual discoveries. Their "present," it turns out, is as mysterious as the Trinity itself—not self-evident, not even actually present, and by no means ordinary. To be constantly praying is to be constantly awakening—not just to the moment, but beyond it into the moment's hitherto unknown significance. As a result, saints are often charged with heresy because their acts of love and service challenge the old paradigms of religiosity. That is, they are charged with heresy *until* the Church catches up with their inspired visions and changes itself to accommodate their greater spiritual reach.

Unlike Joyce's modernist literary epigone Stephen Daedalus or Joseph Campbell's hero "with a thousand faces," Christian saints do not "return to their communities with a boon"; rather, they implode within themselves into God—transforming their communities from the inside out by taking the community's own ideals even more seriously than the community itself takes them. Saints reinstate the lost newness of a faith tradition by living it more deeply and authentically than those who merely conform to its rules and conventions. Thus, Merton converted to an inspired faith, not an institutional religion, moved by the creativity of those odd, passionate religious innovators such as Saint Francis, who gave sermons to the birds, and Theresa of Lisieux, who, as a young tourist, ran past the guards and threw herself onto the floor of the Coliseum so as to mingle with the dust of the martyrs.

Robert Lax's advice to Merton was later echoed by, of all people, the post-Beat writer Charles Bukowski when he wrote:

> If you're going to try, go all the way. Otherwise, don't even start. This could mean losing girlfriends, wives, relatives and maybe even your mind. It could mean not eating for three or four days. It could mean freezing on a park bench. It could mean jail. It could mean derision. It could mean mockery—isolation. Isolation is the gift. All the others are a test of your endurance, of how much you really want to do it. And, you'll do it, despite rejection and the worst odds. And it will be better than anything else you can imagine. If you're going to try, go all the way. There is no other feeling like that. You will be alone with the gods, and the nights will flame

with fire. You will ride life straight to perfect laughter. It's the only good fight there is.[4]

Of course, the hard-drinking Bukowski was not counseling the young to seek Christ, but rather to embrace a brave Nietzschean solitude. Lax, on the other hand, was telling Merton that his desire to be "a good Catholic" required more courage and risk than he had yet to imagine. But Merton was to move away from the Gods of "a proud isolation" toward solidarity with the innocent and downtrodden of this world: away from the egotistical sublime toward the second innocence and exalted humility of the Christian disciple.

Lax understood the communion of saints as a wonderful corrective to a narrow, metaphysically determined conception of Catholicism, for not only did it prove that there were many different ways to follow Christ, but the communion of saints historicized and concretized the Church's theology. The saints existentially embody the values that sustain community: diversity, plurality, and tolerance of imperfection. And their lives represent the most radical virtues of the Christian life: moral imagination, social dissent, and devotional innovation.

Saints remind the Church hierarchy of Christ's humble origins and love for the people, whereas institutions too often value individuals for their place in the hierarchy and their adherence to rules and authority. This is why the organized Church has always had problems with the ingenuity and audacity of its saints—even leading it to employ a "devil's advocate" to smoke out the personal failures and unconscious heresies of its most controversial disciples. Christopher Hitchens, for example, author of *The Missionary Position* and *God is Not Great*, was asked to testify against Mother Teresa's beatification. This was done not only to ensure an objective examination of her life and work, but also to ensure that her values and practices were consistent with Catholic orthodoxy.

In this sense, the communion of the saints functions within the Church much like Kant's notion of "public reason" functions within philosophy: as a court of appeal through which the "private reason" of Catholic doctrine can be thought through with reference to public ideas, premises, and practices. Public reason does not proceed from precise definitions or predetermined ends, but rather seeks to think through the public meaning of concepts originating within otherwise closed systems. Catholic theology insofar as it remains confined to the definitions and ends of the Church can be seen as a form of *private reasoning*. Its sectarian job is to fix false thinking and articulate doctrine, whereas, the community of the saints celebrates the redemption of the fallible and the wisdom of the people living out the faith in the world. Indeed, the lives of the saints represent a public theology coming into being that is often initially at odds with old ideas but orthodox in its values, thereby serving as a court of appeal for the larger universal Church coming into being. In this way, saints recontextualize doctrinal truths by demonstrating what they include and exclude within the emerging sociohistorical reality. They are often exemplars of energetic, transformative, populist religious values where human relatedness and love triumph over rules and regulations.

Oscar Wilde described this plurality of the practical theologies bequeathed by the experimental lives of the saints this way:

> And so he who would lead a Christ-like life is he who is perfectly and absolutely himself. He may be a great poet, or a great man of science; or a young student at a University, or one who watches sheep upon a moor; or a maker of dramas, like Shakespeare, or a thinker about God, like Spinoza; or a child who plays in a garden, or a fisherman who throws his nets into the sea. It does not matter what he is, as long as he realizes the perfection of the soul that is within him. All imitation in morals and in life is wrong. Through the streets of Jerusalem at the present day crawls one who is mad and carries a wooden cross on his shoulders. He is a symbol of the lives that are marred by imitation. Father Damien was Christ-like when he went out to live with the lepers,

because in such service he realized fully what was best in him. But he was not more Christ-like than Wagner, when he realized his soul in music; or than Shelley, when he realized his soul in song. There is no one type for man. There are as many perfections as there are imperfect men.[5]

The saints weaken theology proper while empowering the faith in general. That is to say, they undermine the assertion that there is only one metaphysically true way to be a Christian. This does not, however, lead to moral relativism but to a perpetually self-redefining tradition—as adaptable as process theology but more existentially grounded in the lives of actual individuals. Theology becomes the unfolding, flexible revelation of a God who transcends any and all systems, a God who sides with the poor, the just, the obscure, the innovative, and the personally authentic. This was the kind of "good Catholic" Robert Lax was urging Thomas Merton to become when he advised him to become a saint.

A saint may start from the same point of view as an iconoclastic poet, going against convention and comfort for the sake of an abundant, truthful, and self-sacrificing life, but he eventually arrives at a very different place. Like the hero and the artist, saints live beyond life. But saints are unique among this triumvirate because they do not advance any specific worldly agenda or immanent teleology; rather, they embrace spiritual solitude as part of the price one must pay for a creative dependence upon God. They die to the values of this world in order to live in the life of the spirit. Or, as G. K. Chesterton described it, the Christian must seek his or her "life in a spirit of furious indifference to it; he must desire life like water and yet drink death like wine."[6] The hero and the artist, by contrast, drink life like wine and death like water—that is to say, their indifference to the world is stoic, not religious, and so their hope is placed on the future immortality of their work, whereas the Christian lives content within the ordinary graces of anonymity, truth, and love in the eternal presence of God.

Another way to put this is that saints are those who exercise inner balance within the shifting sands of existence. They don't dissolve the chaos but master it by mastering themselves. The hero and the artist have a different calling. Outraged by the chaos they encounter, they seek to set matters right—if only in their work. Saints, by contrast, transform the dangerous and finite pains of personal isolation into spiritual revelations through contact with the energy of love. When Teresa of Avila remarked that all the way to paradise is paradise, she was speaking as someone for whom everything in this world had become a blessing, someone who was no longer in the grip of illusory images, things, or ideas. Because saints do not lay any conditions upon the world, its dark realities do not diminish their hope, but rather inspire them to even greater acts of love, surrender, and sympathy. Twenty-five years after his conversion, Merton would write: "[T]he saints are what they are *not* because their sanctity makes them admirable to others, but *because the gift of sainthood makes it possible for them to admire everybody else.*"[7]

The saint, like the child, pours out love in the moment without ulterior motive—undiluted by any hope of changing the world or him- or herself. A saint's charity is an absolute sacrifice, which to him or her is no sacrifice at all, but an end in itself, free from expectations. To the degree that we are all compelled by our desires to control the situations in our lives, the saint stands over and against us as a reminder that there are other, better ways to live—free from pettiness and scorn, so filled with love that pity itself dissolves into an absolute identification with everyone and everything alive—extending one's vitality and empathetic reach virtually to infinity.

In *The Seven Storey Mountain*, Merton quotes Augustine's claim that human nature is ordered to an end that it is not equipped by nature to attain. And so when Merton visited the Abbey of Gethsemani in 1941 and found a spiritual community organized around this very paradox, he felt he had discovered the center of America—the hidden vortex around which the basic truth of the human condition spun. This community of contemplatives—free from the rush toward economic development—proved by its mere existence that it was still possible to live a life in accord with conscience without being crippled by either Bohemian isolation or middle-class conformity. Merton found in monasticism a way to *be*, not merely to *seem* to be, a Christian. It was a way of embracing the absurdity of the human condition without succumbing to the false solace of superstition or the false pride of an untethered Nietzschean bravado. The monastic life provided a way to admit that his life had hitherto been compromised by all that he had done and had failed to do.

Historically, monasticism was a movement both within and against the Church, a movement within a movement. Its doctrines were orthodox but its suspicion of empire subversive, and as such, it served as a model for building the new world within the shell of the old. Monasticism was a model for how revelation, creativity, and devotion could find their way around the institutional focus of the Constantine Church. What was being reborn in monasteries was not a new form of institutional power but rather the energy, idealism, and independence the Church had lost by becoming an imperial power.

The monastery, in this sense, was a world inside the world but outside the world's conception of itself. As such, it became a refuge for the soul—what Merton called "an earthly paradise because it is an earthly purgatory."[8] That is to say, unlike the secular world, monasteries see themselves as under an inconceivable horizon of responsibility and therefore inherently vain but also open to redemption. Monks are what the Franciscan Richard Rohr calls "lifestyle Christians"—people who define their faith by how they live, not by what they believe. A monk is not a religious seeker so much as a religious "finder"—a spiritual athlete more than a theologian. His primary concern is with moving his head into his heart by living out his faith—not merely describing it or coming to understand its philosophical implications.[9] "Putting one's head into one's heart" is not a metaphor for subjecting thought to feeling. On the contrary, it is a metaphor for bringing one's intelligence into contact with the divine: bringing intellect under the tutelage of the Divine—which is the ultimate goal of the Christian spiritual journey.[10]

This is not the same thing as thinking deep thoughts or theorizing one's place in the cosmos; it is more an act of perception, of *seeing* the beauty and dignity in all things through a change of heart or *metanoia*. Scientists are currently exploring the neural correlates to such altered states of consciousness that Merton and his contemplative predecessors strove heroically to make permanent in their lives.[11]

The split between knowing and feeling is reunited in the monastery through a life of obedience, service, and devotion. Monastic formation is the journey back to oneness with God and with oneself. Conversion is, in this sense, transformation and rebirth into a completely new, open-ended way of life, which we find in Merton's famous prayer, composed in 1953:

> My Lord God, I have no idea where I am going. I do not see the road ahead of me. I cannot know for certain where it will end. Nor do I really know myself, and the fact that I think I am following your will does not mean that I am actually doing so. But I believe that the desire to please you does in fact please you. And I hope I have that desire in all that I am doing. I hope that I will never do anything apart from that desire. And I know that if I do this you will lead me by the right road though I may know nothing about it. Therefore I will trust you always though I may seem to be lost and in the shadow of death. I will not fear, you are ever with me, and you will never leave me to face my perils alone.[12]

Many years later, we find a more mature expression of this perspective in Merton's essay *The Day of a Stranger* (1967),[13] where the result of this transformation upon ordinary consciousness is narrated with a completeness found nowhere else in his writings. Most of Merton's works, from the poems, to the letters, lectures, and reflections, are life writings. That is to say, unlike biography or theology proper, they narrate bits of life reflected upon and purified into spiritual substance. Like the works of his contemporaries Jack Kerouac, Henry Miller, and Norman Mailer, they record the transformation of the self as it happens. *Day of a Stranger* is different in that it completes the cycle: unifying the saint, the tramp, the outside, the monk, and the man of Tao within a single, shared consciousness. Merton writes: "What I wear is pants. What I do is live. How I pray is breath."[14]

It may sound odd to say it, but monasticism—like Christianity and even like writing itself—is a therapeutic action ethic. One gives up worldly status in order to live a nonviolent life in harmony with nature and, therefore, with one's hitherto undiscovered true Self—married to poverty, chastity, and moral stability—for the sake of a life that is more than merely living. This is why Merton says, "The monastery is not an 'escape' from the world. On the contrary, by being in the monastery, I take my part in all the struggles and sufferings of the world. To adopt a life that is essentially nonassertive, nonviolent, a life of humility and peace is in itself a statement of one's position."[15] And that position is an outright rejection of nationalistic propaganda, power-seeking advertisers, self-promoting politicians, and the various other fads and fashions of commercial culture.

The primary antidote to these trends offered by the monastery was contemplation. Meditative prayer and self-recollection serve as an antidote to "identity thinking," where a thing is known only when it is classified in some way. The progress Enlightenment thought made in getting beyond myth and superstition ironically ended up establishing its own mythic goal of controlling nature. Power over things and people came to define progress and replaced the classical domains of thought, which sought understanding as an end in itself, not primarily as a means of control. Humanity no longer sought to incorporate its past with its own deepest biological nature, and instead developed discrete sciences and disciplines designed to gain power over various aspects of experience leading to the creation of an increasingly self-conscious, global "subjectivity" bent on using technical force to abolish all forms of material deprivation.

Calling for a return to the selfless self of the Christian contemplatives in such a context is not an easy thing to do, and Merton went about it with great care and circumspection, for the contemplative arts taught in monasteries are tied to a sophisticated sociohistorical analysis of their own origins, without which they could all too easily turn round on and devolve into mere techniques and end up stewing in their own supernatural ethos.

This may account for the insular (and esoteric) nature of so many of the sermons and essays one reads in the works of otherwise brilliant meditation teachers. Like Merton, their writings provide powerful phenomenological descriptions of the interior life, but, unlike Merton, they make little or no effort to link the interior life to social reality or "manners." Their works do not contextualize spiritual truths so much as reveal them, and this weakens their significance as a form of cultural critique.

To be fair, many spiritual writers simply assume that once one is liberated from conventional ignorance through the experience of Christian *metanoia*, a well-formed social conscience will follow as a matter of course. But the absence of any unified political alliance within religious communities gives the lie to this assumption and helps to explain why Merton's willingness to address political issues from a contemplative perspective was so important and got him into so much trouble. Indeed, his most important contribution to the thought of his time may be his *marriage of contemplative and intellectual awareness into a single prophetic point of view.*

From Merton's contemplative perspective, human injustice remains uncured because it remains unaddressed, and it remains unaddressed because it continues to go undiagnosed. In the global context, the institutional Church finds itself just another player in a political calculus—offset by competing interests and power blocs. And so, like any other stakeholder, it is forced to compromise rather than exert moral leadership. As a result, the socioeconomic order (and not the Kingdom of God) ends up shaping the world's interpretation of the Christ's teachings. To challenge this standard or to question this context requires a reassessment of the historical ground upon which we stand. So, unless clarified by a transhistorical point of view informed by post-Enlightenment categories of thought, even the most practiced contemplative will find it difficult to speak truth to power—caught as they are within an all-prevailing, systematically distorted system of communications.

In the 1950s, Merton became master of scholastics and then master of novices at Gethsemani, which meant that he was in charge of the spiritual formation of many returning World War II veterans. He quickly realized that in order to initiate these war-hardened veterans into the contemplative life, he would have to find a way of explaining the Christian tradition in nontraditional terms. That is to say, he would need to invent a contemporary spiritual pedagogy that spoke to and through their experience.

From these lectures, Merton culled the passages that make up his books *Seeds of Contemplation* (1948), *No Man Is an Island* (1955), and *Thoughts in Solitude* (1958). All three became devotional classics because Merton did not lean upon antique jargon or bury contemporary issues under overworked religious bromides. He spoke to his war-hardened audience of would-be monks about their call to the religious life—rescuing contemplation from its quietist reputation.

Take, for example, Merton's explanation of the identity of Christ in *No Man Is an Island*. "The Spirit of God must teach us who Christ is and form Christ in us and transform us into other Christs. . . . Therefore if you want to have in your heart the affections and dispositions that were those of Christ on earth, consult not your own imagination but faith. Enter into the darkness of interior renunciation, strip your soul of images and let Christ form Himself in you by His Cross."[16] Here is a definition that is not scholastic but contemplative, reminding us that to define Christ, one must experience Christ—not know him as a metaphysical concept or even as a person, but experience him as the revelation of one's own true and deepest self—that is to say, as an intrinsic reality.

Another example of this is Merton's explanation of prayer: "The whole function of the life of prayer is to enlighten and strengthen our conscience so that it not only knows and perceives the outward, written precepts of the moral and divine laws, but above all lives God's law in concrete reality by perfect and continual union with His will. The conscience that is united to the Holy Spirit by faith, hope, and selfless charity becomes a mirror of God's own interior law which is His charity."[17] Again, no scholasticism here, but experiential appropriation and poetic insight. Prayer, in its deepest sense, is a revelation in which there is no separation between oneself and God. Merton even went so far as to warn his postulates: "A man who is not stripped and poor and naked within his own soul will unconsciously tend to do the works he has to do for his own sake rather than for the glory of God. He will be virtuous not because he loves God's will but because he wants to admire his own virtues. But every moment of the day will bring him some frustration that will make him bitter and impatient, and in his impatience he will be discovered."[18]

These ideas reflect some of the best thinking of Urs von Balthasar and Henri de Lubac, whose work greatly influenced the Second Vatican Council, but Merton presents them in a middle style, where the rigor of the thought is tamed by the forthrightness of expression. Both Christ and prayer are contemplative realities, not merely philosophical concepts or historical facts, and so they can only be grasped devotionally—that is to say, feelingly. This is a truth that must be carefully unpacked because its implications are so profound. Scripture, as these mid-century Catholic theologians pointed out, is intimately tied to the traditions and experiences out of which it emerged and can be rediscovered only through a rigorous fourfold hermeneutic that reads the Bible as operating at several levels at the same time.

The body, mind, soul, emotions, intellect, and conscience are all processed differently in competing realms of experience that nevertheless are unified in and through the Christian mythos. The gospels are not to be decoded or systematized metaphysically so much as experienced and reiterated in and through prayer, community, and service. They do not comment on reality so much as add an additional reality to it. They do not explain experience; they are part of experience itself. The resulting iconic meanings cannot be simply or systematically rendered, and any literal interpretation is, ipso facto, heretical. Urs von Balthasar once remarked,

> The doctrines of the Trinity, of the Man-God, of redemption, of the Cross and the Resurrection, of predestination, and eschatology, are literally bristling with problems which no one raises, which everyone gingerly sidesteps. They deserve more respect. The thought of preceding generations even when incorporated in conciliar definitions is never a resting-place where the thought of the following generations can lie idle. Definitions are less the end than the beginning. . . . Whatever is transmitted without a new personal effort, an effort which must start ab ovo, from the revealed source itself, spoils like the manna. And the longer the interruption of living tradition caused by a simply mechanical transmission the more difficult the renewed tackling of the task.[19]

This radical task, the task of a well-articulated orthodoxy—in all its challenging perpetual originality—was picked up by Merton and reflected in his writing.

And so, when the 1960s arrived with their political crises and social unrest, Merton found that he had important things to say about civil rights, the nuclear threat, and Vietnam as well as about religion. As one might expect, he took the side of the poor, the powerless, and underrepresented—openly declaring his progressive contemplative vision in informal essays and poems. "Our vocation is not simply to be," Merton told his fellow monks and novices,

> but to work together with God in the creation of our own life, our own identity, our own destiny. We are free beings and sons and daughters of God. This means to

say that we should not passively exist, but actively participate in His creative freedom, in our own lives, and in the lives of others, by choosing the truth. To put it better, we are even called to share with God the work of creating the truth of our identity. . . . To work out our own identity in God, which the Bible calls 'working out our salvation,' is a labor that requires sacrifice and anguish, risk and many tears. It demands close attention to reality at every moment, and great fidelity to God as He reveals Himself, obscurely, in the mystery of each new situation.[20]

To be a monk, therefore, is to embrace a certain social oblivion that, nevertheless, opens one up to see social reality without illusion. There is a strange clarity of perception that follows from being written off by the world—a world that had largely forgotten why monasteries even existed in the first place. Merton's point of view was interesting to secular readers precisely because it offered such an entirely different critique of the contemporary life and because Merton identified so deeply and completely with his faith—not in a spirit of irony or self-drama, but with purity of heart and real intelligence.

In one of his later lectures, Merton explained the essential nature of the religious life this way:

> There is something about man that when he is not doing what he was made for, he knows it, and he knows it in a very deep way, and it becomes very important to him to change things. . . . How do you explain these things? The thing is not to explain them, the thing is to deepen them, the thing is to live them, and instead of getting by the thing with explanations and forgetting about it, it is much better not to and to get deeply into it. And that's what the monastic life is about. The monastic life is given to us for one reason only, it's to really deepen this dimension of religious reality.

You come to a monastery because you are looking for something, and you stay here because you keep looking for it, and the whole thing about it is that you believe that there is a point to this search and when you get away from this search . . . you begin to hear the voice, "This isn't the job you're supposed to be doing. Get back on the track of what you are looking for. Do the thing you're supposed to be doing." . . . Once a person has received from God the charge to seek what he has to seek, then he puts everything else aside and seeks it. On the basis of truth like this, accepted and lived, you get a Sufi and you get a monk. The beginning of the spiritual life: "I need God desperately and I am blocking him from helping me because I am getting in His way. I am doing my will not His, and I don't really know quite what to do about it."[21]

This impatience infects self-righteous extremists of every political persuasion. None are free from contamination. "Our choice," Merton explained, "is not that of being pure and whole at the mere cost of formulating a just and honest opinion. Mere commitment to a decent program of action does not lift the curse. Our real choice is between being like Job who knew he was stricken, and Job's friends who did not know that they were stricken too—though less obviously than he. (So they had answers!)."[22]

But for Merton, the monastery was not an island of peace and order amid a sea of immoderate extremes. It had become more of an outpost on the frontier of an emerging counterculture, that is to say, a culture counter to modernism. As a result, Merton wrote as a guilty bystander to the cultural changes taking place—changes that were challenging the status quo but that also seemed to be bringing about a more universal Catholic Church at the same time. Merton agreed with Jean Danielou's remark—later enshrined on a plaque at Gethesmani—that "Too often we think of hope in too individualistic a manner as merely personal salvation. But hope essentially bears on the great actions of God concerning the whole world of salvation. It bears on the destiny of all humanity. God cares for all creatures, not just Catholics or even Christians. It is the salvation of the world that we await."[23]

Still, Merton insisted on challenging the easy conscience of the age. Upon reading Aldous Huxley's description of his LSD experiences, Merton, a longtime admirer of Huxley's work, wrote a letter asking him whether LSD could really be said to open the door to the divine if it forced God to reveal himself. If LSD compels a response, Merton argued, it is a forced relationship—and, therefore, not an experience of true grace. Huxley never replied.

Merton continued to address the spiritual poverty of the consumer society. Lenny Bruce read Merton's poems in his nightclub act. Joan Baez visited him at Gethsemani. Jack Kerouac contributed a poem to Merton's journal, *Monk's Pond*, and Allen Ginsberg wrote about him in his journals. As a result, Merton found himself becoming identified with the emerging counterculture, but his contemplative perspective was in stark contrast to one of the signature critiques of Western civilization to emerge in the 1960s: Norman O. Brown's *Life Against Death: The Psychoanalytic Meaning of History*.

In *Life Against Death*, Norman O. Brown argued that Freud had revealed a sober truth about our culture: that despite all our scientific and political gains, we still do not know what we want. This essential ignorance at the heart of our desires divides us from within and from without. Brown went to great lengths to reveal the full implications of this psychoanalytic insight that history itself was a neurotic replaying of past traumatic events, and that it was not a utopian fantasy to suppose that this unhappy replay of self-defeating behaviors might yet be overcome by putting an end to repression. The way out of personal neurosis, he argued, was to recover our capacity to live life on the far side of civilization and its discontents—in a polymorphously perverse kingdom of free expression not yet of this world.

In the final chapter of his book, "The Resurrection of the Body," Brown made an explicit connection between Christian mysticism and Freud's theories. "If Christianity wishes to help mankind toward that erasure of the traces of original sin which Baudelaire said was the true definition of progress, there are priceless insights in its tradition—insights which have to be transformed into a system of practical therapy, something like psychoanalysis, before they can be useful or even meaningful."[24]

And then Brown offered this concluding observation:

> The resurrection of the body is a social project facing mankind as a whole, and it will become a practical political problem when the statesmen of the world are called upon to deliver happiness instead of power, when political economy becomes a science of use value instead of exchange values—a science of enjoyment instead of a science of accumulation. In the face of this tremendous human problem, contemporary social theory, both capitalist and socialist, has nothing to say. Contemporary social theory (again we must honor Veblen as an exception) has been completely taken in by the inhuman abstractions of the path of sublimation, and has no contact with concrete human beings, with their concrete bodies, their concrete though repressed desires, and their concrete neuroses.[25]

These ideas broach a contemplative perspective, but Brown's bold formulation was relatively unschooled in the long re-educative practices of monastic formation. The happiness of the contemplative, as Merton so often reminds us, is not the same thing as "a science of enjoyment," even though both challenge the prevailing consumer economy of accumulation. And though Brown is right to see the resurrection of the body as a *social event,* his understanding of it as liberation from genital fetishism does not do justice to Christ's tragic identification with the dispossessed as the sine qua non of a life lived in accord with conscience and his definition of happiness (agape) as moral joy.

The resurrected body of Jesus, for Merton, is not the resurrected physical body of a redeemed hedonism, but the spiritual body of a fallen humanity animated by love (the Holy Spirit). And so, as the 1960s progressed, Merton's writings featured significant contemporary social criticism—challenging rigid Cold War dichotomies and shifting the conversation away from the bitter rhetorical battle between East and West and toward the search for a universal, nondualistic expression of what it means to live life in accord with conscience. Merton's work from this period began where Brown's critique left off, granting the need for a post-historical (i.e., eschatological) perspective on existence, but also articulating the lost tradition of apophatic Christianity that had already thought through many of these same problems.

This defense of the mystical roots of contemplation led him into a head-on collision with consumer society, and although Merton only watched television twice in his life, when he saw a Tidy Bowl commercial, he felt compelled to write about its iconic and liturgical presumptions—about how it elevated bathroom hygiene to the level of a religious absolute. He followed up this essay with a reading of an Arpège cologne advertisement in the New Yorker—exposing its transformation of beauty into a vehicle for perfume sales via a McLuhanesque interpretation of its rhetoric and form.

Advertisers, marketers, and political propagandists, Merton argued, had become magicians with words—unlike poets, who expose the limits of language and highlight the ineffable truths of experience. Advertisers use words and images as tools and weapons to weave spells—not as precious human resources whose integrity must be preserved for the common good. Poets enter into communion with the world from inside their own experience and so come to know things as aspects of themselves. The readers of poetry enter into empathy with poets, acquiring a greater sympathetic imagination and with it a larger sense of self. The more the reader disengages from his or her own interior noise—from his or her self-conceived dramas and perceived personal failings—the more the poet's experience comes through, and so, with practice, the mind becomes adept at perceiving universals. Great literature can open our eyes to the operations of grace, the unperceived blessings in what first appears difficult, and the love revealed only through loss. Thus, literature became for Merton a very important force working against the misuse of language and the dumbing down of people through the images of the mass media and the misrepresentation of Christian theology by know-nothing television evangelists and fundamentalist radio preachers.

These critiques made Merton popular, but he was suspicious of his own celebrity and tried to combat it whenever he could. "A few years ago," he wrote,

> a man who was compiling a book entitled *Success* wrote and asked me to contribute a statement on how I got to be a success. I replied indignantly that I was not able to consider myself a success in any terms that had a meaning to me. I swore I had spent my life strenuously avoiding success. If it so happened that I had once written a best seller, this was a pure accident, due to inattention and naiveté, and I would take very good care never to do the same again. If I had a message to my contemporaries, I said, it was surely this: Be anything you like, be madmen, drunks, and bastards of every shape and form, but at all costs avoid one thing: success. I heard no more from him, and I am not aware that my reply was published with the other testimonials.[26]

Success is a something to be avoided because a success is someone who identifies with his or her own worldly accomplishments, someone whose self-conception resides in his or her public reputation. Madmen, drunks, and bastards are of a higher spiritual caliber because they do not kid themselves about who they are or think of themselves as superior to others. "The saints are what they are," Merton writes, "not because their sanctity makes them admirable to others, but because the gift of sanctity makes it possible for them to admire everybody else."[27] Everything on earth is beautiful to them except what human beings think or do when they forget their human dignity and the higher aims of their existence.

Of course, Merton is not saying here that one should not try to succeed in completing a project or fulfilling an obligation, but rather that one should avoid objectifying oneself as a success or identifying with the results of one's actions. To postulate such a successful "self" is to become a social construct of one's own making, a myth, egocentric and inauthentic. One's value as a person has absolutely nothing to do with the job one holds, the number of books one's read, or the number of friends one has on Facebook. What defines the quality of one's life is the degree of beauty and dignity one perceives in and through others, which gives birth to humility, gratitude, and love—what Merton once referred to as "supernatural commonsense."[28]

"In speaking for monks," Merton explained, "I am really speaking for a very strange kind of person, a marginal person, because the monk in the modern world is no longer an established person with an established place in society. The marginal man accepts the basic irrelevance of the human condition, an irrelevance which is manifested above all by the fact of death. The marginal person, the monk, the displaced person, the prisoner, all these people live in the presence of death, which calls into question the meaning of life."[29] He goes on to conclude: "There is something deeper than death, and the office of the monk or the marginal person or the poet is to go beyond death even in this life, to go beyond the dichotomy of life and death and to be, therefore, a witness to life."[30]

To go beyond the dichotomy of life and death, you must step outside the phantasmagoria of history, and to do this you need to acquire some standard for the transvaluation of values. Nietzsche found such a standard in his Overman and Heidegger in the clearing of Being made possible by a return to fundamental ontology, whereas Merton found it in Christ's vision of "the Kingdom of God." All three demanded a brave recognition of the absurdity of the human condition, for only with this recognition does one enter into active contemplation, and for the Christian, scripture becomes devotional and emancipatory, and the Church the mystical alternative to an ideologically ridden and power-obsessed world.

Merton's last public talk (delivered on the day he died) was titled "Monasticism and Marxism," which made it clear that he was already thinking about liberation theology. Although Gustavo Gutierrez's A Theology of Liberation: History, Politics and Salvation (Orbis) was not published in the United States until 1971, no one knows, of course, exactly what Merton would have said about its subsequent developments had he lived. He was always unpredictable and always opening new doors, and the only sure thing we know is that his response would have surprised us.

Merton is one of those rare writers (like Emily Dickinson and Franz Kafka) who actually published more works after he died than when he was alive. Almost all his unpublished journals and many of his letters, unpublished essays, and even poems have found their way into print, fueled by the posthumous discovery of his voluminous correspondence with a variety of world-renowned thinkers from every religious discipline and intellectual persuasion, from Erich Fromm to D. T. Suzuki to Sufi mystics.

Throughout his letters and journals, Merton frequently announced his intentions to write essays that he never completed. These unrealized projects reveal the speculative side to Merton's experimental life. Ed Rice, for example, asked Merton to write a piece on Bob Dylan for his journal, Jubilee.[31] He sent Merton all his Dylan records to study, and Merton agreed to write on Dylan as "an American Villon" but never completed the assignment. But the linking of Dylan to Villon is in itself instructive, for both were stylistic innovators who celebrated the poor, the misunderstood, the outcast, and the despised. The connections Merton might have drawn between this fifteenth-century poet who bridged medieval values with the emerging Renaissance and Dylan's bridging of the values of modern and postmodern America would have been fascinating to read.

In a journal entry from May 22, 1967, Merton considered the possibility of writing an essay on monasticism and madness. He had just finished reading Michel Foucault's Madness and Civilization, and he was taken by the possibility of using Foucault's approach to explain the relationship between the rigid rules governing Trappist monasteries that evolved in the nineteenth century and the epistemic paradigm shift brought about during the Enlightenment. He hoped to show how the implicit positivism unconsciously inherited and foisted upon the religious life in the form of rules, strictures, and regulations worked against the contemplative traditions the monks had dedicated themselves to preserving. "The nineteenth century (insane) asylum," Merton wrote, "and its positivist assumptions has very exact analogies to Trappist monasteries as organized by nineteenth-century French abbots. I'd like to do a paper on it. But for whom?"[32] (Had Merton written this piece, it might have sealed his reputation as an ecclesiastical outlaw and all-around Catholic bad boy.)

At the time of his death, Merton was composing a dictionary of mystical terms that would include the key concepts of all the world's major contemplative traditions. Many of these entries can be found in the appendix to his *Asia Journal*, and they show us what a true ecumenicalism might look like: not a mere parallel list of comparisons and contrasts, but an engaged inquiry at the phenomenological level into the experiential meaning of specific contemplative concepts across traditions and cultures.

One sees a version of what Merton was attempting here in Raimon Panikkar's book *The Experience of God*[33] where Panikkar explores the similarities between the multiple gods of Hinduism and the Christian Trinity, not in order to elevate one tradition over another nor to engage in any sort of syncretism, but to honestly work out what these two traditions specifically have in common and how their phenomenological particulars differ. Panikkar explores, for example, how the Trinity functions as an antidote to Western either/or thinking. Rather than bend Western logic to fit Christ's post-dialectical witness, Christian contemplatives used the image of the Trinity to expose the reductive logic of classical metaphysics and to offer an inclusive, nondualistic vision of the whole. The Trinity is revealed as an icon of mystery rather than the literal solution to medieval logical conundrums. Panikkar sees contemplative Christianity opting out of the Hegelian "negation of the negation" for the sake of an outright mystical embrace of the all in one.

Merton also began—but never finished—a book on writing and spirituality titled *Jacob's War*. The notes for this project were not published until the Fall 2008 issue of *The Merton Seasonal*. The piece is undated but appears to have been written shortly after *The Seven Storey Mountain*, and it argues both for and against Merton's own silence. Although Merton never got beyond the first eight pages, it is a complex and paradoxical set of notes in which he remarks, "It is the illusion of a writer to live in his books. Because the writing of them satisfies him, he thinks they are himself. He places himself where there is spiritual comfort, because where a man's treasure is, there his heart is also. And as he imagines that the voice he speaks in his books is his own voice. He thinks he recognizes himself, and he is glad."[34]

But then the rest of the notes go on to insist that the better path is to give up writing altogether for a life of prayer and to forsake the beauty of language for the beauty of creation itself. For "though it is good that men should make their own poems to praise Him," Merton writes. "I now know that it is better for me to sing to Him, when words are necessary at all, in the words of His own Psalms."[35]

None of this, of course, explains Merton's subsequent production of thousands of additional poems and essays, but it does suggest why he was always looking back to the Psalms and forward to Revelation, always bringing an infinite responsibility to bear upon the more eloquent path. Admittedly, Merton never actually described his life as an experiment, but he did once describe it as "only a sketch of the specific perfection planned for its kind. Why should we ask for it to be anything more?"[36]

And so when Merton died unexpectedly in December 1968 and his unpublished letters and journals emerged over the next forty years—giving him a second incarnation, and then a third, and a fourth, changing our vision of who he was and whom he might have yet become with each new bibliographical entry—is it any wonder that we are still just coming to appreciate his place in contemporary thought and that we would do well to read him less as a spiritual guru with eternal wisdom to dispense than as an intellectual scout on the forefront of intellectual history with the unique vocation of reuniting the natural and supernatural realms—recharting the history of the Occidental soul through an archeology of his own interior life?

2

Contemplation as Critique

"If I were a doctor and I were allowed to prescribe only one remedy for all the ills of the modern world, I would prescribe silence. For even if the Word of God were proclaimed in the modern world, it would be choked to death with noise, it would not be heard because there is no silence. Therefore, create silence."[1]

—Søren Kierkegaard

"It is not as an author that I would speak to you, not as a storyteller, not as a philosopher, not as a friend only: I seek to speak to you in some way as your own self. Who can tell what this may mean? I myself do not know. But if you listen, things will be said that are perhaps not written in this book. And this will be due not to me, but to the One who lives and speaks in both of us!"[2]

—Thomas Merton

As the above Merton quote makes clear, Merton tried to erase any external ecclesiastical authority from his writing in order to reinscribe himself as a co-reader of his own texts in a space shared by his readers with the Holy Spirit. Writing was enacting the search for meaning—a search that was, by force of grace, never entirely under his control. It wasn't the consistency of his voice or the meaning of his message that mattered to him, nor was it the authority he possessed as a priest, but the meaning coming into existence in and through his shared discovery of his own true self.

Many modern writers—like D. H. Lawrence, Virginia Woolf, and Samuel Beckett, to name a few of the most obvious—had long assumed a significance to their writings that transcended their own conscious intentions. But few, except perhaps Merton's mystic contemporaries Henry Miller and Jack Kerouac, ever attributed that transcendent significance *directly to God*. Part of Merton's uniqueness as a literary innovator was that he did just that: seeing in the literary avant garde (and in his own works) an expression of an apophatic faith premised on the unknowable, unnamable transcendental presence of the divine in his own felt perceptions. This faith in a true Self deeper than his own ego allowed him to see affirmation in negation and negation in affirmation—without opting for a radical skepticism or embracing any Hegelian notions of some hidden, but knowable, dialectical totality.[3]

For Merton, Christian faith revealed another world—a reality at once here and not here. In this sense, *The Seven Storey Mountain* was both a conversion story and an exposé of the forgotten truths of Christianity still living unassimilated within the warp and woof of Catholicism as embodied in the lives of the saints.

By explaining this truth, Thomas Merton rescued the lost contemplative culture to its former exemplary status. *The Seven Storey Mountain* was, in this sense, a *bildungsroman*—articulating how Merton moved from being a modernist bohemian to a contemplative monk and from an experimental novelist to a visionary poet and essayist. His story helped to fill postwar monasteries and created a wider audience for Jean LeClerq's masterful study of monastic culture, *The Love of Learning and The Desire for God* (1957), because it narrated exactly how monastic formation, like Christian initiation itself, involves a process of spiritual transformation characterized by a dark night of the soul (or critique) in which one sees through the pretenses of one's world and oneself. This period can last quite a while until a new life and a new, selfless self emerge on the far side of culture, and with them a radical new critique of contemporary life also emerges to awaken the initiate to "the mythology that lies behind the ideology in which their society indoctrinates them."[4]

Merton's rediscovery of contemplative Christianity as a basis for both affirmation and critique was based less upon any personal leap of faith than upon his reclaiming of the world of the spirit that had been far too quickly "understood" and dismissed by modern rationalists. This spiritual world was more akin to the a priori *intentionality* of consciousness than to consciousness itself. It describes the preconditions to conditionality rather than the conditional itself. To find God amid the modern wasteland, Merton told us, we had to give up all of our ideas and images of Him—a painful process that involved questioning the commitments and beliefs residing in the deepest levels of our psyche.

But it would be necessary to endure such self-scrutiny if we were to achieve an authentic spiritual maturation on the far side of Enlightenment thought. Those who cling to reassuring but outmoded (that is to say, no longer credible) images of God have a difficult time attaining this second innocence. Merton's writings reassure us that letting go of our images of God may feel like a loss at first, but it is necessary in order to transition to a deeper faith in the God beyond God where the mystery of creation is experienced directly—not as a classical or metaphysical idea or as a medieval image per se, but as a living reality at one with the living mystery of our very own truest selves.

Such a post-Enlightenment return to spiritual sources is not new by any means. Tolstoy attempted a similar return a century earlier, as did Blake, Coleridge, and other Christian Romantics. But Merton returned to that fork in the road located just prior to Eliot's "disassociation of sensibility" and worked his way from the medieval synthesis forward. And by living a contemplative life, not just professing its virtues, and testing its intellectual viability against his own modern subjectivity, he rediscovered many religious truths and practical insights that had been driven underground or lost among the vagaries of scholastic jargon. While filling in these gaps in our historical-spiritual understanding of ourselves, it became clear to Merton—as it had to Kierkegaard—that the Enlightenment world had become antagonistic to the spirit insofar as it had come to see its conception of the world as a "thing" as having an undeniable "objective existence" to which the subjective lives of individuals had to acquiesce.

Such a conception drove subjectivity underground—into superstition, ideology, and irrational expressions of the will—and so modern thinking could not take seriously the existence of any interior life—even an interior life of "reason." If it were to open itself up to reason again as an expression of the interior life, modern society would have to suspend its belief in its own object-hood. But upon what basis and to what end could this be done?

For Merton, the answer lay in *contemplative experience*. By turning inward in silence and purifying one's intentions, one could gain (with grace and persistence) direct phenomenological access to the self—and through the self. A living culture cannot be centered upon any mere method or technique but must be historically grounded so that it can integrate the changing relationship between its objective circumstances and the source of its own inward existence.

As Paul Ricouer has pointed out, "the self is the person that we represent to ourselves as a project to be realized, one whose actions would be congruent with its existence."[5] And so, without history, there can be no self, and, therefore, no culture. Without history, we enter into Nietzsche's epoch of "the last man"—a condition in which mere survival and its whims replace freedom, autonomy, character, community, and hope.

Western civilization could be preserved from such a fate through the renewal of contemplative religion. Since the triumph of the Cartesian ego, none of the contemplative, mystical forms of religious life had been properly considered, qualified, or understood—either by the Western philosophers or by the institutional

Church. Yet many of these contemplative traditions—from Christian mysticism to Sufism and Zen Buddhism—serve the contemporary need for psychological depth (sacred connection) and cultural breadth (many-sidedness).

In each of these approaches to the divine, religious texts can perform their spiritual function only when they are read devotionally, that is to say, meditatively. And so both the higher criticism and fundamentalism—insofar as they both emphasize the cognitive content of scripture at the expense of its mystical significance—undermine its true value. As inspired, visionary poetry, scripture requires a deeper—or should I say different—way of reading, a way of reading that *changes the person in the act of interpreting the text.*

"The contemplative life," Merton explains, "isn't something objective that is 'there' and to which, after fumbling around, you finally gain access. *The contemplative life is a dimension of our subjective existence.* Discovering the contemplative life is a new self-discovery. One might say it is the flowering of a deeper identity on an entirely different plane from a mere psychological discovery, a paradoxical new identity that is found only in loss of self. To find one's self by losing one's self: that is part of "contemplation." Remember the gospel, "He who would save his life must lose it."[6]

Of course, contemplation is not the only apophatic path to such a conversion. Negative dialectics and many of its postmodern philosophical offshoots do something quite similar—deconstructing philosophical antinomies, but usually within a materialist metaphysic.[7] But for the Christian contemplative, antinomies need not be overcome, but merely accepted as complementary concepts that perpetually shift back and forth. And while contemporary philosophers use concepts taken from Hegel or Wittgenstein to unmask the illusions created by one-dimensional thinking, Merton employs the literary tropes provided by Saint John of the Cross and Thomas Aquinas to accomplish essentially the same thing. But he is more Kierkegaardian than Hegelian in his thinking—preferring to embrace ironies rather than to dialectically subsume them with more inclusive synthesis. (Perhaps this is why Merton never wrote much about process theology per se except by way of his reflections on Teilhard de Chardin, in which he applauds Teilhard's mysticism but questions his developmental optimism.[8])

Merton's originality as a thinker does not only come from his going backward to contemplation in order to recast it as a critique of contemporary culture, but also from his bringing it forward as a set of terms and ideas for liberating the individual from the ideologies of progress and "the non-thought of received ideas."[9] "Modern man," Merton tells us, "in so far as he is still Cartesian is a subject for whom his own self-awareness as a thinking, measuring and estimating self is absolutely primary. The more he is able to develop his consciousness as a subject over against objects . . . the more he tends to isolate himself to become a detached observer cut off from everything else in a kind of impenetrable alienated and transparent bubble which contains all reality in the form of purely subjective experience." Imprisoned in his or her own consciousness, the Cartesian subject is "isolated and out of touch with other such selves, in so far as they are all things rather than persons."[10] "But," as Merton explains, "when God becomes object, he sooner or later 'dies,' because God as object is ultimately unthinkable."[11] Hence the emergence of death-of-god theologies by those alienated modernists who would pull themselves up by their own Cartesian bootstraps.

In the last year of his life, Merton published an essay addressed to unbelievers that apologized for the impertinences that had been inflicted upon them in the name of religion. He felt compelled to write it because the manipulative antics of popular evangelists embarrassed him and because it seemed to him that their defenses of cheap grace constituted a falsification of religious truth.[12]

> Faith comes by hearing, says Saint Paul, but by hearing what? The cries of snake-handlers? The soothing platitudes of the religious operator? One must be able to listen to the inscrutable ground of (one's) own being, and who am I to say that (the atheists') reservations about religious commitment do not protect, in [them],

this kind of listening? [. . .] While I certainly believe that the message of the Gospel is something that we are called upon to preach, I think we will communicate it more intelligently in dialogue.[13]

We need not choose between faith and dialectics or religion or science—just as we need not choose between Christ and the world. In fact, according to Merton, we can only properly choose Christ by choosing the world as it is revealed by Him.[14] God is not an object or thing, but the ground of each of us. Atheists exist in God as much as anyone else does; they just do not call the ground of being God—if they call it anything at all.

In his essay "The Contemplative and the Atheist," Merton honored the honest confusion many atheists experience as a product of the infantile conception of God foisted upon them by know-nothing evangelists. No wonder atheists reject the naive idea of God, which Merton explains "makes Him appear to be a 'thing' in a merely finite and human sense. [But] those who are familiar with the apophatic tradition in theology and mysticism are fully aware that the temporary or permanent inability to imagine God or to 'experience' him as present, or even to find him credible, is not something discovered by modern man or confined to our own age."[15] Indeed, the life of the Christian contemplative was never a life of willful concentration upon a few clear and comforting ideas but rather an experiential inner journey in which the monk, like Christ in the desert, is tested by—among other things—a direct confrontation with the absurd.

Mysticism holds the key to discerning a human place in the ever changing gestalt of human history because it refuses to locate the true self in any narrative of private or group existence and makes perpetual self-transcendence the sine qua non of person-hood. But unlike dialectics or even process theology, mysticism abolishes the autonomous self as illusory. Only mysticism leads to a total identification with and immediate participation in the all-encompassing mystery. The mystic embraces a foundationless foundation in Christ.

This makes the apophatic Christian tradition the most obvious place to look for a solution to the problem of contemporary nihilism posed by post-liberal theology. And it enabled Merton to remain tragic and existential while Christian—not given over to either ego psychology or Lacanian deconstruction. In an essay titled "How to Read Lacan," Slavoj Zizek explained the problem of postmodern psychoanalysis as the problem of dealing with desires one knows aren't worthy of one's personhood—which is the very same problem postulates face when undergoing monastic formation (and the problem addicts face when trying to overcome their physically dependent false selves). "Protect me from what I want" means "What I want, precisely when I seem to formulate my authentic innermost longing, is already imposed on me by the patriarchal order that tells me what to desire, so the first condition of my liberation is that I break up the vicious cycle of my alienated desire and learn to formulate my desire in an autonomous way." Zizek concludes, "To accept fully this inconsistency of our desire, to accept fully that it is desire itself which sabotages its own liberation, is Lacan's bitter lesson."[16] But it is also the "good news" of Merton's eschatological faith. We do not belong to ourselves any more than our worldly desires represent our true selves.

When Merton speaks about "The Kingdom of God," he is talking about a dynamic epiphany experienced by believers of a triune Godhead in the process of realizing itself in and through relationship. It is not some other world or timeless totality. It appears and is real only insofar as it is the active process of negating our fallen history and misnamed cosmos. As the process theologians have taught us, the kingdom is always effecting an absolute transformation of the world, but, as the mystics and Merton remind us, the world itself isn't really going anywhere. It has already arrived.[17]

The god Christopher Hitchens did not find great was not a god Merton ever knew or believed in, and the "believers" Hitchens attacked as fanatics and lunatics don't seem to be believers at all but rather insecure, faithless souls who use religion to soothe their anxieties and justify their false "certainties."[18] At the close of his essay on "Godless Christianity," Merton writes:

It is a truism to say that the "god" supposedly demolished in atheistic reasoning is no God at all. This straw god is in fact a contingent, limited, fallible, powerless object, a thing among things, at the very best, a counterfeit. Such a "god" has no right whatever to exist, but the atheist has very little reason to be proud for seeing it. Yet if he persists in thinking that he has really made a discovery in proving the non-existence of this shadow, it is probably because so many religious people—indeed so many religious books—give the impression that such a shadowy or limited being is indeed the God of religious faith. It is unfortunately true that for many "believers" the God they believe in is not the living God but an apologetic hypothesis.[19]

Merton never rejected the scientific method, viable secular wisdom, or established historical knowledge. In fact, to him such things were the very fruits of faith, not its antitheses. "What [the Christian contemplative] learns," Merton explains, "is not a clearer idea of God but a deeper trust, a purer love, and a more complete abandonment to One he knows to be beyond all understanding."[20] Yet in this abandonment of any definitive conception of the divine, one gains a healthy skepticism toward all forms of abstract reductionism, sympathy for the paradoxical nature of truth and its metaphoric expression, as well as an appreciation for the analogical structure of the human mind. As such, contemplative apophatic faith is the living expression of a Christian ethnology open to universal, transpersonal experiences of our species as a whole.[21]

The apophatic Christian's view of God as conceptually unknowable conforms to the atheist's view that God is not an object of precise knowledge. But where the atheist's experience of God is purely negative, the experience of the contemplative, as Merton puts it, is "negatively positive." That is to say, the believer responds to our cognitive limitations with a reversal—turning the epistemological objection into a positive ontological condition where one understands that not everything experienced can be precisely named. The nonbeliever, unfortunately, responds to this limitation by redoubling his or her calculative ambitions.

Merton put it this way: "The inner self of the mystic, elevated and transformed in Christ, united to the Father in the Son, through the Holy Spirit, knows God not so much through the medium of an objective image, as through its own divined subjectivity. . . . Intuition reaches [God] by one final leap beyond itself, an ecstasy in which it sacrifices itself and yields itself to His transcendent presence. In this last ecstatic act of 'unknowing' the gap between our spirit as subject and God as object is finally closed, and in the embrace of mystical love we know that we and He are one."[22] As a friend of mine once put it, we know that God exists in the same way we know when we've had an orgasm: it is an intimate, personal, interior certainty.

From this perspective, the faithful are more philosophically skeptical than the skeptics in that they suspect their own intellectual powers and the efficacy of concepts per se.[23] By relinquishing any attempt to grasp God conceptually, they find themselves experiencing Him existentially or not at all. "Here," Merton notes, "we enter a realm of apparent contradiction which eludes clear explanation, so that contemplatives prefer not to talk about it at all. Indeed in the past, serious mistakes have been made and deadly confusion has arisen from inadequate attempts to explain this mystery."[24] Perhaps this is why Saint John of the Cross found the fullest expression of the divine in nothing ("Nada").

To some, it may seem that the mystics are making the skeptics' case for them, but what they are really doing is turning away from any attempt to define the undefinable. To the question "How do you know God exists?" the mystic's reply is "Who is asking?" This is not a clever evasion of the question but a shift in perspective such as we see in the discourse of Zen masters, modern poets, and psychotherapists. It is a turn that exposes the illusory position from which the interrogator's inexperienced Cartesian ego holds forth.

When Merton wrote this essay on contemplation in 1968, he felt that medieval ideas of God, which were based on medieval ideas about the cosmos, earth, physics, and the biological and psychological structure of man, were out of date, but that "the reality of experience beyond concepts, however, was not itself modified by changes of culture."[25] The Christian experience is based upon a radical recognition of the infinity (or ecstasy) of the Other—not upon a mapping of New Testament words and images against the contemporary arts and sciences.

"If the deepest ground of our being is love," Merton writes, "then in that very love itself and nowhere else will I find myself, and the world, and my brother, and Christ. It is not a question of either/or but all-in-one."[26] In this sense, the Cartesian God-object simply does not exist. What does exist is a presence revealed through the love that rises in us out to what lies beyond us. Or, as Rainer Maria Rilke once put it: "we fling our emptiness out of our arms into the spaces we breathe so that the birds might feel the expanded air with more passionate flying."[27]

This image of gratuitous self-giving—open to believer and nonbeliever alike—expresses the culture that is emerging on the far side of the modernist divide beyond both atheism and blind faith. This is the nondualist culture where contemplatives, mystics, scholars, and scientists have always labored, and now that the skeptics have vented some of their resentments and the fundamentalists have had their day in the sun, perhaps a real conversation about the eternities can begin—free from invective, straw-man arguments, and polemical grandstanding—a conversation Merton tried to initiate with the publication of his autobiography more than sixty years ago. (But I wouldn't hold my breath.)

"Faith means doubt," Merton wrote. "Faith is not the suppression of doubt. It is the overcoming of doubt, and you overcome doubt by going through it. The man of faith who has never experienced doubt is not a man of faith. Consequently, the monk is one who has to struggle in the depths of his being with the presence of doubt, and to go through what some religions call the Great Doubt, to break through beyond doubt into a servitude which is very, very deep because it is not his own personal servitude, it is the servitude of God Himself, in us."[28]

Perhaps the contemporary significance of Merton's perspective on faith and belief can best be illustrated by contrasting his thoughts on prayer to those of Jacques Derrida, whose works turned to religious themes in his later years and whose essay "Circumfession" (1991) reads like a parody of traditional religious introspection.

At a conference in Toronto in 2002 titled "Other Testaments," Derrida described his own prayer life and was asked by an attendee to whom he prayed because he was an avowed atheist. Derrida attempted to explain his prayer as an "absolutely secret" act that was, nevertheless, expressed through "common ritual and coded gestures." His prayer life, he explained, was fundamentally "childish" in that it regarded God as both a "harsh, just" father and a "forgiving" mother. But he also held to a skeptical "suspension of belief and certainty" in the realization that both the object and subject of prayer are indeterminable. Who or what "God Is" is left in suspension as well as who and what Derrida *is in himself* when he prays.

This radical opening to the Other—and to the Other in oneself—puts at risk all one is; all one has ever thought oneself to be; and all one has ever thought, read, or surmised in a radical receptivity to the as yet unconceivable. "When I pray," Derrida explains,

> I am just thinking about negative theology, about the unnamable, the possibility for me to be totally deceived by my belief and so on and so forth. It's a very skeptical prayer. I don't like this word—a very skeptical prayer. Skepticism is part of the prayer. Instead of skepticism I would call it "epoche"—the suspension of belief—the suspension of certainty (not of belief)—is part of the prayer. And then I consider that this suspension of certainty, this suspension of knowledge—the inability to answer your question "To whom it is you expect to answer this prayer?" is part of what the prayer has to be to be authentic. If I knew, if I were simply expecting an

answer, that would be the end of the prayer, that would be another way of ordering a pizza. My assumption is to give up any expectation, any certainty as to the one (more than one) to whom I address this prayer if this is still a prayer.[29]

Anyone practiced in any of the major prayer traditions might well sympathize with Derrida's remarks—and yet still find him a bit unschooled in the contemplative experience. Of course, prayer risks everything and is therefore by its very nature a relatively unsophisticated new beginning in one's relationship with oneself and with one's God. But Derrida makes no clear distinction between thought and contemplation. This leaves us (and him) with the impression that thought and prayer are essentially the same thing, and something he can do all the time. Also, there is no distinction here between active and passive contemplation and no acknowledgement of any encounter with the contemplative practices of Loyola, Eckhart, Saint John of the Cross, Rumi, or the Bal Shem Tov.

Derrida holds a very different conception of prayer from the dynamic psychological system of the contemplative designed to restructure the emotions in a quest for purity of heart. Prayer, as Derrida describes it, is at the outer limits of his intellectual life— an intellectual life without boundaries. What makes it atheistic and not a species of negative theology (although he seems clearly motivated by an inspired desire for newness of life) is that he doesn't really allow for the possibility *that what he seeks is already there, inspiring him to pray in the first place.* He does not prepare himself to receive this revelation because he does not believe there is anything like this to receive, and he cannot proceed without this belief.

Consider, by way of contrast, one of Thomas Merton's reflections on prayer:

The purest prayer is something on which it is impossible to reflect until after it is over. And when the grace has gone we no longer seek to reflect on it, because we realize that it belongs to another order of things, and that it will be in some sense debased by our reflecting on it. Such prayer desires no witness, even the witness of our own souls. It seeks to keep itself entirely hidden in God. The experience remains in our spirit like a wound, like a scar that will not heal. But we do not reflect upon it. This living wound may become a source of knowledge, if we are to instruct others in the ways of prayer; or else it may become a bar and an obstacle to knowledge, a seal of silence set upon the soul, closing the way to words and thoughts, so that we can say nothing of it to other men.[30]

The contrast with Derrida is both striking and instructive. The atheist's prayer is an attempt to think beyond one's thoughts. The monk's prayer is a way of seeing through one's thinking. The monk begins with the realization of one's nothingness and helplessness in the presence of God; the philosopher considers the boundaries of his own interior life and the limits of discourse. But, according to Merton, "[t]here is an irreducible opposition between the deep transcendent self that awakens only in contemplation, and the superficial, external self which we commonly identify with the first person singular."[31] This transcendental "self" is clearly not the same thing as the mind.

In another passage, Merton makes an even starker distinction:

The way to contemplation is an obscurity so obscure that it is no longer even dramatic. There is nothing in it that can be grasped and cherished as heroic or even unusual. And so, for a contemplative, there is supreme value in the ordinary everyday routine of work, poverty, hardship and monotony that characterize the lives of all the poor, uninteresting and forgotten people of the world. . . . The surest asceticism is the bitter insecurity and labor and nonentity of the really poor. To be utterly dependent on other people. To be ignored and despised and forgotten. To know little of respectability or comfort. To take orders and work hard for little or no money: it is a hard school, and one which most pious people do their best to avoid.[32]

Merton is not concerned here with the gap between the sign and the signified or between the symbolic and the real. He sees the gap between sign and substance, nothingness and being, as something only God can bridge. In this sense, although it sounds odd to say it, contemplation—unlike Derrida's prayer—is more modest in its aims. Rather than storming the epistemological gates via a hyper-sophisticated self-critique, the monk waits in existential poverty upon providence, and so his word is full (if inadequate), whereas the philosopher's prayer is infinitely dispersed but empty.

So, rather than representing a challenge to theism, Derrida's objectless meditation, his evocation of the unknowable, and his suspension of meaning put him in the odd position of affirming in spite of himself a faith (if we can call it that) in thought (but not in God). Indeed, his prayer is Trinitarian in its syntax: one unknown reaches toward another unknown to embrace a third unknown. What is atheistic here is not that Derrida refuses "to order the pizza," as he put it, but rather his collapsing of the religious dimension into the rational. And so, for Derrida, prayer remains an act of speculation and not an ontological leap. Such a leap, he assumes, is simply not possible within the flat metaphysics of human discourse. Or, to put it another way, Derrida is an ethical man watching himself disappear in thoughts of the absolute and calling the resulting chain of signifiers "prayer," but he doesn't conceive of this act as actually looking into the abyss of his own existence.

Thomas Merton, by contrast, turned to apophatic Christianity, the negative theology that sees God as radically Other and unnamable. This put him in a very different relationship both to the Western onto-theological tradition, in which God becomes Being, and to the natural contemplatives of the East.[33] His mystical theology became the shadow philosophy of Western onto-theology—not its ultimate expression. The contemplative does not get rid of thought; the contemplative comes to understand the role thinking plays in creating his sense of an interior life, and so once this "life" is seen through, the self who thinks it just drops away. Thinking doesn't stop, but it becomes less important than the information surging into us from the senses that are also reforming themselves around the emerging new perceptions.

This kind of revelatory experience is quite a different thing from the hyper-reflections of Derrida, whose theories re-sort themselves through rational inquiry, after which Derrida's resorted philosophical self follows suit. Contemplation, on the other hand, forms a radically different kind of intellectual activity. It is a form of subjective experience freed from concern; the liberation of the senses from the filters of fear, anticipation, and worry. Contemplatives attend to a constantly changing perceptual reality to which they must humble themselves so that they might disappear into the larger Self, which is co-terminus with the cosmos itself. Merton's famous awakening on the corner of Fourth and Walnut in Louisville is a perfect example of this: he "suddenly saw the beauty of (everyone's) hearts, the depth of their hearts where neither sin nor desire nor self-knowledge can reach, the core of their reality, the person that each one is in God's eyes."[34]

To grasp this distinction, it might be useful to compare Merton's apophatic faith to Heidegger's ontological "turn." In one of Heidegger's later essays, "The Fieldpath," he describes a nature walk in language not unlike Derrida's description of prayer. "The Simple has yet become simpler. The Ever-Same appears strange and releases, the message of the Fieldpath is now quite clear. Is the soul speaking? Is the world speaking? Is God speaking? Everything speaks the renunciation unto the Same. The renunciation does not take; the renunciation gives. It gives the inexhaustible power of the simple. The message makes us feel at home in a long Origin."[35]

This long origin is what Merton would call natural contemplation. It is the beginner's mind of Zen, and from a Trappist's point of view, the *first* step toward infused contemplation—where God takes the initiative in an act of self-giving and makes something out of nothing through love. In his essay "The Inner Experience," Merton describes active (or natural) contemplation this way:

> In active contemplation, a man becomes able to live within himself. He learns to be at home with his own thoughts. He becomes to a greater and greater degree independent of exterior supports. His mind is pacified not by passive dependence on things outside himself—diversions, entertainments, conversations, business—but by its own constructive activity. That is to say, that he derives inner satisfaction from spiritual creativeness: thinking his own thoughts, reaching his own conclusions, looking at his own life and directing it in accordance with his own inner truth, discovered in meditation and under the eyes of God. He derives strength not from what he gets out of things and people, but from giving himself to life and to others. He discovers the secret of life in the creative energy of love—not love as a sentimental or sensual indulgence, but as a profound and self-oblative expression of freedom."[36]

It is precisely in reflections such as this that we see Merton's unique contribution to contemporary thought. He doesn't teach us how to pray, but *how to think about what we do when we pray.* Much like Stanislavsky didn't teach actors *how* to act but *how to think about* what they do when they act and so transformed the everyday phenomenon of impersonation into a modern art form, Merton takes the everyday phenomenon of natural contemplation and deepens our appreciation of its powers and limitations as a form of mental activity. By so doing, he helped give birth to the centering prayer movement, leading to a renewal of interest in a whole host of contemplative practices, including *lectio divina* (sacred reading), Eucharist, chant, and sacred pilgrimage. But perhaps even more importantly, Merton reestablished a devotional approach to both the Bible and to Christ in stark contrast to the historic, critical, and literal approaches dominating contemporary theology.

Heidegger, by contrast, had no terms for the gratuitous gift of infused contemplation, whereas Derrida simply denied that it even existed. It is only in post-postmodern thought (perhaps in Zizek's attempts to articulate an atheistic Christianity, for example, where mankind kills his transcendent God only to rediscover his immanence in the Holy Spirit acting in and through concrete individuals,[37] or in Levinas's ethical leapfrog over onto-theology into ethical responsibility) that eternity begins to become intelligible again against an infinite horizon made visible through the Other. In this environment, contemplative prayer finds its way back into the conversation not as an obscure, quietist medieval practice, but as the very essence of an engaged postmodern way to the truth.

Merton ended his first attempt to write a formal mystical theology, *The Ascent to Truth*, with an extended quote from Saint John of the Cross that confirms this intuition. Saint John describes infused contemplation as an event where "the soul believes that God has moved and awakened; whereas that which has moved and awakened is in reality the soul itself."[38] This is a fascinating qualification—if not equivocation—for it says that what the mystic receives from God in his deepest, most profound experience of union is his or her own true self, redeemed and made actual. God still remains veiled and out of reach.

Moreover, it marks a key difference from the *existenz* philosophy of Heidegger and may help explain why he—like D. T. Suzuki—succumbed to the fascist temptation. The access to Being provided by natural contemplation is taken by both of these thinkers as superior to the messy interchanges of the interpersonal relationships of our finite lives because it seems to transcend the contingent and thereby achieve the universal, thus fulfilling the higher value of the exceptional individual.

But Merton made it clear that the Being of beings holds no such ontological priority even in the mysticism of Saint John of the Cross. The human condition is one in which living individuals always remain apart from the eternal truth but united to one another in their incompleteness and love. The monk serves the Lord in humble recognition of his place as the servant to his fellows—not as a higher being or Zen samurai, but as a finite creature made in His image whose "happiness cannot consist in anything that happens to [him], in any experience however sublime, if that experience be seen only in reference to [his] own perfection. God alone is [his] beatitude."[39]

So natural (or active) contemplation is not an end in itself, and our love of other beings—in their insufficiency, indeed in their sin and incapacity—is the way of Christ, and we are saved by Him insofar as he models and expresses who we really are in our deepest capacity to love. But we are not made wise by him. We are transformed, but not entirely freed from personal incapacity. And so contemplation, within the Christian context, is a school of humility, the act of letting God be God within us by letting go of our own false sense of self.

Merton explains:

> Contemplation changes us—not by inculcating in us new habits—but in keeping us open, alive, and aware. Active contemplation is nourished by meditation and reading and, as we shall see, by the sacramental and liturgical life of the Church. But before reading, meditation and worship turn into contemplation, they must merge into a unified and intuitive vision of reality. In reading, for instance, we pass from one thought to another, we follow the development of the author's ideas, and we contribute some ideas of our own if we read well. This activity is discursive. Reading becomes contemplative when, instead of reasoning we abandon the sequence of the author's thoughts in order not only to follow our own thoughts (meditation), but simply to rise above thought to penetrate into the mystery of truth experienced intuitively as present and actual.[40]

In this sense, contemplation can be seen as a form of radical phenomenology in the sense that it is a form of listening that is also an act of questioning: a listening to the process of listening and a questioning both of what one hears and of the person who listens. By watching ourselves watch ourselves, by seeing ourselves be seen, the contemplative radicalizes Husserl's phenomenology—seeking not to objectify consciousness but to bracket the act of objectification itself and then let that bracketing itself be bracketed, not in any infinite regress, but against the horizon of the real defined as the infinite love of Christ incarnate.

In 1948, Merton published a pamphlet titled "What is Contemplation?" It described contemplation as something that is taught by liturgy. Through prayer, music, scripture, reflection, and Eucharist, we are united to Christ, "who is the very embodiment of contemplation—a human nature united in one Person with the infinite Truth and Splendor of God."[41] In this work, Merton didn't try to explain contemplation as a cultural or psychological phenomenon (He did this in a later essay, "Contemplation in a World of Action," written in 1968 and published after his death in a book by the same name), but entirely as a religious phenomenon.

In the act of contemplation, Merton explained, we replace our fictive Beings with an actual Nothingness, and by so doing experience the Absolute through the dark light of self-negation. This is a difficult thing to describe, not just because Western metaphysics defines Being as what exists but because Western metaphysics defines what exists as what is present, empirically verifiable, and ready to hand.

But the "always-already" is a very different thing to the mystic than it is to the postmodern materialist, yet the basic idea of an unknowable reality behind the contexts through which everything is experienced remains much the same. It's just that the mystic sees the real as a mystery, whereas the materialist sees it as a thing. The postmodernist is caught within the prison house of language but sometimes forgets and falls into metaphysics, whereas the mystic is always already with God but sometimes forgets, and so falls into ideology and despair.

The liturgy helps the mystic remember who he is, while critical theory reminds the materialist that he isn't who he thinks he is and that the seeming unity of things is always an illusion covering up the true social hierarchy. Saints' stories are accounts of individuals refusing to fall into separateness through identification with the forgotten and despised—Saint Francis giving away first his cloak, then all of his clothes to the beggar. On the other hand, the milestones of critical theory usually point to some hitherto essentialized aspect of contingent experience that has somehow avoided rational critique—such as Jacque Derrida's deconstruction of Western metaphysics, Edward Said's reappraisal of "Orientalism," and Michel Foucault's critique of the unconscious *epistemes* governing the evolution of the social sciences.

Both the saint and the critical theorist expose false thinking in order to break the cultural trance. In the mystic's case, what is overcome is a false separation, while in the case of the critical theorist, what is overcome is a false identification. Both seem necessary—if seemingly incompatible—and by themselves incomplete. The mystic's wager is not, as it is sometimes falsely characterized, aimed at securing personal salvation, just as the critical theorists' deconstructions are not acts of intellectual anarchy. Both approaches seek to preserve the subject of contemplation. But in the mystic's case, that subject is always already transcendent to itself in and through the Other, while in the critical theorist's case, that subject is always already in conflict with the Other as mediated through various regimes of power that can only be overcome first by theory and then by action.

Seen in the light of Merton's contemplative alternative history of Western spirituality, the story of our time is not that we have moved beyond classical thought to arrive at the end of history and transcendence of the self, but rather that we have succeeded in fooling ourselves into believing that we have already done both when our true situation is really quite different. Our lives have actually become more theoretical, abstract, and morally compromised than ever before, ideological to the core and politicized beyond belief. Our egos have not dissipated into a semiotic sea of floating signifiers, but have actually hardened into tiny rocks of self-seeking—inflexible, indeed almost indestructible, absolutes unto themselves. Hardly liberal, even the most democratic of modern regimes run on a tiny ledger of received ideas, propagated and reified by a mind-numbing explosion of factoids and distractions communicated minute by minute to an overwhelmed public living largely upon dreams and illusions.

"We are living," Merton wrote, "under a tyranny of untruth which confirms itself in power and establishes a more and more total control over men in proportion as they convince themselves they are resisting error. Our submission to plausible and useful lies involves us in greater and more obvious contradictions, and to hide these from ourselves we need greater and ever less plausible lies. The basic falsehood is the lie that we are totally dedicated to the truth."[42]

Zen philosopher David Loy put it this way: "What is destructive about modernity is not rationality but rationality in service to power: instrumental reason, especially technological development and bureaucratic organization."[43] Merton found the Cistercian Order to be an antidote to this tyranny of untruth and power worship. He described the Cistercians as

> the flower of medieval monastic spirituality and mysticism, a Biblical mysticism, centered on the mystery of Christ, a traditional mysticism, centered on the ancient way handed down by Cassian, St. Gregory the Great and the Benedictines, with a generous admixture of all that is best in Augustine and some notable traces of Dionysius. A school of experience, in which personal experience is not so much analyzed and dissected, as expressed fully and poetically in the traditional images and terms of Scripture. Hence the character of Cistercian mysticism is to relive the Scriptural mysteries in one's own personal life, without undue subjectivism.[44]

The way to find the real world is not only to measure and observe what is outside us but to discover our own inner ground.

That ground, that world, where we are mysteriously present at once to ourselves and to others, is not a visible, objective, and determined structure with fixed laws and demands. It is "a living and self-creating mystery of which we ourselves are a part, to which we ourselves are our own unique doors."[45]

Human beings are not just creatures living in environments; they inhabit "worlds." That is to say, they also inhabit symbolic universes where they live inside mental constructs. To reduce the human universe to systems of tiny objects bouncing off one another is to reduce the reality of the human community to the laws governing our environment, thereby eliminating the significance of our subjective lives for the sake of an objective-explanatory-causal science that lays claim to all knowledge. But human beings are not just organisms responding to environments. They are, among other things, "that being in the world whose calling it is to find a name for Being, to give testimony to it, and to provide for it a clearing."[46]

The reason so few people understand this, or bother to try to understand it, Merton tells us, is that

> solitude appears to be nothing but a condition. Something one elects to undergo, like standing under a cold shower. Actually, solitude is a realization, an actualization, even a kind of creation, as well as a liberation of active forces within us, forces that are more than our own, and yet more ours that what appears to be "ours." As a mere condition, solitude can be passive, inert and basically unreal: a kind of permanent coma. One has to work at it to keep out of this condition. One has to work actively at solitude, not by putting fences around oneself but by destroying all the fences and throwing away all the disguises and getting down to the naked root of one's inmost desire, which is the desire of liberty-reality. To be free from the illusion that reality creates when one is out of right relation to it, and to be real in the freedom which reality gives when one is rightly related to it.[47]

The implications of this idea are just now beginning to enter our culture. One of the ironies of Merton's life was that by turning away from contemporary history, he reentered it from the backdoor. By refusing the false optimism of the postwar professional classes, he established himself as an American outsider among an international cadre of honest souls seeking a new moral ground for Western civilization—I am thinking here of such figures as George Orwell, Albert Camus, Simone Weil, Arthur Koestler, Boris Pasternak, Aldous Huxley, and Czeslaw Milosz—who bravely stood up at mid-century for the sacred value of the individual in a world torn by ideological extremes: standing up for what Merton once called the third position of integrity (not to be confused with the "third way" of the non-Allied nations). Merton's influence, like those of these other writers, was profound but largely literary, operating in that history within history experienced by individuals in the solitude of their own hearts, and so not quickly acknowledged as being any influence at all by the powers that be.

In the theory and practice of contemplation as a form of integral philosophical critique, we find Merton's intellectual contribution to our time, but in his poetry and anti-poetry, we find his direct attempt to animate a contemporary Christian culture by bringing these contemplative processes directly into dialogue with modern (and postmodern) life.

3

Poetry as Natural Theology

While it is understandable to think that we stand on blind Homer's and Shakespeare's shoulders, it is perhaps more accurate to say that we stand on a depth in them that was struck hundreds of generations before them by those Upper Paleolithic men, women, and children who made the truly incredible break through from no image of the world to an image. The cathedrals and churches in which humankind passively sits today, listening to watered-down statements based on utterances of visionaries and ecstatics, were, before being in effect turned inside out, active underground "sanctuaries" or "incubational pits."[1]

—Clayton Eshelman

"The entire body of Thomas Merton's poetry can be thought of as a poetics of disappearance: the disappearance of the old, corrupt world in favor of an apocalyptic vision of a new world; the disappearance of the false self in favor of discovering the true self in God; the disappearance of traditional religious imagery in favor of montage impressions and anti-poetry; the disappearance of a supernatural category of the sacred in favor of a direct, humanized and intimate experience of the sacred in the center of the profane. Merton was a man and poet of transformation."[2]

—Alan Altany

59

In an essay titled "Thomas Merton: The Pursuit of Marginality," Lawrence S. Cunningham once famously argued that "Thomas Merton was primarily a monk"—that was the way Merton defined himself from the moment he entered Gethsemani Abbey and that was the way he understood himself to the last days of his life . . . "as a marginal person who withdraws deliberately to the margin of society with a view to deepening fundamental human experience."[3]

The problem, of course, is that Thomas Merton also described himself primarily as "*a writer*" and said so in his introduction to *A Thomas Merton Reader*, published in 1962. "It is possible to doubt whether I have become a monk (a doubt I have to live with), but it is not possible to doubt that I am a writer, that I was born one and will most probably die as one. Disconcerting, dis-edifying as it is, this seems to be my lot and my vocation. It is what God has given me in order that I might give it back to Him."[4] By *writer*, Merton was talking about his identity as a literary intellectual, someone who found himself living inside the philosophical and cultural contradictions of his age and responding to it through poetry, essays, stories, and reflections.[5]

In our time, a literary intellectual is an increasingly endangered species—almost as remote from common experience as a monk. Visual images and video narratives, not ideas or poetic expression, dominate our culture, and technical education dominates our schools. Our society has transitioned from a war of attitudes fought via arguments to a war of attitudes fought through myths, images, and competing media campaigns. We have effortlessly entered the age of McLuhan thirty years after McLuhan's death: an age dominated not by thoughts but by myths and memes; an age in which language itself no longer serves as the guarantor of intelligibility but has itself become a part of the occupying forces of a postmodern, commercialized media culture.

In the book *Plastic Words: The Tyranny of Modern Language*, the novelist and linguist Uwe Poerksen described the way contemporary jargon subdues critical consciousness by enmeshing words within networks of meaningless tautologies. "Information is communication. Communication is exchange. Exchange is a relationship. A relationship is a process. Process means development. Development is a basic need. Basic needs are resources. Resources are a problem. Problems require service delivery. Service delivery systems are role systems. Role systems are partnership systems. Partnership systems require communications. Communication is a kind of energy exchange."[6]

In such a world, Merton's fascination with poetry might seem as antique as his love for the Catholic Church—until we realize that in poetry (as well as in Catholicism), Merton found one of the few remaining weapons through which to dismantle the cloudy jargon of our managed and mediated social environment. If language still shapes (and will always shape) consciousness, and contemporary culture is largely unconscious of the tiny ledger of ideas upon which its "plastic words" actually run, then we desperately need fresh speech to explain our lives to us. McLuhan's famous dictum "the medium is the message" has redoubled its meaning in our time, for the message of a culture without content is the unquestioned value of the media through which it is expressed and nothing more. The meaning of television *is* television; the meaning of the Internet *is* the Internet; its ubiquity is its transparency, and there is no place outside it from which to mount a convincing critique of its viciousness for those residing inside its self-justifying Ouroboros.

Merton's unique contribution as a writer derives from his refusal to accept the terms of the culture within which he lived. Coming of age in the mid-1930s, he could see that the early forms of modernism had run their course and various totalitarian political ideologies had spread their toxins around the globe. Writers like George Orwell, Ernest Hemingway, Henry Miller, and Fernando Pessoa were all seeking ways to give expression to the value of personal conscience by championing the autonomy of the individual and "the word." They had all become *existentialists* of one stripe or another, and Thomas Merton was no exception. This is particularly evident in his early novels and *Secular Journal*, in which he directly questions the direction of contemporary civilization and the ideological self-confidence of its inhabitants. "In the El Greco room, people were shocked beyond measure, violent and bitter, especially women. Their voices got shrill with fear and indignation, and one old woman cried out: "They're all dying of T.B.""[7]

But when Merton converted to Catholicism, he turned away from the high literary modernism of his literary idol James Joyce toward the visionary critical romanticism of William Blake—as did many of the Beats and the postwar avant-garde poets a good ten years later. And so, unlike his more conservative Catholic contemporaries, Merton had no problem with the complexity, irony, paradoxes, and silences of the emerging postmodern cultural innovators, and so was capable of bringing the deep ecumenicalism and spirituality of contemplative Christianity into direct dialogue with the best ideas of his time.

In both his poetry and his prose, Merton addressed the enigmas of the self as they played themselves out in his life, but he never gave in to the common desire for a dogmatic or simplistic articulation of the faith. Perhaps this is one of the reasons he remains a controversial figure within the Catholic Church. For Merton, the writer-monk, faith is worked out in fear and trembling, not certainty, in a direct—if shifting and inconclusive—personal relationship to the Absolute. Jorge Luis Borges once famously described theology as "a branch of fantastic literature"[8] And because the highest expressions of the Catholic faith are communicated through ritual, anyway, theological texts can never be any more than commentary and interpretation—not packaged systems.

The spiritual *gravitas* of the Old Testament and the Good News of the Gospels are not born of the theoretical spirit, but the spirit of irony, humor, and the unexpected as revealed in the everyday lives of the faithful. The Bible is the story of love transforming and overcoming power and of the imagination and spirit reborn on the far side of tragedy, temptation, and sin. Richard Rohr makes this point succinctly when he says that the Bible is more about learning *how* to believe than *what* to believe.[9] And by "how to believe," he is talking about the willingness and the capacity to listen and to wait upon the Lord.

This kind of faith—open and contemplative—not willful or grasping—is undermined by easy answers, categorical thinking, religious dogmas, kitsch and clichés more than it is by honest skepticism or even doubt. Merton remarked in his *Letter to an Innocent By-Stander*, "The true solutions are not those which we force upon life in accordance with our theories, but those which life itself provides for those who dispose themselves to receive truth."[10] This axiom is, for Merton, both a literary and a monastic truism: reality always outdistances thought.

During the years just before and after his conversion, Merton considered the possibility that poetry and prayer were incompatible and that at some point the poet had to give up expression altogether in order to transcend dualism and live within the divine unity. The act of naming took one away from the pure, choice-less awareness of contemplative perception. "The artist," Merton wrote, "enters into himself in order to work. But the mystic enters into himself, not in order to work, but to pass through the center of his soul and lose himself in the mystery and secrecy and infinite transcendent reality of God living and working within him."[11]

Eventually, however, he came to the conclusion that there was no inherent contradiction between poetry and prayer. Indeed, literariness was the best idiom through which religious truths could best be expressed. Poetry overcomes dualism through metaphor, image, and symbol. And, like prayer, it reframes our worldly circumstances in direct reference to the Absolute, thus allowing us to find meaning and value outside of time and the contingencies of the moment without forfeiting our existential presence. History may be written by the victors, but poetry is written by the survivors, displaced persons, nonconformists, and both guilty and innocent bystanders still alive to the moment—those beaten but not bowed individuals who may be exiled from the powers that be but who have, nonetheless, somehow managed to escape enculturation to speak and see anew.

"Love is the infinite addressing the finite," Joseph Brodsky once remarked, "but poetry is the finite addressing the infinite."[12] Another way of saying this is that poetry does not just describe history; it challenges it by encouraging the reader to enter the timeless present. It doesn't solve practical problems, but gives us access to a new reality where those problems make sense in new ways. It shows us how amazing things are but also how challenging life can be and how these two aspects of human existence are combined and inseparable. It teaches us to embrace both the brilliance and the suffering at the same time. When Blake claimed a Christian had to be a poet, he was acknowledging that a spiritual life begins with an acknowledgement of this paradox as the very source of our life in the spirit.

Natural theology is theology shorn of any explicit supernaturalism. It finds the proof for God's existence in the natural order and does not presume the authority of any sacred order before the fact. Poetry is secular scripture: secular in that it makes no appeal to any authority other than itself; scripture in that it describes a sublime order to existence beyond that of ordinary life. Poetry is, in this sense, the expression of a natural theology. At its best, it shows us human subjectivity overcoming time and space, reframing its context, and trumping the tropes defining it from without. Like scripture, it does not teach us the explicit meaning of the past, but reveals the past in the light of a timelessness transcendent to it and already present within us. It is the expression of a living eschatology: what remains of Eden in our fallen world.

This is, perhaps, what Czeslaw Milosz meant when he remarked, "Poetry and religion are synonymous, provided they are authentic, i.e. eschatological."[13] Both speak in figurative terms of ultimate matters. And it may also explain Alain Badiou's cryptic remark, "Far from being a form of knowledge, the poem is the exemplary instance of a thought obtained in the retreat and subtraction from everything that sustains the faculty of knowledge."[14] In other words, the poet returns to the thought before thinking itself became an object of thought, and poetics becomes a form of natural theology to the degree that human experience itself has become interpretive, and, by extension, inherently symbolic.

Martin Heidegger's reflections on Holderlin give a similar epistemological importance to poetic utterance—as did the Frankfurt School in its critique of instrumental reason. Heidegger argued that Holderlin's poetry transcended classical humanism because it "thought" the destiny of humanity's essence in a more original way—a way that brought forth Being through deep remembrance. This was in direct opposition to the forgetfulness of Being exemplified in the facile cosmopolitanism of Goethe and his Enlightenment precursors.[15]

Heidegger argued that if language were to remain "the house of Being," then poetry had to protect it from the soulless machinations of propagandists, marketers, public relations "experts," and bureaucrats—and those "creative" writers who mimicked their ambitions—who use it to market themselves or merely promote so-called progressive ideas. The originality of Heidegger's thesis does not, according to Gianni Vattimo, survive a political reading; it is progressive only as critique.[16] Heidegger points out the limitations inherent to classical metaphysics, but when he finds connections between "the poet" and "der Führer," it is clear he has gone too far.

There is a telling scene in Aldous Huxley's Brave New World (1932) where the slogan-writing emotional engineer Helmholtz Watson has come across some lines from Shakespeare, whose works have long since been banned and forgotten. Impressed, he tries his hand at writing a poem, but when he looks within himself, he discovers that there is nothing there: nothing to say, no interior life, nothing but the most superficial feelings. All he can manage to write is a description of his boredom at having to attend a meeting. "Yesterday's committee/ Sticks, but a broken drum/ Midnight in the City/ Flutes in a vacuum."[17] Huxley's would-be poet represents our contemporary conscience-stricken consciousness—seeking through the humblest of images an object correlative to our own existential oblivion and finding only Eliot-like reflections on triviality and waste. Today's postmodernists might not have been quite so dumbstruck, prattling along in their blogs and tweets—free from any conscience-stricken writer's block—repeating ad infinitum the new untruths of the crowd.

Unlike Huxley's Helmholtz Watson, Merton did not write poems in order to *express himself* but to drive the fallen world out of his false self and his false self out of the fallen world—to be reborn within the interpersonal totality that is God and, thereby, redeem common experience. One can see this in the very first selection in Merton's *Collected Poems*, titled "The Philosophers." The final lines read, "As I lay dreaming in the earth/ Enfolded in my future leaves/ My rest was broken by these mandrakes/ Bitterly arguing in their frozen graves."[18] Amid the noise of dead philosophical debates and confusion, the poet/monk awaits his own rebirth.

This theme of a world awaiting redemption through inward transformation is reflected in many of the poems in Merton's first two collections—*Thirty Poems* (1944) and *A Man in the Divided Sea* (1946). These include "Dirge for the Proud World," "The Blessed Virgin Mary Compared to a Window," "The Sponge Full of Vinegar," and "Ode to the Present Century." This last poem concludes with the lines, "Turn all your hunger to humility and to forgiveness/ Forsake your deserts of centrifugal desire/ Then ride in peaceful circles to the depths of life/ and hide you from your burning noon-day devil/ where clean rock-water dropwise spends, and dies in rings."[19] These lines—representative of his work from this period—call for a reseeding of everyday experience.

Like monks, these early poems attempt to close the gap between knowing and being by transforming individual events into meaningful occasions, memories, and opportunities for overcoming the materialism and the positivist mentality of our time. Just as dreams subvert the reasonableness of common sense and liberate the unconscious, Merton's early poems unite the soul with its origins, articulating a pure and radical phenomenology of innocent presence. And like prayer, they reorient perception by decentering the ego, and like scripture, they reeducate the imagination by synthesizing the concrete with the abstract into a new philosophical category: the symbolic.

In these poems, Merton tried to overcome the contradictions of history via a return to paradise—the paradise of an innocent perception of the Real. Just as therapists often carry their patients' inferior psychological function by modeling it until their client can recognize this capacity within themselves, so too do poets carry our lost awareness of our True Selves. When readers says that a poet or a poem "has changed their lives," what they really mean is that their false self—the self they have lived with habitually and unthinkingly, has been eclipsed by a larger Self awakened within them by the poet—opening up a hitherto unseen psychological space within. A Trappist poet might be expected to record contemplative experiences, and Merton's early poems certainly do just that. But there is also an exploratory side to his early poems, revealing a fascination not just with religious essences and absolutes but with the singular and the transitory nature of everyday existence as transformed by the light of the mind and, therefore, capable of revealing life as if it were being seen for the very first time. This interest in the second sight born of a second innocence eventually evolves into a fascination with the works of Chuang Tzu and the Latin American Surrealists and ultimately blossoms in Merton's later language poems, which he calls *anti-poetry*.

Merton took the term *anti-poetry* from the Chilean poet Nicanor Parra, whose work he translated. Parra used the term to describe his own brand of experimental verse, in which he used common terms, jargon, and business speak to highlight the limitations and tragicomedy of contemporary consciousness, caught as it was within a society of the spectacle where language had become less a vehicle for personal expression and more an instrument of control. Anti-poetry directly addresses the problem of how the poet was to write in an environment where the old forms and symbols had been co-opted. It rejected positive literature written to popular tastes and sought to call attention to the fashionable cynicism and kitsch taking the place of true poetry.

Anti-poetry serves as an antidote to the lazy acceptance of what currently presents itself as literature. And it does this by challenging the ideological frames of reference ruling the prevailing culture, questioning its self-image and conformist morality. A typical line of anti-poetry from Parra translated by Merton reads: "While the sad bride/ weeds her father's grave/ The imperfect lover devotes himself/ to reading a magazine."[20] The deflated voice and the explicitly quotidian imagery expose the easy conscience of the status quo and push back against kitsch by carving out an ironic but free voice of resistance. Anti-poetry is a way of saying "no" to the way things are without immediately getting caught up in a rhetorical context not of one's choosing. It has its roots in Dada but its branches in the Beats.

Before Merton moved more deeply into his (not always successful) literary experiment, there was a brief and glorious halfway point in his career as a poet represented by the remarkable collection *Emblems in a Season of Fury* (1963). In this work, the lyricism of his early contemplative works met the irreverence of anti-poetry in a wonderful, if momentary, balance. This collection contains Merton's poem "Chant to Be Used in Processions Around a Site with Furnaces" (the poem Lenny Bruce used to read in his night-club act), which contains found lines from Nazi commandants. *Emblems* also contains Merton's elegy to Ernest Hemingway, his eulogy to "The Children of Birmingham," his "Song for Nobody," and his lyrical "Hagia Sophia," which most succinctly expresses his emerging Christology. "There is in all visible things," it begins, "an invisible fecundity, a dimmed light, a meek namelessness, a hidden wholeness."[21]

The poetry that came after the publication of *Emblems* picked up on the experimental techniques first used in "Original Child Bomb," published a year before *Emblems* in 1962. In that anti-poetic work, Merton described the bombing of Hiroshima and Nagasaki with the dispassionate objectivity of a military analyst. He highlighted the Christian terms used by the military bureaucracy: the secret test at Almagordo was code named "Trinity"; Enola Gay, the plane that delivered the bomb, was named after the mother of Colonel Tibbets, the commander of the operation. The chilling juxtaposition of such violence against what remained of Christian terminology—now reduced to secret signs through which to deliver mass destruction—was both moving and frightful. The words of family and faith had become parody and their symbolic significance publicly mocked.

"In our mechanical age," Merton remarked, "all words have become alike, they've all been reduced to the level of the commercial. To say 'God is love' is like saying 'Eat Wheaties.' "[22] So, in *Cables to the Ace* (1968), Merton went back to the anti-poetry of "Original Child Bomb" and "Chant to Be Used in Processions Around a Site with Furnaces" to focus almost entirely on the abuse of language.

In "Cables to the Ace," the syntax is interrupted—delayed—which affects the reader a lot like the cutups of William Burroughs: frustrating simple logic and throwing attention toward the larger interpretive contexts that serve as the vehicles for ideology. In fact, "Cables" has the spirit and energy of the best Beat poetry—adopting an intimacy and energy not seen in Merton's more crafted poems.

These cables serve as direct links to the poet's power source (the Ace = Christ) and make the readers feel as if they are discovering things on their own, not just reading reflections in verse. On a literal level, these poems are often hard to fathom, but their emotional impact is as powerful as a news flash. "Today's top announcement is a frozen society/ Publicizing a new sherbet of matrimonial mid ways/ And free family lore all over the front pages/ You will meet frank old middle age/ With bold acquaintance soon forgotten/ In the time sequence/ of an unbearable cycle."[23]

This odd Joycean-cum-William Burroughs way of writing mocks the incomprehensible hype of the commercial press that pretends to express common sense and exposes the silly cleverness of business jargon that we now decipher so effortlessly, to our moral and intellectual peril. The anti-poem's juxtapositions—a form of early hip-hop—reveal this scandal and invite us to see through it by tearing mass-mediated language away from its ideological and grammatical contexts so that they stand revealed not so much as clichés but as clever linguistic tricks that handcuff the imagination.

Merton explains the work this way: "Edifying cables can be made musical if played and sung to full-armed societies doomed to an electric war. A heavy imperturbable beat. No indication where to stop. No messages to decode. Cables are never causes. Noises are never values. With the unending vroom vroom vroom of the guitars we will all learn a new kind of obstinacy, together with the massive lessons of irony and refusal. We assist once again in the marriage of heaven and hell."[24]

Cables to the Ace may be Merton's most successful anti-poetic work, deeply affecting in its sad portrayal of language betrayed and the individuality denied. But *The Geography of Longriare*, Merton's last long poem, although less successful, unfinished, and hopelessly hermetic, was more ambitious in its aims—attempting to expose all the defensive lies, exaggerations, and clever self-justifications of our violence-plagued modern world. *The Geography of Longriaire* expresses a vision of history as an unfolding ironic, paradoxical, tragicomic poem interpenetrating time zones, geographies, and cultures.

In his author's note, Merton warns,

> This is a purely tentative first draft of a larger work in progress, in which there are, necessarily many gaps. This is only a beginning of patterns, the first opening up of the dream. A poet spends his life in repeated projects, over and over again, attempting to build or to dream the world in which he lives. But more and more he realizes that this world is at once his and everybody's. It cannot be purely private, any more than it can be purely public. It cannot be fully communicated. It grows out of a common participation which is—nevertheless—recorded in authentically personal images. In this wide-angle mosaic of poems and dreams I have without scruple mixed up my own experience with what is almost everybody else's. Thus "Cargo" and "Ghost Dance," for instance, cease to be bizarre anomalies and are experienced as yours and mine as well as theirs. . . . Much also has been found in the common areas of nightmare to which we are all vulnerable (advertising, news, etc.).[25]

Hence, the poem is a kind of post-Hegelian raga that reveals the corruption of Western values in its attempts to debunk degraded world mythologies. Merton concludes: "These poems incidentally are never explicitly theological or even metaphysical. The tactic is on the whole that of an urbane structuralism."[26] As Merton was a reader of Michel Foucault, Levi-Strauss, and Roland Barthes before English translations existed, this reference to structuralism is very significant and indicates Merton's precocious grasp of constructivist thought, just then emerging in France. In one recording of *The Geography of Longriare*, one can actually hear Merton laughing as he reads, as if he too is caught off guard by the discoveries he himself had made through his experiment in language.

This poem helps us to see that our identities are dissipated among a lot of things that do not have the value we imagine, so we get lost in them. We know this intuitively, even obscurely, by the way things sometimes disappoint and even sicken us once we get what we think we desire. Yet we still ruin our lives trying to fulfill ourselves with things that are incapable of satisfying us. "When we really come to die, at last," Merton remarks, "we suddenly know how much we have squandered and thrown away, and we see that we are truly annihilated by our own sick desires: we were nothing, but everything God gave us we have also reduced to nothing, and now we are pure death."[27] This is, more or less, the theme of *The Geography of Longriare*. Our postmodern subjectivity is moving further and further away from its origins, whereas all we really seek is a return to sources, those deep wells of the contemplative imagination, a return blocked by our own glib superficiality redoubled by mass-mediated entertainments and distractions.

In both *Cables to the Ace* and *The Geography of Longriare*, Merton synthesizes the prosaic with the tragic—unifying the pain and the absurdity of contemporary life. He also amplifies these opposing emotions—stressing the difference between our intelligence and the moral horror so that the reader registers their incompatibility and their interconnectivity. This double effect (or cognitive dissonance) creates the irresolvable tensions that are the essence of anti-poetry—the disturbing, if inevitable, genre for a postmodern contemplative. Consider these lines: "The sacred books are confiscated by police to keep eyes under sightless dome/ Study famous text in court/ Sacred words kept shut in horny room/

They keep my novels in a box of candy/ Shine continental glad warm being in Law." The reader is affected here by the cheerful tone of the rhetoric, which clashes with the narrator's painful experiences and observations and leads to a mixed response of contempt for the manipulations displayed, concern for a world in which such bland greed is rampant, and delight that someone has at last had the capacity to express it.

Merton's journey in and through anti-poetry, beginning with *Original Child Bomb*, reflects his own journey in and through writing. Once a calling and a destination, literature had become for him a medium and a refuge until its limitations came to mirror his own. And then it became, even more poignantly, a spiritual practice and discipline akin to prayer itself—a form of active contemplation that sought to link the secular and sacred worlds. Its powers illuminated its weaknesses, and its weakness illuminated its power in a classic expression of the apophatic insight that what most needs to be said is often the unnamable and what can be said is often the unnecessary.

In this sense, modern poetry became psalm-like for Merton, a gateway to the numinous, to our innate, unitive, visionary selves, a conduit of the collective consciousness and collective vision—a multicultural form of natural theology. In its therapeutic dimension, it served as an antidote to a runaway technological rationalism and the idolatry of the pragmatic self, dethroning our worldly ambitions by showing us sides to life we have not yet been able to integrate into awareness—helping us to see the world as it is, yet also transcend it. A modern anti-poem is not, strictly speaking, interpreted, but rather gotten inside of and psychologically appropriated. It is largely a transcription of consciousness, a bridge between subjectivities thrown across archetypal space, a pictogram of an evolving person in the process of conceiving itself to itself from within the cultural noise.

This kind of poetry doesn't teach lessons so much as extend awareness. It is research into the actual: the actual defined—not as an objective, neutral, outer world, but as that point at which external reality clashes with our inner ground. This is why a good poem always gives us energy. Even in the pathological shrieks of mad poets, the numinous is trying to reach us, to grow alive within in us. Modern poetry, like prayer and liturgy, moves us beyond the reaches of our intelligence, so it is often felt before it is understood. Perhaps this is why the literary theorist Northrop Frye once described literature as "the imaginal in script."[28]

Frye's use of the term "imaginal" here refers to Henry Corbin's use of the term. A Sufi scholar and mystic, Corbin noted that in Persian literature there is believed to be a realm of reality that exists above our ordinary three-dimensional consciousness and a place in our imaginations where images are real in the sense that they are not being "made up" by someone, but images that have an existence of their own. This is roughly the same distinction Coleridge made in his distinction between the "fancy" and the "primary imagination." One is associative and willfully made up; the other is linked to archetypal reality and presents itself to us intact as a direct representation of a collective consciousness that is as real as anything we see or feel or know intellectually. It comes to us—like dreams—from another realm.

To say that literature is the script of the imaginal is to say that it documents the psychology of the image—it is reception, creation, and interpretation. And insofar as the soul is made of images, literature is the most direct form of spiritual transcription. This is, no doubt, why scripture itself is composed in a literary form and why the Bible remains difficult for those grounded in a rationalist perspective to understand: it only makes sense when read devotionally, that is to say, in full engagement with its images—not in order to translate them into some more systematic intellectual structure, but to let them revivify our lives by immersing us in their alternative mythos.

One is tempted here to try to draw an analogy between Merton's poetics and Han Urs von Balthasar's theological aesthetics, but it remains a bit of a reach. Although Balthasar understood that in our modern era theological understanding was primarily a matter of the feeling life and that rational metaphysics untethered from the experience of faith could never broach the gap between skepticism and revelation, he wasn't a working novelist or poet like Merton, so his understanding of literature was primarily as a reader and a critic, a student of the finished product, not as an experimental, creative artist who viewed the "imaginal" as part of a larger, interior process of self-discovery. Merton understood literature in terms of the same apophatic, negative capability with which he understood God—and this shaped his approach to theology as a perpetual work in progress.

For Merton, the master metaphor for our age is not Hellenization, but Exile. We are not in the early years of a New Global Civilization, but in the last stages of an intellectual and spiritual occupation: the twilight of the Enlightenment. As a result, our goals and ambitions have to be rethought. No longer interested in worldly Kingdoms, our chastised worldly prophets now challenge the very notion of secular power, questioning contemporary institutions and exposing the idols of technological efficiency and bureaucratic standardization. Poets create a nexus of issues, idioms, and concerns through which we can begin to rethink our relationship to Being so that we might make the transition to a new phase of civilization without losing touch with what we have traditionally held most dear: love, liberty, compassion, and freedom of conscience.

Those looking in the rearview mirror of twentieth-century history miss the real story of our time. It is not the story of dialectical thought overcoming itself, nor is it the drama of clashing civilizations. It is, rather, *the unfolding epic of aggrieved pagans rediscovering the Absolute—ourselves included!* We postmoderns are just now relearning what the Romantics knew so well: that we are all spiritual exiles to a greater or lesser extent who have lived far too long in the land of the Philistines, torn away from our traditions and forced to worship alien electronic Gods and Goddesses. To free ourselves from these simulacra of the divine, we need a counter-environment (if only in our heads) that will allow us to detach from the world screen long enough to rename ourselves.

The deepest threat to the West does not come from the outside but from the *non-events* that make it so hard for us to see ourselves as *souls under siege.* Coleman Barks, poet, translator, and interpreter of the Sufis, once asked his spiritual teacher Osho (aka Bhagwan Shree Rajneesh) what the emotional exaltation ("burning") he felt from reading and translating Rumi had to do with his own possible enlightenment. Osho told him he had asked "a dangerous question" because this burning had nothing to do with enlightenment; it was only a form of ecstatic self-hypnosis.[29] This diagnosis holds for all of us living in societies of the spectacle where the mesmerizing presence of charismatic politicians, actors, and celebrities (aided by the technologies of mass media) blurs the distinction between the ontological vibrancy of unfiltered perceptions and the hypermediated world of public relations and professional image making.

This would not be much of a problem if our entertainment industry, politics, and celebrity culture did not trade so constantly on this confusion of realms, but the mass media not only manufactures political consent; it also manufactures self-doubt, which it then turns around and "cures" by encouraging us to buy things and identify with various celebrities skilled at fostering adoration for themselves and their ill-gotten gains. Perhaps this is why the American myth of the self-made man has morphed into the myth of the self-created celebrity of modest talents making it big financially through savvy media manipulations and clever self-promotion—think of Sarah Palin, Johnny Knoxville, Gene Simmons, Donald Trump, Rush Limbaugh, and Tony Robbins, just to mention a few.

Monks have historically stood for the very opposite of celebrities. They are self-aware outsiders living in anonymity, off the grid, beyond the compulsions of wealth and illusion, sustaining their conscience in an increasingly conscienceless age, directly challenging by their very lives the common slander against solitude and intellectual independence. Indeed, the stereotype of the monk as a timid recluse hiding from life, no doubt a product of Reformation caricatures, helped to frame Thomas Merton's books as he challenged the stereotype.

The poets who inspired and interested Thomas Merton were countercultural figures within the counterculture of modernism itself. Dissidents within a dissident movement, they demonstrate for us the continuing relevance of our spiritual aspirations. And though many of them broached the antinomian temptation in that they saw the contemporary West as fallen to one degree or another, few defined themselves in direct opposition to it but rather as reformers from within. They came down from their mountaintops—challenging the complacency of the world and questioning our materialism, our militarism, and our Machiavellian assumptions. The foundationless foundation of their poetic faith freed them from the search for absolutes and, like Merton's two-thousand-year-old contemplative tradition, offered us an alternative to both dialectical and analytical philosophy free from the European Enlightenment's narrow focus upon epistemological certainty. It is grounded in an existential critique born of critical philosophical anthropology, expressing a preferential option for the poor, in the figurative language of the sublime. It also reimagines the biblical epic in global, transcultural, macro-historical terms that defend the inner life from collective violence, diagnose the origins of the irrational, expose the limitations inherent to mass communication, reestablish prayer as a way of knowing and art as visionary probe, and reanimate the tradition of biblical prophecy, the inventiveness of literature, and the moral responsibility of criticism.

It synthesizes Romanticism and Realism within a new, integral, holistic worldview that allows us to rethink theology—not as a system of ideas but as a way of living and a discourse on how one participates directly in the intelligence of God, and so overcomes the essentialist–existential divide, the shame–guilt dichotomy, and the master–slave dialectic.

It exposes the aridity of the scapegoat archetype behind all world mythologies and regimes built upon power and violence; it empowers ordinary people with a way of fighting for justice without becoming like the enemies they resist; it reveals history as a phantasmagoria of the human imagination so as to liberate the individual from the burdens of one-dimensional, conventional identity; and it makes it possible for everyone to experience salvation and Enlightenment by separating these experiences from any metaphysical system per se. The parallels here between the postmodern literary project and the aims of contemporary theology are startling. Once freed from their fruitless disputes with science and the hopeless Enlightenment search for certainty, both disciplines can now speak their visionary minds and embark upon a quest—not only to provide valid alternatives to contemporary ideologies but also to reveal the double-edged effects that Hegelian and Kantian philosophy have had upon our intellectual lives, namely, the emphasis upon epistemology, the separation of truth from values, the search for a totalizing conception of reality, and the rigorous critique of the role of reason within human experience.

If deconstruction undercut materialist metaphysics by exposing it as illusory, and positive science sought to fulfill the goals of materialist metaphysics without fully examining its ground, then it was left to the poets and contemplatives of the orthodox avantgarde to offer a description of our postmodern times in the light of common human hopes and aspirations. Through his poetry and anti-poetry, Merton dared to posit a creative challenge to the misrepresentations of our epoch.

4

A Monasticism of the Last Man

"Whoever talks about God in Jesus' sense will always take into account the way one's own pre-formulated certainties are wounded by the misfortunes of others."[1]

—Johann Baptist Metz

"I asked Mother Teresa, 'Tell me something, what really gives you ecstasy in life?' And she said, 'What gives me ecstasy, Tony, is to see a person die with a smile on their face.' And I thought, 'whoa, you know, not number one on my list."[2]

—Tony Robbins (Motivational Speaker and Success Guru)

In an age when monks and nuns appear on radio and television shows—even run their own broadcasting networks—it is, perhaps, not so surprising to find that prayer, like everything else, is becoming a commodity. And in this commercialization of contemplation, we are witnessing the emergence of "a monasticism of the last man" characterized by silence without obscurity, solitude without anonymity, and service without sacrifice—a *faux* monasticism fueled by inspirational speakers, life coaches, and corporate retreat centers.

CEOs take Buddhist meditation classes on their lunch breaks and move investment capital around in the afternoon free from any concerns as to the contradictions in their actions, and no one calls them on this as Merton once called out his complacent peers in such brilliant works as *The Inner Experience, Conjectures of a Guilty Bystander*, and *Disputed Question*. In fact, Merton's willingness to criticize the prevailing ideology of his time (i.e., the logic by which commonplace injustices like segregation and aggressive war were rendered invisible) may account for both the continuing relevance of his work as well as his controversial status within the Church, for Merton never ignored the socioeconomic context within which he lived but questioned its unstated assumptions in nearly everything he wrote.

Merton's fame as a best-selling writer had given him a taste of the dangers and temptations of celebrity, so he made it a point never to articulate any specific meditation techniques or prayer regimes lest they spawn cults of one form or another. Moreover, he publicly denounced *Mertonism* as an absurd and heretical formulation and fought against the reduction of Christianity to personal piety. In his work *The Inner Experience: Notes on Contemplation*, written mostly in 1959 and revised throughout the early 1960s, Merton strongly denounced what he called "illuminism"—the embracing of a private, religious awakening as an end in itself free from any larger responsibilities to others. This work was not published in its entirety until thirty-six years after his death in 2004. In retrospect, it serves as the missing link between the early Merton (contemplative Catholic and author of devotionals) and the later Merton (Catholic student of Eastern thought, contemplative social critic, and admirer of the social activists Martin Luther King Jr., the Berrigan Brothers, and Dorothy Day).

The Inner Experience begins with an instructive disclaimer that it will not be *inspirational*, nor will it be *proscriptive*. Merton makes it clear that he is *not* writing a "how-to" book. Indeed, he denounces "how-to" books in general as based on a fundamental misunderstanding as to the true nature of spirituality and of his authority as a writer.

Sad is the case of that exterior life that imagines himself contemplative, and seeks to achieve contemplation as the fruit of planned effort and of spiritual ambition. He will assume varied attitudes, meditate on the inner significance of his own postures, and try to formulate for himself a contemplative identity: and all the while there is nobody there. There is only an illusory, fictional "I" which seeks itself, struggles to create itself out of nothing, maintained in being by its own compulsion and the prisoner of his own personal illusion. The call to contemplation is not, and cannot, be addressed to such an "I."[3]

So to whom is the book addressed, and how does Merton intend to communicate contemplative wisdom if the false self is the only "self" listening? "The inner self," he explains,

is not a part of our being, like a motor in a car. It is our entire substantial reality itself on its highest, most personal and most existential level. It is like life, and it is life: it is our spiritual life when it is most alive. It is the life by which everything else in us lives and moves. It is in and through and beyond everything that we are. *If it is awakened, it communicates a new intelligence in which it lives, so that it becomes a living awareness of itself: and this awareness is not something that we ourselves have, as something that we are.* It is a new and indefinable quality of our living being.[4] (Author's italics.)

This is a key point that Merton makes again and again in his writings: the spiritual life is not something the private egocentric individual *does* or *has*. It is an ever-present reality to which one awakens: the reality of one's unity with God and his people. A student of the great French historian Jules Michelet once remarked that he remembered almost nothing from any of Michelet's lectures, but when he listened to him speak, a hidden part of himself somehow came into existence. This student was acknowledging the power of his teacher to invoke in him a contemplative state of awareness. This state of awareness is not, strictly speaking, calming or even pleasant so much as it is liberating and empowering. One feels enlarged and more deeply responsible for everyone else more than one feels comforted. "Inner peace," Merton reminds us, "does not suffice to bring us in contact with our deepest liberty."[5] Our deepest liberty comes with the realization of the nothingness of the exterior self and the subsequent emergence of the Real Self, the inner "I," the soul, that part of ourselves that is in God and in others about which we ourselves may as yet know very little. It is the Holy Spirit as it dwells within us.

In a chapter from *The Inner Experience* titled "Some Problems," Merton coins the term "illuminism" to describe the tendency of some religious seekers to value their own subjective experience over the truth. Illuminism sets happiness as an end in itself and so turns contemplation into a tool of the illusory or false self. Illuminism turns prayer into a technique for gaining personal desires and binds the false self to its projected aspirations, thereby imprisoning the individual more deeply within his or her fallen nature. Illuminism is the antithesis of the spiritual life—a kind of anti-spirituality.

"To live for spiritual experience," Merton explains, "is slavery and makes the contemplative life just as secular as the service of any other "thing.""[6] Here, Merton is extending Bonhoeffer's notion of "Cheap Grace" into an entire psychology of religious mystification. "What matters," Merton tells us, "is *not what we feel, but what really takes place beyond the level of feeling or experience*. In genuine contemplation, what takes place is a contact between the inmost reality of the created person and the infinite reality of God.[7] . . . "To serve Him *who is no object* is freedom."[8] (Author's italics.)

To argue over what exactly *is* "beyond feeling and experience" (God, Being, Oneness, or Awareness) may not seem particularly germane for the religious seeker who values experience over labels, yet Merton thinks it is important to make a distinction between contemplation *as an end in itself* and contemplation that *operates in the service of something greater than one's own interior life.* This insistence on a fundamental separation between God and the self makes it clear that Merton was not a closet Vedantist, as some have claimed.[9] At this level of nondual experience, such distinctions may seem too subtle to matter, but Merton is adamant that to the degree illuminism is focused upon a merely personal appropriation of the experience of grace, it blocks one's access to an authentic Christian life in and through love for others.

This is why even prayer, contemplation, or meditation—once they become merely therapeutic techniques—can end up reinforcing the false self's desires—however refined or moral those desires might be, and this, in turn, can foster cults and movements, guru worship, anti-intellectualism, political quietism, fanaticism, and "happiness" training programs for the military. (Think of Martin E. P. Seligman's positive psychology movement, in which happiness is explicitly declared to be the goal of life, and whose clients include a universal cadre of pragmatic "illuminists" from corporate "raiders" to military snipers).

Again, "illuminism" values the experience of illumination more than it values what that experience illuminates, and thus happiness becomes an end in itself, has many faces, and can serve a variety of purposes. For Merton, however, monastic contemplation is illuminated but not self-directed. No one can enter into it without first embracing the possibility of personal transformation, self-forgetfulness, and social obscurity. "Anyone who thinks he or she knows what it (contemplation) is beforehand prevents himself from finding the true nature of contemplation, since he is not able to 'change his mind' and accept something completely new."[10] Contemplation is not something one does so much as it is a by-product that emerges from making space within for the Holy Spirit. One's prayer life discloses the deeper significance of one's goals; it does not just further them. It is a counter-practice to practical reason that aids thinking by suspending the *cogito* within an interior space larger than reason itself.

When pressed to describe how he prayed, Merton would defer to his own mentors within the Catholic tradition: Cassian, Saint

Teresa of Avila, Saint John of the Cross, and other visionary poets and mystics whose words he found both inspiring yet irreducible to the "psychobabble" of popular "metaphysicians." Merton never claimed to possess any extraordinary insights beyond those discernible through ordinary philosophical dialectics and the common, everyday religious channels of grace, prayer, hope, faith, charity, liturgy, and the sacraments. Yet he insisted that what he learned from these things directly challenged conventional wisdom both within and without the Church.

Richard Rohr recently wrote a book that provided links between the traditional teachings of the Christian mystics and those of contemporary spiritual writers such as Eckhart Tolle, Byron Katie, and Ken Wilber.[11] He calls this link "The Lost Tradition" and explains its primary assumption this way: "The ego self is the unobserved self. If you do not find an objective standing point from which to look back at yourself, you will almost always be egocentric—identified with yourself instead of in relationship to yourself. Ego is not bad; it is just what takes over when you do not see truthfully and completely. . . . The Christian name for this stable witness is the Holy Spirit."[12]

Rohr goes on to describe some specific techniques for achieving such awareness but is quick to point out that "God gives us real practices every day in our lives, such as irritable people, long stop lights, and our own inconsistences."[13] The simple tasks of everyday honesty can transform our relationships to language and to ourselves if we let them. Faith is precisely this opening up to the Other, to an awareness of a reality beyond our fears and desires, a letting go so that something greater than our own minds can hold on to us. It is a light in the darkness, a way of beginning again by trusting in something greater than our own personal concerns and ideas. He concludes: "[I]mmediate, unmediated contact with the moment is the clearest path to divine union; naked, undefended, and non-dual presence has the best chance of encountering Real Presence."[14] This unmediated contact with the moment is not a bad description of the basic act of contemplation.

The problem, Rohr argues, is that the faith of the mystics somehow got separated from Catholic Church doctrine, and this created "a two-tiered system that allowed mainline institutions to resist non-dual thought."[15] Both tiers (the spiritual lives lived by the religious within various monastic and mystical orders and the Diocesan Church hierarchy) serve important functions, and one of Merton's unique contributions to Catholicism was to build a bridge between them. Merton's book *The New Man* (1961) may be his most ambitious effort in this regard. Consider, for example, this telling observation of what unified both of these perspectives:

> To awaken to the realities of the spirit and to discover the image of God within us is therefore something quite different from a Platonic awakening to the spirituality of our formal essence as distinguished from the concrete materiality that weighs us down. The Christian view does not make an abstract division between matter and spirit. It plunges into the existential depths of the concrete union of body and spirit which makes up the human person, and by clearing the spiritual temple of all those ways of thinking which obstruct our inward vision, opens the way to an existential communion at the same time with ourselves and with God in the actual, subsisting spiritual reality of our own inviolable being.[16]

In other words, nonduality, within the Christian tradition, works both ways: matter is spirit, but spirit is also matter. Love transcends both material *and* spiritual reductions.

Many New Age writers also believe in a true Self that is transcendent to the ego. This true Self stands outside ideology, although our understanding of its nature can be manipulated and redefined by various ideologues. This ideological vulnerability of even our highest, most profound conceptions is a point often lost on New Age "metaphysicians," whose politics tend to be either unconscious or naive. Too often, these gurus do not take the time to contextualize the meaning of their transcendent experiences within the particular social context, and so their teachings lack historical consciousness and thereby remain inherently reactionary.

Merton, by contrast, explicitly contextualized religious truth and contemplative awareness—not within epistemological taxonomies or metaphysical rubrics, but with reference to the prevailing ideological mystifications and social practices of history. Hence, his controversial and groundbreaking *Letters to a White Liberal* and *Cold War Letters* exposed the social damage generated by political self-deception and delusion. In other words, Merton's power as a contemplative critic did not derive simply from his perception of a nondualistic reality that transcended the binary dilemmas of Karma and dialectics, but from his literary capacity to stay true to its wisdom while still critically analyzing society as a whole. As a result, Merton was far less scholastic than Ken Wilber and even less evangelical than Marianne Williamson or Deepak Chopra. He made no explicit attempts to recruit converts—although his writings had the effect of doing just that. Nor did he publicly proselytize his monasticism through advertising or public relations campaigns. Rather, he wrote serious books examining the meaning and significance of his own religious tradition to his time and used his unique spiritual experiences to raise previously unasked questions about current social values and open up conversations with critics, skeptics, and believers alike—surveying the uncharted seas of our as-yet unwritten meta-history in the spirit of his Christian intellectual contemporaries Marshall McLuhan, Ivan Illich, and Dietrich Bonhoeffer.

All three of these figures, as well as Merton, believed that Christianity offered an advanced perspective on contemporary existence. It just needed to be refigured to free itself from contemporary ideological mystifications. In a passage from "Day of a Stranger," Merton described the social function of his hermetic way of life this way: "*Up here in the woods is seen the New Testament: that is to say, the wind comes through the trees and you breathe it. Is it supposed to be clear? I am not inviting anyone to try it. Or suggesting that one day the message will come saying NOW. That is none of my business.*"[17]

By removing himself from society and entering a community outside the mass media society of the spectacle—an alternative community where death and the absurd were a part of everyday life, continually remembered and perpetually acknowledged—Merton became a twentieth-century version of Kierkegaard's Knight of Faith—steeped in the stark presence of the Absolute, freed from any desire to save others or win favor, a stranger, mysterious even to himself. He then moved into a hermitage for greater solitude, where his life became more intellectually intense, but less obsessed; more purposeful, but less driven; increasingly focused upon God, not personal recognition.

He continued to write out of an inner compulsion to grasp the full meaning of his own inner experience of grace, and so each moment in his monk's life, if well lived—that is to say, if encountered honestly, without neurotic dodges or ideological explanations—had the capacity to change him. And so prayer became, for Merton, the defining metaphor for how all things are to be experienced—not through the ego or will or the stories of the illusory self, but through the Holy Spirit.

In his last public address, "Marxism and Monastic Perspectives" (1968), delivered in Bangkok on the day he died, Merton described a monk as "essentially someone who takes up a critical attitude toward the world and its structures."[18] There "has to be a dialectic between world refusal and world acceptance."[19] Unfortunately, Merton observed, far too many monks have acquiesced to "the legal surrender of things that perhaps they should not have surrendered."[20]

He didn't explicitly say what these "surrendered things" might be, but he did name them later in the essays published after his death, which he was writing at the time of this address. He was talking here about the surrender of one's social conscience to the systemic injustices of a global economic order predicated on the exploitation of the weak. He was talking about surrendering one's energies to the materialist demands of practical life and, thereby, forfeiting one's call to sainthood in the name of fiduciary responsibilities or custodial obligations. (In the back of his mind, he might even have been thinking about the surrender of silent manual farming at Gethsemani for the more efficient, noisy new tractors and the marketing of cheese.)

In calling for a new dialectic between world renunciation and world acceptance, Merton was calling for something that had never been fully articulated before: a socially engaged hermeticism. And perhaps he was also anticipating the coming generation of liberation and creation theologians who would struggle with reconciling the inner and outer responsibilities of faith. Had Merton lived longer, he would no doubt have had to face some unexpected economic and political developments not considered by his Frankfurt School mentors, Herbert Marcuse and Eric Fromm.

When he died, Merton's view of the world was very similar to the one Mr. Jensen—the corporate executive in Paddy Chayefsky's prophetic screenplay *Network* (1976)—delivered by the populist TV show host Howard Beale.

There are no nations. There are no peoples. There are no Russians. There are no Arabs. There are no Third Worlds. There is no West. There is only one holistic system of systems. One vast and immanent, interwoven, interacting, multivariate, multinational dominion of dollars.

Petrol dollars, electro dollars, multi dollars. Reich marks, rins, rubles, pounds and shekels. It is the international system of currency which determines the totality of life on this planet. That is the natural order of things today. That is the atomic . . . and subatomic and galactic structure of things today.

And you have meddled with the primal forces of nature. And you will atone.

Am I getting through to you, Mr. Beale? You get up on your little 12-inch screen . . . and howl about America and democracy. There is no America.

There is no democracy. There is only IBM and ITT and AT&T . . . and DuPont, Dow, Union Carbide and Exxon. Those are the nations of the world today What do you think the Russians talk about in their councils of state? Karl Marx? They get out linear programming charts, statistical decision theories, and compute price-cost probabilities of their transactions and investments like us. We no longer live in a world of nations and ideologies, Mr. Beale. The world is a college of corporations . . . inexorably determined by the immutable bylaws of business.

The world is a business, Mr. Beale. It has been since man crawled out of the slime. And our children will live, Mr. Beale, to see that . . . perfect world . . . in which there's no war or famine, oppression or brutality. One vast and ecumenical holding company, for whom all men will work to serve a common profit. In which all men will hold a share of stock, all necessities provided, all anxieties tranquilized, all boredom amused. And I have chosen you, Mr. Beale, to preach this evangel.[21]

And yet in his last speech, Merton told his mostly Catholic audience that monks must always play a counter-hegemonic role to the values of the world—reeducating individuals to see through the illusory social spectacle by embracing marginality and encouraging them to recalibrate their lives with reference to their true selves in God as opposed to their false selves as self-interested individual profit maximizers. As Merton's friend and correspondent Czeslaw Milosz put it in his last book of poems, "The sublime doesn't have fame or money on its side. But it persists, it renews itself in every generation. Because in thought some greatness of soul keeps being born."[25] Christian contemplatives must not adapt themselves to what the future holds because God's Kingdom is not a part of society, but a sublime counterpoint to it.

5

Merton's Most Dangerous Idea

"The impossible is not there in order to make thought capitulate, but in order to allow it to announce itself according to a measure other than that of power."

—Maurice Blanchot[1]

"Ethics is not—as we normally think of it—primarily a moralistic exercise of distinguishing right from wrong; it is more fundamentally an exercise in self-transformation during which we move from lower to higher levels of being."[2]

—Huston Smith

Merton's most dangerous idea was his belief in the possibility of a world without war. In the Old Testament, the Gospels, the teachings of the early Church, and the reflections of the desert fathers and mothers, he found a nonviolent repudiation of worldly authority. And his study of pre-history led him to the conclusion that organized conflict is a markedly recent development in an otherwise relatively peaceful anthropological record.[3] The Chumash of Central California lived for more than three thousand years in peace with other tribes. And there are many other examples of indigenous groups with even longer records of peaceful coexistence. What we call civilization is largely the record of organized conquest—the rise and fall of empires over a mere four thousand years. Yet the human cultures preceding that record, though seldom discussed, do not seem to have been nearly as destructive to the environment or to each other.[4]

By adopting a natural history perspective on human development, Merton was able to place the prevailing Cold War conception of history as a contest between strategic interests and spheres of influence into a much broader context. And as a monk, he identified with the marginalized cultures of the world—particularly those that flourished in pre-Columbian Central America before the rise of the Incan and Mayan Empires.

Merton believed, like Thomas Mann, that war was a cowardly escape from the problems of peace[5] and that modern man exists within a lower order of consciousness than the far more inclusive, mytho-poetic sensibility of native people.[6] This may be part of the reason Merton didn't lobby for specific governmental reforms or engage in many public policy questions; rather, he lived an alternative life in the hopes of building a new society within the shell of the old. Through his writing and public service, he tried to articulate a higher order of existence over and against the prevailing economically driven political order—what Herbert Marcuse called "the one-dimensional society." Merton did feel forced by circumstances to speak out against racial injustice, the threat of nuclear annihilation, and the war in Vietnam.

Robert Kaplan addressed many of the same ethical concerns as Merton in his much more recent book *Warrior Politics: Why Leadership Demands a Pagan Ethos* (2001). Like Merton, his view of the world is not primitive, modern, or postmodern, but rather *ancient*. That is to say, both see the world coming of age aware of the continuing clashes of civilization and the infinite potential of humankind for both good and evil. It is a world, as Kaplan put it, "that, despite its technologies, the best Chinese, Greek, and Roman philosophers would have understood, and known how to navigate."[7] Sun Tzu's *Art of War*, Augustine's *City of God*, and Hobbes's

Leviathan have all taken on an odd new contemporary relevance. But unlike Merton, Kaplan argued that we need a new *pagan* ethos that is "ruthless and pragmatic but not amoral."[8] By this, I think he means a wiser, historically grounded neo-pragmatism.

It is not surprising that Kaplan became popular in the years right after 9/11. He was praised by former Secretary of State Henry Kissinger, former Secretary of Defense William Cohen, Newt Gingrich, Bill Clinton, and the CEO of Lockheed Martin. But what is surprising is that Merton, fifty years earlier, had anticipated Kaplan's argument and prepared an alternative. For Merton, such a defense of survival and rational self-interest lacks reach and ducks the bigger questions: survival for what? And what exactly *is* in our self-interest?

Merton had anticipated these problems quite succinctly in this celebrated passage from *Conjectures of a Guilty Bystander*:

> We are living in the greatest revolution in history—a huge spontaneous upheaval of the entire human race: not the revolution planned and carried out by any particular party, race, or nation, but a deep elemental boiling over of all the inner contradictions that have ever been in man, a revelation of the chaotic forces inside everybody. This is not something we have chosen, nor is it something we are free to avoid. . . . We do not know if we are building a fabulously wonderful world or destroying all that we have ever had, all that we have achieved! All the inner force of man is boiling and bursting out, the good together with the evil, the good poisoned by evil and fighting it, the evil pretending to be good and revealing itself in the most dreadful crimes, justified and rationalized by the purest and most innocent intentions.[9]

Although Merton's understanding of philosophy is *ancient*, his reading of the present is *modern* and his ethic *radically Christian*. Kaplan's neo-pagan ethos, by contrast, simply assumes he stands atop a hierarchy of being his own naturalist assumptions deny. This is why Merton argued for a circumspect political agenda, one that tempers our worldly ambitions with moral caution and a sense of irony. For Merton, the man of principles is always suspect—especially when he invokes the Machiavellian axiom that "All armed prophets succeed; whereas unarmed ones fail."[10] The future can't be understood through the categories of the present any more than the categories of the past, and human calculations of self-interest are simply not prescient enough to shape our goals beyond mere expediency. The pagan virtues of Pilate may be virtues of a sort, but they are also short sighted and inaccurate, however clever they might have seemed to the men of the hour.

Still, let us not miss Kaplan's point. By bringing the realities of coercion and violence into the discussion of social policy and morality, he makes it clear that—in this world—ethical action can never be *merely* an extension of our highest idealism. If we are serious about furthering the good, the true, and the beautiful, we must factor in those forces working against them. Acquiring an ethical vision of life cannot be divorced from acquiring an understanding of what is really going on (both within ourselves and in the world around us).

What Kaplan fails to acknowledge, however, and what Merton understood so well, is that Orthodox Christianity has already been through the pagan ethos and back again. In fact, Christian social ethics is what is left of classical thought after history has been seen through as a power play. It doesn't try to improve the times, redirect, or even change them, but just describe them, and by so doing liberate us from the tyranny of those philosophers and petty tyrants who would subject us all to their misguided long-term ambitions.

Christianity exposes the need pragmatists have for long-term rationales and scapegoats, and it replaces such plausible, if unfounded, "solutions" with real hope—not that the world is getting better or that our desires will be fulfilled (it's not, and they won't), but that life itself is a great good and that love, courage, and justice matter here and now. Love, courage, and justice are ends in themselves and not the vehicles of some greater, more perfect world to come. This is the Christian response to the pagan ethic of Pilate, which we forget at our own peril and which Merton strove to articulate.

Perhaps the modern theologian who offered the most sophisticated and successful take on the role religion plays in contemporary power politics was Reinhold Niebuhr. Like Merton, he began his intellectual life as a Marxist but converted to Christianity, and after World War II Niebuhr saw that "moral" individuals could inhabit "immoral" societies, and that the clash between a private ethics and the public good needed to be rethought.

Niebuhr came to the sobering conclusion that politics could not give us all that we see, but the only way to know what we could realistically seek was to test our ideals against political realities by acting, however piecemeal, in an already fallen world. Christian realists were needed to temper the utopian excesses of both left- and right-wing political purists *without giving up on the possibility of marginal progress.* The liberal West may not have the solution to every social problem, but if we were honest enough to admit that no easy solutions existed, this tragic awareness in itself offered more hope for slow, sustained worldly improvements than the facile answers offered by ideologues.

For Niebuhr, the biblical ideal of the Kingdom of God stood in radical judgment not only of current social reality but also of every conceivable alternative to it. Cultural and social achievements, however impressive, could provide no final good. History was driven by an insatiable human desire for more. We are best able to direct our energies toward reform only when we understand what is really going on, and in most cases what is really going on is not merely a clash of competing ideals but also a clash of competing interests and knowledge of the facts.

A realistic Christian ethic has to take into account all of the factors in a situation, especially those born of unconscious self-seeking and entrenched privilege. Any perspective that ignores these forces may allow its advocates to feel good about themselves while committing base acts. These are the beautiful souls who opt out of historical guilt for the moral comfort of an illusory absolute, as opposed to engaged Christian realists who own up to their limitations as flawed human beings but, nevertheless, do what they can to help real people in a complex, morally compromised world.

Given Niebuhr's perspective, the fanaticism of Pontius Pilate is the fanaticism of all good men who do not know that they are not as good as they think they are. Pilate represents the moral mediocrity of those in authority who simply cannot distinguish between a criminal and the Savior because they judge everything by the same measures.[11] Or, as John Milbank put it, "In Pilate, precisely, we see what human rule and reason is: the slaying through indifference and impatience of the God-man or the human future."[12] As a result of this common human failing, political decisions often come down to choosing the lesser of two evils. Prophetic leadership can challenge this narrowing of possibilities, but it is seldom, if ever, successful. The best one can hope, Niebuhr argues, is for a hovering self-irony that keeps the powerful subject to perpetual self-criticism and open distrust.

But educating the American public to the paradoxes and ironies of history is a tricky business, given the assault upon traditional ethical thinking that had already taken place through the propaganda barrages of World War II. "Christian realism" pitched to a frightened and cynical postwar population could very well justify a tendency to shoot first and ask questions later. This is one of the reasons why Thomas Merton's *The Seven Storey Mountain* (1948) resonated so powerfully with those looking for alternatives to the ideologies of the new superstates. To meet the dangerous new power alignments of the postwar world, a new America had emerged: corporate, consolidated, internationally connected, and militarily ready, run by professional managers, social scientists, and experts. The most pressing question of the era was not how the country's unique democratic character was going to be preserved (it was to some degree already gone), but rather whose interests was this new superstate of technocrats going to serve?

Merton offered a refreshingly frank answer to this question. The new America would serve exactly the same interests as the old one: money, power, and development. The Allies' victory may have saved the world from entering a new dark age, but it was failing to recognize the empty cultural forms that had preceded the war and that threatened to follow in its wake. There was a very real danger that the Allied victory could become hollow.

For Merton, like Gandhi, history was "the record of every interruption of the even working of the force of love."[13] History was an account—and this was confirmed by the GIs returning home from the war—of the accumulated sins of the fathers visited upon the sons, shadows playing upon the inside of a cave, a nightmare from which we were still all trying to awake.

As the allusion to Dante in the title of *The Seven Storey Mountain* makes clear, Merton saw the modern world as a purgatory where the most profound human values were being exiled, left for dead, or buried at sea. The Allies, in an instinctual reaction to the militarism of the totalitarian states, had themselves embraced the same values of production, might, and control, and, in the process, had lost track of their single greatest moral: the ascetic ideal. If Western civilization was going to survive, Merton suggested, it would have to get in touch again with its own spiritual core.

> The way to find the real world is not merely to measure and observe what is outside us, but to discover our own inner ground. For that is where the world is, first of all: in my deepest self. This "ground," this "world" where I am mysteriously present at once to my own self and to the freedoms of all other men, is not a visible, objective and determined structure with fixed laws and demands. It is a living and self-creating mystery of which I am myself a part, to which I am myself my own unique door.[14]

In its conversation with Enlightenment skepticism beginning in the seventeenth century, Protestant America accepted the epistemological preoccupations of the new sciences as central and became so concerned with evidences for the faith that it never fully came to grips with the ancient wisdom tradition hidden within its own contemplative roots. As a result, America's itinerant, invented Protestant self longed for a spiritual home but, given its preoccupation with Cartesian certainties, had no means for arriving there. This produced an ambitious, rootless, idolatrous people always defining themselves in opposition to others.[15]

Merton argued that the Catholic contemplative tradition, updated by a healthy dose of existentialism, could bring the Western religious imagination back in touch with its roots again and, thus, go William James one better by moving beyond the philosophical reasonableness and moral helpfulness of faith to achieve, again, what Søren Kierkegaard called "the absolutely, paradoxically, teleological placed" radicalism of the apostle.[16] This radically prophetic anti-pagan stance stands in stark relief to both Kaplan's antique ruthlessness and Niebuhr's "realism."

The events of 9/11 confronted Americans with a problem not faced since the Cold War: What do we do with an implacable, relentless enemy sworn to our destruction? Niebuhrian Christian Realism argues that we must simply own up to the fact that life itself is a tragic affair, that there will always be those who oppose our interests and plans, even those who wish our destruction. We cannot make them our friends, whatever we do, because we cannot in good conscience change ourselves to reflect their values, nor can we physically eliminate them from the face of the earth. And so we must temper our ambitions with a longer view of things that recognizes our human limitations.

George W. Bush's mixed strategy of sending both bombs and humanitarian supplies to Afghanistan and Iraq does not quite qualify as Niebuhrian irony because Bush never owned up to the hopelessly contradictory nature of his policies. For him, the bread and the bombs were simply the carrot and the stick of "infinite justice." Niebuhr, however, would caution against such a naive view. Bombs don't just eliminate enemies, they also create them; while humanitarian aide generates goodwill, it also creates dependencies. A Christian realist would have to look upon the wrong one was doing in being an "effective" strategist—if being a subtle strategist was, in fact, what Bush was attempting to be.

Jean Baudrillard described the American war in Iraq as "the continuation of non-politics by other means," and his point is well taken.[17] If no conversation was taking place between the West and the Islamic countries before the war began, the war itself certainly didn't cure that; it simply continued the silence more violently. Christian realists could accept this state of affairs as the tragic context within which all of us must work out our destiny— accepting our moral culpability, our partial virtue, and our limited vision, tempering our confidence in ourselves and our country with faith in a universal God greater than both. However, Christian contemplatives, like Merton, might suspect that even this measured, reasonable approach could be a radical misreading of our true situation, and that only through recollection, prayer, and the perceptions of a heart nurtured by a contemplative culture might our collective illusions be lessened and our national conscience clarified and refined.

If Niebuhr pointed out the ironies of American history, then Merton threw his life into the mystic abyss in order to reveal our hypocrisies and complicities. Merton wasn't interested in distinguishing between the lesser of two evils so much as in describing the impact our politicized world was having upon our ability to attain purity of heart and, therefore, the capacity to perform moral deeds. He described our modern situation this way:

This is no longer a time of systematic ethical speculation, for such speculation implies time to reason, and the power to bring social and individual action under the concerted control of reasoned principles upon which most men agree. There is no time to reason out, calmly and objectively, the moral implications of technical developments which are perhaps already superseded by the time one knows enough to reason about them. Action is not governed by moral reason but by political expediency and the demands of technology—translated into the simple abstract formulas of propaganda. These formulas have nothing to do with reasoned moral action, even though they may appeal to apparent moral values—they simply condition the mass of men to react in a desired way to certain stimuli. Men do not agree in moral reasoning. They concur in the emotional use of slogans and political formulas. There is no persuasion but that of power, of quantity, of pressure, of fear, of desire. Such is our present condition—and it is critical![18]

To transcend this ethical paralysis, we must learn how to act upon the greater reality of our transcendent identities—our true selves known only to God. We can say "Yes" to Niebuhrian Christian Realism only to the degree that we go beyond it to embrace the unseen potentialities lurking within our own lives (and those of our so-called enemies). This means that uncertainties need not be covered up by Pilate-like deferrals of responsibility, but humbly accepted as a reminder of the cost one must pay to do God's business in Caesar's world.

In his essays on nonviolence, Merton spoke out as an outraged public witness and guilty bystander, describing the unspeakable crimes of his times from the perspective of a contemplative—someone who sought justice as an end in itself, not merely as the means to greater social progress. Perhaps this is why Merton felt a particular affinity toward Gandhi and Martin Luther King, Jr., two other religious thinkers who embraced nonviolence as an important wager on the higher destiny of man. Like King, Merton understood that, given the nuclear threat, civilization needed to get beyond the assumption that people only responded to force or might not survive.

Nonviolence offered a way for the common man and woman to fight back without killing and to act directly upon the political order without succumbing to mere political logic. It was prophetic, not ideological, and it placed self-transformation and ethical achievement above only achieving one's goals. Nonviolence remains misunderstood by the public at large—even by some of its advocates—because it is predicated upon a contemplative, nondualistic perspective on existence where tactics take a backseat to authentic dialogue. But until the complexity of the Other becomes as clear to us as the complexity of ourselves, we do not exist in a real relationship—we are in an ideological fantasy, or what is sometimes called "a mental" relationship.

Politicians, journalists, and pundits traffic in mental relationships, and so the nonviolent soldier of truth must continually question their analyses. Within the prevailing one-dimensional neoliberal point of view, all life is reducible to clashes of self-interest—and so even nonviolence itself is reduced to a political tactic and not what it truly is: a way of life. Therefore, without nonviolent dissenters and soldiers of truth, modern civilization is doomed to endure an endless series of wars against war.

Merton remarks:

> Has nonviolence been found wanting? Yes and no. It has been found wanting wherever it has been the nonviolence of the weak. It has not been found wanting when it has been the nonviolence of the strong. What is the difference? It is a difference of language. The language of spurious nonviolence is merely another, more equivocal form of the language of power. It is used and conceived pragmatically, in reference to the seizure of power. But that is not what nonviolence is about. Nonviolence is not for power but for truth. It is not pragmatic but prophetic. It is not aimed at immediate political results, but at the manifestation of fundamental and crucially important truth. Nonviolence is not primarily the language of efficacy, but the language of *kairos*. It does not say, "We shall overcome" so much as "This is the day of the Lord, and whatever may happen to us, He shall overcome."[19]

In 1965, Merton published a selection from the writings of Mahatma Gandhi titled *Gandhi on Nonviolence* (New York: New Directions, 2007). He selected many passages in which Gandhi expressed his admiration for violent resistance over passive acquiescence in order to make it clear that Gandhi hated injustice even more than he hated violence.

Violence, Gandhi claimed, was not in itself evil, but evil was always violent. And violence could be invisible, structural, respectful, civil, even lawful. To practice nonviolence, one must refuse to profit from unjust coercion in any form whatsoever—even if it was invisible, unnamed, and seemingly impossible to correct. In other words, Gandhian nonviolence—or *ahmisa*—required a degree of moral development and personal integrity not encouraged by a world economic order built upon the self-interested, profit maximizing, expedient choices of so-called rational actors.

But if we could evaluate world progress in terms of its capacity to liberate individuals from all forms of coercion—including economic and political power—then we might be able to establish a very different yardstick by which to measure the achievements of history—a measure more in tune with actual human liberation than material development or the refinement of sensual pleasure.

Most people simply fail to comprehend that modern civilization itself—its laws, its economics, even its popular culture—constitutes a form of violence against various excluded individuals and groups. Mystified by the ideology of progress, most first-world citizens have a hard time seeing any suffering as trumping the claims of economic necessity—including wars against other sovereign nations. Such violence is accepted because no one believes there is any higher order to reality beyond that of the materialist status quo. In this sense, Gandhi, King, and even Merton, for that matter, were less political activists than moral teachers—calling for a transformation of the ethical imagination to include the lives and reality of Others, and with that, an end to war. What they stood for hasn't yet been understood, not because it is hard to express, but because the world as currently constituted just doesn't want to hear the message.

Nonviolence—as a call to think differently about history; indeed, to feel differently about thinking—is, by its very nature, hard to fathom because it questions all that we think we know about ourselves and human nature. It is not—as its misnomer implies—a preference for peace at any cost. Rather, it seeks to confront and, thereby, redress injustices caused by objective forms of violence. It does this by challenging the cultural assumptions that give legitimacy to violence built into the system. "Far from being a manifestation of misguided idealism," Merton tells us, "non-violence demands a lucid reason, a profound religious faith, and, above all, an uncompromising and courageous spirit of self-sacrifice."[20]

> [It] seeks to "win" not by destroying or even by humiliating the adversary, but by convincing him that there is a higher and more certain common good than can be attained by bombs and blood. Non-violence, ideally speaking, does not try to overcome the adversary by winning over him, but to turn him from an adversary into a collaborator by winning him over. Unfortunately, nonviolent resistance as practiced by those who do not understand it and have not been trained in it, is often only a weak and veiled form of psychological aggression.[21]

Nonviolence has a longer history than commonly acknowledged—emerging in the Axial Age as part of a larger critique of the militarized cultures, then emerging throughout the world, and it can be seen in the teachings of Zoroaster, Buddha, Isaiah, Confucius, Lao Tzu and Jesus.[22] Each of these teachers invoked his own version of the Golden Rule as the counterpoint to the emerging military ethic of might makes right. And although this ideal has been invoked again and again in response to the violence of our new militarized understanding of history, as a criticism of modern industrialization, and as an ideal connecting us to our ancient past, it was not renewed until the nineteenth century in the writings of Henry David Thoreau and Leo Tolstoy.[23] They advocated popular resistance to oppressive totalitarian structures, such as slavery and economic oppression, given institutional sanction by governments and business cartels.

But it was Gandhi and Martin Luther King (and their disciples Lech Walesa, Vaclav Havel, Bishop Tutu, and the dissidents of Tiananmen Square) who put this ethos into contemporary practice on a mass scale with admittedly mixed results, rendering its strengths and weaknesses visible and, thereby, complicating our understanding of the meaning of nonviolence as a method, medium, and worldview. Martin Luther King Jr.—perhaps the greatest advocate, practitioner, and theorist of nonviolence in our day—liked to quote John F. Kennedy's remark that those who make peaceful revolution impossible make violent revolution inevitable. But for Kennedy, this was an axiom of political pragmatism, whereas for King, it was a tragic ethical truth. Thomas Merton's place in this history of nonviolence, although certainly not as important as Martin Luther King's, was, nevertheless, vital and unique, for he brought its logic into dialogue with the fourfold hermeneutic of contemplative Catholicism. And, like King, his views were constantly oversimplified (and so misunderstood) by his friends almost as often as by his enemies.

King had scheduled a retreat with Merton at Gethsemani just a month before King was assassinated in Memphis. Merton had witnessed, firsthand, the dramatic unfolding of the American civil rights movement—the lunch counter sit-ins, the bombings, the bus boycott, and the March on Washington. And although Merton wrote telling critiques of white liberalism and the need for a more radical response by whites in support of King's visionary leadership, he didn't participate in any of the freedom rides or public demonstrations. And unlike the Berrigan Brothers and Dorothy Day, he was never arrested. Perhaps it was simply because he saw monasticism itself as an act of a social protest: his way, as he put it, of saying "NO to all the concentration camps, the aerial bombardments, the staged political trials, the judicial murders, the racial injustices, the economic tyrannies, and the whole socioeconomic apparatus which seems geared for nothing but global destruction in spite of all its fair words in favor of peace."[24]

In a letter to Dorothy Day written in 1960, Merton wrote: "It seems to me that the most basic problem is not political, it is apolitical and human. One of the most important things to do is to keep cutting deliberately through political lines and barriers and emphasizing the fact that these are largely fabrications and that there is a another dimension, a genuine reality, totally opposed to the fictions of politics, the human dimension which politicians pretend to arrogate entirely to themselves. . . . Is this possible."[25] Merton wasn't discussing strategy here; he was attempting to delineate a theology of resistance born of his contemplative commitments to a higher reading of history. He was defending the inner life of public protest so that it would not fall prey to what Jacques Ellul called the political illusion—the illusion that in the modern world all things are political.[26] Nonviolence was the public enactment of a clear conscience born of inner peace and a more universal frame of reference.

"Like ordinary political action," Merton wrote,

> (nonviolence) is no more than "the art of the possible."
> But precisely the advantage of non-violence is that it lays claim to a more Christian and more human notion (read "more just, visionary, hopeful and transformative notion") of what is actually possible. It extends the horizon beyond the wall of economic and political "realities" to include all of creation. Whereas the powerful believe that only power is efficacious, the nonviolent resister is persuaded of the superior efficacy of love, openness, peaceful negotiation and above all the truth. For "power can guarantee the interests of some men but it can never foster the good of man.[27]

And yet some Catholic Church officials still found Merton's attempts to articulate a theology of war resistance too politically charged for a monk and censored his writings. Merton published them anyway in a series of privately circulated mimeographed letters that became known as *The Cold War Letters*.[28] This put him in the awkward position of being both inside and outside the antiwar movement, and inside and outside the Church. But from his point of view, this was the only place an ethical human being could be.

Merton argued that nonviolence—correctly understood—was a creative act in which one risks violence to oneself for the sake of exposing the flaws in lower-order political thinking. By so doing, it educates the people about their rights and broadens the ethical imagination of the powerful. Like the fourfold hermeneutic of *lectio divina*, it reads history integrally, exposing the limited assumptions at the common-sense level by reference to a new, more inclusive social space in which the shared values of justice and equality can acquire new, more inclusive meanings. Gandhi confronted British colonizers with the emptiness of their professed democratic ideals—just as Martin Luther King challenged America's commitment to equality and Mario Savio exposed the emptiness of his university's commitment to free speech.

All three of these movements succeeded in changing the public conversation (for a while) by introducing new meanings to old words, although occasional slips into coercive tactics left lasting scars on the body politic, giving rise to reactionary backlash and violence. Gandhi did not heal the religious divisions in his own country, and there was significant white retaliation to the Black Liberation movement in the election of Ronald Reagan and the conservative culture warriors that followed in its wake.

Thomas Merton, like King, had tried to short-circuit such developments. In his *Letters to a White Liberal*, Merton argued that the so-called "Black Problem" was more truly a "White Problem." The poverty, political disenfranchisement, and cultural neglect blacks had had to endure was as much a result of white people continuing to define themselves in opposition to their Afro-American neighbors. A higher consciousness would end the oppositional logic and begin to heal the racial divide. As a result, whites (including white *liberals*) had to face up to the fact that they were still defining themselves, even if unconsciously, by a racial myth. The self-professed tolerance of white liberals was self-congratulatory and self-deceived, and so their support for egalitarian reforms could not be counted on to survive the more difficult political struggles ahead, which would require the abolition of all forms of white supremacy—including the notion of liberal largess!

Here, Merton was too far ahead of his time to be widely understood by either the right or the left. Slavoj Zizek ends his book *Violence: Six Sideways Reflections*[29] with a sentiment Merton expressed more than forty years prior. "The threat today is not passivity, but pseudo-activity, the urge to 'be active,' to 'participate,' to mask the nothingness of what goes on. People intervene all the time, 'do something'; academics participate in meaningless debates, and so on. The truly difficult thing is to step back, to withdraw. Those in power often prefer even a 'critical' participation, a dialogue, to silence—just to engage us in 'dialogue,' to make sure our ominous passivity is broken."[30] In other words, it is not enough to actively pursue reforms if by your attitude you reinforce your own social privilege. The monastic vision has always placed *being* before *doing* or *having*.

Merton's ambivalence toward public protests is sometimes misread as a conservative streak in his thinking—which is hardly the case. He simply distrusted the self-righteousness of reformers. He preferred to change individuals' beliefs and perceptions as the precursor to authentic social transformation because the country had made a fetish out of action. Prayer, meditation, and contemplation introduce a real alternative to the objective violence of existing institutions and to the neoliberal pragmatism that in and of itself cannot embrace any higher reality than its own success. Through meditation, our senses are cleansed to perceive the ever-changing, unfinished reality of God's ongoing creation: that all-encompassing, mysterious web of unfolding relationships to which the loving heart must give itself again and again.

In other words, prayer, meditation, and contemplation open up an unpredictable, nonconformist, medieval countercultural idiom within the modern, reductionist body politic. It is based upon the recognition that one's own aims are never as pure as one might believe, that all practical politics as well as all common life are based upon the values and perceptions of our false and limited selves, and that "the twentieth century"—to quote Australian social scientist Alex Carey—"has been characterized by three developments of political importance: the growth of democracy, the growth of corporate power, and the growth of propaganda as a means of protecting corporate power against democracy."[31]

So we must be suspicious of our own good intentions and factor in the possibility that unconscious factors are at play behind our backs. We may think we are acting free from illusion, but until our beliefs are tested against the horizon of the Other, we are not truly testing them.

One of the turning points in Merton's views on nonviolence occurred when Roger Laporte, one of the members of the Catholic Peace Fellowship and former novice, committed suicide in protest over the war in Vietnam. This event struck Merton as a clear signal that the Catholic peace movement had gotten off track, so he resigned from the group.

"The nature oriented mind," Merton explained, "treats other human beings as objects to be manipulated in order to control the course of events and make the future conform to certain rather rigidly determined expectations. Person oriented thinking does not lay down these draconian demands, does not seek so much to control as to respond. All it seeks is openness and free exchange in which reason and love have freedom of action. In such a situation the future will take care of itself."[32]

Remaining resolutely committed to higher values in the face of present injustice might have struck a radical like Laporte as a little fatalistic, maybe even socially irresponsible, yet Merton remained committed to contemplation and the reality of a higher order to history as the sine qua non of any authentic movement for social justice. Those inexperienced in prayer, where one is never in control of God's response, cannot grasp this logic. Like prayer, nonviolence is an experiment in truth, not a planned operation. It puts our ends as well as our means into question and mobilizes our cognitive, intuitive, and revelatory capacities, putting all of our self-conceptions on the line. Man is, indeed, something that must be overcome, but in this case, it isn't our latent humanism that must be overcome, it is our Promethean pride.

Merton's insights into nonviolence, as important as they were, remain hidden within a future still yet to emerge. Until we begin to ask the same questions that Thoreau, Tolstoy, Gandhi, and Martin Luther King asked, such as "How do we end war," we will have little use for Merton's insights. As early as 1961, Merton wrote:

> There can be no question that unless war is abolished the world will remain constantly in a state of madness and desperation in which, because of the immense destructive power of modern weapons, the danger of catastrophe will be imminent and probably at every moment everywhere. Unless we set ourselves immediately to this task, both as individuals and in our political and religious groups, we tend by our passivity and fatalism to cooperate with the destructive forces that are leading inexorably to war. It is a problem of terrifying complexity and magnitude, for which the Church herself is not fully able to see clear and decisive solutions.
>
> Yet she must lead the way on the road towards nonviolent settlement of difficulties and towards the gradual abolition of war as the way of settling international or civil disputes. Christians must become active in every possible way, mobilizing all their resources for the fight against war. First of all there is much to be studied, much to be learned. Peace is to be preached, nonviolence is to be explained as a practical method, and not left to be mocked as an outlet for crackpots who want to make a show of themselves. Prayers and sacrifice must be used as the most effective spiritual weapons in the war against war, and like all weapons they must be used with deliberate aim: not just with a vague aspiration for peace and security, but against violence and against war. This implies that we are also willing to sacrifice and restrain our own instinct for violence and aggressiveness in our relations with other people. We may never succeed in this campaign, but whether we succeed or not the duty is evident. It is the great Christian task of our

time. Everything else is secondary, for the survival of the human race itself depends upon it. We must at least face this responsibility and do something about it. And the first job of all is to understand the psychological forces at work in ourselves and in society.[33]

Just as the contemplative life found new forms and patterns in the radically incarnational vision of post–Vatican II hermeneutical theology, so too had nonviolence begun a new dialogue with history before it was shut down, lost, and misrepresented again at the close of the century. Until the contemplative, religious roots of nonviolence are recovered and taken to heart, the many popular protests invoking its name will remain merely tactical actions—spectacles in a world of spectacles, without any deeper transformative effects.

In a commencement day address at Williams College in 1984, Joseph Brodsky helped us to see the essence of nonviolence as Merton understood it when he remarked,

The surest defense against Evil is extreme individualism, originality of thinking, whimsicality, even—if you will—eccentricity. That is, something that can't be feigned, faked, imitated; something even a seasoned impostor couldn't be happy with. Something, in other words, that can't be shared, like your own skin: not even by a minority. Evil is a sucker for solidity. It always goes for big numbers, for confident granite, for ideological purity, for drilled armies and balanced sheets. Its proclivity for such things has to do presumably with its innate insecurity, but this realization, again, is of small comfort when Evil triumphs.[34]

Nonviolence functions as a therapeutic intervention into the life of the body politic only insofar as it injects a note of authenticity into an otherwise bogus social enterprise. And like a psychoanalyst looking for the exact moment and image through which to reveal the repressed, the nonviolent soldier of truth must select the exact scenario and phrase, such as "I am a Man!," to reveal the cognitive dysfunctions within the body politic. Only then can the traumatic misperception underpinning the prevailing social mystification be exposed and, hence, overcome.

One loves one's enemy as one's self not out of any sentimental desire for personal perfection, but in order to gain access to the images necessary for simple sanity. The method of nonviolence, or noncooperation with evil, transforms the misplaced energies too often directed at one's foe into a direct, transparent opposition toward a particular injustice. In this way, one's energies are not wasted fighting appearances or engaging in vendettas. In a letter to Dorothy Day written in 1961, Merton explains the clarifying effect a commitment to nonviolence has in shaping apt responses to social stereotyping and political repression.

> To shut out the person and to refuse to consider him as a person, as another self, we resort to the impersonal "law" and to abstract "nature." That is to say we block off the reality of the other, we cut the intercommunication of our nature and his nature, and we consider only our own nature with its rights, its claims, its demands. And we justify the evil we do to our brother because he is no longer a brother, he is merely an adversary, an accused. To restore communication, to see our oneness of nature with him, and to respect his personal rights and his integrity, his worthiness of love, we have to see ourselves as similarly accused along with him . . . and needing, with him, the ineffable gift of grace and mercy to be saved. Then, instead of pushing him down, trying to climb out by using his head as a stepping-stone for ourselves, we help ourselves to rise by helping him to rise. For when we extend our hand to the enemy who is sinking in the abyss, God reaches out to both of us, for it is He first of all who extends our hand to the enemy. It is He who "saves himself" in the enemy, who makes

use of us to recover the lost goat which is His image in our enemy.[35]

Merton was suspicious of any claims to moral superiority by anybody, including himself and his fellow peace activists. This was also why he opposed the religious and moral justifications for the war in Vietnam offered by conservative bishops and cardinals. If the corporate-military-industrial complex was ever going to be seen through, it would require a degree of self-sacrifice and inward conversion not yet available to most Americans. Most people were, as yet, simply incapable of the difficult art of love in action, which is a very different thing from simply participating in a social movement. It was something few—if any—really knew how to do on a grand scale, and so far only tragic world-historical figures like Dorothy Day, the Berrigans, Martin Luther King, Jr., and Gandhi seemed willing to try.

In *JFK and the Unspeakable* (2008), James Douglass takes off from Merton's book *Raids on the Unspeakable* to argue that John F. Kennedy had come to understand that peace through war was not possible. At best, it could only create a "Pax Americana" fostering resentment among the conquered and sowing the seeds of future wars. Douglass contends that when Kennedy found his conscience, sought peace with the Russians, and confronted the unspeakable, "he had to be killed."[36]

Whether or not one accepts the idea of Kennedy's change of heart, there is no doubt that the American public stood by helplessly while John F. Kennedy, Malcolm X, Martin Luther King, Jr., and Robert Kennedy were murdered in the streets, and so they became—against their will—silent accomplices to the unspeakable, providing cover for those schooled in "plausible deniability."[37] Douglass quotes a letter from Merton written in 1962 describing his take on Kennedy's politics in terms not unlike those many progressives used to describe President Barack Obama during his first term.

"I have little confidence in Kennedy," Merton wrote,

I think he cannot fully measure up to the magnitude of his task, and lacks creative imagination and the deeper kind of sensitivity that is needed. Too much the *Time* [magazine] and *Life* [magazine] mentality. . . . What is needed is really not shrewdness or craft, but what the politicians don't have: depth, humanity and a certain totality of self-forgetfulness and compassion, not just for individuals but for man as a whole: a deeper kind of dedication. Maybe Kennedy will break through into that someday by a miracle. But such people are before long marked out for assassination.[38]

In that same letter, Merton commented, "Those who are at present too eager to be reconciled with the world at any price must take care not to be reconciled with it under this particular aspect: as the nest of the Unspeakable."[39] The Unspeakable, Douglass tells us, represents for Merton, not only willful evil, but also the void of any agenda for good, the amorality that destroys those who indulge in it—whether it be through the dropping of atomic bombs or drone attacks upon civilians.

"The Christian," Merton wrote,

can renounce the protection of violence and risk being humble, therefore vulnerable, not because he trusts in the supposed efficacy of a gentle and persuasive tactic that will disarm hatred and tame cruelty, *but because he believes that the hidden power of the Gospel is demanding to be manifested in and through his own poor person* (author's italics). Hence in perfect obedience to the Gospel, he effaces himself and his own interests and even risks his life in order to testify not simply to "the truth" in sweeping, idealist, and purely Platonic sense, but to the truth that is incarnate in a concrete human situation, involving living persons whose rights are denied or whose lives are threatened.[40]

Nonviolent dissidents don't act because they know what must be done; they act because an overt injustice must be called into question, and if they have misread things, they are the only ones who suffer from their own miscalculations. The nonviolent activist is, therefore, comforted—even in defeat—by the realization that the truth has been served. In a letter to his friend Jim Forest, a Catholic Worker active in the antiwar movement, Merton wrote:

> Do not depend on the hope of results. When you are doing . . . an apostolic work, you may have to face the fact that your work will be apparently worthless and even achieve no result at all, if not perhaps results opposite to what you expect. As you get used to this idea, you start more and more to concentrate not on the results but on the value, the rightness, the truth of the work itself. And there too a great deal has to be gone through, as gradually you struggle less and less for an idea and more and more for specific people. The range tends to narrow down, but it gets much more real. In the end . . . it is the reality of personal relationships that saves everything.[41]

In his essay "The Sacred City," published in *The Catholic Worker* in 1967 as a rejoinder to Harvey Cox's *Secular City*, Merton used then recent discoveries reported in the journal *Mexican Archaeology and History* to explore the larger theme of civilization and its discontents.[42] The two thousand warless years of Monte Alban, he pointed out, have been largely ignored in Western histories of the world. Not that such an agrarian-based civilization would be possible today, but the fact that such a peaceful culture actually existed for more than two thousand years proves that peace is not just an idealistic dream but an actual part of human history. "It is important that we fit the two thousand war-less years of Monte Alban into our world-view," Merton argues, "because it may help to tone down a little of our aggressive, self-complacent superiority, and puncture some of our more disastrous myths by a sober view of the undoubted success achieved by the Zapotec Indians."[43]

Merton then offered this extended speculation worth citing at length:

> The "sacred cities" of Monte Alban and of Guatemala, as we see them, looked back rather than forward. They were the fulfillment of a long development of a certain type of culture which was agrarian and which flourished in small populations. With the growth of populous societies, the accumulation of wealth, the development of complex political and religious establishments and above all with the expansion of invention and resources for war, human life on earth was revolutionized. That revolution began with what we call "history" and has reached its climax now in another and far greater revolution which may, in one way or other, bring us to the end of history. Will we reach that end in cataclysmic destruction or—as others affably promise—in a "new tribalism," a submersion of history in the vast unified complex of mass-mediated relationships which will make the entire world one homogeneous city? Will this be the purely secular, technological city, in which all relationships will be cultural and nature will have been absorbed in techniques? Will this usher in the millennium? Or will it be nothing more than the laborious institution of a new kind of jungle, the electronic labyrinth, in which tribes will hunt heads among the aerials and fire escapes until somehow an eschatological culture of peace emerges somewhere in the turbulent structure of artifice, abstraction and violence which has become man's second nature?[44]

Confronted by a technological disorder in which ideological tribes actually do hunt heads among the aerials and fire escapes, Merton's prophecy has come literally true. Can an eschatological (i.e., contemplative) culture of peace emerge out of this turbulent structure of artifice, abstraction, and violence? It seems unlikely, yet Merton still had the faith and the resolve to suggest a way out: "It is when we love the other, the enemy, that we obtain from God the key to an understanding of who he is, and who we are. It is only this realization that can open to us the real nature of our duty."[45] But it takes a contemplative perspective to grasp what these words mean beyond their sentimental appropriation as simple bourgeois universalism. Not everyone wants the same world we do, and the awareness of this fact is fundamental to any honest understanding of the human condition.

Such a view, however, remains under assault—not only by political ideologues of every stripe and persuasion, but by a systematically distorted mass communication system that narrows life to a small set of prefabricated possibilities. To understand where our true social responsibilities lie, that is to say, to make art, revolution, and true philosophy possible in opposition to these increasingly backward, totalitarian trends, we have to challenge the givens of our shared social experience through openness to the Otherness of the other (and the Otherness within ourselves).

In his Pulitzer Prize–winning book *The Denial of Death*, Ernest Becker describes what might be the best single description of Merton's kind of Christian social activist:

> The problem with conventional faith for Kierkegaard is that it can serve as a barrier to one's confrontation with *pure possibility* and so substitutes itself for the rebirth of the self that is necessary for true Christian faith. We must first break through the bonds of our own given cultural heroic in order to be open to the true self. By so doing, we link the secret inner self, our authentic talent, our deepest feelings of uniqueness, our inner yearning for absolute significance, to the very ground of creation. Out of the ruins of the broken cultural self there remains the mystery of the private, invisible, inner self which yearns for ultimate significance and cosmic

heroism. This invisible mystery at the heart of every creature now attains its cosmic significance by affirming its connection with the invisible mystery at the heart of creation. This is the meaning of faith. At the same time it is the merger of psychology and religion.[46]

Merton's posthumously published social essays brought Becker's vision to life when they were first published in the 1970s, only to be met by a conservative backlash both within and without the Church that has lasted for more than forty years. Fueled by wounded national pride, a false sense of affluence, and an unchecked sense of entitlement and privilege, the American middle class continues to celebrate its own self-defeating pursuits by electing opportunistic leaders who reflect those same jingoistic aspirations. The old Jeffersonian dream of economically independent farmers became the search for financial independence via multimarketing schemes, real estate clubs, hedge funds, and then, after the crash, Lotto tickets. And as the nobility of our democratic aspirations withered, our imaginations turned away from the egalitarian sublime and toward the worship of the rich and the exotic. Media became spectacular and specious, political rhetoric increasingly shrill, and the Internet more perverse. Merton's social witness remains as contemporary as ever—perhaps even more so—if we can only muster the courage and imagination to follow up on what he had to say.

Conclusion

Refiguring the Faith

"The East emphasizes liberation from the human condition, while the Western spiritual traditions place special value on the human incarnation in its own right, and we are more interested in fulfilling the meaning of incarnation than in going beyond it or in finding release from it. To bring these two together is an important evolutionary step."[1]

—John Welwood

"A few years ago someone posed a question to the great theologian David Tracy. What is the future of theology in the United States? He answered without missing a beat: 'For the next two hundred years, we'll be trying to catch up with Merton.'"[2]

—John Dear S.J., Hiroshima Day Address, June 2005

Thomas Merton gave us a fresh conception of an ancient faith. He questioned the assumptions at the heart of our dreary rationalisms and prefigured—through his turn to monasticism—the birth of a neo-medieval, post-metaphysical creation theology in which God and thought were once again reconciled through the art of contemplation. He did this by a return to the patristic tradition of the fourfold hermeneutic informed by a postmodernist poetics in which the Bible is read as a literary and devotional classic and not as the proof text for dogmatic religion.

But it is one thing to argue that God is more of an experience than a concept by citing texts and making theological arguments, and quite another to demonstrate the consequences of this view by reading scripture in its light, absorbing its wisdom into one's life, and then expressing its ultimate meaning and significance through poetry, prayer, and political dissent. This is what Thomas Merton did, and in the process, he helped to refigure the Christian faith within our modern and postmodern contexts and to rescue it from both the ideological simplifications of the religious fundamentalist and the intellectual obstinacy of established orthodoxy. In other words, the life and work of Thomas Merton provide us with *a spiritual allegory for our times—indicating where our real heroism lies, where our resignation is required, and where our imagination still needs to be stretched.*

Thomas Merton was not the first to point out that modern individuals live in a confusion of idioms and warring "realisms"— inside a weave of interpenetrating worlds that disorient us by multiplying our social roles and responsibilities without revealing the ultimate necessity of any one of them. As a result, we spend a lot of time struggling with the myths and memes that live through us, lost in a semiological house of mirrors that hides the mystic core of things behind a plethora of distractions and illusions. And so like many of the most important artists of the last seventy-five years, from James Joyce and Rainer Maria Rilke to John Coltrane and Andy Warhol, he sought to overcome his alienation through a quixotic return to myth and mysticism—but in a distinctly postmodern fashion.

If T. S. Eliot mirrored back the modern chaos—creating a poetics of dislocation based on an updated mythology of the failed harvest—then Thomas Merton and his avant-garde Catholic cohorts (Karl Rahner, Hans Urs von Balthasar, and Henri De

Lubac) crossed that Wasteland to rescue the Kafkaesque monk starving in his cell at Burnt Norton.[3] But in order to perform this rescue, they had to expose the instrumentalist logic of late modernity still lurking within the contemporary zeitgeist. And they had to call into question the prevailing assumption that whatever can be done technologically *must* be done.

In his influential essay "The Age of the Worldview," Martin Heidegger argued that the philosophical essence of the modern world is our reduction of the world to our views of it. Nietzschean perspectivism had become our last metaphysical concept, and only by a return to fundamental ontology could Western civilization escape from this philosophical dead end. What is called *thinking* today, Heidegger argued, is nothing like the classical reflection upon essences that constituted our first philosophical inquiries, but is something more akin to *interpretation*: the mind sorting experience according to its own categories and premises in order to further some pragmatic or sophistic end. "Truth" now must remain in parentheses—although unschooled ideologues would continue to confuse their will to power for an independent Absolute. To get back to truth as the great mystery and ground of our existence, Heidegger contended, we needed to think Being, not merely calculate the consequences of our actions or interpret the meaning of things according to our own ends, values, and schemes.

But for Merton, Heidegger knew nothing about Being because Being cannot be known conceptually. The only way to think Being is through prayer, meditation, communion, and contemplation because it is only through these disciplines that the Cartesian cogito can be dismantled along with its endless hermeneutical ploys. Only then can the logical (Hegelian) and natural (Gnostic) orders of the world be overcome. And it is this seeing through metaphysics that makes up the second innocence of Christian faith. Merton, echoing Thomas Aquinas, put it this way:

> There is a paradox that lies at the very heart of human existence. It must be approached before any lasting hap-

piness is possible in the soul of man. The paradox is this: man's nature, by itself, can do little or nothing to settle his most important problems. If we follow nothing but our natures, our own philosophies, our own level of ethics we will end up in hell. This would be a depressing thought, if it were not purely abstract. Because in the concrete order of things God gave man a nature that was ordered to a supernatural life. He created man with a soul that was made not to bring itself to perfection in its own order, but to be perfected by Him in an order infinitely beyond the reach of human powers. We were never destined to lead purely natural lives, and therefore we were never destined in God's plan for a purely natural beatitude. Our nature, which is a free gift of God, was given us to be perfected and enhanced by another free gift that is not due it.[4]

The man who sees the world through different views of it, however moral or engaged he may be, defines himself in opposition to other views and so lives in division. Merton explains.

When a man constantly looks and looks at himself in the mirror of his own acts, his spiritual double vision splits him into two people. And if he strains his eyes hard enough, he forgets which one is real. In fact, reality is no longer found either in himself or in his shadow. The substance has gone out of itself into the shadow, and he has become two shadows instead of one real person. Then the battle begins. Whereas one shadow was meant to praise the other, now one shadow accuses the other. The activity that was meant to exalt him, reproaches and condemns him. It is never real enough. Never active enough. The less he is able to *be* the more he has to *do*. He becomes his own slave driver—a shadow whipping a shadow to death, because it cannot produce reality, infinitely substantial reality, out of his own nonentity.[5]

This description of self-annihilating restlessness anticipates the endless activities of post-structuralist man—fabricating meanings with his desires but never arriving at any common cause. Any attempts at overcoming this perspectivism—the last Western Metaphysical Idea—must fail because as long as the cogito remains our ultimate source of identity, we cannot fathom any form of existence beyond the self. By constantly flattering the tyrant within to whom we remain subject, we modern (and postmodern) souls never realize that we are already one with creation, already home, and so the death of our egos coming at the same time as the death of our bodies seems to be absolute existential extinction, as opposed to what it really is: a return to the whole.

It is hard for many moderns to imagine dying fulfilled or with any gratitude for their transitory existence because they remain so alone in the isolation of their conceptions of themselves and in the irreality of their own imagined failures and achievements. The soul (or true Self), however, is revealed only in and through love, sacrifice, and suffering (i.e., Christ), and these are the only things that retain being once the individual disappears. And so if one has never identified with anything greater than the self, death, indeed, becomes a confrontation with despair, and there can be no greater scientific project than the quest for everlasting biological life (never mind who or what is to become immortal).

Merton's essays and later work sought to expose our easy acquiescence to this technological "manifest destiny" fostered by the engineering capacities compelling us to build atomic bombs, travel into outer space, and clone our own biological doubles. For him, such achievements were not necessarily benchmarks of human progress but continuations of our long-standing ambition to master death and turn ourselves into Gods—with the culminating event something now referred to as *the singularity*: that projected point in the future when human beings will have engineered their own extinction and replaced themselves with better, more adapted, thinking machines.[6] To stop this descent into oblivion, we have to see through the self that directs all this change—the self that posits itself as an independent entity—so that we can refuse the temptation of transforming our species into the servant of our own incarnate will to power given objective existence through our machines.

In his poetry, prose, prayers, and reflections, Merton reminded us again and again that we are not our *minds*, nor are we our *calculating power*, nor are we merely the *tools of an abstract intelligence* that has evolved from us and now threatens to transcend us. And should we ever find ourselves obsolete—ghosts inhabiting worlds managed by our digital masters—the crucified Christ will become an even more poignant image of who we really are, and monasticism an even more relevant way back to ourselves.

By making this turn to contemplative living before the "coming singularity" arrived, Thomas Merton showed us that a postmodern culture can be inclusive of our pre-Cartesian past yet still universal in its spiritual reach. And even though Merton stumbled on his way to this eschatological humanism, it was his fits and starts, his evolving theology, and his travels through the back roads of scholastic jargon—Buddhism, Sufism, and other religious polemics—that allowed him to overcome the prevailing philistine notion that faith is one thing and thinking another.

Rene Girard, like Merton, sought to return Christianity from its contemporary status as a supernatural insurance plan reconciled to political violence[7] back to its original essence as a transformative contemplative practice. For Girard, Christ exposed the lie at the heart of scapegoating and, by so doing, undercut the moral and psychological authority of all worldly mythologies, empires, and regimes. Christ did not correct the world's injustices, but unmasked their false justifications. Through Him, God identifies with the scapegoat, not the scapegoating mob, affirming that the Absolute is always in opposition to regimes. This truth, however, can only be comprehended through compassion and care, for no metaphysical system is capable of thinking pure Being.

Christ's passion, therefore, placed an increased burden upon humanity, for the responsibility to love one another now rests upon every one of us. Political authority has been exposed as an expedient fiction, and Augustine's two cities now stand starkly before us as the reigning antinomy of history—irreducible to any Hegelian dialectic. We can repent and resist the contagion of violence through which the world is controlled, or we can hasten a worldly apocalypse by puruing power and, thus, tighten the spiral of violence until we annihilate one another. Either way, we stand under the judgment of the passion of Christ.

Let me explain the logic here using a passage from Franz Kafka.

"Many complain that the words of the wise are merely parables and are of no value in daily life, which is the only life we have. When the sage says: 'Go over,' he does not mean that we should cross to some actual place. He means some fabulous yonder, something that he cannot designate more precisely and therefore cannot help us get there. All these parables really say is that the incomprehensible is incomprehensible, and we know that already."

"Concerning this 'a man said: Why such reluctance? If you only followed the parables you yourselves would become parables and with that rid of all your daily cares.'

"The first said: 'I bet that is also a parable.'

"The second said: 'You have won.'

"The first said: 'But unfortunately only in parable.'

"The second replies: 'No, in reality: in parable you have lost.' "[8]

The point here is that literature—parable, scripture, the imaginal—expresses a different reality from that of literal history, yet remains real—if otherworldly. To seek only the practical or historical meaning of things makes life seem significant in the world's terms, but it actually destroys its value as an end in itself because in the process of becoming applicable to life, the words of the wise lose their value as *literature*—that is to say, they lose their value as a cathartic, symbolic reconciling of the conscious with the unconscious, and the soul with God.

Every time we turn a parable into a moral tale or a historical allegory, we become deaf to its mythic meaning and deeper challenge. We replace the question it is asking us to confront with a less demanding worldly truism. Thus, by preferring the objectivity of the subjective to the subjectivity of the objective, we deny the spiritual meaning from which the story emerged and by which it becomes true as myth. Or, to put it more simply, when our reading of scripture or our reading of experience is reduced to a search for knowledge about the world and its patterns, we no longer see the text as a reflection upon our existential choices—and it is then through our choices that faith, love, hope, and charity make themselves known to us.

Those who attempt to fashion a single God's-eye view of the universe—whether they're materialists, idealists, fundamentalists, or radical skeptics—miss the whole point of the literariness of scripture. Kafka knew, as did Girard, Merton, and the Desert Fathers and Mothers, that the interior life is neither a means to an end nor a mere epiphenomenon built upon some more real material existence. It is, rather, the place where life comes to know itself—the expanding center of order, the evolving "I" of creation moving outward in an ever more inclusive and empathetic love. The high medieval fourfold hermeneutic provided Merton with a way to overcome the Cartesian preoccupations of modernity, while at the same time giving him a critical tool for sorting out life's multiple dimensions of experience.

Every time scripture is read or God is experienced, our previous knowledge of Him is altered, as is our understanding of ourselves in relation to Him. And so the contemplative life, like devotional reading of scripture, deepens, that is to say, changes our relationship to who we are and what we know. The hermeneutical circle is not exactly overcome but extended. One enters it through faith, and through faith, scripture is understood, and that understanding raises new questions, making new conceptions necessary.

This fourfold exegesis, with its looping iterations, overcomes both the fundamentalists' fears of being excluded from the truth and the postmodernists' fear of being imprisoned by it. But even more than this, it also makes interpretations matter to other interpretations and other disciplines. This is a much bolder agenda than either perspectivism or relativism can provide, because it suggests that competing meanings and approaches are part of a dialogue-coming-into-being that is larger than any single ideology. This deep ecumenicalism is a system that furthers systemlessness without collapsing into chaos. That is to say, this integral interpretive approach makes possible a pluralistic culture of readers seeking a single, inclusive reading of multiple significances as opposed to a single reading supporting a one-dimensional, ideology that demands universal allegiance. But caution is needed here.

Merton once wrote that there is "a basis of truth in the vitalist imagery of man bringing God into being in the world by his own creativity *but only if this language is understood not as theology but as poetic mythology concerned with man's own creative self-fulfillment beyond and above the demands of his nature.*"[9] This is an important—indeed critical—qualification. Christian faith affirms life, not just in terms of the evolution of biological forms or even in terms of an evolution of consciousness, but in terms of an extension of freedom, individual choice, and the one-of-a-kind loves and achievements of which only unique souls are capable.[10]

Seen in the light of Merton's apophatic Christianity, radical phenomenology—that form of phenomenology that attempts to describe its own premises—offers the beginning of a secular appropriation of contemplation because it reflects upon the source of the eidetic reductions in an attempt to objectively behold, as in prayer, the very source of our own subjectivity. Of course, the phenomenologist is tempted to believe he or she can force a peek behind the veil of the pre-given, whereas for Merton, this can only be accomplished through grace. Indeed, this is one of the distinctions that separates "infused contemplation" from "natural contemplation" within the Christian tradition. The former is experienced as something done to us from beyond as opposed to something we do for ourselves.

Contemplative Christianity offers an alternative to both materialistic metaphysics and instrumentalist science. On the one hand, its suspicion of worldly values fits in nicely with progressive social movements and modern aesthetic revolutions; on the other, its practices are historically linked to some of the most ancient elements in World civilization. As a result, the answers it offers to the problems of modernity remain largely hidden in the intrapersonal sphere of experience and in the critiques of history offered by various outlaw Christian theorists, poets, and novelists. Its defense of the tragic and existential dimensions of human experience refigures the language of religion as literature rather than metaphysics. Religion, therefore, becomes a language game that can either play itself into reality or play itself into delusion depending upon the sanity, intellectual reach, and imagination of its practitioners.

Merton played the language game of Christian spirituality by the rules of patristic contemplation. And in the process, he challenged Catholic triumphalism, the kitsch iconography of the 1950s Church, mindless fundamentalism, atheistic overreach, and the pious sentimentality of the new, conformist trembling lambs. His works demonstrate a radical suspicion of neoliberal assumptions, a systematic decentering of Enlightenment assumptions, a preferential option for the poor, a proto-theology of liberation, an emphasis upon concrete human experience, and the value of a plurality of religious expressions. Moreover, they provide a reading of history in which technological progress stands under judgment as a Faustian gamble upon the endless deferment of moral responsibility.

He knew that the cultural task at hand was no longer to "get an audience" for one's ideas or to "market" one's program, but rather to let the performance-driven society, with its experts and celebrities, die a peaceful death through nonparticipation in its inanities. We have only to turn our attention away from the Society of the Spectacle to defeat it—a feat far less complicated but much more difficult than organizing a movement against movements on Facebook or attempting to making oneself world famous.

We know now—and it's been confirmed by biology and evolutionary psychology—that our best work is motivated by love—and not love in the abstract, but felt love—biologically based affection and care. And if we are not actually feeling positive regard for one other, we are probably not doing each other (or ourselves) any real good. The value of Being, expressed, by and large, better by the poor than by the moneyed elites, is available at all times to everyone through generosity and selfless presence. This is not—as Merton made abundantly clear—primarily an intellectual achievement, but an act of the heart to which we must recommit ourselves over and over.

In Leonard Cohen's little essay "How to Speak Poetry," he warns writers not to assume false personas through which to extort the admiration of their readers and he sums up far better than I can the prescient gift Thomas Merton's work has offered the world:

> What is our need? To be close to the natural man, to be close to the natural woman. Do not pretend that you are a beloved singer with a vast loyal audience which has followed the ups and downs of your life to this very moment. The bombs, flame-throwers, and all the shit have destroyed more than just the trees and villages. They have also destroyed the stage. Did you think that your profession would escape the general destruction? There is no more stage. There are no more footlights. You are among the people. Then be modest. Speak the words, convey the data, step aside.[11]

When I first read this several years ago, I didn't really understand how apt it is as a description of what Thomas Merton has accomplished. By telling us his story, he exposed all the traps of ego and expertise. And although he didn't live to see the birth of the Internet, I'd like to think he would have seen it as I do: as an infinitely expanding nineteenth-century Parisian brothel where anything is possible and everything is sold. But after coming across Cohen's remarks, I see the Internet and the new social media more as an attempt to construct a new "stage" for performers. It may seem revolutionary because it has an open mike, and we are witnessing some new gimmicks. But as Peter Block, the brilliant business consultant, has pointed out, there can be no community without shared space.[12] The so-called virtual communities on the Internet are not communities at all because everything expressed there is part of the conjured-up reality of commerce and public display. There is no "place" on the Internet where the performers can meet without their social masks on. And without such a shared physical space, everything on the net becomes a performance—and every performance a service delivery system of one kind or another.

Thomas Merton stepped off the stage by entering a monastery, and he wrote about what he discovered in that liminal space between the twelfth and the twenty-first centuries, and between solitude and community, anonymity and fame. He found that beyond the impasse in critical theory and at the very limits of negative dialectics stands the Absolute—unbowed but powerless to explain itself. And so within each of us there is a meeting taking place between Christian mystics, Buddhist monks, Sufi poets, Hasidic ecstatics, and ordinary people that constitutes the *imago mundi* of our times.

At the very moment political demagogues warn of a clash of civilizations, many individuals throughout the world have begun an unforeseen return to spiritual sources—seeking truth through silence, humility, and service. Thomas Merton saw this coming more than sixty years ago and prophetically described the future we are all currently living through.

Appendix

Some Milestones of Merton Scholarship

Kurt Vonnegut opened his futuristic science fiction novel *The Sirens of Titan* (1959) with the lines: "Everyone now knows how to find the meaning of life within himself. But mankind wasn't always so lucky. Less than a century ago men and women did not have easy access to the puzzle boxes within them. They could not name even one of the fifty-three portals to the soul."[1]

Not that we can name those portals now, but, thanks to Thomas Merton and the many other contemplative thinkers who have followed in his wake, we have come a lot closer. What we see in Merton's works (and in twentieth-century avant-garde Christian writers like him) is an ambivalent relationship to the world and a skepticism toward human projects in general.

Like most monks, Merton was not very concerned with proving Christianity to be true so much as with describing the kind of life and truth Christianity offered to those who lived by it. He wrote about its mysteries not as theory or science, but as an affirmation of life so authentically liberating and sublime that it was experienced by its practitioners as salvation.

Merton's relatively early death at age fifty-six and the sheer volume of his works published after his death (well over twice what he published during his lifetime) combined to make him one of the most prolific (and popular) spiritual writers of the twentieth century. With the release of each previously unpublished work, every previous critical study was set back slightly on its heels, keeping Merton's ideas before the public and rendering any final assessment of his thought difficult—if not impossible—to define. New letters and essays continue to be discovered to this day, increasing the size of his oeuvre and further securing his standing as our contemporary.

Merton's first readers after World War II were largely religious (lay Christians, for the most part), but that slowly and steadily changed as his reputation as a literary stylist and social critic grew. Merton also profited from a dedicated group of scholars who were not only students of his work but also spiritual seekers in their own right. They approached his writing not as judges weighing its worth or as academics looking for contradictions, but as fellow students of the human condition—testing Merton's insights against their own and looking for common ground.

But if Merton's monasticism kept his work sequestered in a Catholic literary ghetto of sorts for most of his life, it also saved him from being subjected to the fashions of academic scholarship, with its shifting critical trends and sophistic controversies. He was, for many years, simply dismissed by literary professionals and academics as an interesting religious partisan—but not a particularly important "American writer." (No one, to my knowledge, has yet written a reader response analysis or neofeminist critique of *The Seven Storey Mountain*—although I am sure they are on the way.)

As a result, Merton's works remained popular and relatively unmolested by the academy for years, but also relatively unremarked upon and ignored by most non-Christians. As his full correspondence and journals were published over the years and his essays on secular issues became more well known, it became clear that Merton was not a simple religious partisan, but he had been in rigorous conversation with thinkers from all faiths and intellectual backgrounds—atheists, poets, novelists, feminists, Muslims, Protestants, Byzantine Orthodox, and communists, his entire life. If Merton's work was essentially Catholic apologetics, it was certainly a very different version of apologetics than was previously understood.

In the first ten years after Merton's death, a flood of previously unknown primary material was published that changed the way Merton's entire oeuvre had been received. These included his *Secular Journal* and his novel *My Argument with the Gestapo* (both written before his conversion) and *The Asian Journal*, written during his fatal trip to the Far East. These works deepened our understanding of Merton's early life and clarified his interest in Eastern religions. Moreover, they were published at a time when the United States was experiencing a cultural revolution of sorts in which Christian visionaries and contemplative culture critics played an important role. Those reading Teilhard de Chardin, Ivan Illich, Norman O. Brown, and Marshall McLuhan found a colleague in Merton: a religious intellectual with literary reach and mystical proclivities.

In 1969, John Howard Griffin—a personal friend of Merton and the author of *Black Like Me* (1961)—took on the task of writing the first official biography of Merton. He was unable to finish the project because of poor health, but he did publish an essay to accompany his many photographs of Merton, titled *A Hidden Wholeness*, in (1970).

Edward Rice, Merton's longtime college friend, also wrote a personal memoir titled *The Man in the Sycamore Tree* (1972) in which he lovingly described his friend as a "Buddhist Catholic Hippie Monk." The book captured Merton's trickster personality and spoke to the youth movement. A collection of essays by Merton titled *Contemplation in a World of Action* came out in 1973 that clarified his thoughts on social justice issues. And the psychotherapist James Finley, who had had Merton as his spiritual director when he was a novice at Gethsemani, published *Merton's Palace of Nowhere* (1978), which explored Merton's monastic distinction between the true and false self. Finley brought Merton's understanding of spiritual direction into conversation with psychotherapy, as did Eugene Gendlin in his classic *Focusing* (1978) and the transpersonal psychologists John Welwood and David Richo (whose books, however, were not published until the 1990s.) Parker Palmer also published a pamphlet on Merton titled "In the Belly of Paradox" in 1979 and then went on to write a series of groundbreaking contemplative works on education and spiritual change influenced by Merton including *The Courage to Teach* (1997) and *A Hidden Wholeness* (2009).

From the perspective of the late 1970s, however, Merton's analysis of the Vietnam War and his trenchant warnings as to the insufficiency of white liberals to carry home the promise of the civil rights movement, first published in the early 1960s, seemed, in retrospect, to be downright prophetic. Readers from all religious and anti-religious perspectives wanted to know more about this dissident Catholic—just as his readers in the 1950s and early 1960s had been fascinated by his asceticism. In 1979, Ross Labrie published *The Art of Thomas Merton*, one of the first serious attempts by a professional literary critic to gauge Merton's contributions as a writer—another important step in Merton's transition out of his Catholic ghetto. (In 2001, Labrie published *Thomas Merton and the Inclusive Imagination*, building upon twenty years of thinking about these issues.)

The 1980s saw an explosion of Merton biographies, important collections, and critical works that articulated his cultural significance both inside and outside the Church. *The Literary Essays of Thomas Merton* (1981), edited by Merton's former secretary Brother Patrick Hart, instantly established Merton as a serious literary critic. Monica Furlong's biography *Merton* (1980) explored his private life, including his controversial love affair with Margie Smith. John Howard Griffin published a journal about his own failed attempt to write Merton's official biography, titled *The Hermitage Journals* (1981), and then *Follow the Ecstasy* (1983), a description of Merton's last years.

Anthony Padavano's eloquent book *The Human Journey: Thomas Merton: Symbol of the Century* (1984) also made a case for Merton's world-historical significance, as did Michael Mott's official biography *The Seven Mountains of Thomas Merton* (1984), which remains the definitive Merton biography to this day. Mott combed through thousands of documents to separate the myths and errors in Merton's own writings and memory against the facts. And if the writing was not always eloquent and the book a bit lengthy, its contribution to the historical record is undeniable. There are simply no Merton biographies as inclusive or as balanced to this day. Both Padavano and Mott helped to introduce Merton to a larger readership, and in 1984 the Twayne American Author's Series came out with a critical biography on Merton by Victor Kramer. The theologian Anne Carr published *A Search for Wisdom and Spirit: Thomas Merton's Theology of the Self* in 1988, one of the first and still one of the best articulations of Merton's theological importance and originality.

But perhaps the most important posthumous Merton publication of the 1980s in terms of altering the world's understanding of Thomas Merton as a writer and as a cultural figure was William Shannon's collection of letters *The Hidden Ground of Love* (1985). It revealed—in a direct and hitherto underestimated way—Merton's dialogues with many of the important thinkers of his time. These letters showed the depth of Merton's engagement with secular thinkers and the reach of his concerns, throwing a whole new light on his exemplary willingness to engage intellectual antagonists and critics.

With the coming of the so-called "culture wars" and the elections of Ronald Reagan and Margaret Thatcher, religion became increasing politicized and dumbed down. There was a rise in the ratings (and fortunes) of televangelists like Jerry Falwell, Pat Robertson, and, to a lesser extent, Mother Angelica. In this cultural milieu, Merton's deep ecumenicalism became harder for general readers to fathom, and so his status as a spiritual master-cum-culture critic became a bit confused. His works were far more nuanced and difficult than what was passing for religious thinking at this time, yet he was so clearly a man of faith that he could not be easily dismissed even by the new fundamentalists.

When Ronald Reagan invited Mother Teresa to the White House for a photo opportunity, the press coverage focused almost exclusively on her criticisms of abortion, not on the progressive

Catholic social justice ethic out of which her (and Merton's) selfless social work had emerged. And Merton's works criticizing empires, war, and psychological exploitation were increasingly falling upon deaf ears.

In 1989, David D. Cooper published *Thomas Merton's Art of Denial: The Evolution of a Radical Humanist*, which responded to these trends—making a brave attempt to bring Merton's ideas into dialogue with the culture at large through the radical thesis that Merton was, at heart, more a writer and a humanist than a religious extremist. That is to say, he had more in common with intellectuals and artists like Eric Fromm, Albert Camus, Erik Erikson, and Henry Miller than he did with Mother Angelica or the fanatics and entertainers on "Christian television."

The 1980s also saw the publication of Robert Daggy's collection of the prefaces and introductions that Merton wrote for foreign editions titled *Introductions East and West* (1981) and later reissued as *Honorable Reader* (1989). These prefaces, most of them written in the mid- to late 1960s, had never been published before in the United States, and they revealed Merton's surprising reassessment of himself. A sort of meta-Merton emerged in these prefaces, transcending yet again the categories of his own thought and providing a new understanding of his works—works that were being translated into other languages for the very first time.

In 1989, when the Soviet Union collapsed and the Solidarity Movement triumphed in Poland, due in no small part to the moral and intellectual stature of Pope John Paul II, Catholicism was seen in the United States primarily in its anti-communist aspect, sending Merton critics and scholars to their new computers to explain and defend his legacy as an engaged contemplative culture critic. The 1990s were dominated by the publication of four more volumes of Merton's letters and seven volumes of his journals. Lawrence Cunningham's masterful anthology, *Thomas Merton: Spiritual Master*, came out in 1992, followed by George A. Kilcourse's examination of Merton's Christology, *Ace of Freedoms: Thomas Merton's Christ* (1993). These works were supplemented by memoirs and reflections of many of Merton's aging colleagues and friends—most notably Jim Forest, whose biography *Living with Wisdom* (1991) offered a very intimate, encyclopedic view of Merton's life from the point of view of a lifelong Catholic worker and colleague. Ron Seitz's *Song for Nobody* (1993) offered an equally heartfelt but more lyric remembrance of his friendship with Merton as spiritual mentor and fellow poet.

A *Courage for Truth: Letters to Writers*, selected and edited by Christine M. Bochen, was published by Farrar, Straus and Giroux in 1993. Although its full impact was not immediately felt, it has proven to be one of the turning points in Merton scholarship, refocusing attention upon Merton *the writer* as opposed to Merton *the monk* or Merton *the Catholic*. Over the years, Merton scholarship has both profited and suffered from a primary focus upon his ideas over his literary achievements. The seriousness and sincerity with which his spiritual journey has been examined has suffered from a certain ideological rigidity when dealing with his writing *as writing*.

This, I believe, is one of the reasons he is often falsely earmarked as a "liberal" by conservative Catholics or misread by spiritual seekers as a prototypical New Age guru while his achievements as a writer—whose subject matter just happened to be the interior life—go unrecognized. Bochen's collection of letters on literary themes encouraged Merton scholars to forgo the task of threading the needle of competing ideological simplifications of Merton's work that all too often pit his most general ideas against Hinduism, the entire Buddhist tradition, or atheism proper—forgetting that what makes him worth reading is the way his writing challenges *the way* we talk and think about ourselves.

But this turn to "the Literary Merton" did not happen right away. M. Basil Pennington published his memoir, *Thomas Merton: Brother Monk*, in 1997, the same year William H. Shannon published *Something of a Rebel*, an influential biographical introduction to Merton's work from the point of view of a contemplative. Shannon's book was reissued in 2005 under the title *Thomas Merton: An Introduction*. I published *Thomas Merton's American Prophecy* in 1998 with the hope of placing Merton's work within the context of American intellectual history. John Milbank's groundbreaking *Radi-*

cal Orthodoxy came out in 1999, and although it doesn't mention Merton, its themes certainly resonate with Merton's work—connecting spiritual theology to social theory, placing liturgy and love at the heart of Biblical exegesis, and, by so doing, demonstrating the contemporary relevance of traditional faith in a post-secular world.

By the turn of the twenty-first century, Merton had become an established spiritual master read by people of all faiths as well as by atheists and agnostics who find in his work an early anticipation of many of the most thoughtful insights in contemporary theology. And although the first ten years of the twenty-first century were dominated by wars and military adventurism, Merton's works retained their spiritual depth and theological relevance.

The job of explicating Merton's works for the general public reached its apotheosis in 2002 with the publication of *The Thomas Merton Encyclopedia* by Orbis Press. This compendium of essential summaries and explications, written by William H. Shannon, Christine M. Bochen, and Patrick F. O'Connell, provides sharp, insightful overviews of Merton's major and minor works and is one of the great milestones in Merton studies—culminating nearly four decades of critical readings and clearing the ground for new interpretations and applications of his works.

Perhaps no series better exemplifies this transition than the Fons Vitae Merton Series. These are collections of new essays exploring Merton's relationship to other religions and spiritual practices. They include *Merton and Sufism* (1999), *Merton and Hesychasm* (2003), *Merton and Judaism* (2003), *Merton and Buddhism* (2007), *Merton and Taosim* (forthcoming), and *Merton and Art* (forthcoming). But, once again, it was William H. Shannon who offered the most important contribution to scholarship by editing and publishing Merton's *The Inner Experience: Notes on Contemplation*. This book of notes and reflections, begun in 1948 and finished in 1958, has been long known to Merton scholars with access to his papers. Chapters had been published over the years, but never a full text. When Shannon's edition came out in 2003, it was clear that we had another Merton masterpiece on our hands published thirty-five years after his death. Not that there was anything surprising or new in this book, but its eloquence, reach, and confirmation of Merton's genius renewed interest and admiration for his work in toto.

In 2005, Lynn Szabo edited a collection of Merton's poems, *In the Dark Before Dawn*, which restored a more focused appreciation of the diversity and quality of Merton's poetry. Orbis published two important collections in 2006, *Signs of Peace: The Inter-Faith Letters of Thomas Merton* and *The Cold War Letters*, Merton's infamous mimeographed circular censored by the Church. Roger Lipsey published *Angelic Mistakes: The Art of Thomas Merton*, containing many never-before-seen reproductions of Merton's calligraphy and brush drawings, that same year, following up on Jonathan Montaldo collection of his prayers and line drawings, *Dialogues with Silence* (2001), which showed a side to Merton's artistic sensibilities not generally appreciated.

More than half of the letters in Merton's archive still have yet to be published, and each year the International Thomas Merton Society holds biannual conferences examining these and other materials, extending the range and significance of his influence. In the past seven years, several volumes of Merton's lectures delivered to the novitiates at Gethesmani have been published for the first time. These include his work on *Cassian and the Fathers* (2005), *Pre-Benedictine Monasticism* (2006), *Introduction of Christian Mysticism* (2008), and *The Rule of Saint Benedict* (2009), providing important new primary materials that bear directly upon our understanding of Merton as a teacher and student of monasticism.

An unfinished manuscript on writing and the spiritual life, "The Sign of Jonas," was published in *The Merton Seasonal* in the fall of 2008 by Paul M. Pearson, director and archivist at the Thomas Merton Center at Bellarmine University in Louisville, Kentucky. Pearson was also responsible for publishing Merton's early stories in 1996 and continues to be the primary source for new Merton materials, including a growing number of volumes featuring both sides of Merton's correspondence with Czeslaw Milos, Robert Lax, Rosemary Ruether, Jean LeClerq, James Laughlin, Catherine Doherty, and others.

The International Thomas Merton Society holds biennial conferences in both the United States and the United Kingdom. Its publications, *The Merton Annual: Studies in Culture, Spirituality, and Social Concerns* and *The Merton Seasonal: A Quarterly Review*, edited by Patrick F. O'Connell, offer a steady stream of new scholarship. Essays by Michael Downey, Victor Kramer, George Kilcourse, David Belcastro, Donald Grayston, Grey Matthews, Monica Weis, Judith Hardcastle, Robert Grip, and Angus Stewart, among others, all have appeared in their pages. The Merton Institute for Contemplative Living, also located in Louisville, offers workshops on Merton and publishes a series of study guides based upon Merton's life and teachings.

Students of Merton's works are now offering contemporary synopses and overviews of his overall contribution. Paul Elie's masterful best seller, *The Life You Save May Be Your Own* (2003), weaves Merton's life into the lives of other innovative mid-century Catholics such as Flannery O'Connor, Dorothy Day, and Walker Percy. James Martin, S.J. included Merton in his survey *My Life with the Saints* (2007). And John Eudes Bamberger's essay in the collection *Thomas Merton: Prophet of Renewal* (Collegeville, MN: Cistercian Publications, 2005) brought Merton into dialogue with recent developments in theology, psychology, and emerging social movements. Christopher Pramuk's *Sophia: The Hidden Christ of Thomas Merton* (2009) also offers a rethinking of Merton's Christology in dialogue with some of the best theological thought of our time.

Another area of Merton scholarship not always formally acknowledged but key to any understanding of Merton's ongoing intellectual significance includes those writers and thinkers deeply influenced by his work but who do not explicitly write criticism or commentary on it. I am thinking of writers like Annie Dillard, author of *Pilgrim at Tinker Creek* (1974) and *Holy the Firm* (1977); and Henri Nouwen, whose entire life was a response to Merton's spiritual witness and whose book *Thomas Merton: Contemplative Critic* (1981), although brief, remains one of the most succinct introductions to Merton ever written. Matthew Fox, heir to Merton's socially engaged creation spirituality, continues to produce groundbreaking works (see especially his *Sins of the Spirit, Blessings of the Flesh* [1999], not to mention his *Original Blessing* [1983], *The Coming of the Cosmic Christ* [1988], and *Creation Spirituality* [1991]). In fact, you could name almost any influential contemplative writer of the last sixty years—Huston Smith, Richard Rohr, Cynthia Bourgeault, Anthony De Mello, James Martin, S.J., the Dalai Lama, Thich Nhat Hahn, Ken Wilber, Jacob Needleman, John Main, Kathleen Norris, Mark Nepo, and Bonnie Thurston, among others.—and you will find Thomas Merton lurking somewhere in the wings as an influence or interlocutor. He is one of the sources from whom most—if not all—contemporary spiritual writing has emerged, in both its popular and its more theologically serious manifestations. I include here Richard Foster, author of *The Celebration of Discipline* (1978); Michael Casey, author of *Toward God: The Ancient Wisdom of Western Prayer* (1996); Joan Chittister, author of the spiritual memoir *Called to Question* (2009); and Brother David Steindl-Rast, author of *Gratefulness, The Heart of Prayer: An Approach to Life in Fullness* (1984). All of these writers acknowledge their debt to Merton as a spiritual mentor and literary model.

Gerald May's books on psychiatry, such as *Will and Spirit* (1982), often pick up where Merton left off on the theme of spiritual direction, as do Thomas Moore's book *Care of the Soul* (1992) and the books and tapes of the Franciscan Father Richard Rohr—particularly his *Everything Belongs: The Gift of Contemplative Prayer* (1999) and *The Naked Now: Learning to See as the Mystics See* (2009). Ronald Rolheiser's devotional reflections *Against an Infinite Horizon* (2002) and *The Shattered Lantern* (2005) also owe much to Thomas Merton's teachings and example.

Although it might be too much to credit Merton with inspiring the centering prayer movement, for its roots run much deeper than Merton's own relatively more recent contribution to contemplative thought, there is no doubt that Merton's writings helped lay the groundwork for the successful reception of Thomas Keating's *Finding Grace at the Center* (1978). The writings and lectures of

Cynthia Bourgeault, particularly *The Wisdom Jesus* (2008), also deepen and carry forward the contemplative tradition—so bravely advocated by Merton—into important new territory, as do Bruno Barnhart's *Second Simplicity* (1999) and the *Future of Wisdom* (2007) and Laurence Freeman's powerful book *Jesus the Teacher Within* (2000).

Let me not forget to mention that Beverly Lanzetta's *Path of the Heart* (1986), *Radical Wisdom: A Feminist Mystical Theology* (2005), and *Emerging Heart: Global Spirituality and the Sacred* (2007) all grow out of a deep encounter with Thomas Merton's writings, as do the writings of Paula Huston—see especially her book *The Holy Way* (2003)—and Wayne Teasdale, particularly his book *The Mystic Heart* (2001), a stunning synthesis that carries Merton's deep ecumenicalism forward by linking it to Bede Griffith's work.

But Merton's influence is not limited to spiritual directors. Catholic social justice activists John Dear, James Douglass, Jim Forest, Bryan Massingale, Ken Butigan, and the Berrigan brothers have also invoked Merton's name since the early 1960s as a source of inspiration and direction.[2] John Dear, S.J. even credits Merton with having brought social justice inside the Catholic tent—a view shared by the civil rights historian scholar and Quaker Vincent Harding (colleague and friend of Martin Luther King), who believes that had King survived to make his scheduled retreat with Thomas Merton in the spring of 1968, he would have been astounded to find a Catholic sympathetic to his cause, never having met one before. But even more than this, King would have met a Catholic schooled in the social justice traditions of the Church and quite vocal about it—a Catholic who was struggling to bring the teachings of the Church into dialogue with the critical tradition of the Frankfurt School as well as the Eastern religions.

Other activists and scholars also found Merton's political views challenging: Gordon Zahn, Ronald Powaski, and Patricia Burton, to name just a few. And I don't think it's too much of a stretch to include among this group James Carroll, author of *Con-*

stantine's Sword (2002), who clearly has differences with Merton—seeing him primarily as a disciple of de Lubac and Vatican II—but who, nevertheless, shares Merton's reading of Church history.

But if Merton has influenced scholars and activists of very different intellectual interests and backgrounds, his celebrity has also inspired far less rigorous studies. There has already been one novel published depicting him as a suicide and secret Vedanta convert, as well as several other speculative biographies focusing primarily upon the melodrama of his personal life, including one novelistic hallucination depicting Merton as philanderer,[3] as well as an increasing number of self-published works by various fans and fanatics, leading to a whole subgenre of Mertonian kitsch. (A character named "Thomas Merton" even appears in the film *Quiz Show* as a portly, slightly pompous dinner quest of Mark Van Doren.)

As disturbing as some of these misrepresentations may be (as far as I know, there are as yet no Merton bobbleheads), I have no doubt that his reputation will survive even this current "public comment" phase of his career, provided serious readers and students of his work follow his contemplative lead and do not confuse such opinions and misrepresentations with his actual thinking. In light of these developments, it is fitting to give Merton the last word as to how he might best be read:

> Active contemplation is nourished by meditation and reading and, as we shall see, by the sacramental and liturgical life of the Church. But before reading, meditation and worship turn into contemplation, they must merge into a unified and intuitive vision of reality. In reading, for instance, we pass from one thought to another, we follow the development of the author's ideas, and we contribute some ideas of our own if we read well. This activity is discursive. Reading becomes *contemplative* when, instead of reasoning we abandon the sequence of the author's thoughts in order not only to

follow our own thoughts (meditation), but simply to rise above thought and penetrate into the mystery of truth which is experienced intuitively as present and actual.[4]

I can think of no more succinct summation of the meaning and method of Merton's contribution to contemporary contemplative culture.

Notes

Epigrams

1. *Belief*, trans. David Webb (Stanford, CA: Stanford University Press, 1999) 62.
2. Postscript to *Saving God: Religion After Idolatry* (Princeton: Princeton UP, 2009).

Introduction. Everything Old Is New Again

1. I am paraphrasing here the enthusiasm Hannah Arendt expressed upon first reading Martin Heidegger when she wrote, "Thinking has come to life again; the cultural treasures of the past, believed to be dead, are being made to speak, in the course of which it turns out that they propose things altogether different from the worn-out trivialities they had presumed to say. There exists a teacher." Quoted in Michael Murray, ed., "Martin Heidegger at Eighty," *Heidegger and Modern Philosophy* (New Haven: Yale UP, 1971) 295.

2. Henri-Marie de Lubac (1896–1991) was a French Jesuit priest whose writings and research shaped the Second Vatican Council. He was one of the founders of the "ressourcement" movement for the renewal of the Catholic Church by going back to the methods and sources of the Patristic Era. His study *Exégèse Médiévale* (1959–1965) revived interest in the spiritual exegesis of Scripture. Along with Jean Daniélou, Yves Congar, Hans Balthasar, and Karl Ratzinger, Lubac was part of the "nouvelle théologie"—a group of theologians who questioned the rationalist

approach of the neo-Thomist revival—toward union with God. They argued that rational arguments for belief were powerless without the perceptions of the heart.

3. Hans Urs von Balthasar (1905–1988) was a theologian and priest who, like Karl Rahner and Bernard Lonergan, offered a Christian response to modernism. While Rahner made faith comprehensible to modern minds and Lonergan worked out a historical critique of modernity, Balthasar challenged modern sensibilities through a radical Christian aesthetics of the whole.

4. I am referring, of course, to Dietrich Bonhoeffer's formulation of this concept in *The Cost of Discipleship* (New York: Touchstone, 1995): "Cheap grace is the grace we bestow on ourselves. Cheap grace is the preaching of forgiveness without requiring repentance, baptism without church discipline, Communion without confession. . . . Cheap grace is grace without discipleship, grace without the cross, grace without Jesus Christ, living and incarnate." (44)

5. By transcendental self-reflection, I am referring here to the philosophical approach that seeks to describe the fundamental structures of being in terms of emerging knowledge and not in terms of any theory of Being or ontology (Kant, Fichte, Hegel, Gadamer, et al.). This seems to me the most fitting analogy to what the Desert Fathers and Mothers were attempting, although it is admittedly more of an analogy than a definition.

6. The goal of all structuralist activity, whether reflexive or poetic, is to reconstruct an "object" in such a way as to manifest thereby the rules of functioning (the "functions") of this object. Structure is therefore actually a *simulacrum* of the object, but a directed, *interested* simulacrum, because the imitated object makes something appear that remained invisible, or, if one prefers, unintelligible in the natural object. Structural man takes the real, decomposes it, then recomposes it; this appears to be little enough (which makes some say that the structuralist enterprise is "meaningless," "uninteresting," "useless," etc.). Yet, from another point of view, this "little enough" is decisive: for between the two objects, or the two tenses, of structuralist activity, there occurs *something new*, and what is new is nothing less than the generally intelligible: the simulacrum is intellect added to object, and this addition has an anthropological value, in that it is man himself, his history, his situation, his freedom and the very resistance which nature offers to his mind.

From Roland Barthes, "The Structuralist Activity," reprinted in *Criticism: Major Statements*, 4th ed., ed. Charles Kaplan and William Davis Anderson (New York: Bedford/St. Martin's, 1999).

7. This approach to understanding Merton's process as a writer is also reflected in Fred Herron's essay "A Bricoleur in the Monastery: Merton's Tactics in a Nothing Place," *The Merton Annual* 19 (2006): 114–27.

8. For an insightful treatment of the theological development of the notion of kenosis and its central role in distinguishing Christian orthodoxy from the logical (Hegelian) and natural (Gnostic) processes of history through the "shining forth of God's omnipotence through love," see Hans Urs von Balthasar, *Mysterium Paschale* (San Francisco: Ignatius Press, 1990).

9. For a full account of Merton's relationship to the Catholic Peace Fellowship in the 1960s, see the account in Michael Mott's *The Seven Mountains of Thomas Merton* (Boston: Houghton Mifflin, 1984) 427–33.

10. An influential French poet and author, Charles Pierre Péguy (1873–1914) converted to Catholicism in 1908. His conversion reshaped his creative work and socialist political views. He enlisted on the first day of World War I and was killed by a bullet through the forehead while leading his men in a charge during the Battle of the Marne.

11. Jacques Maritain was a French philosopher who converted to Roman Catholicism in 1906 and published *Art and Scholasticism* (1920), *The Degrees of Knowledge* (1932), *Art and Poetry* (1935), *Man and the State* (1951), and *Moral Philosophy* (1960). He argued for the value of poetry and mysticism as legitimate ways of knowing, the value of the person over the political order, and the importance of interfaith dialogue in the formation of political institutions and civic order.

12. I could include the entire canon of the Romantics here, from Goethe and Blake to Wordsworth and Whitman et al.

13. Merton's expression of Christian kenosis through his critical Romantic Catholic contemplation and social activism differs in kind from Martin Heidegger's Neo-Scholastic ontology and Nazism.

14. *Love and Learning*, ed. Naomi Burton Stone (New York: Farrar, Straus and Giroux, 1979) 123.

15. See Carol Zimmerman, "Thomas Merton Scholars Upset by Monks Absence in Upcoming Catechism," *Catholic News Service* 7 January 2005.

Chapter 1: An Experimental Life

1. *New Seeds of Contemplation* (New York: New Directions, 1962) 31–32.

2. See Dennis Q. McInery's important essay "Thomas Merton and the Tradition of American Critical Romanticism," *The Message of Thomas Merton*, ed. Patrick Hart (Kalamazoo, Cistercian Publications, 1981).

3. *The Seven Storey Mountain* (San Diego: Harcourt Brace Jovanovich, 1976) 237–38.

4. "Roll the Dice," *What Matters Most Is How Well You Walk Through the Fire* (New York: Ecco Press, 2002) 408.

5. Oscar Wilde, *The Soul of Man Under Socialism and Selected Critical Prose: Oscar Wilde*, ed. Linda Dowling (New York: Penguin Classics, 2001) 137.

6. G. K. Chesterton, *Orthodoxy* (Hollywood, FL: Simon & Brown, 2010) 99.

7. *New Seeds of Contemplation* (New York: New Directions, 1962) 57.

8. *Sign of Jonas* (New York: Harcourt, Brace, Jovanovich, 1953) 186.

9. Father Henri Nouwen once said that each of us is on a quest to discover our own individual prayer of the heart. To find it, he suggested, we must "stand in the presence of God with our minds in our hearts." *Reaching Out* (Grand Rapids, MI: Zondervian, 1992) 130.

10. For a profound treatment of the full meaning of this image, see Cynthia Bourgeault's *The Wisdom Way of Knowing* (Hoboken, NJ: John Wiley & Sons, 2003) 83–86.

11. See, for example, Andrew Newberg, M.D., and Mark Robert Waldman, *How God Changes Your Brain: Breakthrough Findings from a Leading Neuroscientist* (New York: Ballantine, 2010).

12. "The Merton Prayer," *Thoughts in Solitude* (New York: Farrar Straus and Giroux, 1958) 89.

13. *Day of a Stranger* (Salt Lake City: Gibbs M. Smith, 1981).

14. Ibid. 41.

15. *Honorable Reader: Reflections on My Work*, ed. Robert Daggy (New York: Crossroads, 1989) 107.

16. *New Seed of Contemplations* 156–57.

17. *No Man Is an Island* (New York: Harcourt Brace Jovanovich, 1983) 41.

18. *New Seeds of Contemplation* 55–59.

19. Urs von Balthasar as quoted by Henri Lubac in his *Funeral Eulogy for Urs von Balthasar* available on-line at http://www.crossroadinitiative.com/library_article/757/Hans_Urs_Von_Balthasar_Eulogy_de_Lucac.html.

20. *New Seeds of Contemplation* 32.

21. From Bernadette Dieker, "Merton's Sufi Lectures to Cistercian Novices 1966–1968," *Merton & Sufism: The Untold Story: A Complete Compendium*, ed. Rob Baker and Gray Henry (Louisville, KY: Fons Vitae, 1999) 146–47.

22. *Faith and Violence* (Notre Dame, IN: University of Notre Dame Press, 1968) 145–46.

23. Quoted by Kathleen Kennedy Townsend, "America's Progressive Catholics: Another Side of the Church," *The Atlantic* 29 June 2011.

24. Norman O. Brown, *Life Against Death: The Psychoanalytic Meaning of History* (Middletown, CT: Wesleyan UP, 1959) 309.

25. *Life Against Death* 317–18.

26. Naomi Burton Stone and Brother Patrick Hart, eds., *Love and Learning* (New York: Farrar, Straus and Giroux, 1980) 10.

27. *New Seeds of Contemplation* 57.

28. *No Man Is an Island* 113.

29. Informal talk delivered in Calcutta, 1968, republished in Thomas Merton, *Spiritual Master: The Essential Writings*, ed. and introduction by Lawrence S. Cunningham; foreword by Patrick Hart; preface by Anne E. Carr (New York: Paulist Press, 1992) 227.

30. Ibid.

31. *Learning to Love: The Journals of Thomas Merton*, vol. 6, 1966–1967, ed. Christine Bochen (San Francisco: Harper San Francisco, 1997) 134.

32. *Learning to Love: The Journals of Thomas Merton*, vol. 6, 238.

33. *The Experience of God: Icons of Mystery*, trans. Joseph Cunneen (Minneapolis: Fortress Press, 2006).

34. *The Merton Seasonal* 33.3 (Fall 2008): 4.

35. Ibid. 5.

36. *No Man Is an Island* 128–29.

Chapter 2: Contemplation as Critique

1. Quoted by Peter Kreeft, C.S. *Lewis for the Third Millennium* (San Francisco: Ignatius Press, 1994) 141.

2. *Honorable Reader: Reflections on My Work*, ed. Robert E. Daggy (New York: Crossroad, 1991) 67.

3. John Bowker, ed., *Oxford Dictionary of World Religions* (New York: Oxford University Press, 1997) 81. "Apophatic theology is another name for 'theology by way of negation,' according to which God is known by negating concepts that might be applied to him, stressing the inadequacy of human language and concepts used to describe God . . . found in the works Gregory of Nyssa and Pseudo-Dionysus the Areopagite A.G.H."

4. This definition of criticism comes from Northrop Frye and is quoted by Richard Single, *The John Hopkins Guide to Literary Theory and Criticism*, 2nd ed. (Baltimore: John Hopkins Press, 2005) 4.

5. David Pellauer, *Ricouer: A Guide for the Perplexed* (New York: Continuum, 2007) 31.

6. *Contemplation in a World of Action* (Garden City, NY: Doubleday, 1966) 340.

7. Listen to Slavoj Zizek's description, for example, of the postmodern subject. "[P]ostmodernism passes from the 'emptied subject' to the subject qua emptiness of the substance. This is homologous to the reversal from the matter qua substance that curves space into matter qua curvature of the space in the theory of relativity. In its most radical dimension, the 'subject' is nothing but this dreaded 'void'—in horror vacui, the subject simply fears himself, his constitutive void." Slavoj Žižek, "Grimaces of the Real, or When the Phallus Appears," *October* 58 *Rendering the Real* (Autumn 1991): 67.

8. See Thomas Merton, "Teilhard's Gamble," *Love and Living*, ed. Naomi Burton and Patrick Hart (New York: Farrar, Straus and Giroux, 1979). I could find no evidence that Merton ever ready anything by Charles Hartshorne or Henry Nelson Wieman.

9. Milan Kundera coined the phrase "the modernization of stupidity." Stupidity was once equated with illiteracy; now it has become the inability to think outside the consciousness fostered by received ideas—or common memes.

10. *Zen and the Birds of Appetite* (New York: New Directions, 1968) 22.

11. Ibid. 23.

12. Ibid. 205–06.

13. Ibid. 210, 212.

14. Merton's views here are directly in line with the Process Theologians.

15. *Contemplation in a World of Action* (Garden City, NY: Doubleday, 1966) 168.

16. "How to Read Lacan," *Che Vuoi? Empty Gestures and Performances: Lacan Confronts the CIA Plot*," 1997 <htpp://www.lacan.com/zizciap.html>.

17. For a wonderful overview of contemporary process theology, see Roland Faber, *God as Poet of the World: Exploring Process Theologies*, trans. Douglas W. Stott (Louisville, KY: Westminster John Knox Press, 2004).

18. See *God Is Not Great* (New York: Twelve, 2009).

19. In *Faith and Violence* (Notre Dame, IN: University of Press, 1968) 286–87.

20. *Contemplation in a World of Action* 163.

21. For a thoughtful analysis of just such a project, see John McManus and Eugene G. D'Aquili, *Brain, Symbol and Experience: Towards a Neurophenomenology of Human Consciousness* (New York: Columbia UP, 1992).

22. *The Inner Experience* 68–69.

23. In an interview with Leonardo Boff by the *Estado de Minas* newspaper, Wednesday, 9 April 2003, the Liberation Theologian remarked, "If God exists as things exist, then God does not exist, because God is not an object which one defines. God is that energy which permits all of the universe, that mysterious reality physicists call the quantum vacuum or the fecund vacuum. That energy of mysterious base, from which comes all things and which is a metaphor of that which we say to be God as Creator, that which put all into motion."

24. *Contemplation in a World of Action* 168–69.

25. Ibid. 172.

26. Ibid. 155–56.

27. This is a paraphrase from Rilke's first *Duino Elegy*.

28. *The Seven Storey Mountain* (San Diego: Harcourt Brace Jovanovich, 1976) 228.

29. *The Seven Storey Mountain* 228.

30. *No Man Is an Island* (New York: Harcourt Brace Jovanovich, 1983) 50–51.

31. *New Seeds of Contemplation* (New York: New Directions, 1962) 7.

32. *New Seeds of Contemplation* 250.

33. See "Nhat Hanh Is My Brother," *Faith and Violence* (Notre Dame, IN: University of Notre Dame Press, 1968) 106.

34. From *Conjectures of a Guilty By-Stander* (Garden City, NY: Doubleday, 1966, 1971) 156–57.

35. Martin Heidegger, "The Fieldpath," trans. Berrit Mexia, *Journal of Chinese Philosophy* 13 (1986): 455–58.

36. *The Inner Experience* 59.

37. See Slavoj Zizek and Boris Gunjevic, *God in Pain: Inversions of Apocalypse*, trans. Ellen Eleas-Bursac (New York: Seven Stories Press, 2012). For a popular discussion of Zizek's views on "Atheistic Christianity," see Jack Miles's interview with Zizek at <http://www.phatmass.com/phorum/topic/123186-slavoj-zizek-god-in-pain-inversions-of-apocalypse-conversation/>.

38. See *Living Flame of Love*, trans. David Lewis (New York: Cosimo Classics, 2007) 122.

39. *Ascent to Truth* (New York: Harcourt, Brace 1951) 135.

40. *The Inner Experience* 59.

41. *Spiritual Direction and Meditation and What Is Contemplation* (Hertfordshire, UK: Anthony Clarke, 1975) 96.

42. *Conjectures of a Guilty By-Stander* (Garden City, NY: Doubleday, 1971) 56.

43. *The World Is Made of Stories* 66.

44. Thomas Merton, *An Introduction to Christian Mysticism*, ed. Patrick F. O'Connell (Kalamazoo, MI: Cistercian Publications, 2008) 171.

45. *Contemplation in a World of Action* 154–55.

46. This famous phrase from Martin Heidegger is quoted in Walker Percy, *The Message in the Bottle: How Queer Man Is, How Queer Language Is, and What One Has to Do with the Other* (New York: Picador USA, 2000) 158.

47. *Learning to Love: The Journals of Thomas Merton*, vol. 6, 1966–1967, ed. Christine Bochen (San Francisco: Harper San Francisco, 1997) 320–21.

Chapter 3: Poetry as Natural Theology

1. *Juniper Fuse: Upper Paleolithic Imagination & the Construction of the Underworld* (Middletown, CT: Wesleyan UP, 2003) xxv.

2. From "Thomas Merton's Poetry: Emblems of a Sacred Season" <http://www.thomasmertonsociety.org/altany1.htm>. See also Alan Altany, "The Transformation of the Idea of the Sacred in the Poetry of Thomas Merton," diss., University of Pittsburgh, 1987.

3. *Christian Century* 6 December 1978: 1181–83.

4. "Introduction," *A Thomas Merton Reader*, ed. Thomas P. McDonnell (New York: Harcourt, Brace & World, Inc., 1962) 17.

5. In his "Letter to an Innocent By-Stander," addressed to contemporary intellectuals, Merton explained his use of the term this way:

> By intellectual, I do not mean clerk (although I might mean clerc). I do not mean bureaucrat. I do not mean politician. I do not mean technician. I do not mean anyone whose intelligence ministers to a machine for counting, classifying, and distributing other people: who hands out to this one a higher pay check and to that one a trip (presently) to the forced labor camp. I do not mean a policeman, or a propagandist. I still dare to use the world intellectual as if it had a meaning.

Raids on the Unspeakable (New York: New Directions, 1964) 54.

6. Uwe Poerksen, *Plastic Words: The Tyranny of Modern Language*, trans. Jutta Mason and David Cayley (University Park: Penn State UP, 1995) 63–64.

7. *The Secular Journal of Thomas Merton* (New York: Farrar, Straus and Cudahy, 1959) 20.

8. Quoted by David R. Loy, The World Is Made of Stories (Somerville, MA: Wisdom Publications, 2010) 13.

9. For an extended treatment of nondualistic thinking as central to Christian thought, see Richard Rohr's book *The Naked Now: Learning to See as the Mystics See* (New York: Crossroad, 2009).

10. *Raids on the Unspeakable* (New York: New Directions, 1966) 61.

11. *The Literary Essays of Thomas Merton*, ed. Brother Patrick Hart (New York: New Directions, 1981) 350.

12. "The Keening Muse," *Less Than One* (New York: Farrar, Straus and Giroux, 1986) 44.

13. *The Land of Ulro*, trans. Louis Iribarne (New York: Farrar, Straus and Giroux, 2000) 165.

14. *Theoretical Writings* (New York: Continuum, 2006) 238.

15. See Martin Heidegger, "Letter on Humanism," *Basic Writings*, ed. David Farrell Krell (London: Rutledge, 1999) 242–43.

16. See *The End of Modernity: Nihilism and Hermeneutics in Postmodern Culture* (Baltimore: John Hopkins UP, 1991).

17. *Brave New World* (New York: Harper Perennial Modern Classics, 2006) 122.

18. *The Collected Poems of Thomas Merton* (New York: New Directions, 1977) 3.

19. Ibid. 122.

20. Ibid. 978.

21. Ibid. 363.

22. *The Springs of Contemplation* (New York: Farrar, Straus and Giroux, 1968) 1992) 9.

23. *Cables to the Ace or Familiar Liturgies of Misunderstanding* (New York: New Directions, 1968) 34.

24. Collected Poems 396.

25. Ibid. 457.

26. Ibid. 457.

27. *The Inner Experience: Notes on Contemplation*, ed. William H. Shannon (San Francisco: Harper San Francisco, 2003) 59–60.

28. Quoted in David Loy, *The World Made of Stories* (Somerville, MA: Wisdom Publications, 2010) 100.

29. The text of this entire dialogue is available online <http://www.oshoworld.com/biography/innercontent.asp?FileName=biography10/10-44-sufism.txt>.

Here is an excerpt:

Coleman, you have asked a very dangerous question!—because burning has nothing to do with your enlightenment. On the path of enlightenment there is no question of burning. But because you are in love with Mevlana Jalaluddin Rumi . . . I also love the man. But you have to understand that Sufism still depends on a hypothetical God. It is not free from the hypothesis of God. And particularly Sufism has the concept of God as a woman. Love is their method—love God as totally as possible. Now you are loving an impossible hypothesis, and totality is asked. You will feel the same kind of burning, in a more intensive way, as lovers feel on a smaller scale. . . . So although I love Sufis . . . I don't want, Coleman, to hurt your feelings, but I would certainly say that you will have one day to change from Sufis to Zen. Sufis are still living in imagination; they have not known the state of no-mind. And because they have not known the state of no-mind, however beautiful their personalities may become, they are still just close to enlightenment, but not enlightened. Remember, even to be very close is not to be enlightened. . . . You are asking, "What do the burning and the fire have to do with my own enlightenment?" Nothing at all. You are enlightened in this very moment; just enter silently into your own being. Find the center of your being and you have found the center of the whole universe. We are separate on the periphery but we are one at the center. I call this the Buddha experience. Unless you become a Buddha—and remember, it is the poverty of language that I have to say "Unless you become . . ." You already are. So I have to say, unless you recognize, unless you remember what you have forgotten . . .

Chapter 4: A Monasticism of the Last Man

1. Johann Baptist Metz, A Passion for God, trans J. Matthew Ashley (Mahwah, NJ: Paulist Press, 1997) 2.
2. Quoted by Peter Sagal on "Wait, Wait, Don't Tell Me," National Public Radio 28 August 2010.
3. The Inner Experience: Notes on Contemplation, ed. William H. Shannon (San Francisco: Harper San Francisco, 2003) 5.
4. Ibid. 6.
5. Ibid. 8.
6. Ibid. 106.
7. Ibid. 108.
8. Ibid. 106.
9. This is the thesis of Paul Hourihan's speculative novel The Death of Thomas Merton (Redding, CA: Vedantic Shores Press, 2002).
10. Ibid. 117.
11. The Naked Now: Learning to See as the Mystics See (New York: Crossroad, 2009).
12. Ibid. 166–68.
13. Ibid. 107–08.

14. Ibid. 105.

15. Ibid. 108.

16. *The New Man* (New York: Farrar, Straus and Giroux, 1961) 64.

17. "Day of a Stranger," *Thomas Merton Spiritual Master*, ed. Lawrence S. Cunningham (New York: Paulist, 1992) 217.

18. *The Asian Journal of Thomas Merton*, ed. Naomi Stone, Patrick Hart, and James Laughlin (New York: New Directions, 1973) 329.

19. Ibid. 329–30.

20. Ibid. 329–30.

21. The entire script of the film *Network* is available at <http://www.script-o-rama.com/movie_scripts/n/network-script-transcript-paddy-chayefsky.html>.

Chapter 5: Merton's Most Dangerous Idea

1. *The Infinite Conversation*, trans. and foreword by Susan Hanson (Minneapolis: University of Minnesota Press, 1993) 43.

2. *Beyond the Postmodern Mind* 67, quoted in Dennis Ford, *The Search for Meaning: A Short History* 211.

3. See Paul Shepard and Florence R. Shepard, *Coming Home to the Pleistocene* for a contemporary version of this argument (Washington, DC: Island Press, 2004).

4. Steven Pinker's recent book *The Better Angels of Our Nature* (New York: Viking, 2012) argues that, statistically, the world is actually getting less violent. His figures are convincing from within the historical record, but his take that Pleistocene cultures were primarily characterized by feuding and raiding is precisely the kind of sweeping historically clichéd generalization that recent anthropological findings are calling into question. In some cases their behavior was even worse; and in other cases, much better.

5. As quoted in Edward R. Murrow, *This I Believe* (New York: Simon and Schuster, 1954) 16.

6. In a 2012 study published in the journal *Trends in Genetics*, Dr. Gerald Crabtree argues that human intelligence peaked at the time of hunter-gatherers and has since declined as a result of "genetic mutations" that have slowly eroded the human brain's intellectual and emotional abilities.

7. Robert Kaplan, *Warrior Politics* (New York: Random House, 2001) vii.

8. Ibid.

9. *Conjectures of a Guilty By-Stander* (Garden City, NY: Doubleday, 1966) 54–55.

10. Quoted in Kaplan viii–ix.

11. Reinhold Niebuhr, *The Irony of American History* (New York: Scribner's, 1962) 160.

12. John Milbank, "Knowledge: The Theological Critique of Philosophy in Hamann and Jacobi," *Radical Orthodoxy: A New Theology*, ed. John Milbank, Graham Ward, and Catherine Pickstock (London: Routledge, 1999) 30.

13. Quoted in Krishna Kripalani, ed., *All Men Are Brothers* (Ahmedabad, India: Navajivan, 1960) 83.

14. *Contemplation in a World of Action* (Garden City, NY: Doubleday, 1971) 234.

15. See Morris Berman, *Why America Failed: The Roots of Imperial Decline* (New York: Wiley, 2011).

16. *The Present Age*, trans. Alexander Dru (San Francisco: Harper and Row, 1962) 105.

17. Jean Baudrillard, "L'esprit du terrorisme," *Harper's* Feb. 2002: 18.

18. Merton, *Conjectures of a Guilty By-Stander* 56–57.

19. From "A Footnote From *Ulysses*: Peace and Revolution" (1968), *The Literary Essays of Thomas Merton*, ed. Patrick Hart (New York: New Directions, 1981) 28.

20. Thomas Merton, preface, *Nonviolence and the Christian Conscience*, by P. Regamey (London: Darton, 1966) 14.

21. *Faith and Violence* (Notre Dame, IN: University of Notre Dame Press, 1968) 12–13.

22. For an interesting, if somewhat controversial, take on this transition, see Riane Eisler, *The Chalice and the Blade* (New York: Peter Smith Publisher, 1994).

23. Tolstoy pointed out in his *Confession* that in order to think critically, one must adopt the stance of a nihilist—assuming nothing, suspecting everything, and questioning every value. Socrates, Buddha, the author of Ecclesiastes, and Schopenhauer set the standard for believing nothing and trusting no one, and all three arrived at the conclusion

that it would have been better not to have been born. The poor are less susceptible to this logic than the rich, and so, by default, the most economically privileged among us end up defining what is rational—often in ways that mirror their own sense of personal meaninglessness. Tolstoy, to his credit, turned away from the ingratitude of the aristocracy to the faith of the peasants as a way out of this intellectual cul-de-sac, and in the process he developed a proto-liberation theology that netted him nothing but scorn from his contemporaries—with the notable exception of a young Hindu named Gandhi, who wrote him admiring letters.

24. *Honorable Reader: Reflections on My Work*, ed. Robert Daggy (New York: Crossroads, 1989) 65.

25. *Hidden Ground of Love* (New York: Farrar, Straus and Giroux, 1985) 272.

26. See *The Political Illusion* (New York: Vintage, 1972).

27. "Blessed Are the Meek" in *Faith and Violence*, 20.

28. Thomas Merton, *Cold War Letters*, ed. Christine M. Bochen and William H. Shannon (New York: Orbis Books, 2007).

29. Slavoj Zizek, *Violence: Six Sideways Reflections* (New York: Picador, 2008) 334.

30. Ibid. 217.

31. From *Taking the Risk out of Democracy: Propaganda in the US and Australia* (Sydney: University of NSW Press, 1995) as quoted in "Letter from Noam Chomsky" in *Covert Action Quarterly 1995*.

32. *Faith and Violence*, 26.

33. From "The Root of War," *The Catholic Worker* #28 Oct. 1961.

34. *Less Than One* (New York: Farrar, Straus and Giroux, 1986) 385.

35. *The Hidden Ground of Love*, ed. William Shannon (San Diego: Harcourt Brace Jovanovitch, 1985) 141.

36. James Douglass, *JFK and the Unspeakable* (New York: Orbis Books, 2008).

37. *JFK and the Unspeakable* (Maryknoll, NY: Orbis, 2008) xvii.

38. *Letters from Tom to W.H. Ferry* (Scarsdale, NY: Fort Hill Press, 1983) 15.

39. Ibid.

40. *Faith and Violence*, 18–19.

41. From a letter written by Thomas Merton to Jim Forest dated 21 February 1966. Published in *The Hidden Ground of Love: Letters by*

Thomas Merton, ed. William Shannon (New York: Farrar, Straus and Giroux, 1985).

42. Later published under the title *Ancient Oaxaca*, ed. John Paddock (Stanford, CA: Stanford UP, 1966).

43. Thomas Merton, *Ishi Means Man* (Greensboro, NC: Unicorn Press, 1976) 70.

44. Ibid. 71.

45. Letter to Dorothy Day in *The Hidden Ground of Love* (1985) 141.

46. *Denial of Death*, 91.

Conclusion: Refiguring the Faith

1. From John Welwood, "Double Vision: Duality and Nonduality in Human Experience" <http://www.johnwelwood.com/articles/DoubleVision.pdf>.

2. This speech, titled "Thomas Merton and the Wisdom of Nonviolence," is available online in its entirety at <http://www.fatherjohndear.org/speeches/thomas_merton_wisdom.htm>.

3. Kafka wrote, "Believing means liberating the indestructible element in oneself, or, more accurately, being indestructible, or, more accurately, being." The Third Notebook, 30 November 1917. *The Blue Octavo Notebooks*, ed. Max Brod, trans. by Ernst Kaiser and Eithne Wilkins (Cambridge, MA: Exact Change, 1991) 27.

4. *The Seven Storey Mountain* (San Diego: Harcourt Brace Jovanovich, 1976) 169.

5. *No Man Is an Island* (New York: Harcourt Brace Jovanovich, 1955) 119.

6. Computer scientists and artificial intelligence researchers (e.g., Ray Kurzweil) have speculated that with the creation of smarter-than-human machines, human beings would have engineered their own intellectual extinction. Then the event horizon of history would have disappeared into a conceptual black hole as machines would have designed ever more capable machines that would then have created even more powerful forms of intelligence in an infinitely ascending trajectory metaphorically divine in its power—qualitatively transforming the very nature of life and existence. See Eliezer Yudkowsky, *The Singularity: Three*

Major Schools <http://yudkowsky.net/singularity/schools>. Also see works celebrating the posthumanities, such as Ian Bogost, *Alien Phenomenology, or What It's Like to Be a Thing (Posthumanities)* (Minneapolis: University of Minnesota Press, 2012).

7. See *The Rivers North of the Future: The Testament of Ivan Illich* as told to David Cayley (Toronto: House of Anansi Press, 2005); and René Girard with Pierpaolo Antonello and João Cezar de Castro Rocha, *Evolution and Conversion: Dialogues on the Origins of Culture* (London: T & T Clark, 2007).

8. Trans. by Willa and Edwin Muir in *The Basic Kafka* (New York, Pocket Books, 1979) p. 158.

9. *The Merton Seasonal* 27.2 (Fall 2002): 8.

10. This view puts Merton in agreement with the classical Christian humanists but also with contemporary thinkers like Michel Henry, the French Christian phenomenologist who influenced Bruce Parain, another writer whom Merton greatly admired. Both are now finding their way into English translations, although Merton read Parain's work in its original French editions. Michel Henry's basic thesis is that Husserl needs to be radicalized. Husserl's idealism and transcendental ego turn subjectivity into an aspect of Being, whereas life itself as experienced is prior to Being. Phenomenology without this turn toward the pre-givenness of Being stays within the limits of Cartesianism.

11. *Stranger Music* (New York: Vintage, 1993) 287–88.

12. See Peter Block, *Community: The Structure of Belonging* (San Francisco: Berrett-Koehler Publishers, 2009).

Appendix: Some Milestones of Merton Scholarship

1. Kurt Vonnugut, *The Sirens of Titan* (New York: Dial Press, 1998) 1.

2. See John Dear, *Living Peace* (New York: Image, 2004); and James Douglass, *JFK and the Unspeakable* (New York: Simon & Schuster, 2010) and *The Non-Violent Cross* (Eugene, OR: Wipf and Stock, 1968).

3. Glenn Kleir, *The Knowledge of Good and Evil* (New York: Tom Doherty, 2011).

4. Thomas Merton, *The Inner Experience: Notes on Contemplation*, ed. William H. Shannon (San Francisco: Harper San Francisco, 2003) 59.

Index

bildungsroman, 36

Blake, William, 10, 37, 62, 64, 147n

Blanchot, Maurice, 91, 156n

"*Blessed Virgin Compared to a Window, The*" by Thomas Merton, 66

Block, Peter, 129, 160n

Bohemianism, 10, 17, 36

Bonhoeffer, Dietrich, 86

Borges, Jorge Luis, 61

Brodsky, Joseph, 63, 64, 110

Brown, Norman O., 26–28, 133, 149n

Bruce, Lenny, 26, 68

Buddha, 103, 155n, 157n

Buddhism, 39, 80, 124, 137, 155n, 157n

Bukowski, Charles, 12, 13

Burnt Norton by T.S. Eliot, 121

Burroughs, William, 69

Bush, George W., 98

Cables to the Ace by Thomas Merton, 69, 70, 71, 154n

Cambridge University, 9, 10

Campbell, Joseph, 12

Camus, Albert, 58, 136

Carey, Alex, 107–108

Cartesian ego (*cogito*), 3, 38–40, 44, 121, "certainties," 98,"God object," 40

Casey, Michael, 141

Cassian, 56, 83, 139

Catholic Worker, The, 114, 158n

Catholic, apologetics, 132, "a good" 10, 11, 13, 15, avant-garde, 120, "bad boy," 32, church, 6, 25, 61,

62 145n, church officials 105, contemplatives, 62, contemplative tradition 98, 104, dissident, 134, doctrine 14, 85, faith, 62, literary avant-garde, 132, 134, News Service, 147n, Peace Fellowship, 4, 108, 147n, social justice, 136, 142, social thought, 4, theologians 1, theology 14, 22, tradition 83, triumphalism, 128, worker 114, 137

Catholicism, 3, 4, 8, 11, 13, 36, 61, 62, 85, 136, 147n

"celebrity culture," 29, 75, 80, 128, 143

"*Chant to be used in Processions Around a Cite with Furnaces*" by Thomas Merton, 68, 69

Chayefsky, Paddy, 88

"cheap grace," 2, 7, 40, 82, 146n

Chesterton, G.K., 4, 15, 145n

Chopra, Deepak, 86

Christ, 5, 10, 11, 13–15, 21, 22, 27, 30, 32, 41, 44, 45, 51, 53, 54, 56, 69, 123–125

Christian, "a good," 4, aesthetics, 146n, apologetics, 4, civilization, 4, converts 11, critical romanticism, 10, culture, 58, disciple, 6, 13, ethnology, 43, experience, 45, faith 36, 116, 120, 121, godless, 42, humanists 160n, initiation 36, intellectual, 86, *kenosis* 3, 147n, life, 83, "lifestyle Christians" 17, 85, *metanoia,* 20, monasticism,

6, mysticism 17, 26, 39, 84, mystics, 130, mythos, 22, Orthodoxy, 147n

Christian Realism, 95, 96, 98, 99

Christianity, v, 3, 5, 10, 19, 26, 36, 80, 94, 95, 124, 131, apophatic 28, 43, 49 atheistic 52, 152n

Christology, 68, 136, 140

Chumash Indians, 91

Circumfession by Jacques Derrida, 46

Cistercian, Order, 4, 56, 149n

City of God by Augustine, 92–93

Civil Rights Movement, 4, 7, 23, 104, 134

Clinton, Bill, 93

Cohen, Leonard, 129

Cohen, William, 9

Cold War Letters, The, by Thomas Merton, 86, 105, 139, 158n

"Cold War, The," 7, 28, 86 92, 98, 105, 139n, 158n

Coleridge, Samuel Taylor, 10, 37, 73

Coliseum, Roman, 12

Collected Poems of Thomas Merton, 66

Colonel Tibbets, 68

Coltrane, John, 120

Columbia University, 9, 10

Communion of Saints, The, 13, 14 (*see also* "saints")

Communist Party, 9

Confucius, 103

Conjectures of a Guilty By-Stander by Thomas Merton 80

conscience, 3, 11, 17, 20, 22, 26–28, 61, 65

Contemplation in a World of Action by Thomas Merton 54, 133, 150n, 151n, 152n, 157n

Contemplation, 6, 8, 19, 21, 28, 35, 39, 40, 44, 45, 47–55, 58, 81–84, 107, 108, 119–121, 127, 128, 143, active, 30, 51, 72, 143, commercialization of, 79, infused 50, 52, 127, natural, 51, 127

"Contemplative and the Atheist, The," by Thomas Merton, 41

contemporary thought, 6, 7, 27, 28, 34, 39, 45, 51, 52, 58, 61, 77, 86, 121, 138n, 144, 151n, 153n, 160n

Corbin, Henry, 73

counterculture, sixties, 6, 25, 26, 75, 107

Cross of Christ, 21, 23, 146n, 160n

"Culture Wars, The," 106, 135

Cunningham, Lawrence S., 60, 136, 149n, 156n

Daedalus, Stephen, 12

Danielou, Jean, 1, 25, 145n

Dante, 97

Day of a Stranger,The, by Thomas Merton, 18, 19, 86, 148n, 156n

Day, Dorothy, 4, 80, 104, 111, 112, 140, 159n

de Chardin, Teilhard, 40, 133

De Lubac, Henri, 1, 4, 22, 143, 145n

Dear, John, 119, 142, 159n, 160n

deconstruction, 6, 42, 55, 77

Demian, Father, 14

Madness and Civilization by Michel
Foucault, 31–32
Mailer, Norman, 19
Mann, Thomas, 92
March on Washington 1968, 104
Marcuse, Herbert, 7, 88, 92
Maritain, Jacques, 4, 147n
"*Marxism and Monastic*
Perspectives" by Thomas
Merton, 80
Marxism, 7, 10, 31, 87, 95
materialism, 3, 66, 76
McLuhan, Marshall, 28, 60, 61,
86, 133
"Medieval Synthesis" 1, 6, 37
metaphysics, *v*, 39, 54, 73, 121,
128, classical 32, 65, Kantian,
4, materialist 77, 127
Merton Seasonal, The, 33, 139,
140, 149, 160n
Merton, Thomas
as a religious thinker 1, 3, 4, 5,
7, 24, 25, 37, 39–41, 52, 63,
81, 82, 109, 122
as constructivist, 71
as existentialist, 61
as experimental novelist, 36
as literary intellectual, 60,
as monk, 5, 18, 19, 23, 24, 60,
75, 87, 89
as mystic, 36, 42, 44, 45, 49, 50
as poet, 65–71, 75
as social critic, 28, 30, 56,
68, 70, 74, 80, 88, 92, 104,
112–117
as teacher, 1, 21, 145n
as writer, 1, 6, 7, 18, 19, 21,
25, 28, 31–36, 58, 60–62,
72–74, 80

Blake and, 10
Cambridge years, 9, 10
Christian Realism and, 95
Columbia years, 10–13
contemporary significance of,
7, 20, 23, 24, 42, 51, 58, 61,
62, 66, 77, 80, 119, 120, 124,
127, 129, 130
contra Heidegger, 50–51, 121
contra Kaplan, Robert, 92–94
contra New Age, 86
contra Niebuhr, Reinhold, 95
conversion of, 10–13, 17–18
critical romanticism of, 10
death of, 33
duality in, 10
Foucault, Michel and, 31–32
Huxley, Aldous, and, 26
Lax, Robert and, 10
life of, 9–33
modernism and, 10, 13, 40, 126
monk or writer? 60
most dangerous idea of, 8,
91–117
negative theology of, 49, 50
on Bob Dylan, 31
on Catholic Social Thought, 4,
22, 25, 26, 31, 99
on Cheap Grace, 82
on Christ, 21, 27, 28
on Christianity, 5, 36, 86, 95, 124
on Cistercian Order the, 56
on contemplation, 4, 8, 17, 18,
20, 21, 37–39, 4, 44, 50–54,
76, 81–83, 86, 89, 98, 108,
116, 124, 127, 128
on desire, 42
on faith, 45, 46, 62, 63, 121,
122, 127

science, 2, 5, 14, 19, 27, 41, 45, 57, 67, 74, 75, 77, 87, 97–99, 105, 112, 127, 130
scientific method, 43
scripture 1–3, 22, 30, 39, 54, 56, 64, 66, 73, 120, 125, 126, 145n
"second innocence," 10, 13, 37, 67, 121, 142n
Secular Journal by Thomas Merton, 61, 133, 153n
Seeds of Contemplation by Thomas Merton, 21
Seligman, Martin E.P., 83
Seton, Saint Elizabeth, 6, 7
Seven Storey Mountain, by Thomas Merton, 1, 3, 5, 16, 33, 36, 96, 97, 132, 145n, 151n, 159n
Shakespeare, William, 14, 15, 59, 65
Shelly, Percy Bysshe, 15
silence, 33, 35, 38, 48, 79, 99, 107, 130, 139
Simmons, Gene, 75
"Singularity, The," 123, 124, 159n, 160n
sixties, the, 6, 23, 26, 28, 80, 104, 134, 136, 143, 147n
skepticism, 36, 43, 46, 63, 73, 74, 97, 131
Smith, Huston, 91, 141
"society of the spectacle," 67, 75, 87, 128
solitude, 13, 15, 57, 58, 75, 79, 87, 130
Spinoza, Baruch, 14
spirituality, 4, 6, 11, 33, 55, 56, 62, 80, 82, 85, 128, 140–142

"*Sponge Full of Vinegar, The,*" by Thomas Merton, 66
Stanislavsky, Konstantine, 51
stories, 2, 55, 60, 87, 139, 152n, 153n, 154n
"structuralist activity," 3, 146n, 147n
"sublime, the," 53, 64, 76, 89, 131, egalitarian, 117, egotistical, 13
Sufi mysticism, 31, 39, 93, 130, 154n
supernaturalism, 2, 20, 59, 64, 122, 124
Suzuki, D. T., 7, 31, 52

television, 28, 29, 61, 79, 136
Teresa of Avila, 16, 83, 84
Theology of Liberation, A, by Gustavo Guiterrez, 31
theology, 2–4, 6, 13–15, 17, 19, 29, 31, 40–42, 46, 47, 49, 50, 52, 59, 62, 64, 72, 73, 74, 76, 77, 105, 110, 119, 124, 127, 138, 140, 145n–147n, 150n, 157n, 158n, weak, 15
Theresa of Lisieux, Saint, 12
Thirty Poems by Thomas Merton, 66
Thomas Merton Reader, The, 60, 153n
"*Thomas Merton: The Pursuit of Marginality,*" by Lawrence Cunningham, 60
Thoreau, Henry David, 103, 104, 109
Thoughts in Solitude by Thomas Merton, 21
Tiananmen Square Revolt, 104

Tolstoy, Leo, 4, 10, 37, 103, 109, 157n, 158n
Tracy, David, 119
Trappist Order, 31, 32, 50, 67
Trinity, 11, 23, 32, 49, 68
"true self," 7, 9–11, 19, 21, 36, 41, 42, 52, 59, 67, 85, 89, 100, 116, 123, 133
Trump, Donald, 75
Tutu, Bishop, 103, 104
twentieth century, 1, 3, 6, 7, 74, 87, 107, 131, 132

"unspeakable, the," 100, 112, 113, 153n, 158n, 160n

Van Doren, Mark, 9, 143
Vatican II, 4, 22, 110, 143, 145
Vietnam War, 4, 7, 22, 92, 108, 112, 134

Von Balthasar, Urs, 4, 22, 23, 73, 120, 121, 146n, 147n, 149n

Wagner, Richard, 15
Walesa, Lech, 119, 133, 159n
Warhol, Andy, 120
Warrior Politics: Why Leadership Demands a Pagan Ethos by Robert Kaplan, 92
Watson, Helmholtz, 65, 66
Weil, Simone, 58
Welwood, John, 119, 133, 159n
Wilber, Ken, 84, 86, 141n
Williams College, 110
Williamson, Marianne, 86
Wittgenstein, Ludwig, 39
World War II, 21, 95, 96, 132

Zen, 44, 50, 53, 56, 150n, 155n
Zizek, Slavoj, 107, 150n, 12n, 158n
Zoroaster, 103